PERIPHERAL VIEW

A novel of love, courage,
and the triumph of the human spirit

PERIPHERAL VIEW

A novel of love, courage,
and the triumph of the human spirit

RITA KUEHN

LANGDON STREET PRESS
MINNEAPOLIS, MINNESOTA

Langdon Street Press
212 3ʳᵈ Avenue North, Suite 290
Minneapolis, MN 55401
612.455.2293
www.langdonstreetpress.com

ISBN - 978-1-934938-34-8
ISBN - 1-934938-34-3
LCCN - 2009924825

Book sales for North America and international:
Itasca Books, 3501 Highway 100 South, Suite 220
Minneapolis, MN 55416
Phone: 952.345.4488 (toll free 1.800.901.3480)
Fax: 952.920.0541; email to orders@itascabooks.com

Cover Design by Tiffany Laschinger
Typeset by Kristeen Wegner

Printed in the United States of America

LᴀɴɢᴅᴏN
Sᴛʀᴇᴇᴛ
PʀᴇSS

To Rick

and in memory of

Lucille Noonan
(1933-1993)

and for Lexa

Acknowledgments

First, I thank God for all of His blessings and for being there for me. I feel lucky with the way that God has things worked out, being there for me (and you) twenty-four seven, and all. Praise be to God.

All of the following individuals gave generously of their time: reading, editing, suggesting, and/or providing unconditional support and encouragement. Their insights and enthusiasm went further than they could know in bringing this book to its finish. I thank each of them with all my heart for their kind words, tactful suggestions, guidance, and, most of all, for their dear friendship. They helped make this book better than it would have been without their help. When the road seemed too long and the journey seemed too precarious, I heard their voices telling me to keep writing. I thank them for sharing the excitement of this book with me. May God bless each of them as they have blessed me. I love you all very much!

My father and mother, Russell and Rose Engel, provided me with important information that I needed to round out the story. I thank them for taking the time to do that and for their constant encouragement throughout my writing.

Several wonderful people read the book in its early drafts, and I've not forgotten their generous contribution. Becky Thaisen offered wonderful suggestions and wrote encouraging Post-it notes that made me smile and believe—I've saved them all! My sister Roxann Dunst, Terry Fligge, and Carl Fligge also offered valuable feedback and support. I hope they are all very pleased with the novel—they helped get it there.

Karen Romness and Jerry Romness are some of the nicest people I've ever met. I loved how they really "got" the heart of my story. They made me believe that I had a good story to tell and that others just might want to read it too.

Kathleen Costello is always ready with a caring heart and an open ear. Her friendship is immeasurable and greatly appreciated. Besides all of that, in an eleventh hour reading of my work, she found some pesky final edits. I think she's missed her calling!

Members of Women in Touch (WIT), my small church group, play an important role in my life. Members: Sue Keller, Denise Fossen, Debra Correll, Julie Heifort, Peggy Schultz, and Betty Anderson cheer me on and provide me with endless amounts of wisdom and enthusiasm. May we all continue to step out of the boat!

Also, I really have to mention the following very important people:

Everyone should have a big brother like Randy Engel. He's strong, confident, and entrepreneurial, but his heart is as soft as a marshmallow. My baby brother, Roger Engel, is funny, talented, and brave, and I like the way he calls me just to talk. Also, I've been blessed with three sisters, Roxann Dunst, Ruth Engel and Robin Ashe, each of them a real firecracker! We don't see each other often enough. (Yes, gentle reader, our names all start with the letter R.)

Then, of course:

My daughter, Lexa, my precious gem, I thank you for blessings beyond measure. The light of your smile, your wonderful spirit, are only a few of the wonderful things about you that make my heart soar every day.

And most of all, I thank my husband, Rick, for believing in my writing, encouraging me to continue, and for the countless hours spent patiently reading and rereading (and rereading, and rereading. . .) my many "this is my final" drafts. Also, for your continual encouragement and love, I thank you.

Chapter One

Pearl had often dreamed about breaking out of the tidy little box in which she lived—the one that allowed others to live more comfortably with her existence. She had played out the fantasy many times over the years, first rolling it about in her mind, and eventually scoring it on her heart. But tonight she was through fantasizing; she was about to bring her dreams to life.

As she prepared for bed, she held a close check on her nerves. She would lie beneath the bedcovers in the cold, spartan room and wait for just the right moment to make her move; she'd wait until the way was clear. Her throat was dry from the anticipation of it, and she hoped the time would pass without incident. With trembling fingers, she worked the sash on her bathrobe, fearing the wait would overwhelm her sensibilities. Finally managing to get the robe tied, she stood still for a moment, inhaled a deep breath, and tried to calm down.

She thought about the emotional havoc she'd experienced over the last few hours: she was first happy, then anxious, then excited, then filled with longing, then felt girlishly giddy, then fearful, and then she was back to happy. It was knocking her psyche to pieces, but she would endure whatever it took to bring her dream to life. Her emotions would not dictate her actions this time.

Pearl wanted everything to appear normal. For her roommate Karoline's benefit, Pearl yawned loudly while sitting on the bed, pulling off her slippers. Then, with her back against the headboard, she picked up the Agatha Christie novel she'd started the night before. However, making any sense of the words she was reading proved difficult; she at least made it look like she was reading for a good hour before lying down. She'd never had a problem falling asleep, most nights nodding off when her head hit the pillow. So she closed her eyes, hoping that everyone would believe she'd easily fallen asleep. Karoline was already asleep. But there were others.

Lying still was nearly an impossibility. The risk of what she was about to do sent butterflies fluttering through her stomach. The excitement of it, the fear of it, turned those flutters into a painful knot of nerves. She began to toss and turn as if in rhythm with her emotions: roll left, flutter and knot, roll right, flutter and knot, roll left.... Still, she kept her eyes shut and her ears alert, and she waited.

Suddenly, a noise outside her room startled her. By now, she could easily recognize the soft thud of a rubber-sole shoe. She tossed the covers over her head. The hard thump of her heartbeat competed with thoughts of who might be out there. As she tried to calm her rising panic, her thoughts raced. It could be anybody: front desk staff, maintenance, someone on their way to the bathroom. It wasn't necessarily the warden, she reasoned.

Abruptly, the steps stopped—near her door, but not at it.

A door squeaked, and Pearl heard the murmur of voices. Then there were more footsteps, this time walking away. Listening closely, Pearl held her breath until she could no longer hear the sticky tap of rubber on tile.

With a sigh of relief, she rolled back the covers. The cool air felt good on her face and she breathed it in, savoring the respite. She cast a quick glance at the open door and knew the staff had to be close to settling in for the night. Things were not going too badly, she decided, just before ducking back beneath the covers.

Soon she would have a new life. Forcing her concentration back to that notion, she hoped to calm herself. Yet unwanted thoughts of all that could go wrong flashed through her mind. Someone might see her, and the consequences would be dire if the wrong person discovered her plan. Maybe it wasn't the right thing to do—well, it wouldn't be by *their* standards, she mused. However, Pearl had carefully thought the plan through, and whether they liked it or not she had a set of standards too. But if they found her out . . . . Round and round these thoughts went. Annoyed, she finally reasoned that staying calm, like lying still, was an unattainable feat.

She was already beyond her limits when an urge to sneeze suddenly grabbed onto her and wouldn't let go. It was the damn cleaning solution—the stinging odor of chemicals—beginning a slow burn up her nose. The cleaning crew was sanitizing her wing, and she hadn't figured them into her escape plan. They worked in teams of two or three and spoke to each other in a foreign language. Thai, she thought. They used harsh cleansers, supposedly to reduce the risk of staph infections. However, Pearl suspected that certain employees of Glory Heights feared catching one of the many infirmities spread throughout the community of patients and thus had the place regularly fumigated.

Pearl scrunched her face and held her breath to try and stop the threatening sneeze. However, the tingle was unbearable and the report was about to go off, causing her to momentarily wonder if one sneezed while one was sleeping. She thought not, and quickly clamped her hand around her nostrils with a hard grip, stifling the sneeze with only a small sputter getting loose. Fortunately, there were no further flare-ups, and her nose remained quiet until she could no longer hear the slopping of wash pails and mops in the hallway. That left her to focus on the cramp in her left leg.

The effort to stem her movements had stiffened her leg muscles enormously, and as she tried to relax them, she mused that it was like bringing the dead back to life. However, soon she would need to move quickly, which wasn't something she was used to doing. So, starting with her toes and working upward, she spent a few minutes tensing and then relaxing each muscle group. However, the exercise soon proved less therapeutic than she'd hoped, and as her mind wandered in anticipation of her imminent adventure, she gave it up.

Pearl rubbed her stomach, trying to calm it. Nervous energy for what was about to happen was all it was. Her nerves were objecting to their part in her plan. Yanking the twisted hem of her robe, she stiffly rolled over. With an exasperated breath, she tried to stay still, but another complaint coursed through her chest. She swallowed back the acid and thought about the bottle of Maalox on the old bed stand. It was within reach, but she wasn't going for it. Not a chance. She couldn't risk anyone noticing that she was awake. Neither her fears nor her stomach would dictate her movements this night. Having put up with the rumblings until now, she would hold on for a few more minutes.

Although she felt that impatience seemed only to mark the slowing of time, not its advancement, she checked the clock. Peeking out from the covers, she opened one eye and glanced at the clock radio on her bed stand. She opened both eyes and blinked hard at the glaring display. Her muscles loosened. It was, thankfully, finally, time to go.

Pearl wiped her nose on the sleeve of her bathrobe and then guardedly rose from the twin bed, praying that its old springs would not betray her. Once on her feet, she dared a glance toward Karoline, hoping that the soft squeak of brittle metal had not woken her. Fortunately, Karoline lay with her eyes closed and her mouth slightly open, still asleep. Pearl let out a long breath.

Then, moving as if her life depended upon it, Pearl stole across the floor, feeling with heightened anxiety that the room was enlarging and distorting before her, threatening to absorb her into a heavy fog before she reached her destiny. However, she reached the door within seconds and clung to it as if its portal were her lifeline. Taking a moment to steady herself, she got control of her heaving breath. Then, cautiously, she peeked around the doorframe. She listened for voices, but heard only the wails of those

4

bound to their beds, those prone to wander from their rooms at night, as Pearl was about to do.

A shudder spread through her limbs as the laments rose and chipped away at her confidence. Although familiar and normally ignored, tonight the sounds worried her. She began to wonder if she could carry out the plan. Looking over her shoulder, she gazed back at the bed. It would be so easy to just turn around and climb back into it. As she leaned her head against the door to regain her composure, she swallowed and felt her dry throat muscles constrict. Nothing about her life had been easy. But this dream of hers was worth something, and she trembled at the cost of giving it up. She looked longingly out the door as her resolve vacillated beyond her control.

The building was finally quiet and perfect for carrying out her plan. The vacant corridor seemed a sign of good luck, and she had a flush of courage as she surveyed both ends of the hall. If she was going to make a move, now was the moment. She nearly took a step forward when, quite suddenly, an imagined shadow sprawled across the floor. With a gasp, she pulled back into the room. Her hands shot to her mouth as she tried, unsuccessfully, to squelch the nervous shriek.

With her heart beating hard and fast, she gulped air and tried to slow her breaths, tried to think rationally. She was alert, maybe too alert, and ready to go, but God, she hated this. The fact that she had to behave like this at all was demeaning. Shaking and near tears, she briefly wondered why a moment ago she'd thought she was having such good luck.

Pearl glanced over her shoulder; her roommate had not moved. She began to relax but swiftly changed her mind when a sound erupted from the hallway in front of her. She spun her head around to look, but nothing was there. A heavy sigh escaped her lips, and her chin dropped to her chest. Shaking her head in dismay, she realized that her own fear must have made her imagine the sound, just like the shadow. Tears rolled down her cheeks; it was all too difficult.

Wiping away the tears, she allowed a deep breath for

courage, but inhaled her own nervous sweat. Irritated by the odor, she opened her robe, pulled at her clothing, and attempted to dry out her armpits while warily studying the hallway. A chill fell over her despite all the clothing she had on and her skin prickled with goose bumps. She rubbed her arms and thought about the future—what she stood to lose if she didn't go forward with her plan.

Suddenly she'd had enough. She knew what she wanted and she was going to get it. Without allowing another thought, she decided to make her move. On tiptoe, she quickly retreated into the room and removed her robe. The modest red sweater and gray skirt she wore beneath it were utterly crumpled, but she could do little about it. Smoothing her hands over the stubborn wrinkles barely changed the result of the hours under cover. It was dismaying; she had wished to look her best, but other important issues were before her.

Pressing onward, she quickly moved back to the door. For the last time, she listened and looked into the corridor. Satisfied that the way was clear, Pearl took a deep breath and stepped out of the room.

Determination replaced her fear, and with it grew girlish excitement. On unsteady bird legs and with a hand braced against the wall for support, she scurried toward her destination. She safely made it to the end of the first hall. Squinting from the hallway's fluorescent lighting, she peered back from where she had come. Then, she looked around the corner to where she would go.

Turning the corner, she set her sights on the double doors ahead. She was going to make it. She was sure. At least, she hoped she was sure. Life waited on the other side of those doors. Silently, she prayed that no one would catch her. The sound of wailing, a backdrop to her journey, reminded her of potential consequences.

Suddenly, the doors seemed to move away from her. Nervous spasms raked her stomach muscles. Her legs moved faster, seemingly of their own accord. Nevertheless, after a few hurried, albeit shaky, steps, she muffled a frustrated cry and reluctantly stopped. Her body could not keep up with her will. She leaned her head and hands against the wall, breathed heavily, and struggled to stay on her feet. Drops of sweat trickled from her forehead, slid down the side of her face, and tickled her overheated cheeks. Wiping the irritating beads away, she realized that her whole body was moist with exertion. She fretted over her favorite sweater, willing the perspiration to stop. She wanted to look and smell her best, and had even sprayed a little perfume behind her ears. The thought of it made her giddy. A giggle escaped her lips, but abruptly stopped.

Voices sounded behind her—familiar voices. Panic instantly spread through her, piercing every nerve in her body. She slapped a hand over her mouth and listened. It was Nurse Charlotte and the warden. They mustn't catch her out of her room, she thought. With a difficult push off the wall, Pearl awkwardly propelled herself forward. She extended her arms and splayed her hands out before her. Her eyes felt like they were boring holes in the doors ahead. The voices grew louder, closer. Hurry, she told herself. Hurry now. Pearl zigzagged across the hall, her bowed shoulders banging against the walls. She was going to make it. She had to make it. Her fingers briefly touched the door. Then, suddenly, a high-pitched scream filled the hallway—a human yelping that was more startling with each protracted second.

Although the noise might have frightened many patients in the rooms along Pearl's path, she herself heard nothing. Her collapse onto the hard tile floor was instantaneous. Those approaching heard the powerful thud of Pearl's head hitting the granite floor.

Pearl's quest for the night was over.

In a seldom-used stock room filled with bed linens, towels, and soap, Sonny woke from a nap—he'd had the time, having been there since visiting hours ended. He checked his watch and then hurriedly finished the preparations. It was to be a cozy place of celebration. Taking a step back, he reviewed his work. A small overturned box was a table for cheese, crackers, two plastic glasses, and a bottle of carbonated grape juice. He would have liked something stronger, but Pearl wasn't supposed to drink alcohol and he wouldn't take any chances with its effects. The room wasn't the lovely place his Pearly deserved but it was all they had for now.

Feeling impatient, he left the room to watch for her, and that's when he heard the cries. He rushed to the double doors where they were to meet, and looking through the window, his jaw went slack. Sonny saw Pearl go down. Oh no, he thought, oh no. Poor Pearly. He gave her a sympathetic look—one she could not see. Pearl lay on the floor, unconscious, in a display of twisted arms and legs.

He needed to help her. He was about to push through the doors when, above the screech, concrete voices suddenly rose and drew near. With a jerk, his gaze left Pearl and went further on down the hall. Sonny froze. Nurse Charlotte and the warden were rushing toward Pearl. Sonny couldn't let them catch him in the building. Moving like a mouse recognizing the trap, he snapped back from the doors and crouched down below the window.

"It's Pearl Witherby," Charlotte told the warden.

"What in God's name is the woman doing out here at this hour?" the warden replied.

The sound of the warden's voice sent its own icy tremor up Sonny's spine. He was afraid to move further, as much for Pearl's sake as for his own. The last thing he wanted was for the warden to discover him waiting for her. Yet, the warden didn't have much control over those who didn't live at Glory Heights. That's what Sonny believed, anyway.

He chewed his thumbnail, already ragged from gnawing on it. What should he do now? Turn and run? Wait? For what? With a dispirited heart, he realized that he should go. He knew there was no longer a reason to stay.

Suddenly, the shrieking stopped. While startled by its finality, Sonny resisted the urge to jump up and look. He wanted to see what was happening, but it was too risky. Nurse Charlotte and the warden were mere inches from the door he crouched behind. He needed to get out of Glory Heights.

Still, he couldn't help himself. Rising and being careful not to lean against the swinging doors, he stretched his eyes above the bottom of the glass in the window. He saw Pearl. Nurse Charlotte was kneeling over her, holding her hand and rubbing her forehead. She was far too busy attending to Pearl's needs to notice Sonny. The warden was now nowhere in sight. If he went for help he'd be back soon, or he'd send others. Sonny had to leave, before they arrived.

He knew that Pearl would have some big explaining to do when she recovered from her epileptic seizure. An ache was growing in the pit of his stomach, and he swallowed hard to quell its rising bile. He also swallowed the feeling that he was abandoning her. After sneaking one last look at her, he turned and ran down the hall, around the corner, and out to the street.

Chapter Two

Paramedics delivered Pearl to her room on a stretcher, with Charlotte efficiently walking alongside, murmuring words of comfort. They transferred Pearl to her bed while the metal stretcher clanged against the metal bed frame and the bed linens rustled. Pearl winced as the noise broke through her subconscious. By the time they'd jostled her into bed her eyes were open and she was returning to consciousness.

Pearl thought she heard Nurse Charlotte's voice, heard her tell Karoline to go back to sleep. So, Nurse Charlotte is here, she thought. But what was this about the warden? She was remembering something about the warden. Had he been there too? Oh, she was beginning to remember. She'd had a seizure. In the hall. Yes, the warden had been there all right, but he'd conveniently disappeared. If Pearl hadn't known the trouble she was in, she might have laughed at him. The warden was known for his inability to stomach patient realities—maladies others lived with on a daily basis—although no one dared to confront him with the irony of his position as Glory Heights Healthcare Facility's administrator.

The paramedics left, and Pearl didn't feel like laughing at all. She was fully aware of what had taken place and began to cry, trying to keep it to herself. The darkened room offered some protection. Charlotte worked only by the fluorescent lights over-flowing from the hallway. After she gave Pearl a shot of phenobarbital, she applied a warm washcloth to her forehead, giving some small comfort with the gentle swabbing. During the fall, Pearl had suffered a painful bump and bruise at the base of her head and an abrasion on her cheek, although they weren't the reason for her tears.

She felt old and tired and closed her eyes against it, but unwillingly her thoughts drifted to the makings of her fifty-two-year-old life. The life she wanted to leave behind. It had passed under someone else's watch: they told her what to do and not to do, when to go and when to stay. Most people, like Nurse Charlotte, were kind enough. But no one asked about her aspirations. If they did, it would surprise them to learn that she had many. Of course, it would make no sense to them, under the circumstances. Her life was one with a peripheral view. Theirs, not hers: marginal looks and thoughts, as if her yearnings for love, family, and home were no longer relevant, as if the illness had somehow evaporated her feelings.

Those of a healthy mind and strong body barely considered her. On a sidewalk, they gave her a peek and moved over to allow space between her and them. Oh, they'd give a glance at the dark leather helmet, wondering if its purpose was to waylay the bang and bruise of a fall. Perhaps they'd quickly check for a mouth guard and wonder if she bit. And the space between them hurried wider. Well, her own sister, the U.S. senator, reacted the same way, for gad sakes. Susan, the one who had devised this fate for her.

Pearl tried to ignore the tweak in her heart, but tears continued to roll down her cheeks. She wasn't bitter; she just wanted something more. Needed it. Like anyone else, she had a right to it. Abandonment, sadness, and loneliness were the feelings that held her at night. She was hurt—hell, yes. However, no good ever came from harvesting ill will and, with much emotional effort, she'd risen above any challenges to do so. She realized that some people, her sister included, might be afraid of those they deemed different. It was no one's fault that she had epilepsy or that she sometimes looked frail and unsure with halting steps and a slight stutter when she was nervous. She tried to keep this in mind whenever someone slighted her.

The nurse nudged her from her thoughts as she helped Pearl with her nightgown. "Pearl, what were you doing up, dressed, and in the hallway at eleven o'clock at night?"

Nurse Charlotte had whispered it—although her Southern accent was detectable even in hushed tones—because apparently she didn't want to awaken Karoline. Nurse Charlotte needn't worry, thought Pearl. Karoline could sleep through anything. She hadn't stirred from her sleep; she was in the same position she had been in when Pearl had left her.

Pearl smiled at Nurse Charlotte, whom she liked, but she didn't offer an explanation. She didn't want to lie or explain. Immediately following the assault of her nervous system, Pearl couldn't recall her reason for being in the hallway; she could've honestly answered that she didn't know. But Pearl sadly realized her failing. She thought about how she must have looked sprawled out on the floor. Embarrassment burned her cheeks. Surely, Sonny saw everything through the windows of the doors where they promised to meet, she thought. Beyond that, the worst of her heartbreak was the realization that her plans had ended in ruin. No, even worse was that they'd found her out.

Nurse Charlotte repeated her question, whispering again. A stream of light spilling across her face allowed Pearl to see the earnestness with which her nurse spoke. Still, Pearl thought her safest option was to claim ignorance. After a seizure, Nurse Charlotte just might believe it. She might even let it go. She could tell the warden it was an isolated incident. Nurse Charlotte was new at Glory Heights. She had come on board only a few months ago and still had that startled, sympathetic look that Pearl often saw in new witnesses to her seizures. Pearl decided to test Nurse Charlotte.

Pearl whispered back, "I don't know what you're talking about." Then she repeated it: "I don't know what you're talking about."

She didn't know what else to say, so she said it a third time. She was blowing it, but she didn't know how to help herself, and she wasn't going to tell Nurse Charlotte the truth. Although, by now Pearl feared she had repeated herself too many times to be believable. She looked sharply at Nurse Charlotte, who was now pulling covers up to Pearl's chin, tucking her in.

"I really don't know what I was doing out there," Pearl said. Then she thought, God almighty, and nearly rolled her eyes. But she caught herself, and only her dry lips twittered with silent scolding while offering Nurse Charlotte an innocent, wide-eyed blink.

"Hmm," was all Nurse Charlotte said.

For one frightening moment, Pearl thought Nurse Charlotte would challenge her denial. But when Nurse Charlotte peered into Pearl's eyes, as if searching for the truth, Pearl noticed something in Nurse Charlotte's eyes, and it looked like sympathy. It surprised Pearl that she even recognized the look. Maybe it wasn't sympathy. Maybe Nurse Charlotte was getting ready for that challenge.

But then Nurse Charlotte simply smiled warmly, patted the bedding next to Pearl, and said, "It's okay, Pearl. Get some sleep now."

Relieved at the good fortune of not having to explain herself further, Pearl shut her eyes and relaxed into the mattress and pillow beneath her. She would have let herself loll in the serenity she often felt after a spell if the disruption in her plans did not bother her so. The potential consequences of them catching her were also disturbing.

She was off the hook with Nurse Charlotte, but the warden had seen her too. A blade of prickles shot up her back. Pearl rolled to her side, curled into a fetal position, and then pulled the covers up over her ears. It was something she had done in childhood, when she was so afraid that a monster would come in the night and cut off her ears.

The warden might have guessed where she was going. She spent a lot of time with Sonny on game nights. The warden most likely knew about that. Pearl didn't care what the warden thought, as long as he didn't do anything to her. Still, she sighed heavily, thinking about it. A midnight wail came from the lock-in area down the hall, too close to her room. She slid further beneath the covers and shuddered with fear. She didn't want to think about what the warden could do.

She wanted to think about Sonny. Had he made it safely out of the building? She wondered. Then a pleasant thought came to her and she smiled in the darkness. If the warden had caught Sonny, she would have heard about it. The tyrant would not have let it go; he would've taken the time to proclaim disastrous outcomes to the peccadillo. That the warden had disappeared after her seizure truly was good news.

Convinced she wouldn't be hearing from the warden anytime soon, she mentally brushed all thoughts of him away and drew Sonny into her mind. She and Sonny Capshaw had plans. She didn't have to worry as long as she had Sonny. Tomorrow she would really set their plans into motion, she decided. Pearl switched onto her back, lifted her chin, and pushed the flimsy synthetic blankets down to her chest in comforted determination. She then let the lingering feelings of a post-traumatic calm wash over her.

Chapter Three

Despite the dismal wake of the previous night's failings, Pearl rose a half hour before the morning bell echoed through the halls of Glory Heights. She had already bathed at the communal bathroom and combed through the thick salt-and-pepper waves surrounding her face. Her gold barrette—a Christmas gift from Sonny—was in place at the side of her head. Out of habit, to be certain her treasure was securely there, she occasionally stroked its jeweled clasp as she sat at the small desk in her room. She was looking over her work. Tapping the pencil against her chin, she re-read the letter she had just written, and a satisfactory smile spread over her face.

Sonny crossed her mind, although he had never quite left it to begin with, and her smile faltered some. She was eager to see him, to explain why she had failed to meet him the previous night. Although, she mused sadly, he probably already knew the answer.

She wondered how he had fared. They'd come so close to being caught by Nurse Charlotte and the warden. Actually, Pearl had been caught. Just the remembrance of it had its impact. She placed a hand on her stomach to dissuade the beginnings of a knot. Closing her eyes, she shook her head to erase any notion of them finding out what she was up to. Before it was time, anyway. The warden, at least, would try to stop her. She struggled to shove the thoughts aside. The consequences were too much to bear. But she admonished herself; she had to think positive. Silently, she repeated it: "Think positive, think positive, *think positive*." Then she had one final, positive push for her thoughts: Nurse Charlotte and the warden could suspect something, but they knew nothing. Of this Pearl could assure Sonny.

While she was in a hurry to see him, rising early didn't get her to him any sooner. Glancing at the letter she'd written, she figured she'd passed the time well. Dressing would take but a minute, and then she would have to wait for the 6:30 bell. That bell started the morning ritual of breakfast in the cafeteria followed by her daily dose of medication. After that, patients allowed to work at Brambles Brads and Bolts lined up at the front door. Fortunately, she was one of them. There they received an allotment of money for snack and pop machines—lunch was provided—before boarding transportation to the factory. At the factory, she would see Sonny.

When the bell went off, Karoline brought her gray-haired head out from beneath the covers. Pearl slid her rose-scented stationery into the desk drawer. When Karoline wrestled her way into a sitting position, Pearl was seriously inspecting her cuticles with a smile on her face. If Karoline wondered about it, she didn't say. Karoline was a heavy woman of late middle age. She suffered from muscular sclerosis, so it was with difficulty and stiffness that she lumbered from bed, donned slippers, and shuffled toward the door. She yawned and said a thick-tongued "good morning" to Pearl before leaving the room.

When Pearl no longer heard the flip-flop of Karoline's slippered feet, she rose and moved to the open door. Other patients herded by. Those fortunate enough to walk by themselves, but unfortunate enough to be without baths in their rooms, walked past in bathrobes, holding their personal toiletries. The noise of people constantly shuffling by out in the hallway was often unbearable. Pearl wanted to slam the door on it all, but it was against Glory

Heights' policy.

Pearl rolled her eyes at Glory Heights' policies and did her best to tune out the echolalic Cora Wilson, who repeated everything she heard four times. She closed her mind to the demonstrative Kenny Holmes. He never stopped waving his arms and talking about the braided bracelets and necklaces that he made every day in his art class, never noticing that no one was listening. She ignored them and the many others who were life's castoffs parading by, struggling for recognition within the sanitized walls of Glory Heights Healthcare Facility. Yet, she knew she was one of them.

Pearl watched until the flat, wide backside of Karoline disappeared through the bathroom door. God of wonder, thought Pearl. She could only hope she didn't look as bad from behind. Having seen enough, she hurried back to the desk and removed the letter. Moving to the bed, she lifted the mattress and smoothed it into the hiding place. She smiled.

Humming a nondescript tune, she dressed for work. She pulled drab polyester pants and a long-sleeved cotton shirt from the closet. Both items were ages old, purchased circa 1970, she figured. And it was 1989. Her heart longed for pretty clothes and shoes to wear. Also nylons—the kind with the seam up the back. The money she received each week for her work at Brambles was paltry, and Glory Heights controlled her access to it, so she wore what she had.

Twisting a broken thread hanging from her pants leg, she considered that getting money out of her account wouldn't be easy. Still, she had to try. Her plans simply warranted a new wardrobe. JC Penney would have everything she needed, and she could order the items from their catalog. In the mirror, her eyes brightened at the prospect. Happy again, she wondered only briefly if nylons with seams were still in style.

Glancing in the mirror atop the dresser, she repositioned her barrette and bounced the ends of her hair with her hands. Ready for the day, she turned from the mirror. But first she stole a look back over her shoulder. She felt sheepish doing it, and it didn't really matter, but she thought her posterior didn't look too bad.

At the door she paused and sighed heavily. An ugly beige helmet with rough leather straps lay on the bed stand, beseeching her. She touched the back of her head. The bruise she received in the previous night's fall from grace still smarted. It made her consider wearing the humiliating thing. However, not for long. Giving a solid pull to the bottom of her shirt, she stretched her neck and chin into a dignified pose. She then turned and closed the door, leaving the helmet behind.

The cafeteria was a minimal room with pea green walls, long rows of tables, and echoes of "good morning" competing with clattering trays. Today's breakfast consisted of warm coffee, cold toast, and lumpy oatmeal. Although the cafeteria was mostly abuzz with the business of serving breakfast and idle talk about the day's weather, chatter was light at Pearl's table. She ate her breakfast with other patients who worked at Brambles. They would have the whole day to discuss any trivia that came to mind. Pearl was thankful for the typical peace and quiet. She had much on her mind, none of which she would discuss with anyone here. However, Rebecca was a friend, and Pearl smiled good morning to her.

Rebecca also suffered from epilepsy. The two women became friends when Rebecca and Pearl signed up for the same experimental drug program—one of many Pearl had volunteered for over the years. They compared their progress until the drug was obviously working for Rebecca, but not Pearl. An increase in seizures forced Pearl out of the program. However, they remained friends. And when Rebecca began working at Brambles, Pearl found comfort in having a female friend with her on the assembly line. Other women worked at Brambles, but none with whom Pearl felt she could decently converse.

Pearl used the last of her lukewarm coffee to swallow one of two phenobarbital pills a nurse had placed next to her cup. The other pill went into her pocket; she would chuck it later. She had taken the same medication for years. No matter how many experimental drug programs she tried, nothing worked. The phenobarbital didn't work that well, either, and she'd recently taken to halving the dosage herself. The side effects of sleepiness and dizziness sometimes bothered her. Assaulted by several seizures a week, she didn't see the sense in doubling up on something that wasn't working for her.

After breakfast, Pearl headed upstairs in the required queue with the rest of the Brambles group. Before going to work, she needed to go back to her room. The letter was still beneath her mattress. Worried that someone would discover it, she'd opted to keep it hidden in the secret place until the last minute.

She politely nudged her way to the front of the line and then hurried down the hall to her room. Thank goodness Karoline was still at breakfast and would not deter her. Pearl was back before the last slowpoke made it to the end of the line for the money handout. When she stepped behind him, the nurse dishing out money didn't seem to notice her.

Waiting in line, Pearl fidgeted, sliding her hand in and out of her pants pocket. Yes, the letter was still there. So was the pill. That she would soon share her good news made her giddy with excitement. The palms of her hands felt damp and warm, making her worry that she would smudge the letter's ink from fretting with it so. While the others boarded the bus, she nonchalantly—at least she tried to be nonchalant about it—moved the letter to her purse. The pill she threw under the bus.

With everyone but Pearl on board, the bus moved away. As it turned onto the street, a black Lincoln Town Car pulled into the circular drive. The sun glinted off its polished chrome wheels. Pearl had never seen a speck of dirt on it. When it came to a stop, the car rocked with the weight of the chauffeur getting out. Dressed in a pressed black uniform and wearing a driving hat, he came around to help Pearl into the Town Car. He said, just as he did every morning, "Good morning, Miss Witherby." Then he closed the passenger door without waiting for a response.

When he got into the driver's seat, Pearl said, "Good morning, Anton. Beautiful day, isn't it?"

Anton nodded at her in the rearview mirror, adjusted his

sunglasses, and pulled onto the road.

Pearl smiled and then looked out the window. She watched the old houses fly by along the residential streets and considered Anton. Quite ceremonious, he rarely said more than "Good morning, Miss Witherby" when he picked her up and "Good afternoon, Miss Witherby" when he retrieved her from Brambles. Occasionally, "See you in the morning, Miss Witherby" surprisingly left his mouth. It used to bother her that he didn't see it fit to speak with her further. His silence had even made her nervous. But not anymore. She had plans, and that was all that mattered. Shifting in her seat and breathing deeply, she tried to parry any crumble in her confidence.

Her spirits ran high, and she disliked the feelings that pulled her down and away from that confidence, destroying her happiness. Was she uncertain about Sonny? No. Of Sonny, she was sure. She struggled to maintain her good spirits. She closed her eyes and shook her head to fight off the wistful moment that would take her back in time to who she used to be. But to no avail. It wasn't so much who she used to be that bothered her, because she had liked her childhood. More to the point, it was what she had lost and, later, what others took away from her that dismayed her most. Her loss of dignity was as clear as if it had just happened yesterday.

She would barely remember the day her life changed if not for her dear mother, Cecilia. Long-gone now, she used to tell the story often, as if it could have somehow changed the circumstances in which the family found themselves. Cecilia and Joseph Witherby may have been as hurt by the change as Pearl was herself, maybe even more so.

As Cecilia told it, it began on a summer morning in 1952. Pearl and her best friend, Amelia, were walking through the swaying wheat fields behind the Witherby house. At the field's edge, majestic bluebirds puffed out their chests and flitted about the poplars and old oak trees. Chickadees cooed and perched among their branches. Hawks looked for unprotected prey. The girls were enjoying the glorious day filled with sunshine and their carefree youth. No one suspected what lay ahead.

Cecilia stooped over her work in the garden, occasionally leaning back on her haunches to wipe sweat from her brow. The sweltering sun, ablaze in a radiant blue sky, pulsated through the back of her thin cotton shirt. With the cracked and drying dirt crumbling beneath her knees, she determinedly pulled at the weeds. Growing profusely under the hot sun, they showed great promise of consuming her string beans. She hoed and pulled, happily aware of the teenage chatter behind her.

The friends had walked away from the house into the woods beyond. Their laughter caught on the light breeze, interrupting the great summer heat, and delicately touched Cecilia's ears. She smiled the smile of a charmed mother. A perpetually happy child, Pearl was the constant twinkle in Cecilia's eyes. Pearl had always played sweetly on Cecilia's heartstrings.

Cecilia had just pulled the last of the miserable weeds from the garden bed when an unfamiliar sound, a high-pitched siren, screeched through the air. She jerked her head up as if a noose had sprung around it and then quickly rose to her feet. She looked toward the highway. Nothing was there. Another cry, a staggering shriek, came from behind her. She threw down the hoe and fled in the direction that seconds before had held her daughter's laughter. The shrieking continued. It was only matched in sound by a scream of volcanic proportions coming from Amelia, whose head bobbed above the bramble in the distance. But where was Pearl? Perspiration covered Cecilia's body and her bowels stirred. Amelia rose and ran toward Cecilia. Amelia, but not Pearl. Frantically, Amelia turned back toward the bramble, and then twisted toward Cecilia again, as if she didn't know which way to go or what to do. Her hands helplessly flapped in the air. "Help, help! Something's wrong, terribly wrong!" Amelia screamed.

Cecilia's stomach shimmied with fear. She ran faster. She counted every pounding footstep, but not the number of tears that sprouted and mixed with the sweat drenching her body. Finally, she spotted Pearl convulsing uncontrollably on the ground. "Pearl, Pearl!" There was no answer. Cecilia kept her eyes on her baby and drove her feet forward.

She collapsed against her daughter, whose body and limbs lashed the air like a desperate fish too long without water. Pearl's eyes rolled back inside her head and her limbs swatted heavily against Cecilia. "Run, Amelia. Call for help. Get Joseph! Get a doctor!" Cecilia howled. Frightened Amelia obeyed at once.

Knowing nothing else to do, Cecilia climbed on top of Pearl. Using all the strength she could muster in her legs, Cecilia spread them over her daughter's legs. Next, frantically arching her back and reaching out her arms, Cecilia grabbed, grabbed, and grabbed again at Pearl's arms, which were slippery with sweat. She gained control of Pearl's right arm and then struggled to secure her daughter's hand underneath her own hipbone. Cecilia then reached for Pearl's left arm just as Pearl's right hand slid from Cecilia's hold. Pearl's arms again hurled into the air. Then, suddenly, the spasm died and the shrill shriek became a gurgling sputter. Pearl's arms fell limply at her sides.

Cecilia jerked her head up and looked into Pearl's colorless face. A groan rose from deep within Pearl's throat. Undiluted fright replaced Cecilia's momentary relief. Pearl's tongue had arched into her throat. She was suffocating. Cecilia grabbed Pearl's jaws and pressed so Pearl's mouth would open. That Cecilia may cause her daughter pain flashed rapidly through her mind, but she couldn't let it stop her. She reached inside Pearl's mouth and grabbed for her tongue. Cecilia's fingers slipped and slithered over the saliva flowing from Pearl's mouth. In desperation, Cecilia did something she had never done before. With an anguished cry, she punched her daughter in the face. Hard. As hard as she could, hoping to wake Pearl. At least, to open her mouth again. With one free hand, Cecilia ripped open her own shirt, barely noticing the buttons snapping against her skin. Wrapping a shirttail around her fingers, she pushed her small fist into Pearl's gaping mouth and grabbed onto her tongue. Teeth gnashed against Cecilia's flesh and blood curled around her fingers. She felt no pain, only what she imagined for her daughter. Cecilia did not let go until Pearl's whole body went limp.

Frightened that death had come to her daughter, Cecilia rushed her shaking hands to cradle Pearl's face. Cecilia checked Pearl's neck for a pulse. She was breathing and her eyes were opening! Overjoyed, Cecilia planted kisses over every inch of Pearl's delicate, sweet face. Pearl was alive and the seizure had passed.

Drenched in sweat, Cecilia pulled away from Pearl and lay down beside her. Cecilia tried to catch her breath. She tried not to think.

Pearl's pants were wet from the loss of bladder control. She began to cry. "What happened, Mama? What happened?"

Cecilia couldn't answer. Exhausted, she rested her head atop Pearl's and cradled Pearl in her arms. Cecilia's own tears fell, landing on Pearl's beautiful head of hair, now wet with perspiration. The fragrant scent of Pearl's favorite shampoo filled Cecilia's heart with sadness. Her tears ran like unrelenting sorrow down her cheeks and chin. Somehow, somewhere inside, Cecilia knew what was to come. Long ago, she had witnessed a friend having a spell like this, but she said nothing of this to Pearl. She only murmured sounds of comfort. Still holding onto each other, they slowly rose and walked back to the house. From across the field, Pearl's father ran toward them. Behind him came Amelia and the first of many doctors that would help set the new course of Pearl's life.

That first seizure rocked Pearl's world and that of those around her. The Witherby family painfully waited for test results. At first, Joseph and Cecilia desperately hoped that the weather, the humid heat of a Wisconsin summer, had caused Pearl to have a mere fainting spell. However, an EEG revealed the presence of electrical discharges in the brain. When the doctor gravely broke the news to Joseph and Cecilia, they knew at once that it was true. Pearl was an epileptic. There was the label no one wanted to hear. On medication, Pearl might finish high school. They would have to wait and see.

No one knew quite what to do. Doctors were consulted. Hearts were broken. Lips were sealed. During the era of world wars, having epilepsy was nearly akin to being insane. While times were changing elsewhere, the stigma still thrived in small-town America. No cure was known. No treatment effectively stopped the hell that broke loose on Pearl Witherby's life.

Before that awful morning when electronic lights buzzed and flashed inside Pearl's pretty head, she had the same hopes and dreams as any teenaged girl: romantic love, a husband, and children. However, those few moments in time changed Pearl's life forever. They silenced the dreams. That first epileptic seizure marked the beginning of a future where no one considered Pearl's dreams relevant. Pearl Witherby, so full of life, was cut off from her hopes and aspirations. It was unfair, unthinkable, and finally unspeakable.

Anton flipped on the radio, the sound of which brought Pearl back to the present, and she was glad for it. She had her future to concentrate on. Shifting comfortably into the Town Car's soft leather seat, she cherished the well-needed privacy. With a pen from her purse, and handwriting that looked like wrinkled geometry, she finished the last few sentences of the letter. She pulled a crumpled stamped and addressed envelope from her purse and pushed the letter inside. It was ready to go. She would place it in the office mailbox on her way to her factory post of counting nails for packaging. If she could count on the U.S. Postal Service, her sister would receive the letter in DC by the day after tomorrow.

Pearl's head jerked and her lips twittered as she imagined her sister's reaction. She placed a hand over the smile forming across her lips; despite the hiccup in the rendezvous of the night before, she was elated. This time no one was going to rain on her parade. Not even Senator Susan Seymour, who decades ago had committed her to Glory Heights.

Chapter Four

Senator Susan Seymour sat in her Washington DC congressional office shaking her head over what she had just read. She didn't know whether to laugh at the absurdity of its contents, or cry at the potent disaster it could cause—and tighten precautions as a result. It was simply unbelievable. There were no other words for it.

Early that morning, Susan had retrieved the letter from her mailbox on the way out of her Congressional Heights apartment building. She knew who it was from the minute she saw the small, nervous chicken-scratch etching out her name, her old name, which was about as exciting as chicken scratch. Pearl was the only one who knew who Susan used to be. Pearl seldom wrote, which Susan greatly appreciated. Any news would be boring news.

Upon arriving at the Hart Senate Building, Susan hastily opened the letter and gave it only a cursory glance. She was certain that it wasn't worth reading. In fact, she had it halfway to the trash can before her mouth flew open and she jerked the paper back in front of her. Hastily then, with a grip on the letter, she wrestled with her reading glasses, upsetting her perfect bobbed-to-the-chin, ash blonde hair in the process. With one good yank and a cuss, she freed the glasses from the tangled strands and got them to the end of her nose. She read the letter, unaware of the tension mounting around her lips, creasing carefully applied raisinberry lipstick into the lines surrounding her fifty-four-year-old mouth.

Taking off her glasses, she pulled the brief note closer to her face and reread it—carefully the second time, searching for the punch line. At that range, the faint floral-scented fumes of the antiquated stationery irritated her nose. She absentmindedly raised a hand and relieved the itch. Then, with glossy French-manicured nails and forced composure, she set the page down in front of her. She lifted her gold-plated Congressional coffee cup and sat for a moment without moving. She stared off into space. There was no punch line.

It was still early morning, way too early to have received this news: Pearl met someone and, God forbid, *she wants to marry him.* How in hell did that happen? Susan silently fumed and thought, Pearl is fifty-two years old and has never lived outside institutional walls, at least as an adult she hasn't. She's an invalid, for Christ's sake. She knows nothing about being on the outside. And if Susan had anything to say about it, which she most certainly did, Pearl would stay at Glory Heights Healthcare Facility. That's where she belonged. Furthermore, just what kind of person could Pearl meet at Glory Heights? Susan shuddered at the thought, tightening her Jones of New York suit jacket around her middle. More absurd than Pearl wanting to marry the guy was that she had written to request Susan's blessing. *Her blessing!*

Susan would rather have dug right into government business than have to deal with that bullshit. All it did was stir up old feelings, things she hated to think about. She sipped the hot black coffee, reacting to its charged bitterness with acrimonious thoughts. From the beginning, she was determined that Pearl's affliction with epilepsy would not ruin her own life. Susan had worked too long and hard to let her sister screw it up now.

She resented having to deal with Pearl at all. Any communication from her only reminded Susan of the past, the only real tie they had with one another. And she'd rather forget that all together. But Susan did remember.

They grew up in Kerry, Wisconsin, a sleepy farming community of no more than a thousand people. The town had three taverns, a combination gas station and hardware store, Mabel's hair salon, George's barbershop, an IGA grocery, a co-op, and Kerry's Café. Other than the schools, the Catholic church, and Peachtree Nursing Home, there was nothing else. It had held no excitement or charm for Susan. Kerry was as clean as a freshly manicured toenail. Susan would give it that. The town's only street cleaner went through twice daily, rain or shine.

It was simply a desolate place with nothing to do but keep the town clean and farm, which is what the Witherbys did. That was, until Cecilia and Joseph Witherby, realizing that neither of their teenaged daughters had a calf's hair of interest in the fetid rituals and backbreaking toils of farming, sold the farm and bought the Silver Dollar.

The rustic tavern came with a home attached alongside—cramped quarters with the yeasty odor of stale draft beer and pungent tobacco smoke emanating from the bar and coming to rest on the home's drapes, rugs, and walls, and, worst of all, their clothing. Patrons hadn't minded the stench, but Susan could still smell it if she lingered on the memory too long.

Susan shook her head, trying to dismiss the old thoughts. That life was decades ago, but she felt contempt for it as if it were yesterday. They'd lived out in the damn boondocks. There wasn't a skyscraper or piece of civilization in sight. She pushed away from the desk, swiveled around in her chair, and looked out the window. Still, the starkness of Pearl's revelation coming by way of the U.S. Postal Service kept drawing her back in time.

They had never been close. Growing up, Pearl's constant cheery chatter merely annoyed Susan. Pearl was incessantly easygoing and of good humor, which made her, not Susan, the apple of their parents' collective eye. High-strung Susan put on a good front only if it got her where she wanted to go, and she resented Pearl for her perpetual good mood.

Although Susan didn't have a best friend or even a close circle of friends, she intrigued many. Conversely, down-to-earth

Pearl had many friends, even a best friend, Amelia. Susan floated in and out of the school's many cliques with ease, attempting to appear mysterious and mystical. She believed it suited her dramatic side, which she liked to test out on unsuspecting young bar patrons.

Joseph and Cecilia did not allow their girls in the tavern on busy nights. However, on quiet nights, Susan stepped inside to steal a glance at the young men, or, to be more exact, let them look at her. At seventeen, she knew her effect on men and used it to her advantage. She stood five feet seven inches and had long legs, a narrow waist, and a bosom that got a normal red-blooded boy's attention. Her high cheeks drew down into a delicate cloven chin. Her blue eyes teased and winked when she felt it enhanced her stakes of getting attention.

She practiced her seduction in her bedroom, standing in front of a mirror. Shaking her wild tangle of auburn hair until it fell loosely around her face and cooing her lips, she imagined herself a famous movie star. She then went into the bar to show off her well-practiced allure on whomever struck her fancy. But, lo and behold, Pearl would already be perched on a stool, batting big brown eyes at Daddy, who easily gave in to her pleas for ice cream, or a bag of peanuts and a cherry soda.

While Susan was a beauty in her own right, resembling their dad's side of the family, Pearl had their mother's small, straight nose, beautiful thick, brown wavy hair, and a sparkle in her eye. Pearl's beauty was enough to make the young men divide their stares between the sisters as they slowly sipped their beers at the end of the bar like they had nowhere else to be anytime soon. Susan noticed it if Pearl did not. Being older, Susan believed the attention rightfully belonged to her, and she didn't like sharing. Rather than joining their dad and Pearl, Susan often stomped back to her room, seething with jealousy.

During these slow times in the bar, their dad and Pearl engaged in long talks about school and friends. While Susan thought the talks pointless, their dad never seemed to tire of his beloved Pearl's endless chatter about all things important to her—high school, Amelia, dances, and boys. Sometimes Susan's curiosity overcame her jealousy. Pearl was known for her gutsy sense of humor and sometimes had a good tale to tell. One story stuck in Susan's mind because it had made even her laugh. The surprised look on their dad's face was priceless.

Pearl had giggled with conspiratorial splendor and told of how she stuffed an overly-dead fish deep into Amelia's school locker. Two weeks passed with teachers and students alike pinching up their noses at the decaying stench. During classes and between, they wondered aloud where the smell could be coming from. Finally, a school janitor found the decomposing walleye beneath a stack of old papers at the bottom of Amelia's locker. Amelia didn't have to ask who did it. Neither did she turn her in. Pearl had simply gotten back at Amelia for the molding Limburger cheese found in her own locker a few weeks before.

How the two girls remained friends, let alone best friends, was beyond Susan. The interesting part for Susan was that she too had suffered with the stench of that old fish for two weeks, completely unaware of her sister's ploy, until Pearl confessed to their dad. While resenting Pearl's relationship with him, it was sometimes worth standing by long enough to find out what they were talking about.

Susan preferred to keep as much distance as possible between Pearl and herself, but the debacle that eventually took over Pearl's life inevitably drew Susan in as well. If Susan resented Pearl for stealing attention before the epilepsy, she grew to hate Pearl for the type of attention received after it.

When classes began in the fall, news of Pearl's illness spread like wildfire through Kerry High School. Classmates began treating both Pearl and Susan differently. Most avoided Pearl, afraid, not knowing what to say to her. Susan's classmates, on the other hand, wanted to talk about it. However, when the curious approached her with questions regarding Pearl's condition, Susan's icy smile was enough to change the subject. Not that she was trying to protect Pearl from becoming the school wacko. She simply didn't want anything to do with Pearl's illness.

At first, a few friends remained social with Pearl. But as her fits increased, so did her friends' fear. In time, even Amelia shrank away. Susan could hardly blame them. After all, what teenager wanted to face the possibility of never getting a driver's license, never going to the prom, never dating again? They feared that if Pearl could get epilepsy, well, then perhaps by osmosis they could too. Susan had thought of this possibility, as well.

Susan thought that having epilepsy would've immediately put a damper on Pearl's lighthearted spirit, but in fact, it took awhile. The loss of Amelia's friendship had been the turning point for Pearl. After being stuck together like glue since first grade, Amelia's rejection devastated her. It was after that time that Susan noticed a marked change in Pearl's demeanor. She grew quieter. She lost the enthusiastic spring in her step. Her clothes hung on slumped shoulders.

While Pearl's life grayed, Cecilia and Joseph kept hope alive for her. In fact, they wasted most of the money saved from the sale of the farm driving back and forth across two states for many consultations with every well-reputed neurological expert referred to them. From the University Hospital in Madison, Wisconsin, to the Mayo Clinic in Rochester, Minnesota, they sought the advice of one renowned specialist after another. Still, the results were the same. Pearl had a hard case of epilepsy manifesting itself in dangerous seizures.

It took months for Joseph to smile after that realization. Bar stool talks between him and Pearl became less frequent. He seemed afraid he would upset her somehow and cause her to go into one of her fits. Susan didn't blame him. He most likely wondered where Pearl had gotten the plague. Susan sure did. Insanity, as Susan thought of the epilepsy then, didn't run in either their dad's or mother's side of the family, not that had ever been reported, anyway. However, if you believed the lore, being Irish meant having a long ancestry of drinking, which killed brain cells. There could've been some relationship between the two problems. It seemed a feasible excuse at the time.

Susan dreaded anything that associated her with Pearl.

Once, during a meeting about the class yearbook, of which Susan was the senior editor, she was summoned to help her sister. Pearl was, as the hall monitor who drafted Susan into service frankly put it, "in the throes of a fit." Susan was horrified. Red-faced with anger and embarrassment, she rushed to find Pearl peeling herself off the floor in front of her locker looking confused and disheveled.

Susan hurriedly ushered Pearl, weak from the seizure's rampage against her mind and body, to the main office. Once there, Susan haphazardly shoved Pearl into a metal chair next to the office's large picture window and then called their mother. She left Pearl waiting for their mother with only the humiliating awareness of classmates moving between rooms and gawking outside the window for company.

Susan promptly returned to the meeting and to her classmates' questioning stares. She offered only a charismatic smile and acted as if no abnormality had occurred. She then swiftly sank back into leading a discussion on the yearbook's final layout. Inwardly, she clenched her teeth and silently thanked God that she had only one year left of high school. After that, she would leave Kerry and everybody in it for more exciting prospects. Her future game plan included studying drama at UCLA and becoming the darling of films. America was going to love her.

Going off to college was the best thing that had ever happened to Susan. She viewed her escape to UCLA, where no one knew her or her sister, as a fresh start. No longer would anyone look at Susan the way the people of small-town, gossiping Kerry had looked at her when she was with Pearl. Between the townspeople's sidelong glances in the IGA grocery and the wide berth students provided in the halls of Kerry High School, they had all laid their distaste before Susan and Pearl.

While Susan was living in LA, Cecilia wrote her once a month with letters that went on and on about Pearl. This doctor recommended this, another that. She fell down here, had a fit there. That she graduated from high school was a miracle. Phenobarbital had controlled the fits enough to get her through school, but not enough to get her a job. No one would hire Pearl.

Susan graduated from UCLA with a degree in theater. She promptly found an agent and began waiting for work as a movie star. She often fantasized about being interviewed by Merv Griffin and Mike Douglas, who would praise her performances in the hottest films. In her wildest dreams, she had won a large mantel's worth of the coveted Oscar. After that, Johnny Carson, the new *Tonight Show* host, would be dying to talk with her too.

Susan gladly took the money her mother sent, often requesting more than she received. After all, it was difficult getting started in any career. She happily continued along this lackadaisical path, attending the right parties and idly waiting for her big break into film. That was until, to Susan's irritation, one letter came sans money. According to Mother, all their money was going to Pearl's care.

Undaunted by her financial drawback, Susan rallied, convincing herself that she was on the road to fame and fortune. Her break was just over the horizon and nothing was going to get in her way. Certainly not Pearl, for whom there was no hope. With Plan A in the dumper, Susan went to Plan B.

First, Susan changed her name. She became Susan Seymour, the actress. Susan Witherby no longer existed. Witherby simply had no sex appeal. It wasn't catchy enough for someone like her. Susan Seymour was a name people would remember. Second, to remedy her financial situation, she found a job hosting at Grago's, one of LA's finest restaurants. It was a place frequented by major stars, directors, producers, and casting agents. The wages were lousy. Nevertheless, Susan knew how to schmooze and flirt, an asset that had a definite impact on the size of her tips. She made enough in tip money to pay the monthly bills on her small apartment. Moreover, she earned sufficient wage money for all the extras she needed in the way of clothes and cosmetics. The next thing she did was beneath her, she knew, but she had to start somewhere. To be in the public's eye while waiting for the roles that would place her in the limelight, she started going to cattle calls for film extras. It turned out to be the catalyst for her real career.

While working as an extra, Susan overheard the star's stand-in talking about a certain charity. It was getting a lot of publicity. Susan listened carefully. He explained that America's celebrity culture, of which he assumed he was clearly a part, had spawned a philanthropy brokerage called Celebrities for Charitable Causes. It thrived on helping celebrities raise their moral quotient by connecting them to an appropriate charitable foundation. Most often, CCC coupled an organization that raised research money for a particular disease with a star who had a loved one stricken by that disease. They were looking for volunteers. They needed anyone able to walk, talk, answer a telephone, or mail flyers. Susan could easily do all of those things, and more.

That same night, she phoned CCC. However, she wasn't about to mention Pearl and get matched up with the Epilepsy Foundation. Susan volunteered to help a charity that raised public awareness about diabetes. She didn't necessarily care about its purpose. In fact, she didn't give it much thought. What she did care about was that she would work alongside others in the film industry, raising her chances for stardom.

The only downside was the requirement that, to be associated with the charity, she had to support the charitable organizations with contributions from her own paycheck. However, Susan conceded that, based on her humble financial situation—having fudged the amount she earned—the donated percentage of income recommended by CCC would be meager at best. Susan figured it was a small price to pay for her impending fame. She chipped in and turned up for publicized charity events hoping to boost her visibility and her career. Important actors, producers, and directors would at least view her favorably, and that couldn't hurt her chances of becoming famous. She didn't know whether it was admiration, love, or simply being in the limelight she craved. It didn't matter. She was going to get it all.

Cecilia continued to write to Susan, without including money, outlining the miserable details of Pearl's existence. It was becoming increasingly difficult for Cecilia and Joseph to care for Pearl. Due to the number of seizures Pearl was having, she needed constant supervision. Consequently, they placed her in the Peachtree Nursing Home right there in Kerry. However, the home was too limiting for Pearl. To her caretaker's exasperation, Pearl frequently wandered out of the nursing home without telling anyone where she was going. Her medication still worked well enough. She had not yet developed the psychosis that often accompanies people who suffer with seizures. It wasn't until later, when the phenobarbital lost some of its effectiveness, that she became afraid to go out on her own, anxious that she would have an epileptic attack.

Pearl's excursions amused Susan. She found her parents' choice of homes for Pearl embarrassing. Susan could hardly blame Pearl for wanting out of the morbid little place for old people. Alas, Pearl slipped out to roam the streets of Kerry once too often. It seemed that she had some remaining spirit for life, and it got her dismissed from Peachtree Nursing Home. Cecilia challenged Pearl's dismissal, saying that she was simply getting some fresh air and seeing what was new at the co-op. But it was to no avail.

According to Cecilia, it was with great sadness that they moved Pearl to a group home thirty miles away. In the group home, they allowed Pearl chaperoned privileges, and she lived in a section with people her own age, although functioning levels of life varied. Susan could only imagine it.

When their dad died, Susan flew back to Kerry for the funeral. It was the first time she had seen Pearl in more than ten years. What Susan saw frightened her. The girl Pearl had been was no more. Her eyes were anxious and slightly dimmed. Her cheeks sagged into jowls. Their mother thought it was from the drugs. Susan thought it had to be something deeper than that. She briefly felt sorry for the girl with the lost smile and wished she had been nicer to her. She was mostly glad that it hadn't happened to her.

At the funeral, Susan covered her head with a black scarf and spoke to no one. Pearl spoke only a few words to Susan, but Susan would never forget it. They were standing side by side over their father at the wake, when Pearl peered into the coffin and then looked back at Susan. "You know something, Sue? With all that makeup on, you look more like Dad now than you ever did!" It appeared that Pearl had not yet lost all of her wit. When Susan arrived back in LA she bought all new makeup.

Susan could not get a break in the movies. She had grown tired of being someone's stand-in or that horror of horrors: an extra. Once at a dinner party, someone easily entertained by her charisma suggested that she go into politics. The power in politics intrigued Susan. The next day she signed up to run for a position on city council, and won. It turned out, much to her surprise, that she enjoyed government. Glamour and recognition could be found in politics too. She decided to stick with it—it was a lot like acting and easier to get a part.

As her political career grew, so did her fear of being associated with Pearl. Susan could tell where her mother's letters were going, with constant reminders that her father was gone and her mother was getting older. Someone would have to tend to Pearl, and Cecilia thought that person should be Susan. But no way was Susan going to have her life tarnished by Pearl's epilepsy. After all, Susan was fine; she was fully sane. That the stigma of insanity was fast becoming an archaic belief briefly touched her mind, but it was certainly not worth pursuing. She did see the need for a faithful, young political assistant and found him in Nick Ballantine. Shortly after Cecilia's death, Susan sent Nick to find a place for Pearl—somewhere she wouldn't be a problem. Taking orders from Susan, he arranged everything. She had scarcely heard a peep from Pearl, until she received the letter.

Having finished her coffee, Susan was ready to make some decisions. She was going to nip Pearl's asinine plan in the bud. But then Susan realized that, as the senator from Minnesota, she had enough to worry about for one day. Considering her position and need for anonymity, someone else needed to deal with the problem. That someone was still Nick Ballantine. She picked up the phone and dialed.

Chapter Five

Nick let the phone ring and thought about not answering it. He knew who was calling. She called him several times a day. The woman's office was next door to his, but could she get off her royal arse and walk over to have a personal conversation? He guessed not. "Nick here."

"Nick, we have a problem. Come to my office at once."

He rolled his eyes. She was unbelievable. "No problem. Be right there."

Without saying "good morning," Susan motioned for Nick to sit, and then, with a disturbed flick of her arm, she handed him a letter.

Nick read it. When he finished, he looked at her with an amused grin. However, after one look at Susan, he lost the smile. "You don't take this shenanigan seriously, do you?"

Susan's expertly dyed blonde hair curved along the sides of her face, pronouncing the tightness in her well-set chin. "Hell no. I'm not willing to take any chances either. Look, Nick, in twenty minutes I'm delivering a speech on the protection of invalids—excuse me, how did you phrase that?—'persons with noncommunicable diseases. . .,'" she said as she glanced over the desk at him.

Nick nodded, indicating that she had said it correctly. Inwardly, he groaned at her incognizance.

She continued, ". . . from being discriminated against in the workplace to the senate Health, Education, Labor, and Pensions Committee. That invalid group includes those with epilepsy. If word got out that I have a sister with epilepsy, it would destroy me. How was I to know that it would turn out to be one of those illnesses? Anyway, it's too late to change course now."

Nick assumed they could easily resolve this. "I don't think we need to get too excited about this. First of all, Pearl's incapable of living without medical assistance. Secondly, she probably doesn't have the mental capacity to carry something like this out. At least not anymore. Thirdly, if you cut off Pearl's insurance, she has nothing." He stopped for a moment, considering. "But if it will make you feel better, I'll give McFinley a call and remind him why we're paying him."

When Nick began working for Susan, he was young, ambitious, naïve, and eager to please his new boss. When she asked him to handle living arrangements for Pearl, he wanted to impress her by doing a good job. Within a week's time, he found Glory Heights Healthcare Facility, located northwest of Minneapolis in Rum River, Minnesota. Without warning or discussion, they whisked Pearl off to Glory Heights.

Nick arranged everything through Daris McFinley, Glory Heights' administrator. McFinley had no idea who Susan was, and he didn't ask questions. For the terms of care Nick laid out, McFinley was an easy payoff. In exchange for more lining in his pants pockets, McFinley wholeheartedly guaranteed Pearl's containment on the premises of Glory Heights. That's what Susan wanted, and that's what Nick got for her. McFinley assured Nick that Pearl would not be free to roam the streets of Rum River.

At the time, Nick thought it was for Pearl's own safety; at least he allowed himself to believe that. According to the monthly report, sent to an anonymous post office box, Pearl's social fears were far beyond the "anticipatory anxiety" associated with having a seizure in public. She had no desire to leave the premises. In fact, Pearl had been terrified of it.

When he thought back on it, any idiot could see that Susan didn't want anyone to know about Pearl. Susan had rooked him into being her liaison. Although, he hadn't had to do too much—the need for contacting McFinley was rare. On the first of each month, Nick sent one check to McFinley and another to Glory Heights, and that was that. The arrangement had worked well for quite a long time, years in fact.

Susan seemed to be considering Nick's analysis of the situation. She brightened. "I believe you are right about her mental condition, Nick. Her medication and seizures have diminished her mental capacity. There's little chance of her doing anything but staying on at the medical facility, indefinitely. Still, the fact is, she's met someone. Now, how in the hell did that happen?" Susan's genial tone snapped as she acknowledged aloud this new revelation.

Nick waved the letter. "It says here they met at work."

Susan drew up in her chair. "I know what the freakin' letter says! I mean, I pay a handsome donation to Glory Heights Healthcare Facility each year. I pay Daris McFinley for his confidentiality and assistance. I pay a chauffeur to escort her to and from work to limit the possibility of her running off somewhere. So how could she get involved with someone enough to think that she needs to marry him?" Having gotten that out, Susan sank back in her chair and continued, almost as if to herself. "Well, maybe there's nothing to worry about. It's not like she has the same feelings as other women. I mean romantically speaking, she lost that years ago."

Nick wasn't so sure about that, but he didn't say so. Susan's peripheral view of Pearl amazed him. How could someone who serves on several Health and Human Service committees be so ignorant? Hell, he knew the answer. It was all ego, and talk. Susan built her career on shrewd ambition and good looks rather than compassion or concern. Others wrote the speeches and initiated the bills. She was the accredited power-head without a heart.

In public, she affected a smooth, refined way of speaking.

With her studied persuasive rhetoric, she was a successful mouthpiece for getting votes through. Her behind-the-scenes foul mouth would flabbergast Minnesota constituents. If they only knew. The senator's other secrets would shock them as well. Having worked with her for so many years, Nick knew more about her than he wanted to, more than she was aware, and he'd been shocked. Still, he had filed the information away. He felt fortunate to have it. In politics, clandestine information was a good thing to have. Sometimes it won votes for good causes.

The senator's treatment of Pearl appalled Nick. Susan was the sister from hell personified. Had Susan treated Pearl with the civility she deserved instead of hiding her away in Rum River all these years without so much as a "Hi, how are ya?", Susan wouldn't have a problem. It wasn't Pearl or her disease that the public would find abhorrent. The Minnesotans who had elected Susan to a democratic senatorial seat were liberal, progressive, and conscientious. They called her constituents "Minnesota nice" for good reason. The senator's unkindness toward Pearl would be her ruin. Although, blinded by her own bigotry, Susan couldn't see it.

Nick looked at her and suppressed a yawn. He was tired of Susan. Lately, he was feeling the need to move on. Nevertheless, he would stay. He would do her dirty work long enough to ensure her "yes" vote on the Great Lakes Water Protection Act. After so many years it was finally coming to fruition, and he didn't want anything standing in the way of that. He was an avid environmentalist, and the act was important to him. The bill would direct the administrator of the Environmental Protection Agency to conduct a study on the environmental effects of oil and gas drilling beneath the water in the Great Lakes. With one-fifth of the world's freshwater supply and its basin the home for over thirty-three million people, the lakes were a vital source of safe drinking water for millions of people. Some politicians, looking for fast alternatives to allay the country's reliance on Saudi Arabia as an energy source, were too ready to drill without studying the effects of such action.

"Nick?" Susan looked as if she had been waiting for an answer. "Don't you agree?"

Nick sat up straight and tried to look attentive. Did Nick agree with Susan that Pearl had no womanly feelings? He wasn't going to touch that. He made a decision. "I'll take care of it. I'll find out what's going on and fix it. Cripes, I'd nearly forgotten Pearl. It's been years since we've had to do anything but send money. The last time was when she started the work program. I'm sure we can easily resolve it, as we did that problem. If work is where Pearl found this guy, work is what we'll fix."

Nick was a man of action and, for that, Susan was grateful. She had laid the problem of Pearl in his hands, and he would take care of it. Susan looked at him now. She wondered how he felt about this mission. It was difficult to know. He had a face you couldn't read, an admirable if not frustrating trait. In twenty years of working together she had found no reason to doubt his loyalty. He was either very trustworthy, or very careful. She wished she knew which.

At forty-five, Nick had not lost the boyish good looks that had drawn her to him so long ago. She had a lustful eye for younger men, beginning with her own daughter's father. Nick had finely honed looks with a solid runner's build and tight buttocks. Moreover, the Celtic and Roman heritage shining through his perpetually tan skin and dark hair should've been enough to send her beyond the edge of reason many times over.

When it came to her sexual nature, she had erred on the wrong side of reason more than once. Susan, shrewdly this time, had kept her hands off Nick. It had not been easy. She often longed to touch the small dark mole set on the right side of his face, tracing it from the curve of his strong cheekbone down to the full pout in his lips. She often wondered how his thick, soft-looking hair would feel in the grip of her fingers. She had these thoughts, but they were never as strong as after some political showcase, from which he drove her home.

After indulging in several glasses of wine inevitably

40

served at those functions, it was hard not to solicit his sexual attention. Even then, especially then, she kept her distance. Instead, she prudently left him, retiring alone to her room. From there, she placed a call to the private service that promised secrecy and gratification. She had kept her feelings well hidden from him. She was sure of it.

Distractedly going from one thought to another, she was wondering again if she could still trust him when he interrupted her.

"What?" Nick asked.

He gave Susan a curious look.

"Excuse me?" She had been frowning from concentrating too hard.

Nick noted that easing the tension between her brows had seemed to take some effort. "You looked a million miles away." Actually, Nick thought, you looked like you were boring a new pore in my face—again.

Susan waved manicured hands in front of her eyes. "I guess I didn't get enough sleep last night. I'd stayed up later than I'd intended studying the notes you'd given me on today's hearings."

Nick smiled at her, indicating he understood. He then handed Susan the letter, thinking she would want to save it. She smiled back at him and took the letter. Then, she ran it through the shredder next to her desk. It was his problem now.

Susan glanced at her watch and then swiftly moved her chair back from the desk. She waved a hand toward the door. "Shall we?"

It was time to give her speech on the senate floor. Before moving out from behind the desk, she opened a drawer and pulled out a compact. She inspected her hair and makeup and straightened the disrupted strands of hair. Nick knew she wouldn't allow a hair out of place; she was meticulous about her appearance.

Looking pleased with what she saw, she smiled at herself and put away the mirror. Nick followed her to the door, and together they stepped into the common hall of the Hart Senate Building.

Seeing another senator, Susan put on a power-smile, fell into stride with him, and started a conversation. Nick stayed behind, watching his boss's brilliant public persona come to life. He thought she was amazing in the worst sense of the word. He also thought that, during their entire conversation, Susan had not once spoken Pearl's name. With some consternation, he turned back toward his office. He had a phone call to make.

Chapter Six

Matthew Kincaid was in his office with the door closed. It was a colorless room, a glaring contrast to the inviting decor shown to the public at Glory Heights. In the reception area, Italian marble flooring complemented green and gold designer walls. Sunlight poured over lush, live foliage adorning every corner. His office had beige walls and brown industrial-strength carpeting. The only bright spot came from the wall with pictures of Cory, his twelve-year-old son. Framed certificates of achievement and diplomas in social welfare from the University of Vermont hung on another wall.

Frowning, he looked around the room. The 10 by 12 space was overflowing with open case files. He didn't know how he would get to them all. Files were stacked atop his desk. An old metal filing cabinet with perpetually belligerent drawers stood in the corner, the top of it piled high with manila folders. Even more lined the floorboards.

Daris McFinley, Glory Heights' administrator, wanted a status report. Matthew didn't like doing them—McFinley was never satisfied. He didn't understand that progress was sometimes slow. Patients healed in their own time, not McFinley's. Still, Matthew was going to give it a shot. He had just picked up a pen when there was an abrupt rap on his door followed by someone walking through it.

Suddenly, the guy he least wanted to see was standing in front of his desk. From the look on McFinley's face, all pinched and pissed, Matthew figured it was a distasteful event in his day too. McFinley had his hands on his hips, and he looked ready to pounce on someone. Most likely, Matthew.

McFinley was a tall man. He tried to be intimidating, but his efforts were lost on Matthew. He reminded Matthew of a large snot-nosed kid with a whine. Behind McFinley's back, most everyone called him the warden. The moniker fit him well. He was cold, unapproachable, and seemingly heartless. Matthew suspected that the warden didn't have an ounce of humanity running through his veins. The warden also didn't get that benevolence was vital to effective social work.

Matthew only had a moment to wonder what had brought him out to Glory Heights. It had to be important, or he wouldn't be there during the day. The state required a once-a-month call to facilities under his jurisdiction. Failing to do so might incur a delay in, or cancellation of, public funding, something near and dear to the warden's position at Glory Heights. Typically, he filled this mandate after residents were in their rooms for the night. Matthew figured that a daylight sojourn brought him too close to reality. The warden had tried it for a while. Being face-to-face with the mentally retarded, epileptic, or manic-ridden had visibly rattled him. Conversely, those people were Matthew's lifework. His master's in social welfare allowed him to work with some of the finest people he'd ever met. Many of his clients had more heart and soul than he'd ever see in people like the warden.

"Matthew, why can't you keep your patients under control?" said the warden.

Matthew had no idea what he was talking about. "What can I do for you, McFinley?"

"I made some changes today. Changes I wished I didn't have to deal with. Because you let things get so out of control with Pearl Witherby, I was forced to put an end to it."

"Pearl Witherby? What are you talking about?"

The warden folded his hands across his chest and looked down his nose. "You don't know?"

Matthew wished he'd get to the point. "Know what?"

"Your Ms. Witherby was scheming to leave Glory Heights and marry Sonny Capshaw." Then the warden added with a tsk, "As if that were a possibility."

Based on his tone, Matthew figured the warden knew about his feelings for her. If he would name a favorite client, it would be Pearl. In deference to his other clients, whom he worked just as hard for, he would never say the words aloud. But Pearl was special. He admired her tenacity to defy whatever life threw at her. She was a trooper, a true survivor. She had come a long way from where she was when Matthew first met her. He had helped her, but she had done the work. Admirably, she had weathered it all.

Matthew knew that she and Sonny spent a lot of time together, even that they really cared for each other. But he hadn't realized it was so serious. Matthew was cautious now. "Really, and how do you know this?" He couldn't fathom the warden getting involved with a resident.

"That's not important." The warden glared at Matthew.

Matthew didn't press him. Instead, he said, "Okay, then. What kind of changes are you talking about?"

"Well, let's just say that Sonny has found a new job."

Matthew was surprised at this. "What's that supposed to mean?"

"Never you mind what it means. Sonny will no longer be working at Brambles. I've taken care of that. Your job is to keep Pearl from seeing him again. He's no longer welcome at Glory Heights. No visiting, no game nights, no nothing."

"That seems a harsh—"

The warden raised his hands. "It's not too harsh, and it must be done."

"Pearl has feelings for Sonny. She can't just shut them off."

The warden looked at him with disbelief. Then, as if

the absurdity of it was too great for him, he sputtered out a half-chuckle and said, "You've got to be kidding me."

Matthew knew that trying to convince him to consider Pearl's feelings would be a fruitless effort. Still, he couldn't help responding, "I kid you not." He tried to control his glare.

"I will not have her carrying on this way. Now are you going to tell her about it, or do I have to do it for you?"

It was far better that Matthew speak to her. "I'll take care of it."

"Good. And make it quick. I don't want to hear any more about it."

The warden then turned on his heels, leaving Matthew to wonder where he got his information. Although Matthew didn't spend too much time on it. Anyone could have tipped off the warden, a nurse or any other employee. Besides, Matthew had bigger issues to deal with. Like what he was going to say to Pearl.

He swiveled in the desk chair to face the window, forgetting the status report. Stretching his legs out, he placed his feet on the sill and leaned back. Outside, black and blue clouds hung low and heavy, creating dark shadows in the dimly lit office. Thunder boomed across the Rum River only a few miles away. Lightning cracked the sky. The weather matched his mood.

Resting his chin on the steeple he made with his hands, he digested the warden's demands. It was late afternoon, nearing his usual quitting time, but he would stay late. If he didn't take care of this right away, he would be thinking about it all night. It would ruin his evening. It just might anyway. He knew how much Pearl enjoyed being with Sonny.

Other thoughts distracted him. He was supposed to take Cory out for pizza and then play some catch that evening. Since the divorce three years ago, Cory spent two nights a week and every other weekend with him. Cory deserved his complete attention, and Matthew wanted to give it to him. He did a quick calculation. If he left work by six, there would still be enough time. Although he'd have to forego his nightly jog.

Skipping tonight meant extending the miles tomorrow

night if he wanted to be in shape for next month's charity run. Although he was a year-round jogger, clocking thirty-five miles a week, he was not a speed runner. This run required extra effort. He began training for it in early April and sometimes wished he'd started sooner. It was his fifth year participating in the 10K Run for the Homeless.

Last year, he took second place. But this year, he hoped to take first and raise a lot of money for the charity. The race pledge form was on his desk and not even half-full of signatures. He would have to perk up enthusiasm amongst his coworkers. He would also knock on strangers' doors to make people aware of the homeless.

Focusing back on his job, Matthew checked his watch. Pearl's chauffeur would soon return her to Glory Heights. He placed a call to the front desk and asked Charlotte to send Pearl to his office when she arrived. Pearl would have noticed changes at Brambles—confusing changes. He didn't feel good about that. Even if he'd known about it, he might not have been able to stop it. He shook his head; the warden was an insensitive bastard.

Matthew couldn't help wondering what this would do to his relationship with Pearl. He'd worked to build up her trust. In him, and in herself. When he first came to Glory Heights, Pearl was on a slippery slide into a lonely, dark place. It began with her previous caseworker suggesting an experimental drug program. Spurred by the natural hope that new meds would better control her seizures, she signed on. For her participation, she earned a $100 stipend. The money, going right into her hands, was an incentive in itself. Matthew couldn't blame her for trying something that might improve her epileptic condition, but he wondered about the caseworker who allowed it.

When Matthew took over her case, she was having several seizures a day. They became more frequent, more powerful, and less likely to predict. He knew that phenobarbital could lose its effectiveness from long-term use, but not to that extent. He did some research and discovered that some of the patients in the program were on a placebo. Pearl was one of them. He immediately pulled her from the program. The clinic wanted their stipend back. He quietly paid it out of his own pocket, allowing Pearl to keep her money.

During that time, she developed the antisocial psychosis that often consumes people with seizures. She refused to go anywhere. She reached her most desolate hour when on the bus ride to work one morning she had a panic attack. As she'd later described it to Matthew, after riding the bus for only a few minutes, she began feeling claustrophobic and was unable to breathe. She feared she was having a heart attack, or a seizure, or both. The alarmed bus driver, concerned for her safety, stopped the bus on the road midway to Brambles. She begged him to let her off the bus. Relenting to her frantic pleas, and those of the other riders, he opened the door. She immediately descended from the bus and fled down the street, running to escape her own fear.

Matthew remembered something else about that time. The warden had flipped out over the incident. Although the driver had coaxed Pearl back to the bus and returned her to Glory Heights, the warden was upset that he'd let her off the bus at all. Although his reaction seemed excessive to Matthew, he'd chalked it up to the warden's concern for lawsuits.

After that ordeal, Pearl stopped going to work. She dreaded the uncontrollable reality of panic attacks and epileptic spells. She fell into the full realm of panic attack syndrome, including agoraphobia and anticipatory anxiety. If not agonized by panic attacks, seizures continually tormented her. Soon, even the thought of stepping outside Glory Heights for a breath of fresh air frightened her. She stayed in her room. Facing those circumstances, Matthew believed he would've stayed home too.

In response to Pearl's situation, the warden suggested something Matthew thought was a bit over the top. Still, he was willing to try anything that might get Pearl out of her room. The warden offered Pearl a driver, who was trained in CPR and managing seizures. She wouldn't have to worry about having anxiety attacks or seizures on the bus, or being humiliated in public. The driver would escort her to and from work. And as mandated in the work program, Brambles had trained personnel on staff to help her once she arrived.

Pearl refused the offer.

She needed specialized medical care. To ensure that she saw the right doctor—a specialist trained in panic attack syndrome and its related phobias—Matthew made an appointment for her. He called Doctor Benjamin, who prescribed Xanax to squelch Pearl's constant state of anxiety and imipramine to counteract her mounting depression. With her anxiety controlled, her mood elevated, and her seizures curbed, she began the long road to recovery. Matthew met with her twice a week with several goals in mind.

He wanted to improve her self-esteem, boost her self-confidence, and ultimately have her gain some control over her life. She struggled with her self-image and feelings of powerlessness. She felt she didn't belong at Glory Heights, that there should be more to her life than what she'd had so far. She was intensely lonely. No one visited her. She felt shut in, but had no interest in socializing. She resisted participating in group activities. Bingo did not fascinate her, she saw no point to shuffle board. She needed something that engaged her mind.

Probing for her interests, Matthew discovered that she enjoyed Yahtzee and a robust game of hearts. He placed a notice in the community hall summoning players. He got a few takers, but found himself playing hearts for the first three weeks to ensure her attendance. She turned out to be a damn good player. Soon, she began to look forward to the newly established game night.

When further discussions revealed that she liked to read, he bought her a stack of books from a bargain bookstore. Before long, Pearl was running in late to their meetings. She had lost track of the time with her nose deep into an Agatha Christie novel.

Within a few months, Pearl felt strong enough to go back to work—even to ride the bus again. But the warden demanded that she go by escort. Matthew challenged him, saying that if she preferred to ride the bus and felt strong enough to ride the bus, then ride the bus is what she should do. The warden was adamant. She would go by chauffeur or not at all. The warden was his boss, so Matthew convinced her to use the chauffeur, suggesting that it was only a temporary situation. Although, the latter turned out to be hopeful thinking on his part.

Matthew sighed heavily and rubbed his face. Hell, he had no idea what he was going to say to Pearl. He had never dealt with that type of situation and wasn't sure of the right course to take. For the time being, he would follow directions, although he didn't like it. Then he would wait, watch, and see. In the end, he would act on his own instincts, as was his typical way of doing things.

A rap on the door stopped his train of thought. Pearl slid her head around it before he could respond. "Nurse Charlotte said you wanted to talk to me?"

A slight stutter halted her speech when she was upset. Matthew observed it now, and it was no less than he expected. He didn't expect her usual jesting, considering what her day must have been like. She hobbled into his office, fussing with her hair and closing her umbrella, both of which were wet and fragrant from the rain.

Rising, he smiled at her while wondering if what he had to say would throw her over the edge. When she returned his smile, he felt some relief, but he knew it wouldn't last.

He helped her into a chair and then sat next to her, conscious of her expectant eyes on him. "I have something to talk with you about. But first, how did your day go?" Coward, he thought. He was only postponing the inevitable. He didn't relish the pain he would undoubtedly cause her. He grabbed a pen and paper from his desktop, as if to take notes.

Her lips twitched as if something funny was on the tip of her tongue, but her eyes darkened as she addressed him. "It seems to me that you already know how my days go, young man. What is it that you want to know?"

Under other circumstances, he would've burst out laughing at her spunk. But he kept a straight face. This was not going to be easy. She had real feelings for Sonny—apparently, the same as any woman had for a man she wanted to marry. But, she could not marry him. Her seizures were often out of control, and she had never lived on her own. And that was just for starters.

Matthew was about to explain the situation when Pearl blurted out, "Sonny wasn't at work today." She moved to the edge of her chair. "I have to call him right away. I hope he's not ill."

She gazed at the phone on the desk, tapped her fingers on the arms of the chair, and then looked back at Matthew questioningly. She was waiting for permission to use the phone.

He realized that she really didn't know why Sonny wasn't there. Shit.

A day at work without Sonny had to have been rough on her. It was a bright spot in her life, Matthew knew. Nevertheless, with a slight shake of his head, he said that she should not use the phone. "I know Sonny wasn't at work. I'm sorry to tell you that he's been assigned to another job." He kept his gaze on her, waiting for a reaction.

She gave him a blank look. "What do you mean he's been assigned to another job? He's mentioned none of that to me."

Matthew shifted in his chair. "I mean he won't be going back to work at Brambles. He only learned of it this morning."

She straightened her back and gave him a hard look. "Why not?"

Feeling like a bastard, he forged ahead. "I know that you and Sonny have become good friends." "Friends" was not the right word, he knew, but it lessened the harshness of the message he was about to give her. For him, anyway.

After meeting at Brambles several years ago, Sonny often visited Pearl at Glory Heights. Several times a week, in fact. Caseworkers rotated chaperoning activities at Glory Heights, so Matthew had seen them together. He came on game nights, he came just to spend the evening watching television with her. The brightness in Pearl's face and personality when she and Sonny were together was undeniable. It was a brightness that was not there when Sonny wasn't. Sonny was an attentive visitor, sweeping frequent watchful glances over Pearl, as if he could shelter her from any oncoming seizures.

Matthew, feeling like an idiot, should have guessed that

they were in love. He should have caught onto it sooner. Continuing their relationship would only mean heartbreak for both. Like it hadn't already gotten to that point.

With a confidence he didn't feel, he continued. "I know that you're very fond of Sonny. And I know how much you've enjoyed his company over the last couple of years."

"It's been four years," Pearl corrected him.

Matthew realized that it was going to be worse than he thought. "Right, four years then."

He was about to begin again, but she interrupted. "Why don't you just spit out what you're trying to say?" Her expression was no longer one of blankness. Her brow was creased, and she began to wring her hands.

He drew in a deep breath. When he exhaled, he turned in his chair and looked directly at her. "Okay, you're probably right about that. It's come to my attention that perhaps you and Sonny are spending too much time together. Given both your situations, I believe it's best if you don't see him again. Either here, or at work," Matthew added, so that she clearly understood his meaning.

Her face paled. He believed it was from anger, and fear. Anger that he would intrude on and try to control something so dear to her. Fear that he had the means to do it. He wanted to apologize for all of it. Instead, he pointed out the potentially dangerous consequences of continuing her friendship with Sonny. "Pearl, you have, on average, five seizures a week. So far, even with all of the medical experiments you've volunteered for, we've not found a drug that eliminates or even lessens the spells." He touched his hand to his chest. "With all my heart, I wish there was one. You need medical attention. Sonny, I'm sorry to say, is not equipped to help you. If we allow you to continue seeing Sonny, it will only lead to more harm.

"Recently, you've either skipped or resisted taking your seizure medication. Because of that, seizures are occurring more frequently. You've also neglected wearing the helmet prescribed to prevent head trauma during seizures." He glanced at her bare head. "You've particularly resisted wearing it around Sonny. That has presented a problem at Brambles. Now, since Brambles no longer employs Sonny, I hope you'll resume wearing your helmet. Then I won't have to worry about you banging your noggin up at work." Matthew let out a heavy breath before continuing.

"I hope you understand that we must do something about this relationship, before it's too late." Please understand, he silently pleaded. He had been clasping his hands tightly together while he spoke, and they were damp with nervous tension. He straightened in his chair and loosened his grip.

She glared at him. Her mouth twittered from side to side before letting out a fusillade of emotion. "You can't do this to me. Sonny Capshaw has asked me to marry him and that's what I'm going to do." She leaned closer to Matthew.

He had the distinct desire to shrink back in his chair, but he stayed put.

"Matthew Kincaid, I cannot believe that you are behind this. It's the warden isn't it? He's unearthed my plans to marry Sonny. He and Nurse Charlotte discovered me in the hallway the other night, and he's trying to get back at me. It has to be him. You wouldn't do this to me." The betrayal she felt was palpable with every word she spoke.

Matthew believed that separating them was in her best interest—after all, he did keep reminding himself of that—and he therefore stood firm in this resolve. And from the look on her face, she knew that he meant to carry it out. He found no satisfaction in this.

She didn't wait for his response before rising to leave. She walked to the door, but stopped and rested her hand on the knob before opening it. With her back to him, he saw her shoulders slump and quake. He thought he should go to her, but when she lifted her head he saw that she was battling tears. A slight hand to her lips and the stammer in her voice gave way to the depth of her pain, and the words she uttered next would haunt him for a very long time. Struggling for a shred of dignity, her voice husky with unbearable sadness, she said: "I'm a person too, you know."

He rose.

But she had walked out, leaving him with the burden of having been party to her pain.

When the door closed, he knew he'd lost her trust, and maybe her respect.

"Damn, damn, damn it!" In one swift movement, he hurled his pen across the room, fell into the desk chair, and spun around to face the window. He sat there for a long time, staring into a black sky, heavy with rain, and silently cursing life's inequities.

Chapter Seven

Pearl left Matthew's office, hurrying down the corridor, looking as distraught as Charlotte had ever seen anyone. With her hands clutching the neck of her shirt and her head bent low, Pearl looked like she was trying to pack her bleeding heart. Tears ran down her face, and her chin trembled. Her step, frailer than usual, seemed out of line with her effort to get someplace before the dam burst. She passed by Charlotte, giving no heed to her questioning look. Pearl seemed not the least bit aware of her presence. Charlotte placed her hands on her hips and wondered what was going on.

Keeping a moderate distance, she followed Pearl to her room and then listened outside the door. Pearl had barely made it inside before the sobs broke loose, the weeping filled with such agony that Charlotte could scarcely bear it herself. Still, she hesitated, trying to figure out what had happened. Matthew wouldn't cause such distress. As caseworkers went, he was one of the best. He was a blessing to his clients. However, she considered, he could have been the bearer of bad news.

Pearl was usually a bright spot on Charlotte's shift with her good humor and kind smile, unwavering even after a seizure. Charlotte didn't know how she did it, and her sadness now was hard to take. She briefly wondered what she could do to help without looking like she was interfering. Then she reconsidered. Well, she was Pearl's nurse, dang it. She was supposed to help. With that settled, she peered around the door, giving it a gentle knock. "Pearl?"

Pearl glanced up, blowing her nose and sniffling before answering, "C-come in."

Charlotte closed the door behind her. The storm outside had darkened the room considerably. Only the lamp on the desk shed a dim light across the floor. It barely reached the bed on which Pearl lay. Hers was one of the nicer rooms, yet not a private one.

Making their twin beds and keeping the room reasonably tidy were Pearl and Karoline's only housekeeping responsibilities. Karoline's blankets were in a heap atop her bed. She had clothes strewn at the end of it. Charlotte couldn't help but notice the contrast with Pearl's side of the room. Pearl hung her clothes in the closet the two women shared. And she made her bed with a white chenille bedspread, embroidered with clumps of cheery yellow daffodils in neat little rows. Although, disheveled by Pearl's form, the daffodils were twisted and strewn about. A sweater lay neatly folded over a chair. Her other personal belongings were tucked away inside the bed stand, the desk, or the closet. Her helmet lay atop the bed stand instead of where it was supposed to be. But it was not the time for a lecture about that.

Pearl sat up clutching a pillow, its casing wet from her tears.

Charlotte seized the Kleenex box from the bed stand and then sat next to Pearl. The bed sank slightly beneath her weight, and her white dress inched up above her knees. Cocking one leg farther up onto the bed, she adjusted her position. She handed over a tissue and then patiently waited while Pearl blew her nose.

Speaking in quiet tones resonating with her Southern accent, she asked, "Do you want to tell me what's wrong? I'd like to help you, if I can."

The kindness motivated bigger tears to fall from Pearl's brown eyes; she held the tissue to her face and wept. Charlotte moved closer and patted Pearl's back, hoping this small gesture would help ease whatever pain she was enduring. She waited while Pearl tried to compose herself enough to speak. Then, clutching Charlotte's hand, Pearl looked into her eyes and tried to speak, but there seemed to be no words to describe her pain. The words did not come. She ducked her chin to her neck and cried harder.

Charlotte gently rubbed Pearl's back and prompted her to try again. "What is it, Pearl? What could be so bad?"

Pearl raised her watery eyes and, with great difficulty, the words finally came. "They've taken Sonny from me." Her head again dropped to her chest, and she wailed uncontrollably.

Charlotte cocked her head to one side and gazed sympathetically at the broken woman before her. The painful words were finally out, but Charlotte needed more information. She didn't understand why anyone would do such a thing. She had seen Sonny and Pearl together. Sonny had a tremendous impact on Pearl. In fact, he was the light of Pearl's life. Anyone could see that. Who would want to put a stop to that?

She couldn't believe that Matthew would take this happiness from Pearl. Someone else had to be involved, and she needed to find out who. She was suddenly aware of how little she knew about Pearl. "What do you mean they've taken Sonny from you? And who's they?"

Through eyes thick with tears, Pearl answered, "Matthew. He said that it's in my best interest to stop seeing Sonny." An angry edge had increased the stammer in her voice. She stopped, hiccupped, cried, and then began again. "They moved Sonny to a new job, and I don't know where. All I know is that he no longer works at Brambles with me." Her voice grew louder between sobs, and Charlotte could barely understand her. But Pearl continued, "It's so horrible. Matthew said that Sonny couldn't come here to visit me anymore."

Charlotte finally figured out what Pearl was trying to tell her. She felt her own eyes soften. "Did Matthew give you a reason for this change?"

"He said that our relationship would only cause pain. That we were getting too close."

In disbelief, Charlotte cocked her head in the other direction. "Why would he say that?"

Pearl looked directly at Charlotte, who straightened her head and looked back.

"Because I want to marry Sonny," declared Pearl. "He asked me to. That's what I want to do. But now they've taken him away from me." Her voice rose and then cracked. "I have a right to love too." Pearl collapsed onto the bed, her face again meeting the pillow with a torrent of tears.

Pearl's last words gave a mighty pull on Charlotte's heart-strings. She finally understood the problem—from both sides of the situation, she had to admit. "Ah, I see." Then she thought: to shut off all Pearl's ties to Sonny seemed an incredible measure. There must be more to this. "Are you sure Matthew is behind this? It doesn't sound like something he would do."

Pearl sat up again, shaking her head. "I can't believe it's him either. I thought he would support me on this, although I hadn't asked him to yet. The warden has to be behind it."

"The warden?"

"He's trying to get back at me for being out of my room the other night."

"Oh, I don't think that's it, Pearl. I spoke with him before he left the other night and explained that you got confused before your seizure and ended up in the hallway by accident." Charlotte lowered her eyelids and then brushed an invisible speck of lint off the bed. "He seemed quite satisfied with what I presumed happened the other night." Charlotte glanced at Pearl.

Pearl's eyes widened. "You told him that? That's what you told him? And he believed you?" Clearly, Pearl couldn't believe that piece of good information.

Charlotte nodded and before she could say any more, she noticed a change in Pearl. A far-off look had taken hold in Pearl's eyes. Charlotte felt uneasy, wondering if a seizure was coming on. But then Pearl blinked, and it appeared as if she were only trying to figure something out. Charlotte breathed a quiet sigh of relief.

A look of comprehension soon replaced the analysis that

seemed to have been going on inside Pearl's head. She shifted her gaze to Charlotte. The nurse hadn't thought it possible for Pearl's eyes to look any sadder, but they suddenly did. Then, just as abruptly, her eyes turned a deeper shade of brown and flashed with anger.

Pearl burst out, "It was my sister!"

It was Charlotte's turn to stammer. "Y-you have a sister? You think your s-sister did this?" She didn't know which surprised her more: that a sister could be responsible for Pearl's pain, or that Pearl had a sister. Pearl never mentioned a sister. In the months of her employment with Glory Heights, she hadn't seen anyone other than Sonny visit Pearl. Feeling a bit contrite for never asking Pearl about her family, Charlotte said, "Do you have other siblings?"

Pearl responded to the last question first. "Just one, and that's enough."

Charlotte smiled at Pearl's wit. Even in her sadness, it was finding its way back to her.

"I wrote to Susan—that's my sister—to tell her about my plans with Sonny."

Charlotte's eyes widened. "You had plans? You and Sonny?"

"Well, nothing concrete. But, we've decided to get married."

Charlotte again saw the problem. With Pearl's seizures and Sonny's mental capacity, a marriage would be the recipe for disaster. Still, Charlotte's heart went out to Pearl. Pearl's haunting words again ran through her mind: "I have a right to love too." There had to be another answer. But before she could contemplate it further, Pearl interrupted her thoughts.

Taking Charlotte's hand, Pearl searched her eyes as if hoping for understanding. "Sonny makes me feel so good," she confided. "When I have a spell, he knows how to take care of me. He wraps his arms around me and squeezes me oh so tight." Dropping Charlotte's hand, she wrapped her arms around herself and rocked back and forth. She closed her eyes and smiled. That was how Sonny would hold her.

59

Charlotte felt the comfort Sonny provided Pearl. The sense of human bonding was overwhelming. Charlotte's own eyes filled with tears. Fortunately, Pearl didn't notice her damp eyes, and before she got a chance to, Charlotte stood up. After straightening her dress around her knees, she turned her back and sniffed back the tears.

Knowing she could not leave Pearl at a time like this, she tried to think of what to do next. She couldn't go against Matthew. She doubted that speaking to him would change things. But, suddenly, she had an idea.

She spun around toward Pearl. The tissue box was empty and the tears were still rolling. Pearl looked at her, helplessly. Charlotte dug into her dress pocket, retrieved a tissue, and handed it to Pearl. Having done that, she broached the subject, not really knowing where it would lead, or if she should suggest it. However, she simply couldn't leave Pearl like this.

"Pearl," Charlotte ventured, "do you have any other relatives? I mean, besides Susan?"

Pearl shook her head and sniffled. "My parents died years ago. That's when I was left here. The only other relative I know of is Susan's daughter, Jordana. But I don't think she knows about me."

"Well," Charlotte began a slow grin, "perhaps it's time she did."

Pearl stopped crying. "What do you mean?"

"Do you know how to reach Jordana?"

"Oh heavens, no. Why, what are you thinking?"

"I'm thinking you should contact Jordana. Tell me what you do know about her."

Pearl seemed reluctant, but finally, she said, "I have a keepsake box. All I know about Jordana is in that box."

"Okay." Charlotte didn't know how much she could push Pearl. "Do you want to show me the box?"

Pearl's gaze lingered on Charlotte; she was probably wondering if she should trust her. She must have decided it was worth the risk, because she reached down and pulled something out from beneath the bed.

The sight of it embarrassed Charlotte, and she hoped her dark complexion would hide the blush. It was a shoe box, decorated in brightly colored fabric. Pearl must have glued it on herself. On the lid, she had written in permanent marker: Pearl's Treasures.

Pearl set the box on her lap and smiled timidly before opening it. "This is Jordana's birth announcement." She handed it to Charlotte.

She took the card and read it. Upon Jordana's birth over twenty-five years ago, Susan, most likely unable to contain her own excitement over the baby, had sent it to Pearl. It read: "Proud parents announce the joyful birth of their daughter, Jordana Kaitlyn Barlow."

Charlotte handed the announcement back to Pearl, and peered into the box.

Pearl cleared her throat, probably dry from crying. "I saved the announcement, along with every letter Susan ever wrote me."

The letters barely covered the bottom of the box.

Charlotte looked at Pearl. "I think a sister could do a little better than this." Then she immediately wished she hadn't said it.

But Pearl didn't make any excuses for her sister. She just smiled, and then drew out her real treasures. For her, the box came to life with anniversary cards, dried flowers, and other mementos from Sonny. For the next half hour, Charlotte forgot that she was on duty and had other patients to attend to. She allowed Pearl time to talk about each gift from Sonny, let her cry in between, and reassured her they'd come up with a plan to help her.

Before leaving, Charlotte helped Pearl get ready for bed. While pleased to see that Pearl had stopped crying and seemed less distraught, Charlotte had a sad feeling of her own. She wondered how many people could sum up their whole life in a five by twelve shoe box.

Chapter Eight

After a restless night of dispiriting dreams, Pearl dragged herself out of bed and went through the motions of dressing for work. She donned another outfit of polyester and cotton. She went to the cafeteria and ate an omelet she didn't taste and avoided talking to anyone at the breakfast table. No matter how she tried, she could not adjust her mind to the dreadful life to which Matthew Kincaid had so painfully banished her. It might not have been his doing, but never mind that. She would never again see Sonny. Having their wedding plans ruined and pulled right out from under their feet was devastating enough. Living without Sonny was more than she could take.

Somehow, she made it to the front gates of Glory Heights. She now stood in the blinding sun with the other residents waiting for transportation to Brambles. She was still in no condition to converse; she barely acknowledged anyone. Rebecca stood behind Pearl and was one whom she felt she should say hello to. Nevertheless, when Rebecca stuck her nose in the pages of a Harlequin romance novel, Pearl was grateful. Her face ached with emotion, and she was bravely trying to contain it.

She lifted her face to the sun—it was a hot one, burning through hazy clouds left from the previous night's storm. However, the warm rays did little to allay the hard, cold hurt within her. Searching through her purse, she realized she'd left her sunglasses behind. Silently, she cursed that realization for more than the sun's glare in her eyes. She held her purse in one hand and guarded her eyes with the other. The shield was as much to keep the sun from stinging her red-rimmed eyes as it was to prevent anyone from noticing the tears that might erupt without warning.

In self-defense, she inhaled a deep breath of fresh air, not yet hot or humid enough to prove stifling. She fidgeted with the gentle waves in her hair and then felt to ensure that the barrette, another reminder of Sonny, was securely in place. As she touched her bare head, thoughts of the helmet fleetingly registered. Today, she didn't much care if she hurt her head in the thrashing a spell could give it. She couldn't see that it would make much difference in the pain she already felt. A seizure, she mused, might provide a few seconds of reprieve from the unremitting ache in her heart.

Waiting with the others seemed an interminable trial. She wished to be alone. She wished to be alone with Sonny. When the bus finally arrived, Pearl gave a half-hearted wave to Sam, the driver. He was a nice fellow who had befriended her. He had been particularly kind to her that day she went berserk on his bus. If he weren't such an empathetic soul, she would still feel like an idiot around him. While she quickly pulled her hand out of its wave to rest it again at her temple, Sam declared with a hearty smile that she should have a good day. In deference to him, she risked a smile. Her feeble emotions showed in the attempt, but she couldn't muster up enough gumption to care.

Standing alone at the curb, she watched the bus leave and waited for her own ride. She almost wished, as on most mornings, that she could take the bus with the others. The nonsensical chatter of her Glory Heights' coworkers would have at least been some distraction from the pain filling her heart. She restlessly rolled her eyes at her own puzzling vacillation. One minute she wanted to be alone, the next, she wished for the monotonous rattle of her cohorts.

She had not known she could hurt this much. It wasn't

just the torment of having Sonny taken away from her, although not seeing him was the most devastating part of it. The fact that it could be done to her at the whim and will of others was demoralizing to her. Believing that her own sister had instigated the whole nightmare both saddened and infuriated her. Susan was the only one who could have done it. But why would she? Pearl would never understand why Susan had abandoned her to a life at Glory Heights. It seemed that Susan was trying to destroy the only happiness that Pearl found for herself.

The Town Car finally made its entrance and parked along the curb. Again, Anton came around to open the door for Pearl. He dutifully placed a hand at her elbow and stiffly uttered his usual "Good morning, Miss Witherby." Getting into the car, even with Anton's assistance, her foot caught on the floor mat and she fell sideways onto the seat. Having no energy to prop herself back up, there she lay. Anton looked at her curiously, as if he thought he should help in some way, but didn't want to put himself out if he didn't have to. Pearl closed her eyes. She stayed laid out in that position until they reached Brambles.

Brambles Brads and Bolts factory was a long pole barn of a building. To get to their assigned positions on the assembly line, employees walked through a narrow entrance and passed by the main office where Mr. Bramble and his staff worked. From there, they entered a windowless, although brightly fluorescent-lit, vaulted room. Inside, several assembly lines ran parallel to each other and extended to the far end of the building. At the back of the building, one door exited to the restrooms, another to the company cafeteria. A third door opened to an employee lounge. Employees used the lounge for fifteen-minute breaks that were done in shifts, once in the morning and once in the afternoon. They could purchase hot food in the cafeteria during assigned lunch breaks, although many toted brown sacks from home. Workers from Glory Heights did not have to purchase their lunch. Brambles provided it as part of their cooperative work plan with Glory Heights.

Pearl went straight to her position on the assembly line, the one she stood at every day. It was her post where she counted the nails for packaging. The canvas gloves Pearl wore gave little protection even on a good day. But today, several nails had poked through the thin protection, pricking sharper and cutting deeper than usual. Blood spots outlined the tips of her fingers. She remained quiet, afraid to give voice to her pain, physical or emotional.

From the men's line where box construction took place came the first questions. Oblivious Kenny Holmes spoke first, and longest: "Hey, Pearl, where's Sonny been? Have you seen Sonny? Wasn't here yesterday, either." On and on. Pearl didn't know how to answer the unwelcome inquisitions. And, with her chin trembling, she didn't answer.

Women on her own line, increasingly aware of Pearl's sober mood, took to staring at her. They knew something was wrong, but not what. Sensing that she needed help, they tried to talk to her. But Pearl spoke only a few words in politeness, for as long as she could endure it. Many of Pearl's coworkers, also residents of Glory Heights, were without experience in social niceties and had no sense of personal boundaries. Therefore, they unabashedly pressed Pearl for comment long after she gave up trying to respond. Although, nearing the noon hour, most everyone began to leave her alone. She was thankful for the reprieve. And with a silent thought to herself, she felt fervently grateful that echolalic Cora Wilson wasn't a Brambles employee. Cora would have caught onto "Where's Sonny?" like a runaway train.

By noon, Pearl was weak from holding her broken heart together while being lambasted by nosey assembly liners. She sought solace in a quiet corner of the cafeteria. She wished to go for a walk outside, but they did not allow it. That was also part of the cooperative work plan. With no Sonny to sit with, she attempted to brave lunch alone. She tried eating a tuna sandwich, but she could barely look at it without feeling nauseous. With no appetite and time on her hands, she tried to think of a way out of the mess she was in. It was then that she first considered acting upon Nurse Charlotte's suggestion to contact Jordana.

But that made her remember the keepsake box filled

with mementos from Sonny, and it brought tears to her eyes. She looked about, hoping no one noticed, and then quickly wiped the teardrops away. Of course, loud-mouthed Hazel Dentry noticed.

"Pearl's crying!" Hazel loudly announced to everyone from across the cafeteria. "What are you sobbing about, Pearl?"

Pearl ignored her. Hazel wasn't from Glory Heights. However, she had assigned herself the task of babysitting the patients, although Brambles had no position with that job description. She worked on the line with everyone else. It was a miracle she hadn't made a scene out of Pearl's disposition earlier.

Pearl wanted to flee, to escape the scrutiny. She thought of running to the ladies' room but she hadn't asked permission. She didn't want to risk losing her job for leaving the cafeteria. It had happened to others. If she lost her job, she would die of rot at Glory Heights. She closed her eyes, hastily wiping more tears from her cheeks. She took a deep breath. Damn, she had to do something. She couldn't, wouldn't live without Sonny. Her only hope was in Jordana. However, Pearl had no idea of how to contact her. Pearl's limited ability to investigate her niece's whereabouts weighed on her. Her head and shoulders bent helplessly over the untouched tuna sandwich.

Later, back on the assembly line, Pearl's distracted thoughts alternated between hopelessly analyzing ways to find Jordana and finding ways to see Sonny. All afternoon, Pearl endured more questions similar to the third degree, feeling like Brambles' spectacle of the day. However, lost in her own thoughts, she succinctly ignored most of the interrogation.

By the time Anton dropped off Pearl at the entrance to Glory Heights, her thoughts were a tangle of emotions that she could not separate. She hadn't figured a way to find Jordana. Other than making a run for it at that moment and escaping to Sonny's apartment, a place she knew the location of but had never been, she could think of no way to reach him, either.

Nurse aides and security guards held sentry at the front door. If Pearl ran, they would most certainly catch her. Then they would lock her in her room and try to sedate her. Once inside the building, she could not freely walk back out. Glory Heights securely locked their doors. She didn't have a phone in her room, so even if she had Jordana's phone number, Pearl didn't have a way to call. She had the same problem with calling Sonny. Feeling like a prisoner, she climbed the steps into the building, mindful of the door closing behind her and the hesitant yawn it made.

She turned to look at the door. Something clicked in her mind, but she wasn't sure what. By the time she reached her room, she had given up trying to formulate the thought. All she wanted was to crawl into bed and stay there. She didn't wish for dinner or, for heaven's sake, any probing conversation with her roommate. Or any other resident. She had simply had enough.

She entered her room, barely noticing that it was not as she had left it—she had no energy to make her bed that morning. However, someone had made her bed. Tucked under the pillowed bedspread lay an envelope with her name on it. That got her attention. Had Sonny somehow gotten a message to her? She quickly opened it. Inside was a note of four lines: "Jordana K. Barlow," a home address and phone number, a work address and phone number at Curic and McCall Global Advertising, and the words "Go for it!"

With eyes wide and mouth agape, Pearl stared at the note. It was from Nurse Charlotte. While Pearl had unsuccessfully labored over how she would find Jordana, Nurse Charlotte had solved the problem for her. Nurse Charlotte had done for Pearl what she could not do for herself. Although Pearl had the evidence right in front of her, it was all too hard to believe. No one, since her mother and father so many years ago, had ever helped her like that. She closed her eyes and cradled the note to her chest. Then, for the first time that day, a smile illuminated her face.

The next thing that happened was even better. The thought she had toiled with upon entering the Glory Heights building came to rest in her mind. She wasted no time in deciding what to do with it.

When Pearl was sure the lobby receptionist would have

left for the day, she made her way to the nurses' station. The lone nurse was filling out charts, wrapping up her shift. Pearl was thankful that Nurse Charlotte wasn't there. It would have made what she was about to do so much more difficult. Pearl would've had to lie to her, and she didn't think she could do that. This nurse was preoccupied with her work. Pearl knew that Glory Heights' nurses, like caseworkers, were overworked. Usually Pearl felt bad for them, the way they had to scramble about their work. However, this time it worked well into her plan.

Having passed the station without so much as a nod to anyone, she walked out to the lobby. It was a long, narrow room filled with lush ficus trees, ferns, and other live plants. She began to pick out a spot when—. Uh-oh. The receptionist was still there. Pearl tried to back out unnoticed, but no such luck.

The young woman glanced over at Pearl. "Can I help you?"

Pearl tried for nonchalance, "Oh heavens, no, dear. Just checking out the weather." She made a point to look out the windows. "Looks like you could still fry an egg out there."

The receptionist smiled, and then she opened a desk drawer and pulled out a purse. "You're lucky to be inside where it's cool."

"Sure am. Lucky to be inside." Pearl nodded her head and smiled back.

"Well, good night, then." The receptionist headed for the main door.

Pearl gave her a small wave, and then pretended to walk back from where she came. She moved slowly and listened. The door opened. She took five steps. The door clicked shut. She smiled.

That was the nagging thought she'd had earlier; the door did not slam shut. It shut slowly. And now she knew there would be enough time for her to escape. She just had to wait for the next person to leave.

Fortunately, the bushiest plants with the biggest pots were in a corner near the door. Acknowledging a blessing came easy to

Pearl. As she crouched behind the ficus, she gave thanks for Glory Heights' plant budget.

She waited until she heard footsteps; then, she got ready. She couldn't believe how nervous she was. The air conditioning again did nothing for her—she was sweating bullets. The tap, tap, tap of footsteps drew nearer, almost to the door. The branches were too thick to get a good view, which meant whoever was there couldn't see her either. He began to whistle, probably happy to be off work, and she knew it was a male nurse leaving his afternoon shift.

She held her breath until he opened the door. Then she sprang up the best that someone with her precarious stability could, and waited only seconds until his whistle waned in her ears. She stepped out from behind the tree. Taking three long steps, she glanced out the door. The man walked toward the employee parking lot without a glance back. She reached for the door. She shouldn't have taken her eyes off it! It was closing! Her fingers grazed the metal without gaining purchase. The heavy door closed with her still inside.

Her heart sunk, and she began to cry. About to give the door a good bang, she heard laughter and ran for cover. It grew louder. Pearl dried her eyes, feeling hopeful again. Two women were leaving. Pearl would not miss the door this time.

The door opened; she waited only until they were through it. Then she ran out from the tree and grabbed the door. Holding onto it, she struggled with its weight, nervously checking over her shoulder and waiting until the two women walked out of sight. Then, suddenly Pearl was scrambling outside, headed for the street. She breathed heartily, although the air was still stifling hot. She didn't mind at all. The sky had never looked so blue, the trees so green. She laughed aloud, experiencing freedom, not once thinking that it might be short-lived.

Pearl knew where to find Sonny. He lived across the Rum River footbridge and two blocks down in a subsidized-housing apartment building. It wasn't far.

After taking a footpath to the bridge, she skeptically maneuvered its old wooden planks. The river gushed beneath the boards, and she was thankful when she reached the other side. With a deep breath, she steadied herself and stepped onto the sidewalk. While waiting for three cars to pass by, she told herself to calm down. Then, she tripped on the curb before descending to cross the street. She again stumbled while ascending to the sidewalk on the other side.

It might be safer, she thought, if she slowed down. Yet, fear kept her going at a good clip. She hobbled along the sidewalk, stopping only once to risk a look back. No one was coming after her. A huge smile spread across her face; she had truly escaped.

Struggling to keep her balance with one hand, she flung the other into her purse to dig for Kleenex. Finding a wilted tissue, she pulled it out and used the inadequate bit of fluff to sop up the sweat trickling down her arms. Wiping more sweat from her brow and pulling her sticky sweater away from her rib cage, she continued, watching each shaky step find its mark on the sidewalk. After stopping half a dozen times to regain her balance and catch her breath, she at last made it to Sonny's apartment.

Knocking on his door, she wondered about the way she looked. Skimming a hand over her hair, thick and coiled from humidity, she adjusted the barrette. Just as she finished, the door opened, slowly. She cocked her head to see inside. For a moment, all she saw was his sad face peering around the crack. Then his eyebrows shot up, and he threw the door open wide. His smile met hers. "Pearly!"

"Sonny!"

They embraced in the doorway for several minutes before he invited her inside, "Get in here, Pearly. I missed you."

The air conditioning would have been a welcome relief, but Pearl, being the more perceptive of the two, thought it would be a mistake. "If someone from Glory Heights is looking for me, this is the first place they'll look. And I'm not going back to Glory Heights until I've finished my business."

"What will we do then?" Sonny was locking his door from the outside, getting ready to go.

"I need a telephone."

"There's a phone booth next to my bus stop."

"Let's go."

Out on the street again, Sonny pointed the way. The phone was on a street corner a few blocks down in the opposite direction from Glory Heights. He held Pearl's hand so tight it almost hurt, but she didn't say anything. She was just glad for the closeness, and they had so much to talk about.

Sonny gave her an earnest look and asked, "What's going on, Pearly? Are we still getting married?"

"They're trying to keep us apart, that's what's going on." Pearl told him about her discussion with Matthew.

Sonny gnawed on a fingernail. "Can they do that?"

"They're obviously trying. We can't give up, though." Then she told him all about Nurse Charlotte. "She's helping me. I can't believe it, but she found Jordana for me."

Sonny knew who she was. "I'm not surprised. She's a real nice lady, always nice to me, too." His brown eyes, round as quarters, began to tear up. Quickly, he grabbed his handkerchief out of his pocket and blew his nose.

Pearl knew that Nurse Charlotte's kindness had touched him. He had a soft heart; it was one of the things she loved about him. After a moment, she grinned and said, "I'm going to call her."

"Who? Nurse Charlotte?"

"No, silly." Pearl playfully pinched his arm. "Jordana."

He put the handkerchief away. "Where does she live?"

"Just outside Minneapolis. Can you believe she's that close, and I've never seen her?"

Then, they stopped walking and stared at each other. Neither knew quite what to say about that.

Finally, Pearl pointed to the phone booth, finally within sight. When they started walking again, she said, "That's enough about me. What happened to you yesterday?"

Sonny looked confused, as if what he was going to say still didn't make sense to him. "A man dressed in a brown suit came to my apartment just as I was leaving for the bus stop."

"Who was it?"

"I don't know. I never saw him before. He was real nice though, and he said that Brambles sent him to see me. He also said I couldn't work there anymore. That Brambles was downsizing, whatever that means. He said I was lucky because another job had just opened up at a warehouse right on my bus line."

Pearl said, "I don't think any of that downsizing business is true. Somebody did this to us, Sonny. I just don't know who yet. Not for sure anyway."

Sonny shook his head, sadly. "Do you want to know about my new job?"

Pearl wondered if Sonny really understood all that had happened. She knew he had limitations. She nodded for him to go ahead, but she wished he didn't have a new job. She wanted him at Brambles with her.

"Well, because it was my first day on the job, the man drove me to the warehouse himself. I thought about you the whole way there, Pearly. I asked him if your job got cut too."

"What did the man have to say about that?" Pearl asked.

"That it was possible. He wasn't sure everyone was as lucky getting another job right away."

The way the man conned Sonny angered her, but she tried to let it go. "What was the warehouse like?"

"Sad." Sonny pulled out his handkerchief again.

Pearl squeezed his arm. "It's okay, Sonny."

Sonny shrugged. "I thought for sure some of my Brambles friends would be there. But no one was. All day I thought you'd show up, or someone else from the assembly line, but no one came."

Pearl thought about how lonely it must have been for him in a strange place all by himself. It was hard enough for her working at Brambles without him. But she, at least, had people she knew around her. Even if they annoyed her to death with their stupid questions. "I'm sorry that happened, Sonny."

"I tried to make friends at the warehouse, but the men are

all different from me. They laughed at me and spit tobacco on the floor. They drive loading trucks inside the warehouse, and I have to run to get out of their way. I'm sure they don't mean to swerve at me."

Pearl felt her blood boil. She couldn't listen to much more of this and was glad that they'd reached the phone booth. Still, she wanted to know one more thing. "What is your main job there?"

"Maintenance, I guess."

"Do you like it there better than Brambles?"

"Oh no, Pearly. I want to be at Brambles with you. Besides, my new boss told me I had to work Saturday mornings. I never had to do that at Brambles."

"I hope we can get your Brambles job back."

Suddenly, Sonny changed the subject. "Hey, did anyone tell you that I tried to call you last night?"

"No!"

"I did. I called the nurse's line at Glory Heights. I needed to talk to you, but the nurse who answered the phone said that you were unavailable. That never happened before. Were you unavailable, Pearly?"

"Of course not. They didn't even tell me that you called."

"I didn't think so, but I didn't know for sure. Because I called six more times, and no one would let me talk to you. And a supervisor came on the line and said that you didn't want to talk to me. I asked them why, but they said they didn't know."

"Oh no, Sonny, that wasn't the truth at all. I wanted to see you more than anything. I was heartbroken without you."

"Well, I didn't know for sure. It made my stomach hurt. Then I had diarrhea explosions so bad that I had to stay home from work the second day on my new job."

"You stayed home from work today?"

"Uh-huh. I hope I still have the job tomorrow."

Having talked it all out, she now wanted to put their troubles behind them and look toward their future. Giggling like a schoolgirl, Pearl pulled at his shirt to get him as close as possible.

He even squeezed into the phone booth with her. The sun was still high in the western sky and the lingering humidity made for sweltering close quarters, but she didn't mind. Sonny sure didn't seem to mind either.

Pearl's thin cotton sweater and calf-length skirt stuck to her skin, but it was of little concern to her now. She was with Sonny and that was all she cared about. He made everything all right. Before getting out her coins for the phone, she touched his round face and smiled. She was with the man she loved, making a phone call to the niece she loved. She loved Jordana even though she'd never met her. It was all so exciting.

Pearl grabbed the phone's handset, which was grimy and sweaty from general communal use and the hot weather. She placed the first coin in the slot, and then stopped. Out of the corner of her eye, she caught sight of a patrol car cruising toward them. For an instant, she panicked. However, she remembered Susan and quickly dismissed the thought of police looking for her. On the off chance that someone had already notified Susan about her escape from Glory Heights, Susan would never involve the police. Susan would send a nice man in a brown suit. Pearl wiped sweat from her brow and continued with the call. Clinging to the metal phone cord, she held her breath and waited for Jordana to answer her call.

Chapter Nine

When the phone rang, Jordana Barlow didn't move to answer it. Curled comfortably into her creamy leather sofa, she was eating salty buttered popcorn and watching the video of *Fatal Attraction*. The movie was just starting. Due to a tight work schedule, she missed seeing the movie when it showed in theaters. She read somewhere that the film grossed over $166 million and was the second-highest grossing film in 1987, behind *Three Men and a Baby*.

She listened as the phone stopped ringing, and then wondered about choosing a movie with Michael Douglas in it over Tom Selleck. She could have had Tom Selleck. Oh well, next time. First she wanted to see what all the hype was about. Glenn Close was to have given an award-winning performance. Scary, dramatic. Jordana could use the drama. Her life certainly was lacking in it.

With a busy weekend ahead of her, she decided to give herself a gift by renting the movie and relaxing at home on Friday evening. Ryan, the handsome coworker with whom she spent her evenings and weekends, was off with "the boys." They went to a cabin up north for another weekend of fishing and golf. How he had gotten all of his corporate accounts reviewed in time to take the weekend off was beyond her. She would be in the office at Curic and McCall Global Advertising on Saturday at the least, reviewing national accounts and analyzing fiscal year-end sales growth. But with Ryan out of town, she was free to kick back and unwind without interruption. At least, that's what she had thought.

The phone rang again. Curious, she smacked the popcorn bowl onto the coffee table and went to the phone.

"Who did you say was calling?" The woman on the other end of the line stammered out an introduction that Jordana must have misunderstood.

"This is Pearl, Pearl Witherby. I'm your mother's sister."

"I'm sorry, you must have the wrong number. My mother has no sisters." Confident that the woman had made a mistake, Jordana almost hung up. But, when she heard her mother's name spoken, she hung on.

"Wait," the voice said. "Your mother, Susan Seymour, is my sister. That is your mother, isn't it?" Without waiting for Jordana to answer, the woman hurried on. "I know this may come as a complete shock to you, Susan's probably never told you about me, but I need to talk to you."

Jordana was alert to the urgency behind the woman's words. "What did you say your name was?"

"Pearl. Pearl Witherby. I'm your mother's younger sister. I need to talk to you," she hurriedly repeated. "Please, don't hang up."

"But my mother's name is Seymour. That's her maiden name."

"Susan changed her name after she left home."

Jordana briefly wondered if her mother would have done that. No, she decided. There was no reason to believe Pearl Witherby. Jordana saw no sense in hearing anything else the woman had to say, either. "Listen, I'm not sure what you're trying to do, but my mother doesn't have a sister and her name has never been Witherby. If this is some weird game you're playing, I'm not interested."

"Please, please, listen to me. I have proof. Your mother sent me a birth announcement when you were born. Your father's name is Trevor Barlow. Your mother is a senator. They were divorced in the seventies. I have letters from your mother. Please. This is not a game. I need your help." The woman took a deep breath and exhaled loudly into the phone.

Between the occasional stammer in the woman's voice and what sounded like a man talking in the background, Jordana had trouble hearing the whole plea. Nevertheless, she had heard enough. She still didn't believe her.

Jordana wondered where the woman was calling from. Also, it seemed that someone was with her. However, other questions preempted those inquiries. "If it's true, and I don't believe it is, why haven't I heard of you before? Why are you calling me now after all these years?"

Jordana sank into the couch. The soft leather provided some comfort for the distress she was feeling. She hadn't bothered rewinding the movie, which had run a good course while she was on the phone. She didn't eat the popcorn either. If she put one kernel in her stomach, she would surely throw it up. Staring off into space, she tried to comprehend what had just happened.

Was it a hoax? Could the woman possibly be Mother's sister? The woman, Pearl she said was her name—no, Jordana wasn't going to give credence to her by calling her by name. But the woman spoke so convincingly. The woman's voice was pleasant and kind as it worked around a nervous stammer. She didn't appear to have any hideous motive behind her call for help, but you never know what people might be inclined to do, Jordana thought. Especially with Mother being a senator. During Mother's congressional tenure, unpleasant incidents most certainly had occurred; however, she had always protected Jordana from them.

The woman certainly had her facts down: the date of Jordana's birth, the date of Mother's divorce, where Mother lived over the years. But wouldn't all of that be public record? Couldn't anyone get that information? Jordana considered this while the air conditioner began to rumble and goose bumps prickled her arms. She pulled the afghan lying across the back of the couch around her shoulders. She sat for a moment before rising to turn off the air conditioner.

On the way back to the couch, she considered the dilemma from another angle. Mother wouldn't have secreted away her own sister, would she? Jordana thought seriously about this and decided that yes, sadly, her mother might if it interfered with her career. Susan Seymour let very little get between her and her career. It was something Jordana both feared and loathed.

As a young child, Jordana constantly worried that she would do something to anger Mother, to lose her love. Mother was always distracted with this event or that act of Congress. Jordana had cherished the bits of time that she had spent with her mother.

As an adult, Jordana could put things in a better perspective. But the little-girl feelings of abandonment seemed to creep back in when she least expected them. Often, it seemed that Mother knew this and used it to control her. Jordana started—she had unconsciously fallen into that unpleasant memory. Shaking her head, she cleared the old tapes from her mind and considered the rest of the woman's story.

She couldn't possibly be telling the truth. She said she has been living in a nursing home for many years, without any family contact. Not even *my* mother would do that to her own flesh and blood, Jordana thought. At least she didn't think she would. No, it's just an outrageous story, she decided—which is all it could be. The woman claims she needs help because she wants to marry someone. What did the woman say his name was? It was something odd for a grown man. In addition, Mother has supposedly conspired—the woman didn't use that word—to stop her from marrying him. Why would Mother do that? The woman said she had epilepsy. She seemed to be functioning well enough. These days there was help for that. Wasn't there?

The pale walls of Jordana's two-story townhouse began to show signs of an evening shadow. Her dining and living rooms were connected as if they were one big room. From the couch, Jordana looked out the sliding glass doors opening onto her deck off the dining room. Although it was still early evening, the branches of huge maple trees had darkened, throwing gray shadows across her cream-colored carpet. The sun was beginning to go down. She had been sitting in this zombie state for over an hour.

She had told the woman there was nothing she could do for her. Why was *she* still thinking about it? With that final thought, Jordana attempted to dismiss the phone call and the woman claiming to be her long-lost aunt. She rewound the movie and picked up the bowl of popcorn. It was probably all a very bad joke, and she wasn't going to waste any more of her precious free time on it.

Chapter Ten

"What'd she say, Pearly? What'd she say?" Sonny had asked the question several times already. So far, all he had for an answer was a mouthed "Shh." Apparently, she didn't want him to interrupt her. It was smothering hot in the phone booth, and his shirt was beginning to stick to him. He wanted to get out in the air. Although, being this close to Pearly and smelling her pretty hair was nice, he thought.

It looked like Pearly was finishing the conversation. Maybe now he would get an answer. He was about to ask again when he realized something was wrong. Pearly was trying to hang up the receiver, but she kept missing the mark. She tried again, clanging it against the phone, as if she couldn't hang it up fast enough. Her eyes looked far away, crazed. She let the phone drop, leaving it to dangle at the end of its cord. Then she yanked herself around toward the door, trying to get out. She couldn't get out. He was in her way. She tried squeezing past him. Sonny froze to the spot, too afraid to move.

"Pearly?" he asked, his voice rising. "Are you all right?"

He tried to put his arms around her, but her wild eyes and flailing arms sought only the door. A desperate groan filled the small compartment. Then, with arms so strong it surprised him, she shoved him aside. He finally realized what was about to happen.

They both struggled with the door. Getting a good hold, he yanked it inward. It scraped across his ankles and banged into her catapulting head. Gaining a narrow opening, he slid through it. Pearl's arms flailed outside the booth after him. He grabbed on and pulled her through. He spotted the bench in the bus shelter and practically dragged her over to it. Then he sat next to her and held her close, as close as he always did at such a time.

Pearl's body began to jerk in one direction and her head thrashed in another. Then came the high-pitched shriek. He held on tight. "It's okay, Pearly. It's okay. I'm here." He tried to control Pearl's convulsions with one arm. With his other, he frantically waved to the police officer cruising the street. The patrol car was coming back their way.

Matthew Kincaid rushed through the doors of North Memorial. Having mastered the hospital's dark and decrepit parking ramp, he didn't know which way to go next. It wasn't often one of his clients ended up here. They normally went to Mercy Hospital near Glory Heights in Rum River. The responding police officer had directed the ambulance to North Memorial. This medical center was in Robbinsdale, another Minneapolis suburb. When Pearl became aware enough to answer questions, she admitted to living at Glory Heights. When the officer placed the call, Charlotte got on the line. She then called Matthew.

It was Charlotte's second call to Matthew. She didn't sound as shaky as she had in the first call. She was relieved, as he was, that they'd found Pearl. Charlotte hadn't given details on how Pearl had left the premises, alone, and at night. He could guess why. How was another matter he would have to address.

Matthew took Cory over to stay with his next-door neighbor. Cory, balking at the arrangement, tried to convince his dad that he was old enough to stay home alone. "Maybe next year," Matthew told him. Then, with hopes of not being gone too long,

Matthew hurried over to the health center.

Ahead of him, he spotted a kidney-shaped information station equipped with a computer and a receptionist. He quickly made his way over to it. Although, once there, he hated to interrupt the young woman behind the desk. She was busy cracking gum, her nose stuck in a romance novel. He looked around. The two security guards near the front entrance didn't look like they would have the answers he needed.

He cleared his throat. "Excuse me? Miss?"

The woman looked up.

"I'm looking for Pearl Witherby. She was admitted here less than an hour ago. Do you know where I can find her?"

Without saying a word, the attendant unhurriedly ran a painted fingernail down a list of names. She then checked a computer previously idling in front of her. She adjusted her phone's headset, cracked her gum, and dialed a number. After mentioning Pearl's name into the headgear and nodding her head into space, she hung up the phone. "Fourth floor, General Care, room 426." She reopened her book.

Matthew rode an elevator to the fourth floor, but finding the room was not that easy. Upon exiting the elevator, he encountered a maze of hallways going in all directions. There was no sign pointing him to room 426 of General Care, so he stopped an orderly and asked for directions. Walking aimlessly through a myriad of hallways and hospital units was a waste of time. He gladly took the expedient route of consulting with someone who knew their way around, particularly since the directions given were lengthy and the way complicated. He didn't want to think about where he would have ended up without them.

At the last leg of his journey, he counted off the room numbers—most of them with doors ajar and faint murmurs of the night's prime-time sitcoms emanating from within. As he walked toward room 426, he considered that the people in this wing of the hospital weren't here for a long stay. Their ailments were not life threatening. Some might have had surgery for removal of an appendix or gall bladder. Most would be going home within the week. Pearl would check out the following day and be transported back to Glory Heights.

Pearl's door was also standing ajar. He was about to enter when he heard a woman talking. He thought it was a nurse. Being careful to ensure Pearl's privacy, he remained outside the room. Then he heard something that piqued his interest. The nurse was saying that in five minutes visiting hours would be over and Mr. Capshaw would have to leave.

Damn, thought Matthew, he's not supposed to be here.

Pearl was asking if they could have a minute alone together. The nurse cheerfully granted this wish and left the room. As she turned into the hallway, she bumped into Matthew. He'd startled her, but after accepting a quick explanation of who he was, she moved on to forewarn the end of visitation to anyone in the next room. Matthew briefly wondered why they didn't just use a PA system. Maybe because no one ever listened to them, or visitors pretended not to hear the message. He supposed he knew that from personal experience.

As Matthew stood outside room 426's oversized, thinly stained door that he had time to notice was missing a few layers of veneer at its bottom, he wondered what he was doing. He was supposed to be keeping Pearl and Sonny apart. Yet here he was, allowing them time alone together. Just like the nurse had. It was time to do his job.

He stepped into the room. His leather boat shoes were silent against the gray vinyl hospital floor; his entry was unannounced. Pearl's bed was on the far side of the room with the privacy curtain pulled nearly closed around it. Matthew opened his mouth to forewarn his arrival, but then he heard the soft tones in Sonny's voice on the other side of the curtain. Matthew inwardly groaned, "Ah, geez." He remained silent a few more moments.

Part of him thought he should follow through with his instructions from the warden. Part of him wanted to hear what they had to say. But most of him wished he had remained in the hallway. He was not an eavesdropper. Moving again would reveal his presence in the private moment, he reasoned. He stayed put.

"Pearly, are you going to be okay in here by yourself? If you want, I'll sleep right out in the family room. They let people wait there. I'll wait all night if you need me to."

Matthew thought he heard a sniffle. Was Sonny crying?

"Sonny, you better go home," said Pearl. "You have to keep that job at the warehouse until we can get you back at Brambles. You said you have to work Saturday mornings. If you stay here all night you'll be too tired for work tomorrow."

"But are you going to be okay? No more spells tonight? I know you're worried about them taking you back to Glory Heights tomorrow morning."

A sob issued from behind the curtain. Matthew thought it must be Pearl. The curtains billowed outward. Sonny had moved closer and wrapped his arms around her. The shadow of two heads bowed together touched Matthew's heart. Silence pervaded the room.

Matthew shifted uncomfortably, studied the hospital's water-stained ceiling, and wondered if he should be concerned about them having sex. It had not entered his mind before. Most of his clients were not involved in intimate relationships. Finding a time and place for romance would prove difficult for someone living at Glory Heights. Pregnancy wasn't a concern; all female patients were on birth control. Besides, Pearl was beyond child-bearing years.

The emotional repercussion of intimacy is what he worried about. Separating two people when there's been sexual involvement was a whole other ball game. Not one he wanted to play. Carrying out the warden's demands might be harder than anyone thought. He shook his head in frustration, and then he cleared his throat and moved to the other side of the curtain.

Sonny shot up and whirled around, quickly wiping his eyes dry. Pearl, wearing a blue, print hospital gown, covered up to her armpits with a sheet, peered around Sonny. She didn't look particularly surprised to see Matthew.

Matthew silently registered the bandage that swelled across Pearl's forehead. She hadn't been wearing her helmet, he thought. He calmly told Pearl and Sonny that Nurse Charlotte had called him, and that he had come to check on Pearl. He wasn't sure why he was explaining his presence to them.

"What are you going to do with her?" Sonny asked, as if horrible repercussions awaited Pearl.

Matthew put a hand on Sonny's shoulder, acting as if he hadn't noticed his watery eyes. He tried not to be imposing, but he was a good five inches taller than Sonny. Matthew chose his words. "I just want to talk to Pearl, Sonny. I know you're concerned about her, but she's going to be fine."

"She's not fine," Sonny's voice rose. "You'll see that she's sent back to Glory Heights. You'll try to keep us apart again." He looked at Pearl and then bit down on a fingernail.

"Sonny, Pearl lives at Glory Heights. I know you're upset that the two of you have been split up, but really, it's for the best." After seeing them together again, Matthew wondered if he still believed that.

The sound of someone entering the room interrupted their conversation. They all turned their heads toward the nurse as she drew up next to the privacy curtain. "Visiting hours are over. Time for you to go," she said, looking pointedly at Sonny.

Sonny batted his eyes between the nurse and Pearl. It was clear he didn't want to go. He finally turned his back on the nurse and focused on Pearl. "But Pearl, I can't go. They'll keep me from you." Sonny jerked his head in Matthew's direction, suggesting who the culprit was.

The nurse looked quizzically at Matthew. Matthew gave her an unrevealing look. Then he remembered something important from his conversation with Charlotte. "Pearl missed her evening medication. Have you administered phenobarbital?"

The nurse nodded. "Pearl's doctor gave us authorization. I gave her a shot of it right after I bandaged her forehead. Pearl has a nasty gash on her head." She nodded at Pearl, inviting her to fill in the blanks of her mishap.

Pearl looked like she didn't want to discuss it. But Sonny turned to the nurse and blurted out, "She banged her head in the phone booth."

"The phone booth?" Matthew and the nurse asked in unison.

Pearl's escape from Glory Heights was of no business to the nurse, although it was obvious that she would love to hear the explanation. Matthew took charge, letting the nurse and Sonny know that he needed to talk with Pearl. Alone. The nurse, with nothing left to do, ordered Sonny from the room. She then made an apprehensive exit herself. Matthew could only guess that she was low on hospital gossip and wished for something juicy to pass along.

Sonny abided only after a few reassuring words from Pearl. She squeezed his hand and admonished him not to give up hope; something would work out for them. Although her voice held little conviction, she attempted a meaningful smile and patted his hand farewell.

Sonny hung his head and left Pearl's bedside, but he stopped at the door. There he turned, and, giving Pearl one last beleaguered glance, hesitantly backed himself out of the hospital room, hanging onto the door frame as if it could somehow, at the last minute, save him. Finally, after a wistful wave to Pearl, Sonny disappeared. He could catch the bus home. Nevertheless, Matthew wondered how Sonny would be when he got there.

Matthew took a deep breath and settled himself in the chair at Pearl's bedside. Pearl closed her eyes. He rested his elbows on the armrests, made a steeple of his hands, and tapped them against his chin. He waited. Was she fatigued or just feeling the calm that often followed her spells? It could be that she was just plain ignoring him. With these recent developments, he had not had time to consider where to begin. He hoped she would be willing to talk. He would need kid gloves for this. Hesitating for another moment, he began. "Pearl?"

Pearl opened her eyes and looked at him. "What is it you want to know, Matthew?"

"As much as you'll tell me."

Pearl looked into Matthew's eyes, as if searching for

him—the caseworker she used to know. He was someone assigned to her case, but he also cared about her, and she knew it. He figured that keeping Sonny from her was most likely confusing her. She probably was wondering if Matthew was still on her side.

"Will you please help me?" Pearl's voice had a desperate edge to it.

"Of course, I'll help you. That's why I'm here."

"No." She was certain he misunderstood her. "I mean, with Sonny."

Matthew pressed forward in his chair, leaning his elbows atop his knees. "Pearl, look what happened tonight. You left Glory Heights without taking your medication. You have quite a bang on your head because you weren't wearing your helmet. You know you need to wear that when you leave the building. Never mind that you were in a secured building—I want to know how you got out and what you were doing in the phone booth."

Matthew couldn't help it; a small smile slid across his face. It was a clever thing to have accomplished, breaking out of a secured health facility.

Pearl smiled back at his growing grin. "I just hid in the lobby bushes until the afternoon shift left. I followed the last one out the door. I guess I can move quicker than you thought, huh? Quicker than the lobby door anyway."

"We'll have to get that fixed."

"I suppose you will."

Matthew lost the smile and adopted a serious tone. "It's obvious you made your way to Sonny's apartment, so let's skip to the part about the phone booth. Who were you trying to call?"

With a resigned look, Pearl confessed. "My niece."

"Your niece?"

Pearl seemed to enjoy the surprised look on his face. He knew Pearl was still hoping that she could enlist his help. She must have thought it was worth taking a chance on trusting him. Pearl filled him in on her call to Jordana. She even confided that she didn't think the call went too well. Jordana had outright said she could not help Pearl. Pearl said she really couldn't blame the poor girl—she surely had given Jordana quite a shock.

When Pearl finished, Matthew sought to address her desperation. He didn't believe for one minute that when she returned to Glory Heights all would be well. And he was beginning to wonder how badly she had conked her head. She wasn't making any sense, talking about a niece. As far as he knew, she didn't have any relatives. He sat back in his chair, resuming the casual air of someone who had nowhere to go and all the time in the world to listen. "What did you want Jordana to do for you?"

Pearl's face registered a moment of shock. She hesitated, as if trying to recall or decide upon the reasoning behind her actions. Then, she meekly admitted that she wasn't sure. "Now that you mention it, I don't really know what I hoped she could do. Maybe just speak up for me. Maybe she could have some influence over her mother."

Matthew was not connecting the dots. "Her mother?"

"My sister."

Matthew stared at her, wondering what was coming next. "Ah, okay, what sister?"

"Yes, Matthew, I have a sister. Her name is Susan. I've not brought her up before because I know she wanted it that way. Susan is behind all of this. She is keeping me from marrying Sonny. I'm sure of it."

Matthew scratched his head in wonder. "Okay, what makes you think that?"

"I wrote her a letter about Sonny and me. The next thing I know, Sonny's lost his job at Brambles, and we're not allowed to see each other."

"I'm sure she's acting in your best interest. Your health warrants constant care. Perhaps she realizes that Sonny could not provide that for you."

"Oh don't be so Pollyannaish," snapped Pearl.

Matthew laughed involuntarily. He hadn't known she knew the word. "What do you mean?"

"Do you know who my sister is, Matthew?"

She was so adamant about her newfound relatives that

he was beginning to believe her. She wasn't the delusional type. He was now wondering how this had escaped his knowledge. He didn't like having to admit that he had not been aware of a sister or a niece. "No, I'm sorry, I didn't know about your relatives."

"Of course you didn't. Susan intended it that way. Many years ago, she checked me into Glory Heights and left me here. She and Jordana are my only living relatives, and Susan makes sure that no one knows that. To Susan, I'm an embarrassment. She's controlled where I live, how I get to work, where I can go, and now whom I can marry. She wants no one associating her with me, her epileptic sister. After all, someone could suggest that this 'insanity' might also run in her blood. That would not do well for her *position* in the world." Pearl shot Matthew a glance, as if to say she had harbored the bitterness for Susan, not him.

The firmness with which Pearl spoke startled Matthew. Her voice had held no stammer. In fact, she had never spoken more resolutely. Matthew kept his own voice even. "What is her position?"

"My sister is Senator Susan Seymour, Matthew. That's whom I have to fight. Now, are you going to help me or not?"

Matthew had a lot to think about. He had left Pearl with the knowledge that he would consider what she said, but he reminded her about the seriousness of her seizures. He explained again that she was in no position to marry Sonny Capshaw. Of that, Matthew was certain. Convincing Pearl of it was another story, although he again mentioned the impact of skipping meds and not wearing the helmet. God, even to Matthew it sounded like a broken record. As for allowing her to see Sonny again, Matthew told her he didn't have control over it—it was the warden's call. Then, after assuring her they would soon talk again, he left the hospital.

It was after midnight and he knew that Cory would be asleep in their neighbor's spare bedroom. Matthew went home, swallowed a scotch, neat, and reflected upon all he had learned that evening. Tomorrow was going to be an interesting day, he knew. If Pearl had a relative in the area, as she claimed, he wanted to speak with her. He had little tolerance for absent relatives. He was going to call Jordana in the morning. Never mind that he felt like a fool for not knowing that Pearl, his longtime client, had a Minnesota senator for a sister and a niece practically in the next suburb.

He was a little irritated with Pearl for not having told him about her family, but it sounded like she had her reasons. Perhaps she had thought it was irrelevant. Before, she didn't have the motivation and conviction to marry Sonny Capshaw. Nevertheless, it should have been in her records. But it hadn't been in her records. He'd read them.

Matthew would have to swallow his "handling everything" pride and make the call. His clients deserved the fullest life possible, and he firmly believed that included having access to family. Pearl had given him Jordana Barlow's phone number and he intended to use it.

Chapter Eleven

Jordana slept poorly. Excerpts of the previous night's phone call with someone named Pearl Witherby claiming to be her mother's sister had breached her usually pleasant slumber. Although it was still dark outside, she couldn't lie in bed any longer. Throwing back the covers, she got up and showered. By the time she'd pulled on pressed jeans, a blue silk tee shirt, and mules, the sun was peeking through the blinds in her bedroom.

In the kitchen, she thought about breakfast, but decided against it. What she really needed was coffee. The Post-It note on which she'd written the woman's number lay on the kitchen counter. She slung her bag over her shoulder, ready to head out, but her eyes went back to the note. She hesitated. Then she grabbed it and stuck it in her purse—why, she didn't know.

With her mind in a fog and sunglasses shielding her eyes from the rising sun, she was on her way to her office. The sky had a pink cast to it, and she wondered about the old saying, "Red sky at night, sailor's delight, red sky in the morning, sailors take warning." She also wondered if it was an omen.

Driving straight to the Wilderness drive-thru coffeehouse, she picked up a large cup of coffee. She then traveled on highways 694 and 94 into Minneapolis. Traffic was light; only a sparse group of weekend workers was making their way downtown. She entered the Midwest Plaza, maneuvered her car into a contracted parking spot, and made her way through the skyway.

In Crystal Court, the area of the building open to small restaurants and novelty shops, she grabbed another cup of coffee at Starbucks. She then took the escalator to ground level and rode the east bank of elevators. Curic and McCall's offices were on the fiftieth floor of the IDS tower. From her office, she had an arresting view of interstate highway 94 as it headed eastward over the Mississippi River toward Wisconsin. As a top national account executive, she had earned her glass-paned office.

Jordana was at her desk reviewing client files, with limited concentration. A tension headache was beginning above her left eye, so she turned to look out the window, hoping to ward it off. Gazing into the wide-open space at fifty stories high did ease the pain. When she closed her eyes to rest them, her thoughts again went to the disturbing phone call.

The woman genuinely thought she needed her help—not that Jordana believed her to be the long-lost aunt she claimed to be. Maybe she was just elderly and confused, although her voice didn't sound that old. Jordana wondered what she should do about it; perhaps someone should know about the call. She reasoned that it wouldn't hurt her to make a simple phone call.

Picking the note out of her purse, she looked over what she'd written. It was the number of the home where the woman said she lived. Jordana had written down the name of the place, too. It was Glory Heights Healthcare Facility in Rum River. Someone there might confirm Ms. Witherby's existence, and her situation. The woman probably had psychological problems—problems that would cause her to seek out a complete stranger for help. Heck, they would probably appreciate the phone call. Why not call and end this mystery? Then she could get back to work.

Reaching for the phone, she was surprised when it rang before she lifted the handset. An eerie chill ran through her, ending in an involuntary jerk. Acid riddled up from a knot in the middle of her stomach. She swallowed hard and wished she hadn't drunk so much coffee. After clearing her throat, she picked up the phone, prepared to do battle over another unwelcome intrusion into her life. However, she was startled out of that stance when the unexpected sound of a smooth male voice came across the phone lines.

"May I speak to Jordana Barlow, please?"

She straightened her back and leaned forward in the leather desk chair. Both hands felt clammy as she tightened them around the phone. She had anticipated the delicate stammering voice from the previous evening, not this confident-sounding man. Still, she thought, she had no reason to feel nervous. She hadn't done anything wrong. Nevertheless, she again swallowed hard to dissipate the unease brewing in the pit of her stomach. Unwilling to admit her identity yet, she asked, "Who's calling?"

"Matthew Kincaid. I'm a caseworker at Glory Heights Healthcare Facility. I'm calling to speak with Jordana Barlow, the niece of Pearl Witherby."

His inference royally piqued Jordana. She had wanted to speak with someone at Glory Heights, but now that that someone was on the other end of the line, she didn't like it much. She assumed she would call them, whomever they turned out to be, not they her. Her plan was for them to take care of everything so she would never again hear from Pearl Witherby, not for them to call her up and all but say, "Your long-lost Auntie Pearl asked me to phone you."

"Ma'am?" His voice was like butter melting.

Jordana hadn't realized she had been holding her breath. She tried to contain her anger. "I'm sorry. Yes, this is Jordana Barlow. That is, I'm Jordana Barlow, but I don't think I'm the niece you're looking for." She cringed at her breathy response.

Matthew Kincaid chuckled lightly. "Well, to tell you the truth, that's why I'm calling. My client, Pearl, gave me your phone number. You met her on the telephone last night?"

Jordana relaxed some at the sound of his easy manner. "Yes, someone by that name called me last night with the most extraordinary story. She called out of the blue, claiming me to be her niece, and asking for my help in some marital caper. In fact, I was just about to call Glory Heights to report the incident. I had assumed she had escaped from some nut house and arbitrarily dialed my number." She laughed lightly at the preposterous situation.

Matthew Kincaid didn't laugh. "I can assure you Glory Heights is not a nut house. It's an upscale health facility attending to the needs of many functioning levels of humanity."

His tone was all she needed to be embarrassed for her shortsighted rudeness. She had not even met this man and he had made her blush twice with her own abnormal behavior. She was not used to this and found no pleasure in it. Nevertheless, she felt the need to apologize. "I'm sorry, Mr. Kincaid, I simply meant that this woman, Pearl, didn't make any sense. She said that she was my mother's sister. My mother doesn't have a sister."

"Is your mother Senator Susan Seymour?" His voice was even, forgiving.

"Well, yes, she is. But as I've stated, my mother doesn't have a sister."

He hesitated a moment before tentatively asking, "Are you sure about that?"

"Of course, I'm sure about that," snapped Jordana. "I think I'd know if my own mother had a sister and me an aunt after all of this time." She picked up a Mont Blanc pen next to the phone and began tapping it on her desk. Something else occurred to her. She stopped tapping. "Do you really take Pearl seriously?"

"Yes, I take her seriously. I'm her caseworker. Pearl has epilepsy, not a mental deficiency, other than some slowness, which has occurred through years of seizures and medication." It occurred to Jordana that the timbre of his voice, deepened with resolve, grew sexier.

She was about to apologize again, but she stopped herself and began tapping the pen against her desk, as if it would help her think straight. This conversation was going nowhere. She needed to persuade him that she was not the person he or Pearl sought. Jordana tried a different approach. "Do you have any proof that Pearl's claim of having a niece, any niece, has any validity?"

"Well, yes, Ms. Barlow, I do."

Jordana dropped the Mont Blanc. "Proof? You have proof?" Her response dripped with a sarcasm she was too nervous to feel.

"There is one document, an old will I found in her history file this morning. It lists Pearl Witherby and Susan Witherby Seymour as dependents of Joseph and Cecilia Witherby."

Jordana gasped, then swallowed dryly, but she let Matthew continue without interruption.

"Joseph and Cecilia Witherby were Pearl's parents and are long deceased. I believe both passed away in the early seventies. By the way, the 'Witherby' after 'Susan' is in parenthesis, as if it was a maiden or previous name. As I said, it's an old document." Matthew continued to talk, as if giving her time to realize the truth of her own heritage. "There's not much in it except instructions for the sale of assets and the distribution of some meager funds to their daughters, Pearl Witherby and Susan Witherby Seymour."

Jordana raked her mind for a defense. "There must be some mistake. Perhaps there's another Susan Seymour." It was weak, and Jordana knew it. Although she had never met her grandparents, she knew their names were Joseph and Cecilia.

"I don't think it's a mistake." Matthew Kincaid's voice softened compassionately. "Look, I'm sorry you had to find out this way. Perhaps you'd like to contact your mother and talk to her about it."

He could not know it, but that thought terrified her. She lashed out at him. "What great good would that do, other than upset our lives? And even if it was true, what would Pearl Witherby's problems have to do with me?"

To his credit, Matthew's voice remained calm, but determined. "Pearl Witherby has no one to call family. Think what that must feel like. It's my hope to encourage you to come visit her, get to know her—"

Jordana, wild with emotion, interrupted him. "Wait. You're going too fast. I have to think. I don't want to visit her. Why should I visit her? No, I'm sorry. I didn't mean that. I . . .

it's just . . . you see . . . I don't know." Then, like a betrayed child seeking comfort, she quietly said, "I have to call my mother," and then she hung up on him.

Jordana didn't really want to call her mother. All her life, Jordana had struggled to keep their relationship on an even keel. She got up, ran to the bathroom, and then returned to pace around her office.

She thought about her mother and their history together, and tried to make sense of what Matthew said. She grew up in private boarding schools, spending holidays and summer vacations in DC or traveling with Mother. While they maintained most of their relationship from afar, the long reach of Mother's influence never left Jordana. As she was growing up, every other night she had to call Mother to report on homework assignments and social activities. At the time, Jordana didn't mind. With no siblings and a father she rarely saw, Jordana clung to Mother, emotionally. Sadly, their relationship was a dichotomy of distance, control, and fear. Jordana supposed it was inevitable with a parent who maintained a demanding career in Washington DC, kept up her social image, and managed a daughter from afar.

Jordana never received what she considered normal motherly affection and attention. She longed for mother/daughter talks, but those kinds of talks never came. Every conversation took its toll, with Jordana wishing Mother would see her as someone other than a "constituent" she rooted for or strove to deter from some misguided path.

Still, she tried to be the good daughter, never rocking the boat. Well, almost never. There was the time Jordana wanted to stay in the Twin Cities after high school. She wanted to attend the U of M, where she had already completed some college-level coursework. Mother insisted that Jordana attend an Eastern school. They had gone round and round on the subject. Jordana loved Minneapolis: the unique city-side lakes and parks where young and old convened to enjoy walking and biking trails and beaches; the skyways for shopping in cold weather; and the culture—just enough to feed her appetite for the arts. She didn't want for popular Broadway performances, thanks to season tickets at the Guthrie. And many small stages like the Chanhassen Dinner Theatre, The Old Log Theatre, and Dudley Riggs' Brave New Workshop provided an eclectic taste of musicals, dramas, and satirical off-beat comedies. Besides all of that, Jordana argued, the U of M was a good school offering programs in her chosen field of study.

Jordana was the first to back down. Several Eastern universities accepted Jordana's application and, according to Mother, Jordana would be very happy at any one of them. With Mother's determined help, Jordana chose the University of New York. Mother, of course, was quite pleased, saying she hadn't paid for private schooling and Jordana hadn't maintained a 4.0 throughout high school to throw it away on any old run-of-the-mill college. Jordana guessed that Mother didn't want to lose money on her investment.

As it turned out, New York had an excellent journalism and mass communication program, and the city was an exciting, multicultural experience. However, when an opportunity rose to return to Minneapolis for a weekend break or a summer job between terms, Jordana took it. At home, she would breathe in the crystal-clean air and appreciate the vast differences between the cities. Upon graduation, she obtained an entry-level advertising position with Curic and McCall in their Minneapolis office. With that, she moved home and completed her graduate work at the U of M. However, New York had its own irresistible charm. She returned there several times a year for long weekends visiting friends, attending cultural events, and touring museums.

As Jordana paced, she wondered how to approach the unnerving subject of Pearl with Mother. The fact that Mother had been hiding a sister all of Jordana's life appalled and confused her. What could she have been thinking? Although she wasn't comfortable talking with Mother on a normal day, Jordana couldn't wait to hear her explanation. This conversation would be beyond ordinary.

How this unearthing would further rattle her relationship with Mother terrified her. Yet, Jordana didn't run away from confrontation with anyone else. She must have inherited that trait from Mother, who didn't seem to mind a good fight.

Jordana didn't know who her mother was anymore. She had obviously duped her own daughter. What kind of person does that? With a burst of indignant anger, Jordana temporarily lost all fear of setting the problem of Pearl Witherby at her mother's feet.

Chapter Twelve

"What, in God's name, is going on over there?" The senator was emoting, had been for ten minutes or more, picking up steam as she went. "They're supposed to be watching her. What in hell does McFinley think I'm paying him to do, sit on his haunches while my sister gallivants around that hole-in-the-wall town making a fool of herself? If that's what he thinks, he's sorely mistaken."

After a phone call from Jordana, Susan went directly to the one person that could help her. She knew that Nick would be alone in the office. On a typical Saturday, personnel wishing to wrap up the past week's miscellaneous items, or get a head start on the upcoming week's demanding schedule, arrived early afternoon. Nick was always in earlier, and he stayed late.

She sped to her congressional offices in her own seldom-used car. She didn't take the time to call a driver. The distance was only a few short blocks. The traffic, both pedestrian and automobile, was light, even for a weekend day. Rushing inside, she did find Nick in his office. Completely forgetting to usher him into the inner sanctum of her elite quarters, they stayed there, a modest space by comparison.

She was sitting across from him in a hard, uncomfortable visitor's chair, while Nick was behind his desk in a fabric-covered burgundy chair, one befitting an aide. Susan caught her breath and mused for a moment that the situation didn't feel right. She glanced at Nick. He seemed quite comfortable—too comfortable for the turmoil she faced. Disregarding it for the time being, Susan raged on.

The utter embarrassment of having an epileptic sister possibly exposed to her public had turned her into a raving lunatic. The potential humiliation was more egregious than the fact that Jordana knew about Pearl, thanks to Pearl herself. Although Susan had to admit to feeling a little disconcerted about Jordana's reaction.

Jordana had all but accused Susan of being deceptive—the audacity of it made her temper spike red. She had saved Jordana from every exposure to the ugly side of life. Jordana had no reason to know about her aunt. Pearl was not a part of their lives. As for Susan not mentioning that she had changed her name so many years ago, what in hell did that matter to anyone but her?

Jordana had been an overly sensitive child, and Susan had to keep close tabs on her. Sometimes at the expense of her own career. She didn't believe in letting her heart rule her mind. She thought she had taught Jordana the same. It appeared that she had somehow failed Jordana in that regard.

Susan made no apologies to Jordana. She tried to soothe her daughter's concerns by assuring her that Pearl would not bother them again. Susan would take care of everything. Never mind about Pearl, Susan had said. Pearl wasn't a part of their lives. She was an epileptic invalid and required constant care. Care that she could only get at Glory Heights. That Jordana didn't fully accept everything her mother told her was troublesome, and new. Susan hoped it wouldn't become a problem, and then she dismissed it from her mind.

Susan stopped her rampage for a moment to ensure that Nick was listening. He appeared to be listening, attentively. However, he was sitting too slack in his chair for her liking. She wanted to shake him down. This was his fault. He was supposed to handle the situation, which meant make it go away. He had obviously failed to do that.

"Nick," snapped Susan. "I thought you were going to take care of this for me. Didn't you make it clear to McFinley that my sister is not to see that man?"

Nick assumed a concerned look. "I did speak with him. We got a guy to take care of Sonny's job. I guess I'll have to—"

"You'll have to what?" She interrupted and all but spat at him. "Talk to him again? A lot of good talking to him did the first time." Nick's casual tone irritated Susan. He obviously was not as upset as she was about Pearl's behavior, or Jordana's. Not yet anyway.

Nick started to defend himself, but she was not finished.

She went on. "You know what really burns me? McFinley didn't call to tell us himself about my sister's escape from the home. He's a damn coward." Then, as an afterthought, "He didn't call you, did he?"

Nick glanced over Susan's shoulder toward the closed door. Reflexively, she looked too. The click and hum of a copy machine had caught his attention. Others were arriving, earlier than usual, most likely to work on the text of the latest Water Protection Act revisions. Nick's baby. They glanced back at each other, silently agreeing to lower their voices.

Nick began by answering her question. "No, McFinley hasn't called me. But, in fairness to him, it is Saturday. Perhaps he's not yet been informed of your sister's activities."

His voice of reason angered her. "Not yet been informed of her activities? He's supposed to be on top of her activities. She walked right out of that *secured* building. She then made her way to that dunderhead she wants to marry. And then she contacted my naïve daughter. All in the same day!"

Nick held his hands up to quiet her, beckoning her to let him finish. "Yes, I understand that's what happened. I'll talk to McFinley to find out how it happened."

"I don't really care how it happened, but it's not going to happen again."

Nick looked wary. "What do you mean?"

Lowering her voice, she assumed a dignified air; what was to come next was only in the best interest of her sister. "I mean that my sister is not well. She's obviously taken to wandering the streets at night. Certainly, they can take measures to prevent that from happening again."

"What measures?" Nick asked.

She studied him, gauging as she often did whether or not she could trust him with what she was about to say. She really had no choice. "I believe that people who try to leave the Glory Heights facility or wander the halls at night are sedated. It works out best for everyone. The patient gets their sleep and the staff doesn't have to worry about them running off. My sister is most certainly an immediate candidate for sedation. I want it done."

Nick's stare made her uncomfortable.

She shifted in her chair. "Well, it makes sense, doesn't it? We can't have her running around to God knows where whenever she feels the urge." She stood up to leave, giving one last order. "Call McFinley. Tell him he has one more chance before we move her to another home. Tell him to do what's necessary to keep her from running away again."

She moved toward the door, but then waited for Nick to respond. He had hesitated a moment too long. Would he defy her? The request wasn't out of line with her sister's needs. Besides, what did he care? He didn't know Pearl; she was nothing to him. Susan raised her eyebrows. "Well?"

Nick was thinking it over.

Chapter Thirteen

In the early-morning quiet at Glory Heights, Charlotte heard the bell buzz at the front entrance and went to check on it. She was surprised to find a female security guard reporting for duty. They didn't have a receptionist in on the weekends, let alone a security guard. But, when Matthew came up the steps right behind her, it started to make sense. While most caseworkers didn't work weekends, Charlotte wasn't surprised to see him—especially after last night, she thought. She supposed he was going to make sure Pearl didn't escape again.

"Good morning, ladies." His tone was upbeat.

The guard, a young woman, stuck out her hand and smiled. "Good morning. You must be Matthew. We spoke on the phone. I'll just set up at the desk over there."

"Perfect."

The guard walked away, but not before giving Matthew's body an admiring look. Charlotte couldn't blame her; he was an attractive man. She was enjoying the view herself. He was dressed in runner's shorts, an olive green tee shirt with "Friends Food Share" printed on it, and running shoes. His long legs were muscular, but not overly so. His chest was broad, and while his shirt hung loosely over his torso, it was obvious that a toned abdomen lay beneath it. His face was flushed and his hair wet with brown waves pressed close to his head. He looked as if he'd jogged from home.

Caught up in his looks, Charlotte almost forgot that she could be in big trouble with him. Suddenly, she wanted to get back to her patients. Still, her Southern upbringing kicked in to chat. "Good morning, Matthew. You're up early on your day off."

He ran his fingers through his hair and looked apologetic, as if he'd noticed her gawking at him. "You'll have to excuse my appearance. I got in a run this morning, and then realized that I was late getting Cory and his friends to swimming lessons." He smiled and said, "It was my turn to drive. I only had time to change my shirt."

"You're fine, don't worry about that." She waved away his concerns.

"I have a few things to do here before I get back to Cory. Another parent is picking up the kids, and I'll have to retrieve him from the neighbor's." Matthew headed toward the lobby desk, and she thought that was her cue to get back to work.

She started toward the nurses' station when Matthew turned back and said, "Hold on just a sec, Nurse Charlotte, I need to talk with you." Although he'd asked politely enough, her skin prickled. She waited in discomfort while he talked to the guard. When he finished, he nodded at Charlotte to follow him.

In his office, she gripped the arms of the chair he'd offered and prepared herself while he took a seat on the other side of the desk. He was probably going to fire her, she thought; he probably got the warden's permission to give her the axe. She could hardly come up with a defense for her part in Pearl's escape. Giving her Jordana's phone number had put ideas in Pearl's head, ones Charlotte hadn't considered.

Lowering her eyes so he wouldn't see how nervous she was, she noticed her exposed thighs. Dang slippery uniforms. Quickly, she gave the hem of her skirt a good yank, and then went back to gripping. She held her breath and waited, hoping she didn't turn purple and die right there on the spot.

Matthew settled himself with a pad of paper and pen, and then he surprised her. In his low-key approach, he simply said, "Nurse Charlotte, I'd like your take on what happened last night. How could Pearl have gotten out?"

Her head shot up, and she stared at him. Wasn't he going to fire her? Then she realized—he didn't know what she had done. Pearl must not have told him. She tried not to smile, and hoped he wouldn't notice the relief in her voice. "It must have happened during the shift change, when people were at dinner. No one seemed to see anything."

He nodded, but didn't say anything. He clicked his pen.

She wasn't comfortable with the silence. "The receptionist's desk is often unattended then."

"I suspected the same thing. That's why I ordered a security guard. I'm sure the warden, I mean McFinley, won't mind, under the circumstances." He smiled at his own faux pas.

Charlotte smiled too, and then she agreed with him. "That was probably a good move."

"Well, we need a guard. Sonny may try to see Pearl. Unless something changes, we can't allow him in here. You might not have been aware of that." He lifted his eyebrows as if it were a question.

She wasn't going to touch it. "I'll keep an eye on Pearl."

She also kept an eye on Matthew as he suddenly stood and strode over to the filing cabinet. She watched him open the lowest drawer, giving the handle a tough pull. He reached into the deepest part of the cabinet and pulled out a folder. The well-worn file had Pearl's name on it.

With the folder in his hands, he turned to Charlotte. "Okay, then." He looked like he wanted to add something else, but then thought better of it.

She thought, is that it? It sure sounded like she was free to leave. While she wondered what he was going to do with the file, she was too afraid to ask. Until this whole episode with Pearl blew over, Charlotte didn't want to get into any further discussion about her. She was going to keep a low profile for a while. "I'll keep an eye on Pearl," she repeated. Then, with an internal "Whew!", she made a quick exit.

Later, Matthew called Charlotte at the nurses' station and asked her to send Pearl to his office. She wanted to ask what it was about, but of course, she couldn't. She just went looking for Pearl. She'd get the skinny out of Pearl afterward.

Pearl was lying on her bed, doing nothing but thinking about Sonny. She'd heard that it was nice outside, apparently not too hot with a slight breeze, so many residents had gone out. Some were getting fresh air with a stroll around the grounds, others were on a chaperoned trip to the Minnesota Zoo. Pearl wasn't interested in fresh air, and her mind felt like a zoo. She had a blistering headache from the previous night's injury to her head. The second injury that week.

Feeling claustrophobic, she decided to go to the community room to see what was on television. She sighed and looked at the helmet on her bed stand. Well, she couldn't put it on now. It wouldn't fit over the gauze bandage.

In the community room, she fell into a recliner and began flicking through the channels, not really concentrating on any of them. All she could think about was that Sonny used to watch TV with her, but now he wouldn't make it through the secured doors of what she felt was her prison. They were still supposed to stay away from each other, per Matthew's instructions. She seethed at the gall of it.

The television set had been blaring for some time without her knowing what she was watching when she heard Nurse Charlotte's voice. "Pearl, Pearl, Pearl. Mm, mm, mm." She was briskly approaching Pearl's chair, wagging a chastising index finger.

Pearl turned and gave her a faint sheepish grin. "Hello, Nurse Charlotte." Her nurse was a welcome interruption to her endless thoughts of Sonny, even if she was about to get a scolding.

Nurse Charlotte stood in an indignant stance, elbows out, hands on her hips. One hip jutted out to the left, the other one lowered as her knee and thigh bent sideways. "Young lady," she began, although Pearl was twenty years her senior, "you gave me quite a fright last night. What on earth possessed you to run off like that? Never mind, I already know what possessed you."

In her agitation, her Southern tongue twanged to a degree Pearl had never before witnessed. She rattled on, but lowered her voice. "I know you went to see Sonny, and I'm assuming you tried contacting Jordana, as well." It was a statement, not a question. "Why, I thought I was going to have to confess to Matthew that I found your niece in *Minnesota's Who's Who* and handed the information over to you. By the way, I don't think I could've found Jordana if her mother wasn't a senator. But never mind that, do you know how my helping you would look to Matthew? Worse yet, do you know that I could lose my job for helping you?"

She stopped for a moment to catch her breath, eyeing Pearl. "Good gad girl, what did you do to yourself?"

Pearl fingered the large butterfly bandage covering her forehead. "I hit my head last night during a spell."

Nurse Charlotte gently touched Pearl's hairline, predictably examining her swollen head. "You got stitches under there?" Then, without waiting for an answer, she peeked underneath the bandage. "I want to know what we're dealing with here. No, just a nasty gash. You weren't wearing your helmet, were you?"

Pearl shook her head in response. She didn't want to talk about the helmet; she wanted to apologize for having caused Nurse Charlotte such grief. It would be a long stretch to be sorry for breaking out of Glory Heights and seeing Sonny. Lowering her eyes, she shrugged. "I didn't mean to get you into trouble, Nurse Charlotte. I just wanted to see Sonny, and call Jordana. I didn't know how else to do it." It occurred to Pearl that this seemed a childish explanation, and it embarrassed her. Being in a position where she could not do as she wished angered her.

When she looked up again, Nurse Charlotte was smiling and shaking her head. "So you did run off to call Jordana. I knew it! You sure have guts, girl, I'll give you that."

Pearl smiled, relieved that she wasn't in serious trouble

with the only person, other than Rebecca, who had befriended her. Matthew was her friend, but the way he banished Sonny from her was heartless. Friends didn't do things like that to each other.

Nurse Charlotte yanked at the skirt on her white dress. It fit snugly across her rear end and rode up the slippery slope of her pale nylons. "I couldn't eat a bite of my dinner last night, nor breakfast this morning. Knowing that I was in cahoots with you, and you taking off on me like that, I bet I lost five pounds in worry over you.

"Well, the whole thing seems to have blown over. Matthew doesn't seem too put out over it, anyway. Never shows it anyhow. He just gets down to work and solves the problem. I don't know what else he would be working on in his office, on a Saturday. Mercy me, how he thinks he's going to solve this problem, I'm waitin' to hear."

This spiked Pearl's interest. "Matthew is here?"

"Yes, ma'am, since bright and early. He's busy behind that closed door. I could hear him talking on the phone. And now he wants to talk with you. So come on. I'll take you to him, but you better tell me what he has to say when he's done with you."

With Nurse Charlotte at her elbow, they hurried to Matthew's office. Pearl had a good feeling about it.

Pearl listened intently, not wanting to miss a word Matthew was saying. He'd checked old files, in hopes of finding anything that would corroborate Pearl's relationship to Jordana. In an old will left by Pearl and Susan's mother and dad, he found Susan's name—her real name. Pearl had forgotten that, it was so long ago. Thank God, Matthew had found proof. She nodded excitedly when he told her that he'd talked with Jordana. He'd actually called her up.

This news really got Pearl thinking. Matthew was now on her side. It did mean that, didn't it? Perhaps now Jordana would be willing to help too, she hoped. Maybe the two of them could even get Susan to agree to her marrying Sonny. Pearl couldn't keep the smile from beaming across her lips.

Matthew looked relaxed in his office chair, holding his pen, as he always did during their meetings. Saturday was normally his day off, but he had come in to help her. At least that's what she thought he was saying. The excitement was overpowering. She had to ask him right out: "Does this mean you're going to help me?"

Suddenly, Matthew straightened up and leaned forward in his chair. That bridled her concentration.

He began, "I want you to understand that I only contacted Jordana in hopes that she might come to visit you. Not because I think she should help you marry Sonny. I still believe that isn't a good idea."

Suddenly, things didn't sound so good to Pearl. Apprehension took its place in her mind. Elation diminished. She was stunned, having given Matthew's interest in contacting Jordana such high hopes. Hopes that were dashed and plunging into the abyss she knew all too well. She should never have put that much faith in someone. It hurt too much to be let down. She missed Sonny so much and there was no help for it, at least with Matthew.

"You mean you *aren't* going to help me?" She had choked out the words, her mouth so dry she was barely able to speak.

Matthew shrugged and said, "I thought I was helping you by phoning Jordana, although I have to admit I'm not sure she'll visit. But she seems like a responsible person, and she might surprise us. I didn't think it would be a good idea to browbeat her into visiting when the whole notion of having an aunt was so new to her. I kind of felt sorry for her. She wanted to talk to her mother, and that's where we left our conversation."

"Well, if Jordana's going to talk it over with Susan, we won't be seeing her anytime soon," quipped Pearl. "But we may hear from Susan, whether we want to or not. I wrote to her hoping she would be happy for me, maybe help me marry Sonny. Boy, did I make a mistake."

Dejected, Pearl slumped hard against the back of the chair. Tears filled her eyes. Taking a handkerchief from her pocket, she blew her nose. Then, she straightened up in the chair and looked pointedly at Matthew. "Is that the extent of your news for me today?"

Matthew winced, probably at the harshness in her words. He wasn't used to that tone from her. He most likely hadn't intended to create any animosity between them. "No, Pearl, it's not." He sounded empathetic. "I would like to talk to you about where we can go from here, without Sonny, to improve your personal health and happiness. For starters, I would like to see what we can do to get your seizures under control."

The words "without Sonny" sliced through her heart. She could almost feel the blood gushing from its wound. She glared at him. "I don't want to do anything without Sonny." The angry words spilled out in a heated stammer. "You want to improve my health and happiness? Harrumph! Seeing Sonny is the only thing that can increase my happiness, and you've taken him away from me."

Embarrassed, she tried to calm her stammer, but it seemed beyond her control. However, what she had to say was important to her, and she had to continue. "If you want to improve my happiness, figure out a way for me to see my Sonny." She glared at him, thickening the space between them with undiluted reproach.

Matthew was a smart man and he wisely changed the subject. "Maybe talking about improving your life isn't the best thing right now. Sometime soon I would like to talk about reducing your seizures, but right now managing your medication isn't foremost in your mind."

She acknowledged this summation with a nod.

He continued, "I didn't mean to upset you. In fact, I had hoped you would be happy with the news that I contacted Jordana. I even tried to convince her to visit. Not that that looks very promising, considering Jordana's resistance to the implication that she had an aunt she had never met. But, for your sake, Pearl, I tried."

A quieting break hung between them. Pearl softened her glare, and then she turned her eyes to the hands wringing in her lap. She could never stay angry with anyone for long, and that included Matthew.

Their caseworker/client connection was going to hell in a handbasket, fast. She knew he felt it too. When it came to marrying Sonny, Matthew said he couldn't do anything about it. Nevertheless, she tried again. "Isn't there something you can do for me and Sonny?"

Matthew sunk into his chair, letting out a heavy breath. He seemed to be thinking something over. Pearl let him do it. A few moments passed before he seemed to have made a decision.

"Okay, Pearl Witherby, let's see if we can come to a truce here. You and I have been together far too long to see our relationship deteriorate this way. You're right. I am not totally behind the warden on his call to keep you from seeing Sonny. Marrying him is another matter. So if I can get a smile out of one of my favorite clients, I would like to make another suggestion."

Pearl hesitated, not willing to give in yet. Not trusting. "Tell me first."

Matthew made a funny face at her. "Smile first."

Pearl had to break a small smile. It was hard to stay angry with Matthew Kincaid. He was a handsome, kind, intelligent young man with an engaging smile, and he had been her staunch supporter for far too long not to give him some slack.

Matthew smiled back. "Well, I happen to know you can do better than that, Ms. Pearl Witherby, but I'll take it."

Then, what he said next surprised her.

"Maybe, if you took your medication correctly, wore your helmet, and duly stayed on premises, for starters, we could offer up some other arrangement with Sonny. Maybe I could get the warden to agree to it."

"R-really?" She was so excited she could hardly speak. She sat up in her chair. "I could give it a try."

Then, as if Matthew realized he was tottering next to condoning her wish to see Sonny, he again exhaled heavily and sat back up in his chair.

She wasn't going to give him a chance to think it over. While she wasn't completely happy with his suggestion that she could possibly "see" Sonny but not marry him, it was a start.

Thanking him from the bottom of her heart, she got up from her chair and left before he could change his mind.

After Pearl left his office, Matthew stuck around long enough to wonder what he had just done. Had he just endorsed her wish to see Sonny?

After seeing them together at the hospital, Matthew had begun to wonder if he really had the right to deny her access to Sonny. Matthew was tempted to take it up with the warden again. But that would mean calling him, and Matthew wasn't ready to talk to the warden about Pearl's escape. And he sure didn't relish the idea of telling the warden that Pearl had seen Sonny. Matthew didn't feel like hearing the warden's dubiously valuable input on Pearl's adventure.

Once Matthew knew about Susan, he wondered who was really behind prohibiting Pearl from seeing Sonny. And about their motive. Maybe someone was protecting his or her own interests. He wasn't sure that person cared about Pearl's well-being. But if he or she did, Matthew could understand why the person wouldn't want Pearl to marry Sonny. After all, Sonny was mildly retarded—had been since birth. He lived in subsidized housing and most likely had insufficient financial assets to care for a wife. Pearl had never lived on her own and had many improvements to make just to take care of herself, let alone a home and a husband. Yet Matthew was an optimist, so in the end he had to wonder: Was it really so impossible? For the time being, yes it was. But with a few changes?

Abruptly, he stood up and tried to wash away his train of thought. His thinking was edging dangerously close to insubordination. When the train continued winding about his mind, he threw down his pen, and then ran his fingers through his hair.

He remembered Pearl in her solemn position sitting across the desk with her weary face emanating sadness and anger. Being responsible for any of her anguish was more than he could take. Frustrated, he picked up his pen and threw it down again, wondering what he was going to do next. Then he smiled and laughed quietly to himself. What the hell, he had been insubordinate before. He cared too much about Pearl Witherby to see her in this turmoil. Finding a solution wasn't going to be easy, but he would do it. With that in mind, he left Glory Heights to spend the afternoon at Calhoun Beach with Cory. Matthew would try to enjoy what was left of his weekend.

Chapter Fourteen

The latest developments in Pearl's life had worn her out. Her head throbbed and she didn't know whether it was from exhaustion or the latest gash to her noggin. Probably both. From her bedside, she opened the bottle of 800 milligram Tylenol prescribed by the emergency room doctor and then choked the pill down with a glass of water. How convenient, she thought, to take a pill to make the pain in her head go away. She wished she had one for the pain in her heart.

Even after talking to Matthew, she felt depressed. If she followed the rules and got her seizures under control, he would see what he could do about seeing Sonny. But Matthew's proposal seemed like such fuss, for which there was no immediate benefit. At least not the gratification she wanted, like seeing Sonny right away. She figured taking a nap and shutting the world out for a while would be the best thing she could do for herself. Thank goodness Karoline had gone to the zoo with the others. Pearl could rest peacefully. That is, if the Tylenol did its job and knocked her out.

She had just closed her eyes when Charlotte peeked her head around the door. "Is everything okay in here? How's your head feeling?"

Pearl propped herself up into a sitting position. Normally, no one cared how she was doing. "I just took some Tylenol. I'm sure I'll be okay after a little nap." Her voice was frail.

Charlotte walked into the room with an evaluating look on her face. "Let me see what we have here." She gently removed the bandage on Pearl's forehead and then inspected the wound, as if satisfying herself that it was healing properly. "It's looking better, but you may have a scar with that one."

Pearl touched it. The nodule had shrunk considerably since morning. She smiled up at Charlotte and noticed the thoughtful look on her face.

"Are you tired, Pearl? Or are you just sad and in need of a diversion?"

"Probably some of each."

With that, Charlotte took charge. "Well, hanging around in here all day would depress anybody. You need some sunshine, girl. It's a gorgeous day out there, and I'm taking you out in it. Fresh air first, nap later. Besides," she winked, "you owe me an update."

Pearl was bewildered—she wasn't used to this kind of attention. Although she had to admit it felt good. A small smile developed on her face as she let Charlotte help her off the bed and escort her outdoors.

Pearl loved the backyard at Glory Heights. It was a stunning medley of well-attended gardens. Showy bougainvilleas, delicate rose bushes, and crisp bee balm were nestled neatly amongst the centuries old maples, pines, and oak trees. Brilliantly hued petals glimmered in the mid-afternoon sun. Bold green leaves shimmered in the light breeze coming across the Rum River. It was a glorious day.

Charlotte led her down the cobblestone path, meandering through the artistic stretch of trees and flowers. The perfume of pine needles mixed with the floral bouquet sent a wonderful aroma into the warm summer air. Pearl inhaled deeply, gratified by this small gift of nature. Pearl and Charlotte passed through the gate on the white picket fence and then stepped down to the wide deck overhanging the banks of the Rum River. Together, they settled themselves on a wooden bench.

They sat for a time in amicable silence, enjoying the sun on their faces. Pearl listened to the sound of the leaves rustling in the breeze. Charlotte sat quietly, as if lost in her own thoughts. Only the squawk of the vivid red male tanager perched atop an ornamental lighthouse perforated their shared silence.

The summer air drifted about Pearl's face and the simple pleasure lifted her spirits. The foliage and songbirds reminded her of the fields behind the tavern where she grew up. Life was a lot simpler then.

It had been a long while since she'd felt such peace. She was even comfortable sitting in silence with Nurse Charlotte, who must have sensed and trusted correctly that Pearl wouldn't try to run away once they were outside. For one thing, Pearl simply didn't have enough energy for another trip like the one she'd had the night before. For another, she was beginning to respect Nurse Charlotte and just wouldn't put her through it again. Pearl smiled. The nurse had insisted that she wear her helmet into the backyard, to which Pearl gave little resistance. Nurse Charlotte said that it was for her own safety. And if Pearl told the truth, she knew that it was.

She opened her mouth to tell Nurse Charlotte about her discussion with Matthew, to see if she saw any hope in it. Although, after glancing at Nurse Charlotte, Pearl chose to remain silent. The nurse's eyes were closed, her face tilted toward the sun. A smile danced across her lips. Pearl let her enjoy the sun. Nurses needed breaks too, and she would soon have to get back to other patients.

Pearl wondered why Nurse Charlotte chose to sit with her. She could just as well have left Pearl in her room, curled up in a ball, all afternoon. Pearl was thinking about this when a jarring thought settled on her—the weekend shift changed an hour ago. What *was* Nurse Charlotte doing sitting here with her?

Then, as if reading Pearl's thoughts, Charlotte opened her eyes and looked over at Pearl. The warm expression on Nurse

Charlotte's face made Pearl feel that she could trust her. She opened her mouth to speak, but Nurse Charlotte spoke first.

"Girlfriend, I understand that you've had epilepsy for a long time."

Pearl grinned at Nurse Charlotte's dialect. Then she nodded her head in acknowledgment but said nothing.

Charlotte nodded back, giving her a sympathetic smile. "That's a tough burden to bear."

The nurse turned in her seat, pulling at her skirt. Then she crossed her legs and laid a hand atop one thigh. She pulled at her dress again, trying to cover some skin. The two women smiled at each other indulgently. With a slight laugh, Charlotte said, "I'm going to have to invest in some pants."

"Maybe so. Pants do cover us up." Pearl smiled at this feminine exchange. Then she patiently waited for Nurse Charlotte to continue what she started. It wasn't often that someone talked with Pearl like this, woman to woman. She was interested in whatever Nurse Charlotte had to say.

"I don't know exactly what you're going through," she began. "No one could. But, I do have some idea. My mother suffered from a debilitating disease for most of her life."

"Oh?"

Charlotte nodded. "Schizophrenia. It's different from your illness, but in some ways it's just as life-prohibiting. She would have been about your age." She dropped her head and then pulled at a thread loosening from her skirt. "She lived in a nursing home down south for the last several years. She hated it just as much as you do. She died last month. Drank too much water, they said. Went into a coma and didn't come out. I guess it was a way to suicide." She swallowed hard. "I thought they were keeping a better watch over her." Charlotte briefly closed her eyes, and then she shook her wiry head of cropped hair.

Pearl reached out and touched the hand pulling on the loose thread. "I'm sorry to hear that." It was barely a whisper. She never had a daughter, but it didn't keep her from having maternal instincts.

Suddenly, Pearl realized that she must remind Nurse Charlotte of her mother. She wondered if that was why Nurse Charlotte helped her. Maybe it somehow helped Nurse Charlotte too. The nurse shifted and straightened herself on the bench, looking somewhat uncomfortable. Pearl quickly drew her hand away.

But with a small sniff, Charlotte quickly recovered from what appeared to be an abnormal confession of personal suffering. Then, she placed her hands on her hips and stared at Pearl. Her black eyes sparkled. "Well, are you going to tell me what Matthew had to say or not? I can't help you if I don't know what the hell is going on, can I?"

The abrupt change in subject surprised Pearl. She smiled and straightened the helmet itching at her head. "Matthew says I have to learn to manage my medication better." She felt sheepish saying this and was certain her face showed it. She shrugged. "I guess he's right about that. I should know better."

"He is right about that, girlie girl. Do what he says. Your seizures might lessen if you take the pills at the prescribed amounts and time. Now what else did he say?"

"That I should wear my helmet whenever I leave the building."

Charlotte gave her a look. "We don't even need to discuss how true that might be."

Pearl touched the hard brown leather attached to her head. "I don't like it. It's embarrassing to me." It was a painful admission. "Maybe I won't have to wear it if I don't have so many seizures."

Charlotte looked sympathetic. "We'll see about that. What else?"

"He said that if I followed all the rules at Glory Heights, he would see what he could do. About getting the warden to allow Sonny to visit me. But I have to prove myself first."

"What about Jordana? Did he say anything about her?"

"Oh yes. Matthew found proof that Susan is my sister and Jordana is my niece. Then he called Jordana, just to see if she would visit me. But, I don't believe she'll be visiting any time soon. She wanted to discuss it with her mother." Pearl rolled her eyes, showing what she thought about that idea.

Charlotte's eyes lit up. "Aha. I thought that's what Matthew was doing this morning. I saw him pull an old folder out from the back of his filing cabinet. I wondered what he was searching for in there. He was checking for facts. He must want to help you. Maybe he'll call Jordana again, to try to get her to visit you."

Considering this possibility, Charlotte inhaled an excited happy breath, clapping her hands together. But upon exhaling, she gave Pearl a sharp, authoritative look.

Pearl wondered what Nurse Charlotte was thinking about. Maybe she was thinking of some way to speed up the process. Pearl had to know. "What? What are you thinking?"

Charlotte began in the scolding voice Pearl had heard earlier that morning. "Are you going to do everything your caseworker, Mr. Matthew Kincaid, has asked you to do? Are you, girlfriend? Because I think it's everything you need to do to take care of yourself right now."

Pearl felt uneasy, knowing that no one was going to give her a choice about making the improvements everyone knew she had to do. "Yes. Yes, I can do those things. I mean, I will do those things." Then she had to ask: "Do you think there's any way I could see Sonny sooner?"

Charlotte looked out over the water and a pensive look shadowed her face. "Pearl, I'm wondering about Sonny. I don't really know anything about him, other than what I've seen of him at Glory Heights. And please don't be offended by this, but he appears, oh, I don't know, as if he has some challenges of his own. I wonder, is he capable of living on his own?"

"But he already does live on his own. Always has." Pearl had more than a hint of admiration in her voice.

"He does?" This was news to Charlotte.

"He sure does. He lives in an apartment, by himself, down the block."

"Does he buy his own groceries, toiletries, things like that?"

"Well, if he didn't, he wouldn't eat and he would smell pretty bad," quipped Pearl. Then, seriously, she said, "Sonny has a few problems thinking things through, but his heart is as good as gold."

Charlotte's face brightened, as if she realized that Pearl's love for Sonny was as good as gold, and his for Pearl. "Well, I don't have control over anything, but I'm a great cheerleader. I'm not sure why I'm getting in so deep, but here goes." Charlotte turned to Pearl, giving her a sly look. "Look, I know you want to see Sonny again real soon, but right now I have something better than that for you."

Pearl looked at her expectantly, incredulous that something could be better than being with Sonny again. "What's that?"

"Hope, my dear friend. Hope."

Pearl didn't understand what there was to hope about. "Come again?"

Charlotte rose, ready to end their venture outside. She talked as they walked, arm in arm, up the cobblestone path to the back door of Glory Heights. "Pearl, sometimes one thing leads to another. You do the things Matthew has asked of you. You know it's only the right thing to do. And let's just wait and see if Jordana calls on you. The girl is how old, twenty-six, twenty-eight? She's actually a woman, with a mind of her own, and it doesn't necessarily mean that it reflects her mother's twisted thoughts. Jordana may see things differently than her mother.

"Matthew can talk all he wants to the warden, but unless you have a relative on your side, it won't do much good. But have faith in Matthew. He always pulls for you, and he has your best interest at heart. So don't be too hard on him. You'll see. He'll call Jordana again. You just wait and see. You may also see Sonny again, sooner than you think."

Pearl didn't believe everything Nurse Charlotte had just said, but she knew it came from her heart. More importantly, Pearl finally had someone on her side. Someone she trusted. Trust was something she could hold onto. It gave her hope. Pearl would try her best to make the improvements Matthew expected of her.

Then she would wait and see, because Nurse Charlotte had asked her to.

Chapter Fifteen

It was Sunday afternoon and Nick was working in his office. He was on the phone with McFinley, trying to save himself a trip to the heartland.

Years ago, Nick flew to Minnesota and met with McFinley in person. During the meeting, several of McFinley's personality flaws surfaced. Nick could only imagine how those flaws had grown over time. Frankly, now more than ever, he didn't need the aggravation. He preferred to handle Susan's dubious request over the phone. She wanted assurance from McFinley that Pearl would not pull another stunt like the other night. Actually, Susan wanted a guarantee.

If restraining Pearl meant sedating her, so be it. According to Susan, anyway. Nick didn't like the idea, and he hadn't wanted to make the call to the warden requesting it. Senseless drugging was inhuman and he didn't want to be party to it. But, he considered, with Pearl running away at night, maybe sedation was the way to go. It might keep her from hurting herself. Still, it didn't pass the smell test. In fact, no matter how he looked at it, Susan's idea stunk.

As an eager-to-please young aide to the senator, Nick had gotten himself in the middle of things years ago. He arranged

Pearl's care, and Susan was an unnamed benefactor. He was a liaison, as it were, to ensure Susan's privacy. After twenty years, he had not yet figured a way out of that role. Although, when Susan had most recently sought his assistance he had made her sweat for it. He let her wonder if he would call McFinley for her, ensuring her anonymity. It served the dual purpose of allowing him time to think it over.

Nick had just explained the situation to McFinley, and it quickly became clear that McFinley had not known about Pearl's escape.

"I don't know where you got your information from, but there was no escape. No one gets out of Glory Heights without my authorization." McFinley was indignant.

"You're wrong, McFinley. Pearl made contact with her benefactor's daughter." Nick always referred to Susan as Pearl's benefactor, although she hardly fit the description. That's all McFinley knew of the person who lined his pockets each month and that was just as well. Who knew the blackmail McFinley would try to extort if he knew the truth? Blackmail had even crossed Nick's mind, particularly in the last few years, but it was beyond his ethical quotient. So far.

"It couldn't have been Pearl. She's always under observation." McFinley didn't sound so sure of himself.

"Apparently, no one was observing her last night. She left the grounds."

"Well, I don't know what to say." His voice turned huffy again.

Nick could almost see his narrow head burning red. McFinley was most likely wondering who he was going to get for this. His discomfiture would be laughable if Nick wasn't already losing patience with the guy.

McFinley made one last attempt. "If it were true, someone from my organization would have informed me."

"That's your problem," Nick said.

He thought McFinley was wondering how this was going to affect his pocketbook, so he stated the obvious point blank.

"McFinley, you're paid to watch Ms. Witherby." Then he waited to see what McFinley had to say for himself and his fine institution of compassionate living assistance.

The phone line was dead silent. Then a sputter came from McFinley's end, as if he was gearing up to say something but couldn't quite get it past his lips. Silence again.

Nick waited.

McFinley finally thought of a response. "I will certainly check into this matter. At once."

Nick was disappointed in him; he thought McFinley could do better than that. "You'll check into it? That's it? That's all you think you have to do? Not good enough, old boy. Not good enough. I guess we'll have to transfer Ms. Witherby to another facility." Nick did not plan to move Pearl to another nursing home, but McFinley had no way of knowing that. Nick let the weight of his words sink in.

Fortunately, McFinley didn't waste any more of Nick's time with dead air. McFinley rose to the occasion with an appeasing chuckle. "No, now, wait a minute, Mr. Ballantine, let's not be hasty. You are right. We can do better." He spoke as if there were no periods at the ends of his sentences, as if fearing Nick would use the time to move Pearl to another nursing home. "You know, and I think I might have mentioned this to you once before, we do sedate patients who are, shall we say, unruly. For their own good, you understand. Is that something you would like to consider?"

Nick would never say the words himself. "Is that what you advise, Administrator?" Nick couldn't let it go so easily. He thoughtfully added, "You'll see that she comes to no harm? That whatever course you take is safe for Ms. Witherby?" He had to know this, to appease his own conscience.

"Yes, yes, I think that in this case it is most justifiably warranted. We always take pride in the great care we give our patients." He coughed after making that statement, as if remembering the reason for the whole conversation.

Anxious to end the conversation, Nick let it go. "Well, if you think you can handle things on your end, we would consider giving you another chance."

"We most certainly will handle this, Mr. Ballantine. Don't you worry."

Nick hung up the phone, slamming the receiver down. Don't worry, my ass. He'd had enough of the senator's personal problems. Sedating elderly women to keep them in line was past his comfort level. The next time the senator needed something done, she could call Daris McFinley herself. Angrily, he turned off his computer and left the office. He had a date. He was taking her to see Pavarotti at the Kennedy Center. If that didn't take his mind off work and Susan's personal life, nothing would.

"Why wasn't I informed, immediately?" spat Daris McFinley. It was Monday morning. The warden had barged his way into Matthew's office, dressed in his usual gray three-piece suit and, without so much as a how do you do, began an explosive tirade over Pearl's disappearing act.

Matthew was expecting this, and he wasn't disappointed. It was as bad as he thought it would be. Fortunately, he had already decided how much he would tell the disagreeable old geezer. Discovering that he knew only half the story made it all the easier.

From the warden's diabolical ranting, Matthew detected that the warden was oblivious to the identity of Pearl's sister. He mentioned a liaison for Pearl's benefactor. Someone named Nick Ballantine phoned the warden to let him know about Pearl's escape. He grumbled over the embarrassment he suffered at not knowing what was going on within his own nursing home.

If the warden knew that Susan was Pearl's benefactor, he would have mentioned it. The senator had kept herself anonymous, and Matthew wasn't going to tell him about her. He first had to figure out what he was going to do with the information himself— on Pearl's behalf.

Matthew glanced up at the warden. He had quit pacing in front of Matthew's desk and was waiting for an answer. Matthew looked at him innocently. Then, in an attempt to foil more theatrics, he gave a nonchalant shrug. "It was the weekend, Daris. I didn't want to bother you with it." Matthew watched the warden take this in. The warden's face darkened with rage. Matthew expected as much. He knew the warden wouldn't like his answer, but that's the one Matthew was giving out.

"What made you think I wouldn't want to know?" Saliva was accumulating at the corners of the warden's mouth.

Matthew wanted to turn away in disgust, or get the guy a tissue. Instead, he smiled. He was pushing the warden's buttons. He would bet his own money that the warden was getting a payoff to keep Pearl under control. There could be no other reason for his inordinate reaction to everything Pearl did that didn't fall within the confining norms of Glory Heights. If the warden wanted to play games, Matthew would accommodate him. Matthew would do anything to protect Pearl from what he already believed to be extraordinary restrictions on her life.

"We have everything under control. Pearl has returned to Glory Heights. In fact, she's off to work at Brambles right now. Everything's back on track." Earlier, he intercepted Pearl leaving for work to ask if she had taken her medicine. She was wearing her helmet, seemed in a better mood, and was almost cheerful. Matthew felt assured that they were making progress.

However, the warden didn't seem to see it that way. He flailed his arms at Matthew and asked, "You let Witherby go to work? Are you a fool? What if she escapes again?"

Now it was Matthew's turn to get angry, and that was something he didn't do often. He stood up and leaned over his desk to get eye to eye with the warden. "I can assure you that I am no fool, McFinley. I take full responsibility for my clients. I trust that Pearl will not try to leave us again. I spoke with her. I have her word."

The warden flinched. He seemed intimidated by Matthew's stature. Nevertheless, the warden's face twisted into a sneer. "You have her word? Her *word*? What makes you think that means anything?"

"I trust my client." Matthew's words were heated, clipped.

"By the way, I'm her caseworker. If you don't like the way I'm handling things around here, just say so."

The warden visibly shrank. Matthew was the senior caseworker at Glory Heights, and he was damn good at his job. He was bargaining that the warden wouldn't want to lose him. Thinking of the grief the warden would receive from Matthew's clients and their benefactors would be enough for the warden to back down. Plus, good caseworkers were hard to find, and the warden knew that.

As Matthew had hoped, the warden backtracked. He was a coward after all. He lowered his voice and said, "I didn't say you weren't doing a good job. Not at all, I didn't mean to imply that. I just don't want anything to happen to any of our clients." Then his face brightened, as if he had thought of something particularly spectacular. "I was just thinking of repercussions. The lawsuit would be enormous."

Yeah, right. The scoundrel. Matthew wanted him out of his office. "Why don't we just leave it rest? Let it go for now." He walked around the desk and opened the door. But the warden wasn't quite ready to leave.

"But, what about Witherby calling her benefactor's daughter? I don't want Witherby bothering anyone."

The warden had missed his calling, thought Matthew. He was so much more suited for a prison. You don't want prisoners bothering people. An aunt calling her niece should be a natural human right. However, again the warden didn't mention who the benefactor was. He didn't know that Jordana was Pearl's niece. Matthew couldn't decide if the warden didn't know, or if he just didn't care. Matthew was banking on him not knowing. The warden possibly wouldn't care either, just as long as the money kept coming in.

Matthew stepped outside the door and extended an arm out, inviting the warden to leave. "I've been in touch with Jordana, the benefactor's daughter. I assured her that she is welcome to visit Pearl, anytime. Whether or not she does is up to her."

The warden's eyebrows twisted at this response. However,

he must have realized that to speak against it would further give away his pension for unnecessary control over something that was clearly Matthew's call. The warden stepped into the hallway muttering something under his breath, but he finally went away.

Matthew shut the door behind him. Leaning against it, he breathed a sigh of relief. He was glad that confrontation was over, although he couldn't help feeling a sense of victory. He had gotten the warden off his back. Maybe now the warden would leave him alone to tend to Pearl's needs. Matthew wasn't going to report his every move to him. It wasn't necessary. Matthew didn't do that with any of his other clients, and Pearl deserved the same privacy. If Pearl kept herself on track, self-managed her medicine and health, maybe she could occasionally see Sonny. Matthew had implied as much to her in Saturday's conversation. He had held Sonny out like a carrot stick, as a reward for acting responsibly. For reducing her seizures, as much as was humanly possible. That alone would be worth her efforts. Of course, Pearl would have to prove herself. Then Matthew would work something out so she could see Sonny. Maybe Sonny could at least come for game nights again. That was something Matthew wasn't going to relay to the warden.

Daris McFinley was fuming. Matthew had all but thrown him out of his office.

Passive aggressively, at that. Daris knew some of their psychobabble. He hadn't been finished admonishing Matthew for his negligence in reporting Witherby's escape. He also didn't get to give Matthew instructions to have Pearl sedated at night. As he'd promised Nick. Daris got none of that in before the door all but slammed behind him. It was a sticky situation. However, he didn't intend to lose his best caseworker over it. He didn't even want to consider the mess that would cause. He would have more than Nick screaming down his back. The money Daris received for watching Pearl wasn't worth that headache. He shuddered at the thought of it.

Stomping through the halls of Glory Heights with a

sour look on his face, he made his way to the nurses' station. As he approached the desk, he tried his level best not to look at the two wheelchair-bound patients coming his way. He kept his eyes averted. However, his mind conjured up nauseating images of the man and woman rolling down the hallway. Their old legs were crossed in their seats and their dilapidated, wrinkled arms arched with great effort over the large, thin wheels of the chairs. He closed his eyes as they passed him, but he opened them again a second too soon. He was surprised to discover that the patients were neither old nor dilapidated, and their legs were not crossed over in their seats. The patients were younger than he, and they were probably not as wrinkled. This was no comfort to Daris. He longed to be gone from there, but he had business to take care of first.

There was a way around asking Matthew to have Witherby sedated. Daris knew what Matthew would think about it, anyway. He would object, saying he needed a doctor's prescription for it. At Glory Heights that was a formality, as far as Daris was concerned. He had assured Nick that he would take care of this situation, and he would. He just had to enlist the help of the right nurse.

Nurse Charlotte was out of the question; she was too new at Glory Heights. She also was a sympathetic character. He wasn't going to bother discussing Witherby's departure with her, although he knew she was on duty that night. He didn't want to hear any more of her excuses for Witherby. Nurse Charlotte had swooned over Witherby the night they found her laid out in the hallway having a seizure. It was ridiculous. She'd rationalized that Witherby, who was fully clothed at 11 p.m., had gotten disoriented. He didn't believe it for a minute, but neither did he have a basis for dispelling it.

That night alone, he reasoned, should've clued everyone in to the fact that Witherby needed sedation. Not that he needed to talk himself into anything. He believed in sedating those whom they couldn't trust to remain in their rooms at night. If Pearl Witherby wasn't a candidate for that, who was?

At the station, Daris asked to see Nurse Shelby. He waited

for her to answer her page, leaning stiffly against the counter, avoiding eye contact with anything or anyone that moved. Within a few minutes, Shelby stepped through the elevator doors and smiled.

"Daris," she exclaimed, looking at her watch. "Did you come to take me to lunch?"

With a look that said, "Not now, you idiot," he quieted her. "No, that's not it. I have something I need you to do for me."

Chapter Sixteen

Bent over his desk, Matthew was finishing his work when a soft tap on the door interrupted him. He looked up to see a beautiful woman with long auburn hair take an apprehensive step into his office. Unconsciously, he stood up straight, stretching his spine to its full length. He tried to be courteous—to keep his eyes level with hers—but he couldn't help himself from sneaking an appreciative look at her long legs and perfect figure. She was wearing a lavender silk suit that looked quite expensive. The suit's color seemed to intensify her vivid blue eyes. It wasn't often he had a visitor like this, never before, in fact, and he didn't want to forget it.

When he finally did meet her eyes, he realized that she had caught him staring at her. He felt his face grow warm at the sexist indiscretion. He thought, could I have made a bigger mistake? Normally, he wasn't so blatant. Stumbling over his words, he tried to make amends. To at least greet her. "Ah, excuse me, I'm sorry. Can I help you?"

The young woman stepped further into Matthew's office. "I'm looking for Matthew Kincaid. That must be you. I recognize your voice."

Matthew's color deepened. Had he met her before and not

remembered it? Oh, he thought, I'd remember meeting her. "Excuse me? I don't mean to be rude, but have we met before?"

She approached his desk and stuck out her hand. "I'm Jordana Barlow. We spoke on the phone Saturday morning?"

Matthew took her hand and gave it a businesslike shake, not wanting to intimidate her any further with his male idiosyncrasies. "Pearl Witherby's long-lost niece. Now I recognize your voice." How hokey did that sound? He wondered.

He noticed that Jordana blushed at his words, although he didn't understand what she would have to blush about. "Yes, well, I spoke with my mother. It appears that you are correct, I am her long-lost niece."

"And you came to visit." Matthew hoped the obvious statement hadn't sounded as lame as it felt saying it.

"Well, yes. Is she here?" Jordana sounded unsure of herself, as if she had decided to visit her aunt but for the life of her wasn't certain it was the right thing to do.

Matthew checked his watch. "Pearl's at work now, but she'll be here soon. You could visit her after dinner tonight."

Jordana looked confused. Matthew didn't know if she was disappointed or relieved that Pearl was currently unavailable. Jordana spoke softly, as if at a loss about what to do next. "Oh, I thought I could see her right away. I didn't know that she had a job. I guess I could wait, go have dinner or something."

A wonderful idea burst through Matthew's mind, but he thought he might scare her away if he voiced it. On the other hand, if he didn't, she might not stay to see Pearl. As uncertain as Jordana seemed, she might just turn around and go home. He was going for it. "I have an idea. See what you think about this. We should have a talk before you meet Pearl. I could give you an idea of what to expect. It might make a first visit easier for both of you." He made a show of checking his watch. "I have time now. How about letting me take you to dinner? We can discuss Pearl. When I bring you back, I'll introduce the two of you." His words rushed out of his mouth faster than he hoped Jordana could think of a reason to reject his offer. Then, before she could answer, he broke out into a big smile. He clapped his hands together and exclaimed, "Pearl is going to be so excited."

Jordana smiled at his boyish glee, but she seemed apprehensive about his suggestion. "I don't want to take up your time. It looked like you were getting ready to leave."

Matthew was not one to give up easily. "I'd like to say that you'd be interrupting some major event in my life tonight, but the fact is, I have no plans. My son is with his mother tonight, my ex, and I have no other commitments. I have to eat and would love the company. Besides, now that you're here, I don't want to let you get away. For Pearl's sake," he quickly added. Then he briefly wondered why he had felt the need to include that he had an ex.

She smiled at him, either impressed by his brazen attempt at securing dinner with her or amused at his audacity. At this point, he didn't care which, as long as she said yes. She gave him an appraising look. "I guess you look harmless enough. I would really like some sort of briefing before I meet my aunt. I really don't know what to expect. I'm not sure if I will know how to act, and a personal introduction might help. I'll take you up on your offer, Mr. Kincaid."

"Matthew. You have to call me Matthew."

Matthew let Jordana drive. He thought she would feel safer that way. After all, she didn't know him from any serial killer. When he followed her to the cherry-red mustang convertible parked out in front, he was glad he did. His beat up Honda Accord would've been embarrassing.

It was easy to relax with her driving. It had been a hot day and the sun was still high in the sky, although it looked as if dark clouds were about to blow in. A storm warning had been issued for the area, and he hoped they wouldn't have to pull over and put up the top. He briefly considered that a downpour would make Jordana's trip back home more difficult too, and he hoped she wouldn't to have to drive through a storm.

The warm air felt good flowing against his face. He decided to take her to Sunset's, a waterside restaurant across town. It was a casual place with great food, and it would be quiet enough on a weeknight. They could get a seat looking out across the water and, hopefully, have a good conversation. He was looking forward to it, for more reasons than one. He almost laughed at his own delight in meeting her. He had to remind himself that Jordana was here to see Pearl, not him.

Jordana interrupted his private thoughts. "What's Rum River like?"

Matthew smiled. "You might be sorry you asked me that!" He loved the little town on the river and was happy to fill her in on it. So, while Jordana maneuvered the Mustang through the two-lane, narrow streets of Rum River, Matthew interspersed his directions to Sunset's with his knowledge of the quintessential small town. He only hoped he wouldn't bore her with his enthusiastic, somewhat historical, account of the city.

"Rum River," he said, "is a charming little place. It has a history anchored in the logging industry. In earlier times, loggers—mainly emigrants from Norway and Sweden—cut timber from Minnesota's dense forestry. Mostly aspens and pines. They bundled the timber into rafts and set them afloat in the Rum, where they bobbled downstream, converged with the Mississippi, and eventually were sold to other settlers for their own homes and businesses."

Matthew stopped with his rendition of Rum River to say that Jordana should turn left on the road ahead. Then he shot her a glance to see if she was still interested in hearing about Rum River. He hoped he didn't sound like a grade school book report. But Jordana nodded her head, indicating that she wanted to hear more.

Matthew continued: "Of course, the logging industry is gone now, but Rum River still has its small-town values of working hard and making a difference. The residents have little regard for snobbery. From the tumbledown houses left over from the 1800s to the well-kept forties-style homes, the families tolerate each other. So, places like the subsidized apartments on Ferry Street where Sonny lives and Glory Heights Healthcare Facility are not contested in as lively a manner as they are in some communities. People simply don't care."

Jordana interrupted to ask, "How far are we from downtown Minneapolis?"

"Kind of a city girl, I take it?"

"Kind of a historian, I take it?"

Matthew smiled. "We're on the outskirts of the last suburb of Minneapolis. Sometimes it feels like Minneapolis is a hundred miles away from us, but in fact, it's only forty. Outside the metro suburbs, the pace is slower."

"I didn't think this was a suburb. You have an actual downtown here, a Main Street." Jordana said.

"Main Street, the whole five blocks of it, is a great place." Matthew said this as if he were trying to convince her to live here. "We have old established businesses such as Froggy's Hardware and Mama's Corner Grocery mingled amongst the eclectic coffeehouses and boutiques." They shared a smile, considering the names.

"Resident entrepreneurs refurbished old buildings that had outlived their original purpose and put them to good use. Two sisters turned the second floor of the old post office into Bronte's Tea House."

Jordana spoke up, "I noticed the Tea House."

"It's quaint, with tables overlooking the river. Other merchandisers divided the first floor into tiny boutiques selling everything from Amish quilts to candles to garden trellises. Two friends from the Lion's Club split the armory in half. They turned one side into an antique shop chock-full of musty old things. The other side is a bookstore where they sell used books for a pittance. Rum River's kind of a cool place, huh?"

"I guess. Do you live here?"

"No."

By the time they arrived at Sunset's, Jordana had quite a feel for the town. Matthew's enthusiastic exposé of Rum River's attributes made the ride over more comfortable. His rich voice was easy to listen to. His earlier excitement, which she could only assume had to do with her decision to meet Pearl, had calmed some, slowing his speech to a soothing timbre.

Jordana could see why Matthew liked the area. It was quite appealing, and he was right: it was a charming little place. Driving slowly through Main Street, she was careful to stop for pedestrians in the prominent yellow-painted crosswalks, and had time to glance over at several boutiques. The welcoming window displays made her want to stop the car and go inside them. Driving past Bronte's Tea House fondly reminded her, a lover of Indian green tea and soft buttery English scones, of a trip to Great Britain many years ago. A Minnesota tea house was a rarity. She longed to share a cozy spot of tea with old girlfriends in an authentic tea house. Or, she thought, looking at Matthew, a new man friend.

After her initial embarrassment, when he'd realized that she was, in the flesh, the confused wonder he'd talked with last Saturday, she'd relaxed some with his easy manner. On the drive to Sunset's she was distracted by the gentleman sitting in the leather bucket seat next to her. More than once she had found herself doing a mental shakedown, admonishing herself to pay attention to what Matthew was saying. Matthew, with his handsome looks, short wavy hair, and dazzling, friendly smile, was quite appealing. His strong, masculine manner encompassed a boyish sweetness and an easy sense of humor.

She tried to ignore those thoughts. It made her think of her mother, who would blow a gasket over Jordana's interest in a mere social worker. Her mother was already in a snit over her Aunt Pearl. If Mother knew that Jordana had come to see Aunt Pearl, she would probably never forgive her, Jordana thought. Besides, Jordana was fond of Ryan, even if he was acting a little distant since his return last weekend from the northern reaches of Minnesota. Mother would approve of him.

The clouds were turning dark, threatening a storm, so when Jordana stopped the convertible in Sunset's rustic gravel parking lot, she put the top up. During the minute it took her to snap it into place, Matthew had come around to her side of the car and opened the door for her. She was impressed with his manners. However, she had the feeling that she might need to remind him that this was not a romantic interlude with someone he had just picked up in his office. On second thought, with one hand harmlessly set inside his pants pocket and the other holding the wide steel door for her, she thought he was probably just being a gentleman. And she was being paranoid.

He was hardly on the make. He was here because he was Aunt Pearl's caseworker and Jordana was her niece. With that self-admonishment, Jordana walked side-by-side with him to the entrance of the café. At the door, he was quicker than she, as they teach gentlemen to be, so she was again left with no choice but to let him get the door.

They took a table with a view of the Rum River. Jordana thought it looked slightly mysterious with dark purplish clouds hanging over a deep blue waterway, wildly cresting with wind blowing in from the east. Thunder cracked angrily in the distance, and jagged bolts of lightning silently answered, flashing one atop another, illuminating the sky. Jordana enjoyed a good thunderstorm, but she was concerned for her drive home. Hopefully, she thought, the storm will have passed by then.

The waiter took their orders, with both of them declining a tempting glass of wine. Then Matthew wasted no time in asking what made her decide to see Pearl. Jordana had expected his question. Nonetheless, she didn't know if she should tell him the whole truth, since she wasn't sure she understood it herself. So she opted for a shorter version. "After confirming that she is truly my aunt, I wanted to see her for myself. I'm not heartless. If I have a relative who needs help, I guess I think it's my duty to check it out." She shrugged, not knowing how else to explain it.

Matthew listened intently, never taking his eyes off her, as if searching for honesty. In the end he seemed to accept her answer. "She doesn't so much need your help with anything as she needs your attention, your occasional companionship."

Jordana was confused. "I thought she said she needed help. She wants to get married."

Matthew smiled at her, appreciatively. "Pearl isn't really in any condition to marry anyone."

His explanation didn't help her confusion. "What does that mean?"

"It means that she's never lived independently, on her own, and she's not always managed her seizure medication properly." He waved a hand in the air. "Those things, along with a whole host of other related issues, make her marrying Sonny inconceivable."

"But, she wouldn't be living alone. If she married, she would be living with her husband. Sonny, is it?"

"Yeah, Sonny. Sonny is mildly retarded. He has been since birth."

Hard rain splattering against the window sounding like microwave popcorn gave Jordana an uneasy feeling. She looked out over the river, relieved to find it wasn't hail. The damage it could do to her unprotected car was unnerving.

Turning back to Matthew, she didn't know what else she could say about Pearl's predicament. Matthew was Pearl's caseworker. He knew the whole situation better than anyone. Instead, Jordana asked about meeting Pearl later. What could she expect?

Matthew's face lit up, as if he couldn't contain his excitement for Pearl. "I think you can expect to find a lonely women who will be extremely happy to see you. You've nothing to worry about. She's not a vindictive person, and she won't hold you responsible for your mother's actions."

Jordana felt a jolt pass through the bottom of her stomach, and involuntarily winced. Fortunately, the waiter arrived and silently placed their food in front of them, giving Jordana the moment to recover from the implication of Matthew's words. However, they both knew that her mother's behavior toward Pearl was appalling. She simply nodded her head, as much to agree with his implication as to invite him to go on. They dug into their dinner and continued their discussion of Pearl.

"Pearl will probably be curious about your decision to visit. If you don't mind, it would make my life easier," he smiled, "if you didn't tell her that you've come to help her marry Sonny."

Jordana laughed, "I'll tell her that I just wanted to see her, meet her. How's that?"

"That would be great, but she may press you to help her see Sonny. Try to stay neutral on that. Let her know that you're here because you cared enough to see her, but there's nothing you can do about seeing Sonny."

"You mean she's not even allowed to see Sonny? That seems cruel." Jordana had laid it out quite simply in only a few words.

Matthew's eyes warmed and his face softened. "Ah, you are a romantic, I see. Well, we have this administrator, we call him the warden, and he's banned Pearl from ever seeing Sonny again. The warden made Sonny lose his job at Brambles, where he and Pearl both worked, where they first met. At least the warden or somebody had the sense to get Sonny another job right away."

When Jordana realized what Matthew was so tactfully saying, she lowered her eyes. She picked the cloth napkin up from her lap and dabbed at her mouth, then spoke softly. "Who told the warden to do that? It was my mother, wasn't it?"

Matthew looked as if he didn't want to admit it, as if he could see her pain in knowing it. He nodded his head. "Yes, he would've been acting on instructions from your mother, Pearl's benefactor."

Jordana tossed her napkin aside, shame burning at the core of her. Her body broke into beads of moisture at its heat and her face blushed with its intensity. Jordana's eyes filled with tears. She was barely audible over the roaring storm outside. "That's a horrible thing to do to someone."

Matthew reached out and covered Jordana's hand. "Hey," he prompted, waiting to catch her eye. She brought her eyes up to meet his. "Have no fear, I have a plan."

"A plan," Jordana squeaked out the words. She cleared her throat, husky with the ache of unshed tears. "Excuse me. What plan? You can't go against your warden's wishes. Can you?"

Matthew looked at Jordana earnestly. "Pearl needs something, someone, in her life, and hopefully she now has you. Pearl also needs an incentive to help herself. I sort of talked myself into letting Sonny be that goal. The other day, I as much as told Pearl I would look into her being able to see Sonny, occasionally. That is, if she could better manage a few things under her control. I know she's capable of it, or I wouldn't ask her to do it. She just needs a reason. It's often hard for someone in her circumstances to come up with a reason to live, let alone manage their health."

Jordana was stunned. "Wow. You do care about Pearl, don't you?"

"You better believe it. Pearl's health and welfare are more important to me than the warden's edicts, or your mother's. Come on, Jordana," he said, now smiling, helping her with her chair. "Let me introduce you to someone special."

Having agreed to forego dessert, Matthew motioned to the waiter to bring their check.

Chapter Seventeen

It was barely 7:00, but Pearl was already getting ready for bed. Without Sonny she had little to do or that she felt like doing. Sometimes she just wanted the day to be over. Working at Brambles just wasn't the same without him. Workdays dragged on forever and the monotony of filling boxes without Sonny there to distract her was as boring as dirt. When he had worked at Brambles with her, she could at least look over to his line for a pick-me-up smile or anticipate lunches and breaks with him. When Sonny was nearby, she didn't give the nails and all the cuts she received trying to get them into cartons a second thought. Now she noticed the sting of every cut. She endlessly missed Sonny but had no way of even talking to him.

That day she had taken her morning medication, all of it. She had worn her helmet to work like a good little girl. Yet, while Matthew said he would work on being able to see Sonny if she did all those things, she knew it was going to be a while. Well, at least she hadn't had a seizure all day. She figured that if she went to bed she would have had a successful day managing her epilepsy. She didn't have much energy left over for much else. Loneliness made her tired.

Just back from brushing her teeth and washing her face in

the women's communal lavatory, she was now maneuvering her way around Karoline in the small room. Her roommate was looking for her glasses, getting ready to head down to the community room for a few hours of television. Pearl knew Karoline hated to miss her shows.

Although they had shared the same room for many years, Karoline and Pearl were not really friends. It seemed they had both concluded, as if by tacit agreement, that their shared living arrangements would work much better if they just kept to themselves and didn't pry into each other's personal life. Standing by that silent creed, Karoline seldom asked about Sonny.

Karoline had found her glasses and was now wearing them and lingering near the bedroom door. Climbing into bed, Pearl noticed Karoline eyeing her. Karoline appeared to have something on her mind. Pearl looked at her curiously. "What is it, Karoline?"

Karoline's low voice was heavy with saliva and tongue, as she valiantly worked around her hard-set muscular sclerosis. Due to the effort her speech required, she didn't talk much. When she did speak, her communication was briefly and simply stated. "Going to bed kind of early."

Pearl nodded as she pulled the covers up and reached for the light on the bed stand. "Yes, it's been a long day."

Karoline wasn't finished yet. Her sad face looked more drawn than usual. Pearl wondered if there was a problem. Had Pearl unknowingly committed some roommate error? Like tossed her clothes onto Karoline's side of the room? Or let the piles of tissues she had used to mop her torrentially tearful eyes cascade behind the wrong bed stand? As preoccupied as she had been lately, she sure could have. She was about to take an investigative look around the room when Karoline drew out what she really wanted to say. "Heard 'bout ya and Sonny. Grapevines talk, ya know. Just wanted to say I feel bad for ya."

Karoline's rare show of kindness touched Pearl's heart. It wasn't that Karoline was an unkind person, she just seldom said enough for anyone to know about it. Pearl thought, you never know what's really inside someone, then grabbed a tissue from the almost empty box and dabbed back a teardrop. "Thank you," she sniffed. "I suppose everyone knows by now."

Karoline nodded at her. "I leave ya alone now. Rest is good for a broken heart."

Pearl watched Karoline leave the room. So many patients enjoyed watching television at night in the community room because most, like Pearl and Karoline, didn't have a set in their room. Rebecca would most likely be there, along with Kenny and Cora. Thinking of Cora made Pearl shudder. She could just hear Cora echoing ardent condolences of, "Sorry to hear about you and Sonny. Sorry to hear about you and Sonny. Sorry to hear about you and Sonny." Or worse yet, a repetitious rendition of those who had not heard the gossip, "Where's Sonny? Haven't seen him. Where's Sonny? Haven't seen him. Where's Sonny? Haven't seen him." Pearl decided it was a good thing she was going to bed early. She had just snapped off the light when there was a knock on her door.

"Pearl?"

Pearl was startled to hear Matthew's voice. She sat up in bed and clicked the light back on. "Matthew? What in land sakes are you—"

The young woman who followed Matthew into Pearl's room stopped her questions. Her heart skipped a beat. She knew who it was, instantly. She climbed out of bed like a schoolgirl and was halfway around it before she lost her balance and grabbed the end of the bed for support.

Matthew immediately stepped forward, offering Pearl his arm. He smiled warmly at Pearl. "Pearl, I have someone I want you to—"

Pearl beamed a smile back at Matthew, and then in her excitement she cut him off. "It's Jordana. I'd know my own niece anywhere."

Jordana, who had drawn closer as Matthew settled Pearl onto the end of the bed, looked surprised by the declaration. Pearl openly beamed at her. "You look just like your mother did when she was young. And, oh boy, was she a beauty."

Jordana smiled nervously. "Thank you. Yes, it's me, Aunt Pearl. Oh, I'm wondering what you would like me to call you. Should I call you aunt or Pearl?"

"You're a grown woman and you may call me what you wish. But, I like aunt. It makes me feel good to be called that." She wrapped her arms around herself, hugged her middle, and then she wiggled comfortably, showing just how good it made her feel.

Jordana and Matthew shared a smile. Then, Jordana turned to Pearl. "Then, Aunt Pearl it is."

Pearl glowed her satisfaction with the title. Then, remembering her manners, she asked them to sit down and apologized for the lack of comfortable furniture.

Jordana took a chair by the desk, but Matthew declined. "I better leave you two to each other. I just wanted to introduce the two of you, but I see it wasn't necessary." He winked at Pearl, then turned toward Jordana to bid her goodbye. He was about to offer his hand to Jordana when a worried look crossed over her clear blue eyes. She stared at him and gave him a nearly imperceptible shake of her head. Pearl noticed it, but she said nothing and pretended not to see the exchange. Jordana wanted him to stay, and he seemed happy to oblige. Pearl understood that this was not an easy visit for Jordana.

Matthew turned to face Pearl. "On second thought, I don't have anything pressing. Maybe I could stay for a while too." He pulled a chair over from Karoline's side of the room and sat down.

If Matthew's sudden decision to stay confused Pearl, she didn't say so or seem to care. It was obvious to Jordana that Pearl was quite comfortable with her caseworker. Jordana, for her part, was relieved that he had changed his mind and decided to stay for their first meeting. Jordana was more nervous than she thought she would be or that she cared to admit. She found it curious that she was comfortable enough with Matthew to let on that she required his assistance through this initial encounter. She was equally amused that he was sensitive enough to pick up on her subtle prompting.

With Jordana at the desk chair, Pearl on the end of the bed, and Matthew positioned between them, a silent moment passed. Jordana became anxious that, now that she was here, she didn't know what to say to her new aunt. The two women knew little about each other. Jordana felt her face flush with embarrassment and watched as Pearl fidgeted with her hair. To Jordana's great relief, Matthew broke the silence. He checked his watch, and then he looked at Pearl. "Pearl, I just realized we got you out of bed. It's early. Are you feeling all right?"

Self-consciously, Pearl ducked her head and patted the ends of her wavy hair, as if for the first time remembering the way she looked. She was wearing a nightgown and no makeup. "Oh, I'm fine. Just a little tired." Then, easily recovering from the slight embarrassment over her appearance, she again beamed proudly at Jordana. "I'm wide awake now. My niece has come to see me."

That Pearl was glad to see her struck a chord with Jordana. She wondered about it. She had expected Pearl to have some animosity toward her—for not coming to Pearl's aid when she phoned last week or for the senator's actions. However, if Pearl felt an ounce of hostility, she hid it well. She hadn't stopped smiling at Jordana since she had entered the room. Pearl's obvious pride in Jordana was unnerving. Jordana felt that she didn't deserve it. In fact, she didn't know whether she would ever see her aunt again. Jordana had not thought that far in advance. Her mother would probably disown her for looking in on Pearl. Mother had unabashedly told Jordana that Pearl was, in fact, her aunt. She had even admitted to stashing Aunt Pearl away at Glory Heights. Nonetheless, Jordana needed to see it for herself to believe it.

It certainly was true. Jordana could no longer dispute it. She began to worry about what Pearl expected from her. Jordana had no idea yet of what she was willing to do for Pearl from there on out. Jordana thought she had better at least make it clear that, as Matthew had suggested at dinner, she wasn't there to help, couldn't help, with Sonny. Then, as if Pearl had read Jordana's thoughts, she asked the burning question. "Are you here to help me marry Sonny?"

Matthew and Jordana glanced at each other. He had known Pearl was that abrupt, but Jordana hadn't expected it. She was conscious of her face turning bright pink, and blotches of the same hue were most likely spotting her neck. It was an annoying announcement of her own unease. She'd had it since childhood and could not control it. Jordana looked into her aunt's hopeful face and hated having to tell her that she could not help her with Sonny. Except, if Jordana was going to have any kind of conversation with Pearl, they needed to get past the questions about Sonny. Jordana was tempted to answer it the way she did a business question she needed more time to think about: sidestep the direct question so that it could lose some of its impact. However, that wouldn't be fair to Aunt Pearl, she knew. Jordana decided to take the direct approach as Pearl had done. "No, I'm sorry, I'm afraid that's out of my hands. But, Matthew tells me he's working on having Sonny come to see you."

Matthew gave her a quick look. He had not actually said he was working on it. He had said he was going to look into it. Jordana had just sped up the process. Even she didn't know whether she had done it on purpose.

Pearl's smile quivered at Jordana's declaration that she couldn't help her with Sonny. That Matthew was going to look into it was something Pearl already knew. It was apparent she had hoped for more from Jordana, but the disheartening news hadn't completely devastated the moment's high spirits for Pearl. Because, to Jordana's surprise, Pearl quickly rebounded with a firm smile. She then readily changed the subject to ask Jordana about her work, whether she was happy in advertising, and what she liked to do in her free time. Relieved to be off the hook about Sonny, Jordana relaxed enough to enjoy Pearl's interest in her. Jordana gave Pearl a summary of her life. After an hour of easy chitchat, during which neither Pearl nor Matthew yawned once, Jordana realized the storm outside had stopped hammering against the windows.

Jordana thought it was time to leave—she wanted to get on the road before it started raining again. She stood up from the hard desk chair and started to say goodbye. Pearl rose too and reached her arms out for Jordana. Jordana, not knowing what else to do, found herself pulled into Pearl's embrace. It wasn't a quick "get it over with" kind of hug. It was a welcoming hug of love, of warmth, of not wanting to let go. Jordana looked over her Aunt Pearl's shoulder at Matthew. He smiled. He knew how much Jordana's visit would mean to Pearl; he had told Jordana as much at dinner. Now, she knew it too.

Just as Jordana thought that they would part from their mutual hug, Pearl held on, squeezing more tightly, and with a desperate appeal whispered in Jordana's ear. "Please come see me again. I've always wanted to know you. Please come. No one will tell your mother."

Chapter Eighteen

Pearl climbed back into bed and turned off the light, although she was no longer sleepy. A ray of fluorescent light extending from the hallway broke the room's darkness, but Pearl was used to sleeping in the half-light. She could hardly think about sleeping: Jordana had come to see her. Pearl silently said the words and smiled. She had hoped that Jordana would come but had never really believed in it. Jordana really had no reason to care about an old aunt her mother had tossed away like a dirty rag. Pearl knew it had taken a lot of guts for Jordana to come, most likely against her mother's wishes. But Jordana had done it.

Cozy under the bedcovers, Pearl was glad that Karoline hadn't returned from watching her television shows. She would probably be downstairs for another hour or so. Pearl wanted to be alone with her thoughts. She had so much to think about. Jordana had said she couldn't help with Sonny, but maybe that would change. As Nurse Charlotte had said, sometimes one thing leads to another. Maybe Matthew would change his mind and help her marry Sonny too. Pearl felt her eyes glowing in the darkened room and blinked. She knew she was getting ahead of herself, but she couldn't help it. Even if Jordana couldn't help with Sonny, Pearl would be content to have Jordana in her life. Pearl had never had much to believe in. Now, oh, did she dare to hope? Jordana might come to see her more often, maybe even on a regular basis. Pearl had assured Jordana that no one would tell Susan that Jordana was here. If only Jordana would come again!

Life had robbed Pearl of having children. Jordana was the closest thing to a daughter Pearl would ever have. She wanted Jordana's friendship, her companionship, and her understanding. Pearl wanted Jordana to talk about her life—to tell Pearl about it. Maybe, somehow, by Jordana telling her about it, Jordana would include her in it. Jordana was a beautiful young woman, and Pearl was proud to call her niece.

Suddenly, Pearl was startled out of her reflection on the evening. The door was pushed wide open and the brilliant light from the hallway stretched over the bed. Shifting herself up onto her elbows, Pearl held a hand over one side of her face to lessen the room's new glare. She squinted at the person who had invaded her privacy. A tall blonde woman stood at the end of her bed. Pearl was surprised to see that it was Nurse Shelby. It had been a while since they had included Pearl on Nurse Shelby's roster of patients. In fact, Pearl hadn't seen Nurse Shelby since Nurse Charlotte started working at Glory Heights.

Pearl supposed Nurse Shelby had come to give her an evening dose of medication. Pearl preferred Nurse Charlotte, especially since she had confided in her about Sonny. However, Nurse Shelby had always been nice enough. Pearl supposed Nurse Charlotte needed a day off now and then. Pearl just hoped they hadn't taken her off Nurse Charlotte's patient list. Pearl knew that the nurse supervisors often changed the rosters and they didn't feel the need to discuss it with the patient first. Pearl hoped they hadn't exchanged Nurse Shelby for her Nurse Charlotte, especially since they had gotten to know each other, gotten close. Pearl couldn't let herself think of that. Not after such a lovely evening. She offered Nurse Shelby a smile. "Nurse Shelby, what a surprise. I haven't seen you in quite some time."

Shelby returned Pearl's smile. Then, coming around to the side of Pearl's bed, Shelby set down the tray she was carrying.

"Hello Pearl, it has been quite a while. I'm glad to see you looking so cheerful."

Pearl suspected her face was still glowing from Jordana's visit.

Shelby continued. "I'd heard that you weren't feeling well lately. Having a hard time over Sonny, I bet. So, I brought you some warm milk, just like I used to do for you."

When Pearl was on Shelby's roster, Shelby had often brought warm milk for Pearl to wash down her medicine with, after which Pearl always slept so well. Pearl appreciated the kind gesture and took the warm cup of milk and the phenobarbital. She sat up and drank the soothing liquid while Shelby fluffed the pillows.

Shelby spoke while Pearl finished the milk. "I saw Karoline in the community room. She said you had gone to bed early, but I see you didn't get much sleep."

Pearl deliberately kept her nose in the cup, finishing the milk as slowly as possible. She wasn't sure how to answer Shelby. Pearl wondered if Nurse Shelby had seen Jordana and Matthew leaving the room. If Nurse Shelby hadn't, Pearl didn't want to give it away. She didn't want to share her precious Jordana with anyone except Nurse Charlotte. Pearl thought of the safest answer possible, and after handing the empty cup back to Shelby, she offered it up to her. "No, I'm still awake."

Shelby wasn't so easily diverted. She laughed at Pearl's simple remark. "No, silly, I mean you had company. I saw Matthew Kincaid leave here with a young woman. I've certainly seen Matthew around here at night, but I've never seen the woman before. Is she someone you know?"

Pearl had easily forgotten that she wanted to keep Jordana a secret, because when the first opportunity arose to tell someone about her niece, as it clearly had done here, she couldn't contain herself. "Yes," Pearl beamed. "It was my niece, Jordana. She came to see me. Isn't she pretty? She's my niece," she repeated proudly.

Pearl could tell that Shelby was trying not to pry too much

by the way she picked up the tray and headed toward the door. Pearl thought it was nice that Nurse Shelby stopped for just a moment to offer a kind word and share in her excitement.

"Oh my yes, she is a beauty," exclaimed Shelby. "I didn't know you had a niece. How nice of her to visit you. And, Matthew stayed for it, as well." Shelby hesitated at the door for just a second before asking, "Do you think Jordana will come again?"

Pearl glowed at the slender, smiling figure standing in her doorway, "I sure hope so, Nurse Shelby. I sure hope so. Thanks for asking, and by the way, thanks for the warm milk, too." Pearl yawned. "I think I can sleep now."

Chapter Nineteen

Jordana stepped into the refreshing night air, welcoming the light rain-cleansed breeze on her face. Matthew walked by her side. After leaving Pearl to tuck herself back into bed, Matthew had insisted on escorting Jordana to her car. It was parked in a lot on the south end of Glory Heights. She wondered if he gave everyone such personalized attention. She wouldn't complain. She had wanted him to stay after introducing her to Pearl. Matthew and Pearl had seemed so comfortable with each other, and Jordana had been nervous. Matthew's confident, composed presence had eased the introduction and subsequent visit.

While daylight saving time extended summer hours to nearly nine o'clock, the sky was thick with blue black clouds from the evening's storm. Coal-black shadows loomed over the parking lot, and it was darker than she would've felt comfortable faring alone. The lone lamppost stationed in the middle of the lot was not enough to illuminate the entire area. Jordana had purposely parked the convertible in a far corner of the lot to ward off dents from carelessly opened car doors. She noticed that most cars were parked closer to the building or to the light. Nearing the corner of the lot, only an inky outline of her convertible was visible, and she was glad to have Matthew with her.

Upon reaching the Mustang, she pressed the remote lock release and then turned to Matthew. "Thank you, Matthew." She offered him her hand. "You've been a big help to me tonight, and it was nice meeting you."

Matthew extended his own hand, which seemed to resonate strength and tenderness. In equal measures. Had he held on a moment too long, or had she? Before pondering it any further, she withdrew her hand, sliding her fingers easily through the warmth of his palm. "I better get going. It looks as if the storm is finished for now."

Matthew opened the car door for her, but water from the storm threatened to fall from the car's roof. He slid his hand across the top of the door, securing the water away from Jordana. "I hope we'll see you again soon. You'll be good for Pearl."

Jordana got into her car, but she couldn't close the door. Matthew was standing in its way, waiting for an answer. She said. "I'm not sure that's a good idea."

A crease formed between Matthew's dark eyebrows. "But why did you come if you didn't intend to become a part of Pearl's life? She needs you. Now, more than ever."

Jordana knew that what he said was probably true. But he had no idea what the visit had done to her. She had hid the shock of it. Walking through the nursing home looking for Pearl's room had scared her. She remembered thinking: How could someone live in a place like Glory Heights for years believing they didn't belong there, believing there was love to be had elsewhere? Between the walls of Glory Heights and her own mother, they had denied Aunt Pearl all that she had dreamed of and hoped for. Even the smallest amenities were missing from Aunt Pearl's life. The ones Jordana took for granted. Jordana owned a lovely townhouse. Aunt Pearl's scarcely adorned room was without even a bath to call her own. Aunt Pearl had no privacy. Jordana was accustomed to the sweet aroma of lilac-scented potpourri kept in leaded crystal bowls throughout her home. Aunt Pearl inhaled the rotted smells of a nursing home, mixed with—What was that smell anyway? Chlorine? And the sounds. Jordana's home was peaceful, quiet.

The sounds of Glory Heights were atrocious, unbearable. Had that been someone weeping in the room next to Aunt Pearl's? Who could handle sleeping with that abominable noise next door? Aunt Pearl must surely be paying the price of sins for many generations of Witherbys. The most unbearable tragedy of all had to be the day-to-day loneliness bestowed upon Aunt Pearl, separated from the only person she ever loved and who loved her.

How could someone live in a place like that? Jordana knew the answer: because Mother forced her to. Jordana felt a fool for what she knew about her mother, and herself. Jordana sadly thought, I must be my mother's daughter.

Jordana looked at Matthew, wondering if he could see the inadequacy in her. "I'm sorry. I just don't think I can do it. My mother . . . " Was she really going to blame her mother for her own cowardice? Yes, before she could stop the inapt words from forming, they were out of her mouth. "My mother, she would kill me if she knew I'd come to see Aunt Pearl. I can't risk her finding out."

Matthew lowered his eyelids, thick with black eyelashes, nearly shading a hurt that had passed across his eyes. It reminded Jordana again of how much he cared for her Aunt Pearl. However, his next words didn't reflect hurt. It was disappointment. In Jordana. "Are you saying you can't come to visit Pearl because your mommy wouldn't approve?" He had said it with a slight laugh, to ease his disbelief. Still, it hadn't softened the blow to Jordana's ego. His words shocked her, angered her. Nevertheless, they were true, and he had been perceptive enough to see through her.

The tension she had felt since first deciding to see Pearl manifested in a gush of angry words directed at Matthew. "How dare you talk to me like that? Do you treat all of your clients' relatives like this? If you do, I bet you don't get a lot of repeat visitors. I have my own reasons for keeping my distance from Aunt Pearl. And, no matter what they are, you can't change them by bullying me into seeing her." Her uncontrolled, displaced anger was humiliating, and if she wasn't already upset enough, her eyes stung with tears she couldn't hold back. She didn't want him to see her cry.

But Matthew had seen the tears. He immediately softened his posture and tone of voice. "Hey, I'm sorry. I shouldn't have said what I did, not the way I said it anyway." He pulled a handkerchief from his pocket and shook the folds out before offering it to Jordana. He looked like he was going to dab her tears away himself, so she quickly seized the linen from his hand and wiped her cheeks and nose with it.

He continued to appease his guilt for making her cry, but he hadn't backed down on his thoughts on why she wasn't returning to Glory Heights. "It's just that I would like you to visit Pearl. I know that you're worried over your mother's reaction to it. It's clear to me that she has quite an influence on you. I don't think that's unnatural. Someone who gets themselves elected to the position of United States senator must have quite a knack for persuasion. You've grown up with it. Maybe it's taken its toll where it shouldn't."

Jordana blew her nose angrily. Damn, when it came to Mother she was like a volcano of pent-up emotions. The uncontrollable feelings rested right beneath the surface of her skin, ready to burst into flames at the merest prick of her senses. It was Mother she was angry with, not Matthew. Embarrassed at her own outburst, Jordana wanted to make amends. She smiled weakly. "How did you get so smart?"

Looking relieved that she had forgiven him, he smiled back. "I have a master's in social welfare. It ought to be good for something." Then his face turned serious. "I have something that I want you to think about. Don't answer me now. Just say you'll think about it."

Jordana knew the answer to whatever he was going to ask her, but she felt she owed it to him to hear him out.

"Friday night, I'm taking a group of my clients, Pearl included, to a concert in the park. It's just the town orchestra; they play in the park every weekend during the summer. We've done it before, and they love it. I'd like you to join us."

Jordana's response was immediate. "Oh, I couldn't do that, I wouldn't know what to do with all of those. . . ." Horrified, she stopped and looked at Matthew, who was staring at her. She hadn't known what she was going to say, but Matthew filled the blanks for her.

In a kind voice he said, "All those what? Crippled, diseased, socially unacceptable aliens?"

Jordana was embarrassed, but she let him continue without interruption.

"Look, I know it's not what you're used to, but I could use some help. I could use another chaperone. You really wouldn't have to do anything but be there. You could get to know your Aunt Pearl. And me. You could talk to me." He was talking fast again, as if trying to keep her from interjecting a rejection to his offer. "Don't say no, just say you'll think about it. I'll call you later in the week and see what you've decided."

His earnest plea was the only thing keeping her from declining now. She started her car, and although she knew what her answer would be, she couldn't tell him. With a cordial smile she delayed the inevitable. "Okay, I'll think about it, but don't expect miracles."

Matthew smiled broadly at her languid consent to thinking over his suggestion. "Great. Great. I'll call you before the concert to find out your decision."

Jordana was tired and couldn't wait to get to the safe harbor of her home. It had been the most exhausting evening she'd had in a long time, and she was incredibly disappointed in herself. She would have to think everything over and sort it all out. She knew the night hadn't been all bad. She had, temporarily, at least, made a lonely woman happy. She also couldn't help thinking what a nice man Matthew was. Too bad they had not met under different circumstances.

Driving from the parking lot, she looked in her rearview mirror. As if to confirm what she thought of him, Matthew was standing in the breaking moonlight making sure she had gotten safely on the road.

Chapter Twenty

Pearl had worked hard at Brambles, but not that hard, she thought. It was early evening and she was already yawning like crazy. She wondered how she could feel so tired after sleeping like a bear in hibernation the night before. It was the best sleep she'd had since having Sonny taken from her. The warm milk from Nurse Shelby had really done the trick.

Sleepy or not, Pearl wasn't ready to go to bed; she wanted to talk to Charlotte. Pearl hadn't seen her since before Jordana's visit, and she was itching to tell her all about it.

Pearl found Charlotte at the nurses' station. She was alone, thumbing through a stack of papers on a clipboard—probably checking her patients' medication charts. She looked quite intent on her work. Pearl hesitated, not wanting to disturb her. She was considering going back to her room when Charlotte looked up from her clipboard.

"Pearl!" Charlotte broke into a warm, expansive smile, her large white teeth contrasting beautifully with her nut-brown skin. "What's up, girlfriend?"

Pearl immediately lost all apprehension. She broke into her own perky grin, barely containing her excitement as she told her best confidante the good news. Her cheeks grew warm as she described Jordana's visit. She thought it was just excitement, or lack of oxygen, but she yawned in the middle of her story. She reported the whole story, from the moment Jordana arrived and she had immediately recognized her to the embrace in which Pearl asked Jordana to come see her again. By the time Pearl finished, she was leaning against the counter. Suddenly, she felt warm, flushed. She yawned again and flapped her hands in front of her face to cool it.

Charlotte smiled. "All the excitement must be wearing you out. We should get you to bed. But first, come here, girlfriend." Opening her arms wide, she gave Pearl a hug. "I'm so happy for you, Pearl."

"Thanks so much." Her voice was happy, but weak. Weariness won over, and Pearl decided to accept Charlotte's nudge to retire for the evening.

Walking down the hallway, Pearl clung to Charlotte's crooked arm, leaning heavily against it. Exhaustion set itself against her every footstep, like a barbell too heavy for its lifter. Yet, in the midst of Pearl's growing fatigue, a comforting awareness existed in knowing that Nurse Charlotte was her friend. The nurse again told her how happy she was for Pearl. Then, shaking a knowing finger into the air, she declared that Jordana was a good diversion, because too many of Pearl's thoughts were wrapped up in missing Sonny.

Sonny's absence still plagued Pearl with sadness, although Jordana's visit had gone a long way to improve her outlook. Pearl lay her head against Charlotte shoulder. "I sure hope Jordana will visit me again. I hope I didn't scare her away."

"What do you mean?" Charlotte asked, sounding surprised.

Pearl shrugged, "Perhaps the way I look. Or by something I said."

Charlotte patted Pearl's arm. "I'm certain that you did nothing to scare Jordana away. She'll be back. Don't lose hope." There was that hope again.

Charlotte tucked Pearl in before going back to work. Pearl

couldn't believe how drowsy she was—probably from all the excitement, as Nurse Charlotte had said.

Too tired to do any reading, Pearl had nearly dozed off when Shelby came in. "I made you some warm milk," she said.

Pearl propped herself up in bed and smiled. "That's two nights in a row now."

Shelby smiled back. "Well, I heard that you were feeling sad about Sonny and I thought this would help you sleep."

Pearl took the cup from her. "Thank you, you are so thoughtful."

"You are very welcome. You look settled in for the night, so I won't keep you. Go ahead and drink it up, and here's your medicine."

"Okay." Pearl didn't need anything to put her to sleep, as exhausted as she was. However, Nurse Shelby had again gone through the extra trouble, and Pearl did enjoy the sweet liquid. So she drank it, using it to wash down her dose of phenobarbital.

Shelby waited for her to finish drinking, and then said, "Good girl. I'll just take the cup with me."

Pearl barely had time to thank her again for her kindness. Only seconds after having drunk the milk, Pearl's eyelids grew too heavy to hold open and she surrendered to a dreamless sleep.

Chapter Twenty-One

Pearl stumbled into the reception area at Glory Heights, headed for her usual Wednesday afternoon appointment with Matthew. She'd taken an early leave from her shift at Brambles. She was pooped. Too pooped to pop. She half-chuckled at the phrase. It had always been such a funny expression to her, but a half-chuckle was all she could muster.

On the drive home she had closed her eyes and tried to catch a catnap. For once, she was thankful for Anton's stoic bent for silence. She thought she might be coming down with something. Her limbs felt too heavy to move properly. She had grappled with fatigue all day. While counting nails into boxes, she had done everything she could to keep from balancing her elbows against the belt running past her on the assembly line.

As Pearl neared the door to Matthew's office, she concluded that she must've caught a flu. Standing so close to everyone on the assembly line at Brambles gave way to catching just about any bug anyone else had. She had not recalled anyone being out sick. Then again, she had not paid much attention to anyone else lately, so absorbed was she with her own problems. Oh well, she thought, after meeting with Matthew she would crawl into bed and sleep it off. By morning, she would most likely be feeling good as new. Or at least as good as she could feel without Sonny by her side. Thinking of him again, she swallowed back a dry crick in her throat. Something she did quite a bit lately.

Matthew was eagerly waiting for Pearl. He hadn't talked with her since Jordana's unexpected arrival at Glory Heights. He couldn't wait to hear Pearl's reaction to it. But, when she struggled through the door, that discussion took a back seat to the one about the way she looked. Her face sagged and she moved with the slowness of an eighty-year-old woman. Matthew stood up to help her into a chair. "Pearl, are you okay? You look tired."

Pearl fell into the chair with a heavy plunk. "I'm sure I'll be fine. I'm just a little tired. I feel like I'm catching something." The words came out tiredly, as if they took some effort.

Matthew worried about her. "Are you up for this? We don't have to meet now if you aren't feeling well."

From Pearl's tired face came a slow smile and a wink. "We have things to talk about. I'm staying."

Matthew was cautious. He knew Pearl wanted to talk about Jordana, and if he told the truth, so did he. He sat in the chair next to Pearl. "Well, if you're sure you feel up to it."

Pearl nodded. "I'm sure."

While Matthew had thought she would start their weekly meeting off with talk about Jordana, he was mistaken. Someone else was still more important to Pearl.

"When can I see Sonny? You said you'd work on it." That subject perked her up.

Matthew laughed lightly. "Boy, you don't waste any time."

Pearl wasn't laughing. "I don't have time to waste. I miss my Sonny."

Matthew lowered his eyes, then spoke softly, sincerely. "I'm sure you do." He shifted in his chair. "The truth is, I haven't done anything about it yet. I said I'd look into it and it's only been a couple of days. Let's talk about you. It looks like you're making progress."

Yesterday morning, he saw her walk out of the building without her helmet on. She had been on her way to Brambles. After one glimpse of him, she touched her head, then turned around and took off down the hall to retrieve it from her room. She had simply forgotten it. She hadn't blatantly left it behind. He had also checked the charts at the nurses' station and found that she had been taking her medicine as prescribed.

Pearl's eyes met his. "I'm doing what you asked me to, if that's what you mean. I haven't had a seizure in three days. I've taken my medicine and worn that disgustingly ugly helmet. Are you happy?"

Matthew looked concerned. "Yes, I am happy that you are taking care of yourself, Pearl, but you should be happy about it too. It's your health we're talking about."

"I'd be happier if I could see Sonny. Jordana said that you were working on having Sonny come to see me. What about that?"

Matthew silently thanked Jordana for causing this upheaval. On Monday, she told Pearl he was working on having Sonny visit her. It wasn't exactly the truth. At the time, he was too shocked to dispute Jordana's innocent mistake, and he was giving her the benefit of the doubt there. The truth was, he had not figured out a good way to defy the warden's orders. That is, without the warden citing him on insubordination, or firing him. Not that Matthew believed the warden would really fire him. Matthew just hadn't figured it all out yet. He told Pearl as much, and then he finally got her on the subject of Jordana.

"Do you think she'll come visit me again?" Pearl's eyes held the light of dubious hope mixed with a glimpse of sadness.

Matthew had already decided what to tell Pearl. It had occurred to him that he might have inadvertently scared Jordana away. He had thought about it all day, cursing himself for the misstep. He should've known better. Considering Jordana's reluctance to return to Glory Heights, he shouldn't have tried to push so much on her at once. Asking Jordana to help chaperone an outing with several Glory Heights clientele may have been a mistake. He had been too eager to see her again himself. Trying to bring her back to both him and Pearl, he had initially thought that an environment outside Glory Heights might be more comfortable for Jordana. But his high hopes of her returning a yes verdict on the offer to accompany them to the concert were soon dashed with realism.

It hurt him to tell Pearl that Jordana had already as much as rejected his offer to visit again. Pearl didn't need any more pain or rejection in her life, but Matthew had to tell her the truth. "I might've blown it with Jordana." It came out wrong, and he knew it.

Pearl's eyes lit on him. She looked physically exhausted, but she was interested in what he had to say. Stifling a yawn, she shifted in her chair. "What does that mean?"

"It means that I'd asked her to come back, this Friday, in fact, to go to the concert with us."

Pearl looked confused. "That doesn't sound like you did such a bad thing."

"Well, all of this is so new to her. It may have frightened her." Matthew admitted.

Pearl raised her eyebrows. The problem had dawned on her, as Matthew knew it would. She was smart. She had an understanding for what Glory Heights must look like to someone on the outside. "I see," she lowered her eyelids and spoke quietly. "It's all too much for Jordana, I suppose. Seeing me is too much for her, let alone being with a group of people like me."

Pearl hadn't said it begrudgingly. She wasn't placing any blame on Jordana. Pearl spoke it as a matter of course. For this, Matthew felt sorry. Having a natural desire to persevere and to help his client, he offered some appeasement. He straightened in his chair and jabbed a finger in the air. "But I've not given up yet. I'll wait a few days and call her. I think there's still hope that she'll come to see you again. I think she liked you. That goes a long way." He hoped he wasn't being too optimistic. He knew he was going to try to get Jordana to see things his way.

Pearl broke into a grin. In a tired voice, she let him know

that she had not given up yet either. "I sure hope so. You can quit frowning now."

Matthew hadn't realized his own distress was so obvious. Learning of it, he didn't much like it. He tried straightening his brow and smiling at Pearl. However, honing in on her apparent fatigue, his forehead again creased with concern. She was moving her legs as if they ached with tiredness, and she looked as if she just couldn't get comfortable sitting up in the chair. "Pearl, are you sure you're okay?"

She yawned a response and struggled to sit up straight.

Matthew checked his watch. "It's already past our session time. Let me help you back to your room." Rising, he offered Pearl an arm to lean on.

Weakly, she raised a hand up to him, indicating that she had something to say. Her eyes beseeched him. "First, promise me you'll work on getting Sonny over here to see me."

Matthew sighed. Pearl had a one-track mind. He had to hand it to her. She wasn't going to give up on this. Nor was she going to let him. He smiled appreciatively and raised his right hand. "Scout's honor. I'll work on it."

She smiled at him, and then she lifted her arm, allowing him to help her from the chair. Rising, Pearl hesitated. Then, she swayed awkwardly, as if an inordinate weight was crippling her struggle to stand. Suddenly, she pressed heavily into Matthew, her hands grappling with his shirt sleeves. Both of their smiles waned in apprehension. Matthew instinctively reached out his other arm to brace her. With unsure, spasmodic motion, Pearl clung to him. Then, to Matthew's distress, he watched helplessly as Pearl's face paled, her eyes rolled back in her head, and her bird-like body collapsed limply against him. He caught her before she hit the floor, balanced her in a chair, grabbed the phone, and called for paramedics.

Although Matthew tried to make her comfortable, Pearl lay with her helmeted head draped against the back of the chair, her mouth agape. He wasn't sure what to do. Thinking that he should try to wake her up, he shook her hands. He patted her face.

He was about to remove her helmet when he heard the rattle of the stretcher and the voices of paramedics shouting to one another. One was giving orders for the other to call Doctor Sotto. The time between Matthew's call for help and when the paramedics sped into his office with the stretcher had been less than three minutes. To Matthew it felt like twenty.

Chapter Twenty-Two

The travel alarm began a slow beep. After a few seconds, it accelerated into double time, blasting an annoying attempt to awaken its owner. Susan stretched across Derek, who lay naked in the middle of the king-sized bed, and with an agitated slap to the top of the small digital contraption, she turned the noisy disturbance off. Then, sitting halfway up in bed, she squinted at the clock sitting next to her travel alarm. Both said 7:00 p.m. She had not overslept. She looked over at what was supposed to be her afternoon's delight and gave him a poke with a sharp fingernail. "Get up. You have to get out of here. Now."

They had started at 3:00 that afternoon. It was shortly after she had arrived in New York and checked in at the Waldorf. After several rounds of sex, both had fallen off into heavy sleep. Now she wanted him to leave, posthaste. She was finished with him, and if luck was on her side, she would never see him again.

While she waited for him to get his ass out of her bed, she thought about the service; it seemed to be slipping. She had specifically requested someone between the ages of twenty-five and thirty-five. Derek was forty-five if he was a day, although he had laid claim to the age of thirty-five. And, his name probably wasn't Derek any more than hers was Bo. The service had time to get it right. She'd placed her order before she'd even left DC.

When Derek arrived at the hotel suite, she thought of asking for his ID—other than the one provided by the service. A driver's license, even. However, she knew he probably wasn't carrying one. It had been too long since she last had sex, so she tried to ignore that he was too old for her appetite. His tanned skin wasn't the smooth velvet of youth, but the rippled flesh of someone trying to keep it together. Ouch. That thought had hit too close to home. The senator groaned inwardly, registering a personal complaint. She slid to the edge of the bed and slipped into a white terry-cloth hotel robe. Grabbing Derek's arm, she gave him a rough shake, acrimoniously urging him out of bed. "I said it's time to go."

Derek moaned. "Wha—? Oh, sorry." He grappled with the bed sheet, pulling it around his thin waist as he stood up. As he looked around for his clothes, he yawned and practically stumbled over his own feet. "Sorry," he said again. "My head feels like it's going to fall off." In his thick, nasal-ridden New York accent, it sounded like a whine.

Susan gave him a disagreeable look. They had consumed several glasses of wine and it must've taken its toll on him. Fortunately, it had only served to relax her enough to squeeze in an afternoon of sex and a nap. Thank God *her* head wasn't hurting. She had a full night in front of her. In less than two hours, she would be appearing on *Larry King Live*. She needed to be at the studio for makeup in an hour. The limousine provided by the show's producers would be picking her up in forty-five minutes. She had to get him out of there and get herself in the shower.

"Your pants are over there," she said, tightening the robe around her body and then pointing to a settee near the window. A sliver of evening sun streamed through an opening in the drapes. Derek lifted his pants and gave them a shake, accidentally snapping them against the curtains before pulling them on. The senator wrinkled her nose as a flock of dust bunnies flew into the air. The Waldorf didn't impress her, and she never really understood all the hype about it. Nevertheless, King's producer booked her here.

Giving Derek a moment to pull himself together and leave,

she went into the bathroom. She wanted to see what damage the boy wonder had done to her hair and makeup. The bath was a suite in itself. Its carpeted, mirrored entrance served as a dressing room. Beyond the dressing room was a pink, marble-tiled vanity and raised bath. She glanced in the mirror over the vanity. Ouch. She would have to pull herself together before leaving the suite. She couldn't look like she spent the afternoon in bed. Makeup artists would work wonders once she arrived at the studio, but she had to do something with herself before she got there. It was imperative that society perceived her as a flawless public servant. Besides, Nick had accompanied her to New York. He would be waiting for her in the overly chandeliered hotel lobby to escort her to the studio. She certainly didn't want him to figure out her afternoon's business.

She picked at her face and hair, and thought about Nick. He typically accompanied her whenever she traveled on political business. But this was a short trip, and she had advised him to stay in DC. Discussions on the Great Lakes Water Protection Act were heating up. In her mind, it would've been better use of his time if he stayed behind to answer constituent questions and take phone calls. However, they would be discussing the Water Protection Bill on Larry King, and Nick thought publicity for the bill was more important. It was his baby. He wanted to brief her up to the last minute on any aspects of the bill she was bound to forget. She had reminded him that they had a script, which he had approved himself, but that wasn't good enough. She could bullshit her way through any conversation, yet he was adamant about coming along. And frankly, she really didn't care that he came along, as long as someone was running the office while they were out. Nick had assured her there would be. If no one was responding to constituents, it would be bad publicity for her.

Since Nick was here, she mused, he could just as well also attend the charity dinner with her following the Larry King show. The Epilepsy Foundation, of all things, was holding its annual benefit. Nick had insisted she attend the opening ceremonies and say a few words of support, since she was already going to be in New York. She considered that it would be good for her public image, and agreed to it.

To get the most mileage out of her attendance at the charitable event, Nick threw a tidbit about it into the Larry King script. Nick also sent news blips to the Minneapolis *Star Tribune* and the St. Paul *Pioneer Press* announcing her appearance on Larry King, with a line about her attendance at the banquet, a $600 a plate fund-raiser. She would've skipped the dinner, wanting to stay as far away from epileptic causes as she could get. However, thanks to Nick, she didn't see any way out of it.

Leaning across the vanity in the bathroom, she moved closer to the mirror, leaving about an inch of space between it and her face, and pulled down her left eyelid. While she did this, she wondered what the hell she was looking for and let go of it, standing up straight. All she did was confirm that, although her head didn't hurt, her eyes were severely bloodshot.

She went out to the bedroom to look for her contact solution, hoping a few drops of that would soothe her eyes. To her dismay, Derek was still there, sitting on the crumpled bed, fully dressed. He appeared to be waiting for her. They handled payment for his services privately; no money exchanged hands between escorts and clients. She wondered what he was still doing in her suite. "Is there something else you need, Derek?"

Derek rose from the bed. Placing his hands inside his pants pockets, he was not yet making a move toward the exit. "Well, ah, I was just wondering if maybe you forgot something."

The senator cocked her head to one side. "Forgot something? Like what?"

Derek took one hand from his pocket and waved it in front of her. "Well, ah, I thought maybe you'd forgotten the tip."

The senator placed a hand to her head as if she were now coming down with the headache. "The tip? There's no tip. There never is. Get out of here, you rapacious slime."

He was unmoved by her words, both in physical position and facial demeanor. He still hadn't moved toward the door. "I recognize you; you're a senator. Senators usually tip."

The agency did not tell escorts the real names of their clients. They trained them not to let on that they knew who you were, even if they did recognize you. This aging Adonis had just exposed her. She looked at him shrewdly, her eyes burning with anger. Was he stupid, or was he cleverly trying to bribe her? Had it worked for him before? She wasn't going to start paying bribes. This was probably the only kind of job he could get, and he wouldn't want to lose his position with the service. Her privacy was essential. She had to play this right. "How long have you worked with this escort service, Derek?"

His eyes lit up. He had caught on to what she meant. "Awhile." He finally took a few steps toward the door.

"Is it your livelihood? Or do you have another line of work to support yourself?"

"Well, I'm an actor. Trying to be, that is. Other than that, this is it. Hey, look, I didn't mean anything by what I said. I just recognized you, that's all. I don't often have a senator."

The senator raised her eyebrows. He still had hopes for his own fame. "Then how do you know they usually tip?" She emphasized the word "usually" with a sneer. "And aren't you trained to keep private both the identity and type of clients that you see?"

His face blushed beneath the well-worn tan. "Hey, just forget it, okay? I'm sorry. I don't want to cause any trouble or nothin'." The senator held her breath. He was almost out of her hair. He quickly walked to the door, speaking over his shoulder. "I'll get out of your way now. I hope you'll forgive me. Maybe we could just keep this between us, huh?" He turned to look at her.

Fire rolled in the senator's eyes. "Just get the hell out."

The Larry King show went well, as Susan had expected. The Epilepsy Foundation benefit was another story. Her fifteen-minute pep talk on the health and labor subcommittee's commitment to education and awareness had gone well. She had covered the government's interest in dispelling old beliefs about epilepsy both in the workplace and in society, and the crowd seemed to buy it. Having wrapped up what she thought was a riveting presentation, she was moving away from the podium when the cross-examination began.

"Senator Seymour, have you ever visited an epilepsy treatment center?"

"Have you ever employed someone with epilepsy?"

To the first question, Susan had answered that she was looking forward to visiting one in the near future. To the second, she lied and brazenly told them a story of her experience working with a man suffering from epilepsy. As the tale unfolded, she glimpsed over at Nick, who was standing off stage. She had caught his look of utter disbelief from the corner of her eye. After a few difficult questions, and a lot of bullshit answers, she managed an inspirational closing comment. When the audience rose to a standing applause for the senator's seemingly unmitigated support, Nick quickly whisked her off the stage and out the door. Staying for dinner might only get the senator in more trouble. Bullshit was one thing, but an outright lie that a savvy journalist could investigate was another.

On the ride back to the hotel, Nick's brooding stare cut through the dark silence between them, irritating Susan. The lights surrounding the limo floor lit upon his face, confirming his distaste for her speech at the benefit. She didn't really care what he thought, but she did care what he might do with his discomfiture. Lately, she had sensed his waning loyalty. She had hoped to bring it back on course with her appearance on Larry King promoting the Water Protection Act that was so near and dear to the environmentalist's heart. She silently harrumphed. After her benefit speech, she had probably erased any goodwill she had mustered up with him.

Nick turned his head to stare out the window. Susan looked, too. The view was minimal; New Yorkers whizzed by. Speeding taxis practically piled on top of each other trying to get a fare or keep from running over people crowding the sidewalks and streets of Manhattan. Susan's thoughts flitted from one miserable issue to another.

She had hated Nick for making her wait while he thought

over whether he would help her with Pearl. He waited a full two days before acknowledging that he had talked with Daris McFinley at Glory Heights. McFinley apparently assured Nick that Pearl would no longer be a problem. But Susan wanted to hear it again. Another disruption from Pearl was the last thing she needed. She wondered whether to broach the subject again.

She also worried that she was too flippant with Jordana when she called with questions about Pearl. Jordana was such a sensitive child. Perhaps Susan should've handled her differently. Most bothersome was that Jordana had not returned her phone calls since that night. Before Pearl disrupted everything, Jordana had always promptly returned Susan's phone calls.

In the end, everything would be okay between her and Jordana. She was sure of it. It wasn't like Jordana would ever have anything to do with Pearl. Jordana had no reason to do that. Although Susan was certain that Pearl was a dead issue for Jordana, she would feel more comfortable hearing it from Jordana. Susan sighed deeply. She was thinking too hard about something so insignificant. She reminded herself again that Nick had confirmed McFinley's promise to keep Pearl from becoming a nuisance. McFinley would sedate Pearl if he had to, to keep her at Glory Heights.

But the banquet—maybe there Susan had gone too far, said too much. She was going to need Nick more than ever on that one. He always knew of a way to smooth things over, to save her political ass, when things got rough. She wanted to ask again about Pearl, but decided that making nicey-nice with Nick was more important, critical in fact, to her career.

She cleared her throat to get Nick's attention. He straightened in the seat, turning his gaze toward her. She tried on a feminine pout. "Nick, I think I may have blown it tonight. I didn't let on, but the harsh questions truly flustered me. Do you think I've done much damage?" She eyed him, searching for a reaction to her attempt at feminine wiles. Nothing registered on his face, but his eyes seemed to brighten at her confession.

He folded his hands, and extending them out across his

knees, leaned toward her. "You're going to have to visit an epileptic treatment center, and soon. As far as the fictitious epileptic coworker, don't bring it up again and maybe it'll pass without anyone looking into it."

The senator smiled graciously. "I knew you could fix it, Nick. I just knew it." She all but batted her eyes at him.

Nick gave her a sideways glance. "Fix it? I've not fixed anything yet. I said we'll sign you up for a tour of the treatment center. On the other issue, we'll wait and see." Then he gave her the bad news. "Taylor Costica was in the audience tonight."

Susan lost her smile. Taylor was an energetic political correspondent with the *Washington Post*. She was Susan's political enemy. As far as Susan was concerned, Taylor's reporting was biased with the right-wing capitalists. They were always looking for a democratic screw-up to take to the ethics committee. She once wrote a damaging article questioning the senator's dedication to the committees she sat on. Fortunately, Nick wrote an elaborate editorial rebuttal that squelched the budding rumors. Rumors that Taylor had started. The good-looking blonde was a thorough investigative reporter, and she could do a lot of damage if she wanted to.

Now more than ever, Susan wished she had kept her mouth shut at the banquet. What a fool she had been for lying about having once worked alongside a person with epilepsy. If Taylor chose to look into that declaration of stupidity, she and the rest of the press would have a field day with the senator's dishonesty. And if Taylor dug further and found out about Pearl, Susan's political career would suffer a ruin from which she would never recover. Susan bent her head into her hand and rubbed the creases from her forehead. Lifting her head, she narrowed her eyes and searched Nick's face. Maybe he knew more than he was letting on. "What was Taylor doing at the banquet?" She snapped. "Isn't it a little out of her realm of journalism?"

Nick gave her a weary glance. "I don't know why Taylor was there, but I presume she was covering your speech." Both of them knew that he meant, "covering the senator's commitment to the cause." He didn't have to say it. "Taylor is another good reason we didn't stay for dinner. She would've tried to get an interview with you. I can only imagine the disaster that would've turned into. Just hope she isn't interested enough to check out your claims."

Somewhere between a satisfied nod and a frustrated glare, Nick grabbed a wine cooler from the limo's ice bucket. Then he sat back in his seat and again turned to the window. Susan fished out two miniature-sized whiskey bottles and went silent as well.

Chapter Twenty-Three

The paramedics wheeled Pearl into her room with Matthew following close on their heels. They raced down the hallway past Charlotte, who rushed into Pearl's room and pushed herself to the forefront. Her only thoughts were of Pearl, laid out on the stretcher, limp and unconscious.

Charlotte turned down the bed with one motion and then helped the paramedics transfer Pearl to the bed by supporting her head. The clang of the metal woke a napping Karoline, who sat up to see what all the ruckus was about. Charlotte glanced at her, but gave no explanation. She attended only to Pearl. Charlotte's face felt warm and tight with concern, a feeling that extended to her neck and the scalp beneath her curly black hair. Pearl was still unconscious from having fainted in Matthew's office minutes earlier, which had been too long a time for Charlotte's sensibilities.

The paramedics checked Pearl's pulse and blood pressure while Charlotte removed the damp, musty-smelling helmet from Pearl's perspiring head. Having shimmied the helmet off, she handed it to Matthew, motioning with her head for him to set it on the bed stand. She called for a paramedic to toss over a damp cloth, which she used to swab strings of swirling dark hair away from Pearl's face.

Charlotte swabbed Pearl and watched for signs of her coming around, but a brush at her hip distracted her. She thought her tight dress had again taken a hike up her thighs while she was leaned over tending to Pearl, and she swung her head around to look. All she needed was for her tush to be hanging out with all these men in the room, she thought. However, the distraction was Karoline. She was sitting on the edge of her bed, peeking around Charlotte's hips at close enough range to smell her. Karoline was apparently trying to get a good look at Pearl's pale face.

With controlled irritation, Charlotte waved Karoline back, motioning for some room to work. The room was crowded, the air warm and stuffy, all from nervous commotion and the excessive number of bodies per square foot. Charlotte pulled on her dress anyway and didn't look up to see who had noticed. She was soon nudged again, on her arm this time, by a paramedic handing her an emergency report. The paramedics were leaving, providing a welcome latitude in the small space. The uncomfortable air and the antiseptic smell of the room were nearly overpowering. However, she didn't care about that and suspected no one else did either. All eyes were on Pearl.

Charlotte gently stroked Pearl's hand and spoke her name. Aware of how frightening it was to come out of a fainting spell— the frantic attempt to unscramble thoughts, to grab onto a shred of cognizance—Charlotte tried to help Pearl focus. "Pearl," she repeated several times. "Come on, girlfriend. It's Nurse Charlotte. You've fainted. You were in Matthew's office when you passed out. We're here with you in your room now."

Charlotte checked the emergency report. According to the report, Pearl's pulse was slow and erratic. Her blood pressure was low. Charlotte looked helplessly at Matthew, wishing the doctor would show up soon. The paramedics had called Doctor Sotto, a generalist on call for Glory Heights. All Charlotte could do was keep Pearl comfortable until he got there. Matthew, looking worried, wiped a trickle of sweat off his own brow. He began to follow Charlotte's lead in coaching Pearl to consciousness. "Pearl, it's me. Matthew. Are you okay?"

Charlotte rechecked Pearl's vitals. There was some improvement. Encouraged, she coaxed Pearl on again, but with no results. She asked Matthew what had happened.

He seemed happy to tell her, just for something to do. "It looked like she fainted; it wasn't a seizure." Matthew ran his hands through his hair. "I just don't know. Maybe the strain of the last couple of weeks has been too much for her. Or maybe she has a bad flu." Matthew put that as a question, wondering if it would explain Pearl's coma.

Charlotte shrugged and nodded; she didn't know what was going on either. She said, "It could be a flu."

Matthew continued to talk about the trauma in his office. Then just as he finished his monologue, as if on cue and having waited to see if he would get the story right, Pearl began to wake up. She was struggling to sit up, asking Charlotte what had happened. At the same time, Doctor Sotto, a small formal man of Asian descent with kind eyes, entered the room. Charlotte could have hugged them both. Instead, she relayed Pearl's vital signs to Doctor Sotto and let Matthew fill both of them in on what had happened. Charlotte added that Pearl had been unusually tired the evening before.

"Any aches or pains?" Doctor Sotto asked Pearl.

With Charlotte's help, Pearl was propped up on pillows. Her face was ashen and drawn. Sweat beaded her forehead. Her lips were dry and cracked from her mouth being slung wide open during the fainting spell. Charlotte used a Q-tip to skim Vaseline across Pearl's lips. Then she handed her a glass of water, watching in case Pearl needed help with it. Pearl faltered and sipped at the water. She shook her head "no" to answer Doctor Sotto. "Just tired."

Doctor Sotto rubbed his chin. "Your heartbeat is a little slow and irregular. What have you been doing to yourself?" He was teasing her and briefly touched her hand with his to show it.

Pearl half-grinned. "Not enough." She clearly liked Doctor Sotto. He had seen her several times for colds and influenza.

He examined Pearl's eyes, and then he rechecked her

pulse and blood pressure. "Fainting could've slowed it." Then he turned to Charlotte. "Have there been any changes in Pearl's medications, in the phenobarbital?"

Charlotte shifted her stance and pulled on her dress, suddenly remembering something. She had acted spontaneously, rushing to Pearl's side after seeing the paramedics and Matthew flying down the hall with her. For a moment, she had forgotten that Pearl was no longer her patient. The change took place several days ago, but Charlotte hadn't found the heart to tell Pearl about it yet. Not being able to let go, she had been checking in on Pearl as if Pearl was still her patient. She assumed Pearl hadn't figured it out, although Pearl could've realized something was up when Shelby also checked on her—bringing her medication in the evening again, as she used to do.

Charlotte never understood why the nurse supervisor removed Pearl from her patient roster. She tried finding the paperwork on it. That's what she was doing when Pearl interrupted her the previous night, although she didn't find anything. Shelby told her about the change, explaining that they regularly modified shifts so that nurses didn't get too attached to their patients. It made them more effective in their work, Shelby had said. Charlotte still felt like the new kid on the block. Because of this, she had accepted what Shelby said. It seemed reasonable. There was some truth to it.

Pearl reminded Charlotte so much of her own mother's plight; it made Charlotte wonder if she was getting too attached to Pearl. Maybe the change was for the best. Nonetheless, Charlotte was sad to lose Pearl as a patient. And now, as Doctor Sotto questioned Pearl, Charlotte realized that she should be deferring the inquiry to Shelby. Worse was that she would have to inform Pearl of the change right now.

"Ah," began Charlotte, "In all of the excitement, I'd rushed in here and forgotten to notify the nurse assigned to Pearl. Nurse Shelby is the one in charge of her now. She's the one you should speak with, Doctor Sotto." Charlotte became aware of Karoline gawking behind her. Turning toward her, Charlotte suggested that

Karoline go catch some dinner or television in the community room. Charlotte tried not to, but she still ended up stressing the word "go." Taking the hint, Karoline left the room.

After Karoline's departure, Charlotte turned to Pearl. She spoke softly. "Last week they gave me a new roster of patients. Nurse Shelby has you now." Charlotte squeezed Pearl's shoulder, trying to express the sense of loss she felt.

Pearl had been resting with her eyes closed. She rolled on the pillow, looked at Charlotte, and simply nodded. Pearl's eyes didn't show much more than sad weariness. She seemed not so much surprised as perhaps accepting of the news. As she had been to so many things in her life.

Charlotte looked at Matthew. The news that she was no longer Pearl's nurse didn't seem to affect him. She turned back to Doctor Sotto, who was nodding "yes," he would like to speak to Shelby. Charlotte straightened her demeanor. Using a professional tone with no Southern twang in evidence, she said, "I'm fairly confident that there's been no change in Pearl's medication, but to be sure, I'll get Nurse Shelby."

Charlotte found Shelby at the nurses' station. When she first approached her with Pearl's condition, alarm flashed across Shelby's face. Most likely, Charlotte surmised, in regard for Pearl's welfare. However, in another flash, Shelby covered the alarm with a professional, detached look. When Charlotte relayed the message that Doctor Sotto wanted to speak with her, Shelby's face colored. Charlotte didn't know what to think about her, but she couldn't take the time to worry over it then.

Entering Pearl's room, Charlotte trailed behind, valiantly taking a backseat to the senior nurse. An introduction between Doctor Sotto and Shelby wasn't needed, both having worked with Glory Heights for quite some time. In his polite way, Doctor Sotto welcomed Shelby with a nod. He was packing up his bag. "Nurse Shelby, what can you tell me about Pearl's medication? For instance, has their been a change in dosage to her phenobarbital?"

Shelby's eyes widened. "No, no changes there. Pearl took Tylenol to ease the pain and swelling of the bump she got on her head last week. That would be the only thing different in her medication."

As Shelby spoke, her eyes slowly averted from Doctor Sotto so that by the time she had finished the last sentence she was no longer looking at him. Charlotte found it curious, but she surmised that Shelby was upset that they hadn't called her in earlier to help with Pearl.

Doctor Sotto's eyes grew keen. He looked at Pearl. "Did you have an accident?"

In answer, Pearl pushed back her hair, showing Doctor Sotto the remains of the gash she received trying to exit the phone booth amidst the seizure the weekend before. "Nothing serious, I just bumped my head during a seizure. See, it's almost healed."

Doctor Sotto touched the nodule. "Did you have a concussion?"

Charlotte, who knew something about this, and Pearl both shook their heads "no." Doctor Sotto turned to Shelby, who added a nod of confirmation to their declaration. "How about headaches, Pearl? Did you have headaches after receiving the injury?"

Pearl pointed to the healing gash on her head. "Just right here. The doctor at the emergency room gave me some extra-strength Tylenol to take for it. It's fine now."

"Where's the Tylenol now?" asked Doctor Sotto.

Pearl pointed to the drawer in her bed stand. "In there. There's quite a bit left."

Shelby opened the drawer and pulled out the Tylenol. "It doesn't look like you took more than the prescribed dose of this."

Apparently insulted, Pearl had recovered enough from her fainting spell to let out an unqualified "Harrumph!" She then clarified it. "What? Do you think I tried to kill myself with Tylenol?"

Matthew, who had remained silent while the medical staff discussed the case, let out a laugh. "I think they're just checking on anything that would make you so tired, Pearl."

"It's just the flu," insisted Pearl.

Matthew addressed Doctor Sotto. "Pearl's had quite a bit going on in her life lately. Enough that would exhaust just about anyone. If you aren't finding anything else medically wrong with her, she just may have the flu or be worn out and needing some rest."

After earnestly listening to Matthew's summation, Doctor Sotto spoke. "Let me explain my initial concern and questions." Doctor Sotto looked at everyone, and then he addressed himself mostly to Pearl. "The preliminary effects of overdosing on phenobarbital or any other sedative are an erratic heartbeat, low blood pressure, and extreme drowsiness. Some viruses might also have that affect on our bodies. If you are not feeling better soon, we will take more tests. But, after talking with all of you, the only thing I will prescribe for our patient right now is complete bed rest." He emphasized the words "our patient" and smiled around the room. He turned again to Pearl. "You have quite an excellent team of caregivers working with you. We'll keep an eye on you for a few days. Get some rest, and I'll soon be back to check on you." He spoke to Shelby next. "Call me if anything changes for the worse, but I think it's something that with good rest will soon pass."

After hearing Doctor Sotto's analysis, Charlotte noted a change in Shelby. She appeared relieved and could finally meet his eyes. With a spring in her step, Shelby walked him to the door and promised to call if there was any decline in Pearl's condition. Quite a charmer when she wants to be, thought Charlotte.

Matthew checked his watch, causing Charlotte to check hers. It was already 5:00. Matthew had a son that probably needed attending to. He could leave now that they knew Pearl was going to be all right. He, too, walked to the door, but before exiting, he pointed a finger back at Pearl. "You do as the good Doctor Sotto ordered and get some rest. I'll call Brambles to tell them that you won't be in to work for the next couple of days. I'm sure they'll understand."

Pearl gave him a lazy smile. "Oh, go on, young man. I'm not going anywhere. But don't forget to take care of that business we talked about."

Matthew shook his head, indicating his dismay. "I'm in deep this time." However, he was smiling when he left the room.

Charlotte wondered what that exchange was all about, but she felt certain it had something to do with Sonny.

After seeing Doctor Sotto on his way, Shelby came back into the room. Charlotte hadn't budged from Pearl's bedside. The two nurses stared at each other. Charlotte wasn't sure why, but she was starting not to like Shelby. Charlotte was the first to step aside, giving Shelby a slight bow in acquiescence before moving from the bed. Charlotte then turned to say goodnight to Pearl. "I have to get going, too. Nurse Shelby will take good care of you now." She intended to leave, but hesitant to do so, she had to ask, "Are you starting to feel better, Pearl?"

Pearl smiled at Charlotte's concern. "I was a little queasy after fainting, but that feeling is gone. I'm just thirsty now."

At that, both nurses reached for the water glass sitting on the table. Before colliding hands at the glass, Charlotte pulled back, again giving in to the senior nurse. The one now in charge of Pearl, she reminded herself at the last moment. After that, she decided to quit torturing herself and exited the room with only a small wave to Pearl. Hurrying through the halls away from Pearl's room, Charlotte reasoned it through. Shelby taking over her favorite patient was affecting her attitude. Charlotte thought she better let it go; she was still the new kid on the Glory Heights block.

Alone in the room with Pearl, Shelby was considering whether to give her the sedative-tainted warm milk along with the phenobarbital that evening. With some shame, she realized that the effects of the phenobarbital had been enhanced by the 100 milligrams of Seconal she had put in Pearl's milk. Sometimes, doctors prescribed phenobarbital as a sedative rather than as an anticonvulsant. She had read Pearl's charts—her prescription was for 200 milligrams of phenobarbital in the morning and 175 at night. That was high dosage for anticonvulsant purposes, but Pearl had a tough case of epilepsy. A single dose could go as high as 200 milligrams if dosage wasn't over 400 in a twenty-four-hour period.

For a moment, she thought of increasing the phenobarbital and skipping the Seconal. However, after her admission to Doctor Sotto that nothing had changed in Pearl's prescribed dosage of phenobarbital, she thought better of it. She wasn't a doctor and wasn't sure what to do. She didn't want to harm Pearl. She had only wanted to stay on the favorable side of McFinley. It had been easy enough. Until now. Frustrated, she silently cursed Daris McFinley.

She looked down at Pearl, whom she had assumed was resting her eyes while she thought over this new dilemma. In fact, Pearl had gone to sleep. She nearly laughed aloud at her silly analysis over an already-sleeping patient. She certainly wasn't going to wake Pearl up to give her a sleeping aid. Having made that decision, she gently pulled the covers up over Pearl's shoulders and left the room. Later, she would check on Pearl again and at least give her the mandatory dose of phenobarbital. Maybe by then she would have decided what to do.

Chapter Twenty-Four

Matthew left Glory Heights and drove home. The evening heat was smothering, but he defied it by changing into jogging clothes and going out for a run. Beginning at his home, he ran through residential streets until he came to a winding wooded path. He took the path down to the edge of the Rum River and picked up a walking trail that followed along the water. After a distance, he climbed the bank to the city park, circled the picnic grounds encompassing the band shell, turned around, and followed the course home. By the time he finished, sweat poured from every pore of his body and he felt as if he had jogged through an elongated sauna. However, the tension from the workday and the trauma of Pearl fainting on him had been relieved. He still didn't know what to make of it, but he hoped she soon felt better.

He stood in front of his brownstone with sweat sliding down his muscular arms and legs. He leaned over, rested his hands on his knees, and waited for his breathing to calm. Then, having almost forgotten, he quickly checked his watch for the time. Not bad. He had run ten kilometers, a little over six miles, in thirty-two minutes. He hoped it was faster than his competitors' best in the upcoming Run for the Homeless race. The faster Matthew ran, the more money he made for the charity. With the race coming up in a few weeks, he was pleased that the evening's run had gone so well.

The pledge forms he sent around at work came back with a decent response. He pumped up coworkers with his determination to win the race and got them to increase their pledges over the previous year. Earlier in the year, he talked the stiff-nosed warden into matching employee pledges with a Glory Heights donation. When the news got out that Matthew Kincaid had moved Mount Everest, coworkers chomped at the bit to raise their pledges even further. His neighbors also supported the race with handsome pledges. He was grateful for all the support.

Matthew stepped from the cool shower smelling of Irish Spring soap. He toweled off, feeling refreshed after sloughing off the day's high heat and humidity. The cold contrast of the air-conditioned house also invigorated him. He suddenly realized how hungry he was. After donning lightweight cotton boxers, he went to the kitchen looking for dinner.

Ice-cold Michelob and some leftover chicken were in the refrigerator. A bag of chips was on the counter. Cory had opened them and left them out. No bag clip attached. Matthew smiled and shook his head. They were probably stale. Oh, well. He loaded the chips and the rest of his dinner into his arms and went into the living room to eat in front of the television.

When Cory was with Matthew, he made an effort to cook. However, tonight Cory was with his mother, and Matthew was looking forward to an evening of solitude. Lately, life felt like a whirlwind without much time to himself.

He settled appreciatively into his recliner and turned on the television. After gulping a generous swig of beer, he flipped through the channels until he hit CNN. A reporter he liked caught his eye. Taylor Costica was a guest reporter on a nightly news broadcast delivering a report on the nation's political climate. He found it interesting enough to give it half an ear while he munched chips and gnawed on a chicken leg. But when she mentioned a name he recognized, he quit gnawing and munching altogether.

As he sat forward in his recliner, a picture of Susan came on the screen.

Taylor was reporting on a fundraiser sponsored by the Epilepsy Foundation. Matthew continued eating, and listened. Susan had delivered an opening address at the event and promised to, said she was looking forward to, touring an epileptic treatment center in the near future. Matthew nearly choked on his drumstick. Taylor reported that Susan had no tour scheduled. Taylor added, "so far," as if to give the senator the benefit of the doubt. Or to cover her own liable butt. The show's host brought up Taylor's previous controversial pieces on the senator; articles questioning her proclaimed commitment to educating the public about problems faced by the handicapped.

Matthew listened for a few minutes, then he sat back in his chair and slugged another one out of the bottle. He thought, Ms. Costica, you are a very smart lady. Senator Seymour is a fraud, and you're just the person to unravel her political ass.

He'd seen enough. He switched off the television, closed his eyes, and let his mind wander. Passing the band shell had reminded him of his offer to Jordana. His thoughts inevitably floated to her. He smiled. He was going to call her later. Partly because he wanted to tell her that Pearl had taken ill, and partly because he was dying to hear her voice again. No doubt, he was attracted to her. She dazzled him with her natural good looks and coloring. He loved her lean body, sapphire blue eyes, and thick auburn hair. Learning more about her was at the top of his list of things to do.

He wondered, briefly, if dating her would cause a conflict of interest for him at Glory Heights. His contract held no clause prohibiting him from dating a client's relative. Well, it hadn't come up before, either. When it came down to it, he didn't really care what anyone at Glory Heights would think about it. His personal life was no one's business but his own.

He got up and retrieved another beer from the fridge. Chuckling, he stretched back into the recliner. Here he was wondering about a conflict of interest, practically assuming Jordana would go out with him, when she might not even be interested in doing so. For his part, he couldn't get Jordana out of his mind. She was a beautiful, intelligent, complex woman, all wrapped up in one package. He smiled. What was there not to like?

He reflected on how conflicted she was over visiting Pearl. The cause of Jordana's battle was due to her mother. From her senate seat in Washington, Susan had wielded her influence over her only child. However, the fact that Jordana had come to see Pearl for herself, against her mother's wishes, meant that she had a heart and a mind of her own. He bet that, in the end, no matter what her mother thought about it, Jordana wouldn't be able to stay away from Pearl. She wouldn't be able to abandon her aunt. Matthew suspected that she knew all too well what abandonment, at least emotional abandonment, felt like. She would be back to see Pearl, and as for him, the sooner the better.

If he wanted to spend time alone with Jordana, he would have to play his cards right. She seemed the type of person who warmed slowly to others. She wasn't going to plunge into anything she wasn't sure of. He could wait; he was a patient man. He would wait, but that didn't mean he wouldn't pursue.

Suddenly, he had a good idea. He smiled and opened his eyes. At least he thought it was a good idea. There was something that might help him further his cause, or at the very least, induce steps in the right direction. He went to the den, clicked open his briefcase, and retrieved Jordana's home phone number.

Jordana was home, sulking. She had met Ryan for lunch at DuJour's, a popular brunch café, midway between their afternoon client destinations. That's where he chose to break off their relationship. For the summer, as he had put it. It seemed that Ryan was having too much fun with the guys and didn't have time to dote on any one girlfriend. Jordana thought that was an excuse for wanting to play the field if she had ever heard one, and she told him so. She also told him that he didn't need to call when summer was over. He needn't think about getting back together when his social life died down, which is the way he probably meant it to be anyway. She had ended the conversation and the lunch on a self-preserving note. Still, Ryan had dumped her, and she knew it.

In self-defense, she reasoned that, because he had kept his distance in the past few months with supposed fishing trips and other lone events, she wouldn't miss him much. Besides, his ego had grown with his advertising account status, and what woman needed that to maintain? Not this one, she thought. A lifetime of tolerating her mother's overpowered ego had caused an aversion to the likeness of it that only strengthened her resolve to avoid that tired characteristic in men.

When Ryan became a top account executive at Curic and McCall, he started wining and dining more female clients than any other account manager ever had. That was the rumor, anyway. Initially, she ignored the rumblings about inappropriate behavior. He had emphatically denied them. She first chalked them up as untruths, and then she thought they were because of jealousy among coworkers. But finally she believed every word, and she hoped he got what was coming to him. She figured a few of the women found him quite charming, as she first did, and succumbed to his futureless advances. If so, he would hang himself with his own stupidity in mixing personal pleasures with business. If he didn't, Curic and McCall's brass would.

She hated feeling vengeful and sorry for herself, as she knew she was doing. But she was hurt and left without a playmate for summer. It felt childish. If she spoke it out loud, it would sound infantile. But who wanted to spend summer alone, particularly if you thought you had someone to do things with, a boyfriend in fact, and now he's pulled the rug out from under you? It occurred to her that she was more concerned about spending time alone during the summer than she was feeling sad about missing Ryan. She decided to hang onto that thought.

She wouldn't have to worry about seeing him in the halls of Curic and McCall. They were both supposed to spend most of their time with clients outside the office. That was a godsend. If it happened that they were in the office at the same time, she would do her best to avoid him. If she had the bad luck of running into him, she would remind herself that she barely missed his presence.

With one last blow of her nose, she ended her grieving period for Ryan. She took a deep breath of her lilac-scented house and decided all would be well. On impulse, she checked the kitchen clock and reviewed her timing. They had met for a late lunch at about 1:30, after which Jordana left for back-to-back client meetings that didn't allow a minute's time to think about him. She got home around 6:30. She poured herself a tall glass of St. Michelle's Cabernet Sauvignon, sank onto the couch, and burst into tears. That had been two hours ago. She laughed and decided that was an appropriate amount of mourning—maybe it had even lasted a little too long.

In her heart, she knew she deserved and could find someone better suited for her than Ryan. He wasn't so much of a loss. As for wanting someone to hang out with, she would simply start making plans to mix with friends. She remembered an article in that day's newspaper. The Aquatennial, Minneapolis' annual civic celebration, would kick off that weekend with the usual Hennepin Avenue Block Party. The festival would last ten days and include forty-eight events. It produced one of Minnesota's largest parades, displayed the nation's fourth largest fireworks show, conducted milk carton boat races, sand castle competitions, and running events. With all of that to choose from, she would surely find something to capture her interest. She could invite someone to go to an event with her. At the very least, she could hang out at the city parks and beaches with the other 800,000 guests the city expected to attend the event. She would people watch and suntan, or get in on a game of volleyball at Lake Calhoun. With that, she promised herself she would not sit home over the weekend.

To get her mind off the breakup, she decided to do some client work. After refilling her wine glass, she found her bulging Coach briefcase. She dug into the soft leather bag looking for a file folder she needed to review. The file contained information on a significant client, a real moneymaker for the firm. Their marketing executive had called complaining of an error, a typo, in the kick-off ad for a major promotion. An error like that was almost unheard of at Curic and McCall. The client had final review of the ad, but that didn't let the advertising firm off the hook. The copy had gone through Curic and McCall's quality control department, but no one caught the error. Jordana had looked at the ad herself and didn't catch it. The client didn't catch it until it was in print. That the faux pas would most likely also go unnoticed by the client's intended audience was beside the point.

She had already reprinted and redistributed the ad for publication in the next day's newspapers, at Curic and McCall's expense. Now, she just wanted to review the issue to see if they required any further compensation. Curic and McCall wouldn't plead guilty, but she wasn't going to lose her client, either. She would offer up some recompense for their pain, like a discount on their next promotional package. Although, paying for the reprint and redistribution of the ad wasn't chicken feed.

The wine was beginning to soften Jordana's senses. A silly thought occurred to her, and she chuckled at it. She wondered how much chicken feed actually cost. She had found the file and was tugging at it, trying to free it from its entrapment in the overloaded briefcase. She was still giggling about the price of chicken feed when the phone rang, startling her.

She jerked her hands out of the briefcase, breaking a fingernail. Hastily applying the finger to her lips, she sucked on it, as if mouthing it would cause the nail to mend. The call made her heart leap, but she hesitated to answer it. She pushed back the hair from her forehead and took a deep breath. It was probably Matthew—calling to ask if she'd decided to attend the concert Friday night. Jordana wasn't going, and she didn't want to talk about it. She decided to let him leave a message. She would then leave one for him at his home number the next day. While he was at work.

However, as she listened to the message, she began to feel guilty. Aunt Pearl had taken ill. Jordana almost picked up the phone, wanting to know: Was her aunt going to be okay? What happened? But when Matthew closed the message with, "If you wouldn't mind returning my call, I would like to talk something over with you," she again hesitated. In the end, she let him finish the message without picking up the phone. She wondered about the call. What did he want to discuss? The concert? Was he interested in her personally? She suspected as much. Was he going to ask her out? Oh no.

Jordana took her finger out of her mouth and jammed the file back into her bag. Hell, she already knew what she was going to do about her big wigging client. It was Matthew Kincaid and Aunt Pearl she didn't know what to do about. She poured another glass of cabernet and sipped on it while she thought it over.

She felt uneasy about hiding behind her telephone. Just who or what was she hiding from, anyway? Matthew Kincaid, Aunt Pearl, Mother? Well, Mother was a given, considering the circumstances surrounding Aunt Pearl. Jordana hadn't told her mother that she went to see Aunt Pearl, and she hoped her mother never found out. Jordana had even temporarily stopped returning her mother's phone calls to avoid telling her about going to Glory Heights.

As for Matthew Kincaid, Jordana would simply tell him she wasn't interested in a personal relationship with him—if the subject ever came up, that was. Never mind about the good leap her heart took when Matthew called, or the tingle that cascaded through her middle when she heard his voice.

Aunt Pearl was harmless. Still, knowing that Pearl had spent her life sequestered in a nursing home, unloved by her only sibling, placed a sad weight on Jordana's heart. She began to analyze what she was going to do about her aunt Pearl. The wine enhanced Jordana's emotions. She went back and forth in her mind about what to do. In the end, her conscience told her that she was going to call and find out the nature of Pearl's illness. Jordana was angry with herself for not having picked up the phone right away.

The fact that she hadn't answered the phone, knowing Matthew Kincaid was on the other end of the line, told her from whom she was really hiding. Matthew Kincaid was a diligent caseworker, strong in his convictions, and emphatic in his belief that she should pay attention to Pearl. Between the strength of his character and the nagging belief that he was interested in something more, Jordana realized she better start dealing with Matthew Kincaid. Because he wasn't going away.

Chapter Twenty-Five

Friday morning, Pearl sat on the edge of the bed, her brow knitted in frustration. She was trying to decide if she could make it down to the cafeteria for breakfast. Yet, when she thought about it, food didn't appeal to her.

Thursday morning, she had sat in the same spot and wondered the same thing. After Doctor Sotto and the others left her room Wednesday evening, she slept soundly until the 6:00 a.m. bell went off. Still, she felt too weak and groggy to get out of bed in the morning. She finally succumbed to the debilitating fatigue and lay back down. But before falling into another deep sleep, she had the presence of mind to wonder about her medication. Had she taken it? A tightness in her left arm called her attention to a Band-Aid covering a piece of cotton. Nurse Shelby must have given her the medication while she slept. Having figured that out, she let herself fall into the slumber her body craved. That had been Thursday.

She hoped Friday would be different. While she pondered her strength or lack of it, Karoline stirred in the bed across from her. She yawned and stretched loudly before crawling out from the covers. Sitting up, she hugged her thick arms around her wrinkled nightgown and gave Pearl an appraising look. "Are ya better this morning? Ya don't look too good yet."

Giving in, Pearl lay back down on the bed. "I'm not sure. But I don't think so. I think I better stay in bed for a while longer. Would you mind asking the morning nurse to bring my medicine and breakfast to the room?"

"Course I'd do that for ya." Karoline then headed for the bathroom.

Pearl so wished she felt well enough to get out of bed. She had things she wanted to do. Namely, she needed to figure out a way to see Sonny. Also, the concert was that evening. If she didn't feel better, she wouldn't be able to go to it. The worst of it was, if Matthew had talked Jordana into coming to the concert, Pearl wouldn't get to see her. Pearl resigned herself to doing what she needed to feel better. She didn't like it, but it looked like she wasn't going anywhere for a while.

She dozed until early afternoon, sifting in and out of dreams about Sonny. Upon waking, she felt some improvement in her condition, and credited it to having seen her man—if only in her dreams. She felt other sensations besides those of being fatigued. Band-Aids prickled her upper arm, one from the morning's shot, the other from Thursday night. Her stomach stirred with an appetite for the first time since Wednesday. She ate the lunch left on a tray for her and started feeling even better. She didn't know if she was getting over the flu, or if the thought of going to the concert in the park was improving her spirit. But, by late afternoon, she felt perky enough to put on a robe, sit at her desk, and read a bit of her latest Agatha Christie: *By the Prickling of My Thumbs.*

She was enjoying the mystery when Matthew popped his head in. "You're up. Does that mean you're feeling better?"

She gave him a warm smile and quipped, "You bet I am. You can't keep me down for long."

Matthew looked surprised, but genuinely pleased to see her feeling better. "Hey, I'm glad to hear that. Are you coming with us to the concert?"

Her answer was immediate. "I'm planning on it." Then she looked at him hopefully. "Is Jordana coming?"

Pearl didn't know if Matthew was aware of it, but his smile faltered at the question. Yet his words were positive. "I'm still hoping to hear from her. Let's keep our fingers crossed. You rest up so you're ready to go tonight. And wear something cool, it's a scorcher out there."

Waving Matthew off, she crossed her fingers for Jordana. Then she crossed her ankles and wondered if there was a way to get a note to Sonny. He could just happen by the concert. She thought a minute, but then decided to leave well enough alone. She had to trust that Matthew would come through for her. She put her nose back in the book.

Before she got too far along in her reading, Rebecca entered the room dressed in a flowered, large-pocketed housecoat. She had a twinkle in her eye and was acting suspicious. Leaning forward, she whispered that she had a surprise for Pearl.

Anticipating a delicious secret, Pearl's eyes lit up. "What is it, what is it?" she asked. A lover of surprises, she had not the slightest guess at what this one could be.

Rebecca made her wait for it, unbearably piquing Pearl's childlike curiosity. Rebecca stepped back to the door and searched down both sides of the hallway. Seeming satisfied that they were alone and that no one was approaching, Rebecca scurried back to Pearl. Then, she pulled a white envelope from her pocket and handed it to Pearl.

Pearl's name was scrawled on the outside of the envelope. She studied the boxy penmanship, but didn't recognize the handwriting. She looked up at Rebecca. Her friend had not sat down, as if she was afraid of being caught with the goods or was preparing to make a quick exit. Rebecca laughed at Pearl's obvious bewilderment. "Open it, silly."

Following Rebecca's instructions, Pearl edged the envelope open, careful not to damage its contents. A letter, written on a small piece of lined notepaper, pulled easily from the envelope. This handwriting she recognized immediately. A blush and a wide smile spread across her face, putting well-needed color back into it. The note was from Sonny. He had disguised his writing on the envelope to conceal the source of the letter from prying nursing staff. Pearl quickly read the message, reread it, and turned to thank Rebecca. But tears welled in her eyes and she couldn't speak.

Rebecca, having forgotten her worries about being discovered, hastened to pull a chair over from Karoline's side of the room. Rebecca sat across from Pearl, her face bubbling with relished excitement. She knew things Pearl was dying to know. "He came by Brambles at noon today, Sonny did, hoping to see you. He rode the city bus over from his work."

Pearl smiled and wiped back tears of happiness. Before long, though, an uncomfortable thought occurred to her. "Oh dear, I hope Sonny got back to work on time. I don't want him to lose his job."

Rebecca patted Pearl's arm. "I think he caught the bus back in plenty of time. Kenny Holmes got a hold of him when he entered the lunchroom. He wanted to be the first to give him any news we had. He didn't even give Sonny a chance to sit down."

The women exchanged a knowing look, and Pearl laughed appreciatively. "What did Kenny tell Sonny?"

"Kenny told him you'd taken ill, had the flu or something. Naturally, Sonny was sad to hear that and downhearted with missing you." Rebecca tapped a finger on the letter in Pearl's hands. "He had this letter all written out and was handing it over to Kenny to deliver to you when I snatched it away from them. Who knows where it would have ended up if loudmouth Holmesy got his hands on it. He would have read it and then blabbed what Sonny had written as well. You know, big man with big news and all. I stuck it in my pocket and, of course, I didn't read it."

Pearl believed Rebecca when she said she hadn't read it. Wanting to share what Sonny had written, Pearl turned the note toward Rebecca. "Look, he's taped his picture to the message. He says he misses me terribly, and he hopes I've not forgotten him. He wants me to write back."

Rebecca eagerly took the letter and read it. "He says not to give up hope." She smiled at Pearl as she handed the letter back to her. "That sounds like something you'd say." Then, she tilted her head to one side, and her expression took on a concerned look. "You've not given up hope yet, have you?"

Pearl shook her head. "No, of course not. Now tell me, did Sonny say anything else? I want to hear everything."

"No, I'm afraid not. After Sonny found out you weren't there and had delivered the letter, he hightailed it out of Brambles before the guard caught him looking for you. I'm sure he made it back to work in plenty of time."

Out of the blue, a cart rattled in the hallway. The two women froze, staring at each other. Rebecca was the first to breathe, to react. Frantically, she whispered, "Put the note away, put it away." She hurriedly stood up to leave, but looked down, and then quickly smoothed over the pockets of her housecoat. She was destroying any residual evidence of the envelope having been there. They would later giggle at almost getting caught passing notes like schoolgirls. But Pearl slipped Sonny's letter into the desk drawer just as Shelby entered the room. She left a cart filled with afternoon medication outside the door.

Shelby looked pleasantly surprised to see Pearl up and sitting at the desk. There was something else there too, but Pearl didn't know what to make of it.

Shelby glanced at both women. "I didn't mean to barge in on you girls. I just wanted to see how my patient is recovering. You must be feeling better, Pearl."

"How nice of you to check on me. I am feeling better, thank you."

Rebecca yawned nonchalantly. "That's okay, I was just leaving. I'm going to catch a little nap before dinner. It's been a long day." She yawned again and extended her arms in an animated stretch.

Shelby turned her back and set about checking Pearl's temperature with an ear thermometer. Pearl looked over Shelby's shoulder to say good night to Rebecca. "Thanks for everything. I mean, for stopping in. Sleep tight and don't let the bed bugs bite."

Grinning, Rebecca shot her friend a conspiratorial wink

before leaving the room.

Shelby checked the thermometer, and then she gave Pearl an appraising look. "This is odd. Your temperature reading is actually low. Sometimes these ear thermometers aren't as accurate as we'd like them to be. But you look like you're in good spirits, feeling okay." Her voice lifted at the end as if she were making a statement and asking a question.

Knowing that hearing from Sonny had gone a long way to lift her spirits, Pearl was instantly on guard. "I'm sure I'm on the mend."

Shelby gave her an odd look, leaving Pearl to wonder if she had somehow found out about the letter. Perhaps Kenny had told Nurse Shelby, she thought, or maybe it had just gotten back to her from him telling everybody else.

To ease the guilt and tension she felt from being so secretive, Pearl told Shelby that she intended to brave the heat and go to the concert. She would be leaving in a few hours with Matthew. Shelby said it was up to her, but she thought Pearl should stay in another day, just to be sure she was over the virus. Pearl began to relax. Maybe that was it. Nurse Shelby didn't know about the letter. She was just being cautious for Pearl having been ill all week.

She was relieved when Shelby finally left to continue her patient rounds. When Shelby was gone, Pearl pulled out the letter. She unfolded it like a lost treasure. Sonny's picture struck her hard, hitting deep in her heart. She lovingly ran her fingers over his face. Then, she pulled it carefully from the letter to dislodge the tape, but not rip the paper. She pressed the picture to her face. Sniffing the letter, she imagined some scent of Sonny's cologne there. She ran her fingers over the writing, feeling comfort in knowing that Sonny had put pen to hand and ink on paper. There was peace in doing these things, knowing that Sonny was thinking of her. In spirit, they were still together.

She was lost in these private thoughts, rereading Sonny's letter, when she had another scare. She heard Shelby talking to someone in the hallway outside her room. Pearl had barely enough time to shoot the note beneath her robe before Shelby passed her door, not coming in at all.

Whew, that was a close call. She couldn't take too much more of that. Pearl tried to get up from the desk, but having risen too fast, she felt faint. She was shaking, perhaps from all the excitement. She sat back down. She stayed in the chair a moment, and then she rose again, with more caution this time. Steadying herself, she maneuvered her way across the room. She leaned on the chair and along the bed, until she got where she wanted to go. There she reached down and hid Sonny's letter beneath the bed in her box of treasures.

Chapter Twenty-Six

Matthew had just stepped back into his office when the phone rang. It was Jordana returning his call, and he took that as a positive sign. If she didn't care about Pearl, she certainly wouldn't have called to check on her. Just the sound of her voice kept him smiling throughout the conversation; well, most of it anyway.

"Your call is good timing. I just looked in on Pearl."

"How is she doing today?"

Jordana sounded apprehensive. He didn't know if it was because of him or Pearl. Still, just the sound of her voice made him smile. "She was sitting at her desk reading a book."

"That's a good sign." He could hear a smile in her voice.

Her apprehension, he thought, must've only been concern for Pearl. It had nothing to do with him. He thought *that* was a good sign. "Yeah, she still looks a little weak, but she says she's well enough to go to the concert. I think she has a bit of cabin fever after so much bed rest. She's anxious to go to the park."

"Do you know what was wrong with her?"

A little embarrassed, he wondered whether his call to Jordana had been premature. Pearl must've only had a twenty-four-hour bug. Well, he thought, it was a good excuse to talk to Jordana. Besides, he had told her that he would call about the concert. He said, "I'm sorry if I alarmed you for nothing. It seems she just had the flu. I'm sure she's going to be fine once she gets her strength back."

"That's good to hear. Well, I just thought I'd call and check on her." It sounded like she was ready to wrap up the conversation.

Before she could hang up, he asked, "What about you? Are you coming to the concert?"

"I'm afraid not."

"Do you mind if I ask why?"

"I just don't think it's something I can do right now. It's just not for me."

"Pearl would love to have you along. She's hoping you'll come." He'd try anything to get a relative in Pearl's life. Even guilt. Now he was thinking about Pearl, forgetting his own agenda.

"No, I'm sorry, Matthew." She was going to hang up.

He tried to hide his disappointment. Still, in a last-ditch effort of hope, he said, "Well, if you change your mind, the van will be leaving Glory Heights' parking lot at 6:45."

Jordana said, "I have to go." Then she hung up.

He sat back in his chair, bummed. All he had to do was talk Jordana into attending the concert, yet he had failed miserably. Failed Pearl. He'd ruined his other big ideas too. After the concert ended, the night would still be young. He had planned to invite Jordana to the Aquatennial Block Party. The outdoor festivities offered several stages with bands, lots of food kiosks, and great people watching. It was an easy atmosphere just made for getting to know her better.

By late afternoon, Matthew couldn't wait any longer. He had packed up his briefcase for the weekend, done the unheard of by cleaning off his desk, and then stood staring out the window for the past ten minutes. The last really was a waste of time. With nothing left to do, he really needed to get going. He had to go home, pack up the cooler, blankets, and bug spray, then grab something to eat and be back at Glory Heights in an hour to assemble the gang for the concert in the park. Only a handful of residents were going. He really didn't need a second chaperone, but for Pearl's sake, he hadn't told Jordana that. He was hoping Jordana would come walking through his office door, but that wasn't happening. With no sign of her, he regretfully left his office and went home to prepare for the outing.

He parked his Honda in the circle in front of Glory Heights behind a company-owned minivan and began transferring the cooler and other supplies into it. With a July heat index of 100 degrees, most of the residents had chosen to stay indoors with the air conditioning. Only five were enthusiastic enough about going to the concert to brave the heat wave. He could hear their excited chatter, impatiently waiting for him. They were lining up just inside the building.

Matthew was wearing walking shorts and a light-weave golf shirt, opened at the neck. He had hoped to be comfortably dressed for the evening. But while loading the van, he had already broken into a heavy sweat. Sam, a well-liked driver for Glory Heights, was sitting in the van. He turned the air conditioner on full blast while Matthew loaded. When Matthew had finished, he leaned into the van and let the coolness still the beads of sweat dripping from his forehead. For a moment, he had a break from the smothering, hot humidity. For another moment, he wondered at the sense of going out in this oven.

Being an eternal optimist, he hadn't told Pearl of Jordana's decision not to attend the concert. He was still hoping that Jordana would change her mind and show up at the last minute. However, with no sign of Jordana, he wished he'd told Pearl about it earlier. She would be so disappointed, and Matthew hated that. What with being sick, missing Sonny, and now this, Matthew felt sorry for her.

She didn't deserve any more bad news. He was going to delay delivering it as long as possible. In so doing, he recounted what he had packed in the van: a cooler filled with pop, a bag with an assortment of chips, and two blankets to sit on the grass with. There really wasn't all that much to count. He slid the van door closed. Like a forlorn puppy, he scanned the road for any sign of a red Mustang hightailing it into the parking lot, but there was no such luck. He stuck his hands in his pockets, hung his head in the uncomfortable feeling of dejection, and walked up the steps.

The queued up concert goers cheered when he opened the doors. Matthew took a handkerchief from his pocket, swabbed sweat off his face, and donned a smile. He wanted to put a positive slant on the group's night out, especially Pearl's, after he explained why Jordana wasn't there.

He prepared to count five heads and then give a set of instructions to the group for an orderly and enjoyable evening, but only four people were in the lobby. Pearl was missing. He wondered where she was. Had she suffered a relapse, or a seizure? Was she running late? He began to ask the others if they knew where she was when something beyond the reception desk caught his attention. Something beautiful. A smile spread across his face, and he went to meet her.

Pearl was dressed in a sleeveless blue print shirt and matching cotton shorts. Her skinny white arms and knobby-kneed legs glared in contrast against the blue. She was wearing a smile as big as Matthew's, her helmet, and a touch of makeup for the special occasion. She walked carefully toward him with one hand moving along the wall for support. Her other hand was clasped tightly around Jordana.

The two women continued toward Matthew. Feeling a tremendous sense of relief, he opened his arms wide in greetings, his excitement bubbling over. "Hey, it's great to see both of you! I'll warn you right now, it's hot out there, but we're going to try and ignore the heat and have a great time anyway. We'll find a shade tree to sit under." He felt like a gushing idiot, but he didn't care much. He was just happy to see Jordana. He didn't know why she changed her mind, and he wasn't going to ask her about it now. He was only glad that she had.

He couldn't help staring at Jordana. Her tan legs stretching out from khaki shorts. Her delicate arms in a sleeveless knit tank top, the stripes of the shirt enhancing her bodice. The strappy sandals revealing painted nails in hot pink. He looked into her blue eyes, at her face, and his heart did a double take at the smile he found there. He could've lingered there forever, but Pearl, having reached the end of the hallway, grabbed his hand for support.

Matthew helped Pearl into line behind the others, with Jordana pulled alongside, as Pearl would not let go of her niece's hand. He caught Pearl's eye and winked. She smiled with her eyes as much as with her lips, and he saw the cheer in her heart mixed with the fatigue of the last few days. He suspected she wasn't 100 percent over the flu, but she would not admit it now for the life of her.

He placed Pearl in line and smiled warmly at Jordana. Then he jolted, as if remembering the others. In his enchantment with Jordana, he had almost forgotten them. He turned to find all of them solemnly, yet curiously, staring at Jordana and Pearl. Pearl lifted her chin and grinned back at them, beaming with pride. She let go of Matthew's hand to hold onto Jordana with both hands. As Pearl addressed the group, a joyful coloring fell over her face, from her neck to the edge of her helmet. "This is my niece, Jordana. She's going to the concert with us. She's my niece," she repeated proudly, gripping Jordana's hand possessively.

At the attention bestowed upon her, Jordana's face flushed pink and her neck began spotting with color. Her eyes met Matthew's, and he comforted her unease with a smile and a nod of appreciation for Pearl's pride in her.

After Matthew delivered the short set of instructions for the outing that included staying together as a group, and the handling of treats and bathroom breaks, they all headed outside. Paying no mind to the temperature, they scurried down the front steps of Glory Heights and into the cool van. Matthew had taken the lead, boarding the bus first, and Jordana took up the back with Pearl, who hadn't let go of her hand. Jordana placed a hand at Pearl's elbow, offering more support as she wobbled up the steps. Pearl managed okay; her enthusiasm seemed to provide the necessary motoring mechanisms. Jordana climbed up behind her, but she came up short when Pearl abruptly stopped at the top of the steps. She had something to tell the driver. "Sam, I want you to meet Jordana. She's my niece. She's going to the concert with us."

Sam peeked around Pearl to say hello to Jordana. Then he turned to Pearl. "Well, that's real good, Pearl, real good. You go ahead and take a seat now, any one you want. It's not often I get to drive you around."

Satisfied that everyone knew who Jordana was, Pearl moved to the back of the bus, pulling Jordana with her. That ended any hope Matthew had of sitting next to her.

Jordana and Pearl sat on the blanket, the music a mere backdrop to their quiet conversation. Jordana filled Pearl in on her life, even giving out tidbits of information about her relationship with her mother. Pearl had listened so intently that Jordana found herself telling her about the recent breakup with Ryan. Pearl reacted with murmurs of empathy and her firm belief that Jordana could have her pick of men.

Then it was Jordana's turn to listen as Pearl described how she missed "her Sonny." "Sonny knows how to take care of me. He holds me tight when I have a seizure and looks at me differently than others do. He doesn't see my seizures as part of me, or if he does, he accepts them as such. That means a lot to me. He buys me pretty things, too, like this barrette." With an embarrassed look, Pearl tapped her helmet. "It's under here."

Jordana followed Pearl's hand with her eyes. "Do you have to wear that often?"

Pearl nodded, reluctantly. "Any time I go out. It keeps me from banging my head if I should have a seizure." She shrugged and admitted, "It's such a humiliating thing, to have to wear a helmet. Especially out in public." Tears welled in her eyes, emphasizing not only her words, but also the peripheral view others had for "people like her."

Shamefully, Jordana hung her head. She was initially surprised to hear that wearing the helmet embarrassed Aunt Pearl. Then Jordana immediately knew her mistake. Why wouldn't that be embarrassing? She would be embarrassed, too, what with everyone staring just as she had done a few moments ago. Aunt Pearl was no different from her. Yet Jordana had been blind to her feelings, as if they didn't exist, as if Aunt Pearl had willingly accepted her lot in life, and therefore had no feelings about it. Jordana wanted to reach out to her, to hug her, to tell her she was sorry for her pain. And to apologize for Mother.

Pearl seemed to know Jordana's thoughts. She lifted a finger to Jordana's chin and gently pulled her head up. "It's not your fault. Life's not fair for anybody. I've had to bear this burden. My epilepsy. It's gotten easier since I met Sonny, or at least it had been easier. I just wanted to make a life for myself and him. I still intend to do that. Somehow."

Jordana looked into her aunt's eyes and saw the determination. If Aunt Pearl received help, maybe it could be done. She would need to overcome obstacles of titanic proportions. Jordana couldn't begin to know what they all were. Then, she didn't know if she should ask, if she was being too personal, but she wanted to know. "Do you have seizures often?"

"Several time a week, but I think they're getting better. I've been taking my medicine better. I promised Matthew I would do that if he got Sonny over to see me. I've not seen Sonny since they took him away from me."

Again, the despondency in Aunt Pearl's voice raked over Jordana's heart. She knew who "they" were. She wondered how Mother lived with herself, with her baseness. Then she looked over to Matthew who was sitting on the other blanket, watching the band play. The music was quite good for a city band. They were playing show tunes with a few classical hits thrown in for variety. Maybe Jordana would talk to him and find out what the status was on Sonny. It would have to be after the concert, when she could have a private word with him.

She didn't want Aunt Pearl to overhear the conversation in case it turned out bad. Aunt Pearl wasn't letting Jordana out of her sight. Jordana was surprised to find that she didn't mind it. She didn't think she deserved the attention, but Aunt Pearl's innocent devotion touched her heart in a way that made turning away inconceivable.

They had said good night to Pearl, who would let Jordana leave only after promising in front of Matthew to come back and see her again soon. Jordana acquiesced, if only to get Pearl inside the building and back in bed where they all thought she belonged. Pearl had looked as if she could barely stand up a moment longer. Jordana walked Pearl to her room while Matthew waited out front for her. He was enjoying the evening air, which had cooled down to a comfortable temperature.

Jordana had parked her car in the lot on the backside of Glory Heights, which explained why Matthew hadn't seen it earlier. He intended to walk her to it. He was going to ask her to the Block Party. He wished he had some idea of what she would say, but he didn't. As he pondered this, Jordana came through the front doors, her long hair swaying around her shoulders. "Wow, I must've worn Aunt Pearl out. She was asleep almost before her head hit the pillow. A nurse came in to give her medicine and some warm milk, then pow, she zonked out."

Matthew had never seen Jordana so animated, and he was enjoying it. They started walking to her car, and he was thankful that she didn't object to the escort. So far so good. "You two seemed to have hit it off tonight."

Jordana turned her head to him and he caught the sweet scent of her perfume. "Yeah, it was kind of nice. She's so real." She turned her head away, and then she shrugged her shoulders as if she didn't know what else to say about it.

Matthew understood. "I know what you mean. She's a caring person. Strong too, although you might not suspect it."

Jordana stopped at her car and leaned against it, as if this time she was in no hurry to leave. "I'm beginning to find that out."

Matthew wanted to ask her about the party. He hesitated,

but then he decided to go for it. "I was wondering, since it's still early," Matthew looked at his watch, as if to prove that the night was still young, and then asked, "Would you like to go down to the Block Party with me?"

She hesitated, and his heart sunk.

"Well, it's funny you should ask. I thought about going to some Aquatennial events this weekend. My boyfriend—"

Matthew perked up. "You have a boyfriend?"

Jordana laughed, "Let me rephrase that. My ex-boyfriend. He dumped me this week, and I decided to celebrate by keeping busy. That's why I came tonight. I couldn't think of a good reason not to, and there was someone here who needed me."

Matthew liked the sound of her laughter. He hated to interrupt her explanation but, relieved to know that there was no longer a boyfriend, he had to ask, "So does that mean you'll go with me?"

Jordana laughed again, this time at his boyish eagerness. "Well, yeah, I guess so. Under one condition."

Matthew could hardly keep from pounding his fist into the air with a great big "yes," but maintaining his composure, he asked what the trade-off was. Whatever it was, he knew he was going to do it.

Still smiling, but with a serious tone, she laid it on him. "Get Sonny in to see Aunt Pearl. Soon. As soon as possible."

Although he was reveling in his good fortune of Jordana consenting to go out with him, for a moment his thoughts held a glint of concern. It passed, and he smiled at her. "Between you and your Aunt Pearl, I don't know who drives a harder bargain. But I can see there's only one thing left for me to do: buy you a drink and swear Pearl will see Sonny next week."

Jordana looked as if she wasn't sure she could believe him. "Promise?"

Matthew spoke confidently. "Promise."

Jordana held out her hand. "Deal."

"Deal."

Chapter Twenty-Seven

When Pearl woke up Saturday morning, three things struck her. The first was the dull ache in her chest, reminding her of how much she missed Sonny. The second was the wonderful memory of being with Jordana at the concert the night before. The third was the heavy fatigue returning to her, impressing upon her that Nurse Shelby must've known what she was talking about. She had advised Pearl to stay in one more day.

Pearl tried to get out of bed, and then she tried to stand up. But she was too weak. Her limbs were too heavy. She fell to the floor, clutching the bed linens for support, but only dragging them down with her. She thought, I must be having a relapse. Her reflexes were functioning worse than usual. And her eyes moved spasmodically, making it difficult to balance even as she leaned against the bed, trying to pull herself back up to it. The muscles in her body seemed to have a mind of their own. She struggled to her feet, then lay back, and pulling her legs with her hands, shifted herself onto the bed. Her body stiffened, and she started to shiver. With great effort, she crawled beneath the sheets and awkwardly pulled a blanket up over her shoulders. For once she wished Glory Heights would turn the air conditioner off. The cold air added to the hard, icy texture of her skin. Pearl could understand having a fever along with the flu, but her body temperature seemed to be dropping.

She would have to buzz for a nurse to bring breakfast and her phenobarbital. Sick or not, she was determined to keep up her end of the bargain with Matthew by taking her medicine on time. On second thought, maybe she would skip breakfast. She really couldn't eat a thing. When the room started spinning, she thought how ridiculous it was to be thinking about eating. Her mouth felt dry. All she needed was something warm to drink. She reached for the call button. It seemed so far away. Had someone moved it? She tried shifting, but nothing moved. Her strength was waning. Her limbs were too heavy, as if pulling her down and away from the button. A frantic, electrifying moment of knowing she wouldn't reach it came over her. She was right. With one last erratic flutter of her eyelids, Pearl fell into unconsciousness.

Charlotte had just come on duty and was looking through the patient charts for information on Pearl's health status. Failing to find a current report, she rechecked the charts. Perhaps someone had misfiled it. Still not finding it, she surmised that the rotating nurse on morning duty had kept Pearl's chart with her. Well, she thought, it couldn't hurt to stop by Pearl's room to check on her ex-patient's recuperation.

Charlotte peeked her head inside the room and found Pearl lying on the bed. She tapped at the doorway, not wanting to wake Pearl if she was asleep. The way Pearl lay stretched across the bed didn't look right. Charlotte stepped into the room to get a closer look at her, but before she reached the bed she knew something was wrong. Pearl's skin was blue. Charlotte immediately reached out to her. Pearl was cold to the touch. Her arm was stretched out across the bed with one finger nearly touching the nurse call button. Charlotte felt her mouth go dry. If that wasn't frightening enough, her forearm was swelling with blood-red blisters.

Charlotte promptly pulled Pearl onto her back and felt Pearl's wrist to see if she had a pulse, when at the pressure of her fingers on Pearl's skin another unsightly blister rose up. Worse,

Charlotte couldn't find a pulse. She wiped away the perspiration on her own upper lip and then moved her fingers to another area of Pearl's wrist, being careful not to puncture the blister. Again, she felt, she waited, but still, there was no pulse. She studied Pearl's chest. There was no movement.

She swallowed her panic and switched her fingers to Pearl's neck. Charlotte cried out, "Come on, girlfriend, come on! Where's your pulse, girl? Let me have it!" Then she said, "Hang in there, girlfriend!" She found a barely audible heartbeat. She turned and ran from Pearl's room to the nurses' station. She grabbed the PA system's microphone from the wall and paged a code red.

Paramedics came running. Charlotte waved her hands in the direction they needed to go. "It's Pearl Witherby. Go! Go!" Yelling to the medics, she explained Pearl's condition. At the same time, she picked up the phone and dialed Doctor Sotto's emergency number. The paramedics flew past her, taking in her speculations, continuously moving toward Pearl's room. The call connected. An operator paged Doctor Sotto. Charlotte tapped her foot on the tile floor, waiting for him to answer. Vital seconds passed. Finally, Doctor Sotto erupted on the other end of the line.

Doctor Sotto directed that they transfer Pearl to Mercy Hospital, immediately. The paramedics were already on it, whirring by, heading for the ambulance parked at a side entrance to Glory Heights. Charlotte yelled after them, "Take her to Mercy. Sotto says Mercy. He'll meet us there." Then, Charlotte herself tore down the hall. She was going along. Something smelled fishy. Pearl had more than a flu bug. She feared Pearl's symptoms were those of a fatal barbiturate overdose. Phenobarbital, a barbiturate, was a controlled substance at Glory Heights, administered only by nursing staff in supposedly the proper doses.

Had Pearl done something to hurt herself? Had someone else done this to her? Charlotte couldn't be sure. She would watch over Pearl until they figured it out—of that she was very sure.

Chapter Twenty-Eight

Pearl lay frozen in a coma at Mercy Hospital with IV lines running up her arms and through her veins. A layer of blankets snugly swathed her body in an attempt to raise its subnormal temperature. Charlotte pulled Pearl's arm from beneath the linens to recheck her vitals. The blisters spattering the insides of her arms and wrists looked better. They weren't as swollen or red, and her skin was warmer and suppler than when Charlotte first found her passed out on her bed at Glory Heights.

Matthew was sitting on the room's extra hospital bed, his eyes anxiously trained on Charlotte. She nodded, and smiled reassuringly. "Better," she said.

Satisfied that Pearl's blood pressure and pulse were improving, although not yet normalized, Charlotte tucked her arm back beneath the blanket. She then watched Pearl's pale face, her closed, sunken eyes, for any sign of coming to. There was none. Charlotte was worried about her; something had gone terribly wrong. She sighed heavily, giving Pearl's shoulder an affectionate stroke. Doctor Sotto arrived just then, and Charlotte stepped out of his way. He would attend to Pearl now.

With nothing more Charlotte could do for Pearl, she thought she'd better call Shelby with an update. She had to keep reminding herself that she wasn't Pearl's nurse anymore. Although, she thought, under her watch this wouldn't have happened to Pearl. Whatever *this* was—they didn't know yet. Not that she was ready to blame Shelby for Pearl's malady. So far, all Charlotte had were suspicions.

Matthew was looking downhearted. She couldn't do anything for him, either. He'd called Jordana, and she was on her way. Nothing much left to do but wait for Jordana to arrive, and Pearl to wake up.

Charlotte left the room in search of a phone. A nearby visitors' lounge was empty, and a phone was on a table next to a sofa. She called the nurses' station and had Shelby paged. While she waited, she prepared herself for Shelby telling her to return to Glory Heights. Her mind filled with potential arguments: Mercy's nursing staff was quite capable of caring for Pearl; being her nurse, Shelby would come to the hospital herself; Matthew was there and that was enough. Charlotte didn't have a good defense for any of them; she only knew she wanted to stay with Pearl.

Shelby came on the line and said, "Charlotte, what's going on with Pearl?" She sounded worried.

"We don't know yet. Doctor Sotto is with her now, and she's still in a coma."

There was silence, then came a weak, "Oh, dear."

Charlotte thought that Shelby seemed as concerned for Pearl as she was. This realization made Charlotte feel a bit guilty for her suspicions. She said, "I know, it doesn't look good. But let's not lose hope."

Shelby was quiet again for a moment. Then she said, "I know it's a lot to ask, but would you mind staying there with Pearl?"

Charlotte couldn't believe her good luck. She didn't understand it, but she wasn't going to question it either. "I'd like to stay with her." Grateful that it had worked out in her favor, she felt compelled to thank the nurse. "I appreciate it."

"No," Shelby said quietly, "thank you."

Nurse Charlotte thought of something: maybe Shelby

could provide some insight into Pearl's illness. "Do you have any idea what happened to Pearl?"

Shelby hesitated, but finally she said, "I just don't know."

Her hesitation was just long enough to raise Charlotte's suspicions again. She decided to put it all out there for Shelby. "I think Pearl has an overdose of barbiturates in her bloodstream."

Shelby gasped, "How could that be?"

"I don't know, but if it's something we should've prevented, there may be lawsuits."

"I just hope Pearl recovers soon." Shelby seemed sincere, but Charlotte thought she heard something else in her voice, too. It might've been fear.

Charlotte hung up, remembering something she'd heard through the powerful rumor mill at Glory Heights. The gossip was that Shelby was sleeping with the warden. It seemed unlikely that the two would plot to sedate Pearl to keep her from running away again. They would lose their jobs, go to jail, for sedating someone without a doctor's prescription. Yet, something was going on, and Charlotte wanted to find out what it was. Only then could she save Pearl from it.

When Charlotte arrived back at the room, Doctor Sotto was gone and Matthew was slumped in a chair at the end of the bed. He seemed lost in his own thoughts. Charlotte considered telling him about her suspicions, but she decided it would be better to wait for Doctor Sotto's prognosis. She leaned restlessly against the wall, tapping her foot.

The movement brought Matthew out of his reverie. "Is Pearl doing any better?" He sounded nervous, more than he would probably have liked to let on.

Charlotte looked at Doctor Sotto's notes in Pearl's bedside chart. "Some. Her body temperature hasn't stabilized yet, but it's improved." There wasn't much else to say about it.

"I hope Jordana can find the hospital okay," Matthew said. "She's not familiar with the area, but I gave her directions along with the hospital's phone number in case she runs into a problem."

He seemed anxious for her to arrive, although Charlotte thought it was too soon to worry about it. He seemed to want to talk, so Charlotte listened.

Immediately after hearing the news about Pearl, he called Jordana. He'd just caught her. They'd made plans at the Block Party the night before to go rollerblading around Lake Harriet, and when he called, she was just leaving her house to meet him.

Charlotte was happily registering what he'd just told her—They'd gone on a date!—when Jordana flew into the room. She was dressed in a cobalt blue jog bra, jogging shorts, and running shoes. Her face and neck were a pink glow.

Matthew quickly rose to greet her, checking his watch. "Jordana, you made good time. You must've busted speed limits to get here so fast."

Jordana didn't answer right away. Rushing to Pearl's bedside, she leaned over and looked into her aunt's face. She ran a hand over Pearl's forehead before looking up. "I guess I did. The hardest part was finding the room."

She glanced at Charlotte, then over to Matthew, as if she didn't know whom to address. "Is Aunt Pearl still unconscious? I've never seen anyone in a coma before. It looks like she's only sleeping."

Charlotte stepped forward, tugging at the hem of her skirt. It had scooted up her thighs as she rested against the wall. "It looks like she's sleeping but, yes, she's still unconscious. We can never know how long a coma will last." Her Southern drawl had come to life under the stressful circumstances.

Jordana looked sharply at Charlotte; the words apparently frightening her. But then she softened her startled reaction with a faint smile. "I'm sorry, I don't think we've met."

Matthew interrupted and made introductions. "I'm sorry, I didn't realize. This is Nurse Charlotte. She used to be Pearl's nurse. It appears she's still looking out for her." He smiled, giving Charlotte a kind, knowing look.

Then he made a swooping motion with his hands from

Charlotte to Jordana. "Nurse Charlotte, this is Jordana. Pearl's niece."

Jordana held her hand out to Charlotte. "So, do we know what's wrong with her? What can be done to wake her up?"

Charlotte's heart warmed. Long-lost niece or not, she spoke to Jordana as she would any member of a patient's family. "Doctor Sotto is Pearl's doctor, the very best doctor. Pearl knows him and likes him. He'll be back soon and you'll meet him. Meanwhile, you should know that he's ordered blood tests to determine the level of phenobarbital in Pearl's blood. Doctor Sotto's preliminary thoughts are that Pearl's had some kind of overdose."

Jordana's baby blues widened and darkened with fear. "An overdose? What kind of overdose?"

Seeing Jordana's distress, Matthew moved closer. He looked as if he wanted to put a comforting arm around her, but he hesitated, and only touched her arm. Charlotte noticed Matthew's tenderness. She let him explain the circumstances to Jordana. Matthew spoke gently. "It may be barbiturates. The medication Pearl takes to control epileptic convulsions is called phenobarbital. It's a barbiturate."

Jordana's face opened up in horror. "She's overdosed on her own medication? The stuff she's been taking for years? I don't understand. How could that happen?" She again looked from Charlotte to Matthew. They looked at each other, not knowing how to respond to this very good question. Seeing that they didn't have an answer, Jordana continued to probe. "Wait a minute. Matthew, you said that Nurse Charlotte *used* to be Aunt Pearl's nurse. Who's her nurse now?"

After Jordana's barrage of questions, Charlotte was eager to drop some kind of hint at what she thought. "Nurse Shelby has been Pearl's nurse for the last couple of weeks." She left it at that, although she was well aware that, in Nurse Shelby's defense, she could've added some qualifying nicety. She opened her mouth to add it, but Doctor Sotto arrived with the test results, saving her from the compromise.

Jordana introduced herself, after which Doctor Sotto confirmed the overdose. Jordana's eyes lit up with anger. "I want to know how this happened."

Doctor Sotto tried to console her. "We all do, and I believe we'll be able to find out what happened once Pearl wakes up. The important thing right now is to get her awake."

With that, they all looked down at Pearl, in tacit agreement of this. The confidence with which Doctor Sotto spoke visibly calmed Jordana. Still, she was eager, as they all were, to get her aunt out of the coma. "Okay, what's next? How do we wake her up?" Jordana rubbed her hands together, ready to get to work.

Doctor Sotto, realizing Jordana's intent to help and her proactive spirit, laughed in appreciation. "We'll talk about that, but there's something else I need to tell you first."

His face turned solemn, and he addressed everyone in the room. "We found something else in Pearl's blood."

The room turned starkly quiet, with only the disjointed lament of Pearl's slumber altering the moment's suspense. Charlotte felt her heart skip a beat. Jordana's face and neck turned a deeper pink. Matthew's face grew more serious. They all leaned forward as if better to hear whatever came next.

"Test results reveal the presence of Seconal along with the phenobarbital that we'd expect to see. Seconal is a sedative used to calm or help people sleep. The two drugs together in her bloodstream caused her to have an overdose. They are both barbiturates, both sedatives, but Pearl has no prescription for Seconal as she does for phenobarbital." Doctor Sotto stopped for a moment, took a deep breath, and let everyone absorb the bad news. As if this bomb of information, of what it inferred, was too much for anyone to yet comprehend the significance of, everyone remained silent, waiting for him to continue. "Having both of these drugs in her system at the same time was too much for her, would be too much for anyone to take. And as we've just discussed, at this time, we don't know how it happened. That is, how the Seconal got into her bloodstream. Or why," he added.

Matthew and Jordana spoke at the same time: "Oh, my God." They were obviously both at a loss for other words. Charlotte felt her dark skin turn an angry hue, but she found her tongue. She was just deciding whether she should bite it. However, before she could assert her thoughts, Jordana found her voice.

Most likely left with no coping skills of this magnitude, Jordana reverted to the best ones she had: her objective business acumen. "Okay, first things first. We'll find out how it happened, as you said, but what are we doing to get her awake, so she can talk to us? You said we'd be able to figure this out if she could talk to us." She looked at Doctor Sotto, expecting an answer. However, before he could respond, another thought appeared to be brewing inside of her. She whisked hair off her neck and shook it out as if she'd grown unbearably warm. "She's not going to die, is she?"

Seeing the emotion on Jordana's face, Matthew moved closer to her. This time he put his arm around her. They both stared at Doctor Sotto, waiting for his answer.

Doctor Sotto looked at them with his warm empathetic eyes, and said, "I do not believe Pearl is going to die, but she is very sick. Have faith, I think we caught this, whatever this turns out to be, in time."

Charlotte wasn't as frightened, anymore; Pearl had been improving. However, she needed to confirm for herself that Pearl was still improving and began rechecking Pearl's vital signs. After a few minutes of checking, she let out a sigh of relief and moved aside to let Doctor Sotto examine Pearl.

He listened to her heart, and then he checked for eye movement under her closed lid. He pulled the covers off of Pearl's shoulders to look at the sores. He drew in a deep breath. "I've given Pearl an IV to flush out the excessive sedatives. She's already improved from when she first arrived." He looked at Charlotte.

She smiled and said, "Pearl's temperature is back to normal."

Doctor Sotto was about to continue when Jordana cried out, "What are those?" She was pointing at the blood blisters.

Doctor Sotto finished examining Pearl's arm, and then he placed it back under the bed linens. He calmly explained to Jordana that blood blisters were symptoms of a barbiturate overdose.

"The sores look better, they've shrunk in size. And Pearl's body temperature has risen to normal. Now we wait for her to wake up. Pray that she will do it soon.

"But to answer your original question, I believe Pearl is out of danger. If she wakes up soon, she has an excellent chance of a quick and full recovery."

Jordana let out the breath she was holding. "Can she hear us?"

Doctor Sotto wasn't sure about that. "It's a possibility. Some believe that a person in a coma can hear. I advise you to speak to her, to encourage her to come out of it."

No one knew what else to say. They stood around Pearl's bed in silence, all wishing the same thing. Then, as if Pearl understood their wish, she rocked her head back and forth across the pillow. Doctor Sotto spoke first, calling her name. "Pearl, it's Doctor Sotto. Pearl, can you hear me?"

What happened next gave them hope. Pearl began struggling against the bed linens tucked tightly around her body. She was trying to get up. A violent rock to the left loosened the bedding. She rose on her elbows and opened her eyes. Jordana and Matthew started talking to her at once.

"Aunt Pearl, wake up, it's Jordana."

"Hey, Pearl, stay with us now. Come on, Pearl. It's Matthew."

Doctor Sotto and Charlotte had seen what Jordana and Matthew didn't. Pearl's dark pupils were unfocused, nebulous. There was nothing behind them. No recognition and no thought.

Suddenly, Pearl turned toward Jordana and moved her head, as if looking into Jordana's face. Jordana gasped and threw her hand over her mouth to squelch her emotions. She'd seen it. The eyes looked straight through her.

The others continued to talk to Pearl, to rub her hand, to stimulate her back to consciousness, but it was useless. After a minute's time, Pearl lay back down and closed her eyes, still imprisoned in the grips of a coma.

Jordana stood up and stretched her arms over her head. It felt good to move, although it wasn't enough to relieve the stiffness from sitting in a hospital chair for the past two days. She wanted a bath and a change of clothing. Other than running out to her car and grabbing an old tee shirt from the back seat to throw over her sports bra, she was wearing the same clothes she had arrived in on Saturday morning. Yet all that took a back seat to seeing Pearl regain consciousness. In the aftermath of the one false alarm, Jordana had experienced an odd combination of horror and hope. The eerie blank orbs, suggesting that Pearl had no awareness of having risen in bed, had devastated Jordana. It also gave her the unscientific optimism that if Pearl's body could reach out, so, eventually, would her mind.

It had only been an hour since Charlotte and Matthew had gone to their homes for some much-needed sleep and changes of clothes. Matthew had been a perfect gentleman at the Block Party Friday night while proving to be an intriguing date. She liked him more than she wanted to admit. When he suggested that she go home with him from the hospital—to take a break from the sheer exhaustion of holding sentry at Pearl's bedside—she knew he meant it in the sincerest sense of the proposal. However, she hadn't wanted to leave. Jordana wanted to be there when Pearl woke up.

She was tired and her body ached. Matthew and Charlotte, whom she'd come to know and like after spending so much time together, weren't in any better condition than she was. They could've taken turns stretching out on the room's second hospital bed, but no one wanted to sleep if the others were awake. The three were in this together, though no one had uttered the words. There was no need. Now Jordana wouldn't climb onto it for fear that she would go to sleep and Pearl would wake up while she was dozing. The odds seemed to work that way, she mused. Then the absurdity of her thoughts occurred to her. She realized that if she thought Pearl would wake up if she went to sleep, then maybe she should go to sleep. Aah. Frustrated and weary, she rubbed her fists against her eyes. This is ridiculous, she thought. I'm so tired I'm not making any sense, and I'm too worried to sleep.

Determined to revive herself, Jordana went into the bathroom and found a washcloth and a bar of Ivory soap. The bathroom smelled like disinfectant. It was the same way Pearl's hospital room smelled when she had first arrived. But after four people without showers, one of them oblivious to bodily functions, had shared the room for two days, the room no longer smelled that way. Maybe Jordana had just become numb to its scent.

Jordana washed her face, enjoying the cool, rough terrycloth rubbing against her skin. She washed beneath her sports bra and then around her neck and shoulders, pressing the cloth into her, awakening her senses, peeling off the worried skin with the refreshing exfolient. Feeling renewed, she went back into the room. In her purse, she found a small bottle of Trésor perfume, which she sprayed along her body. She then sprayed it into the room, hoping to alleviate some of the staleness that had transpired there.

When a nurse passed by the room, Jordana stopped her and asked where she could get a cup of coffee. Graciously, the nurse brought her a cup. Now she stared out the window watching birds flutter and wispy clouds float by in the light-blue sky. She sipped the hot acidic coffee and reflected on what was happening to Pearl.

The first thing that came to mind, that had flitted through it several times in the last forty-eight hours, was her mother. If someone had been sedating Pearl without a doctor's prescriptions, could Mother have ordered it? And if she did, why would anyone carry it out? Maybe it was to better control Aunt Pearl, in effect to keep her down, and too much of it combined with the phenobarbital had driven her unconscious. It seemed unlikely that Aunt Pearl had sedated herself.

After Doctor Sotto told them about the test results, Charlotte had pointed out that Seconal was a controlled substance requiring a prescription to obtain it. Doctor Sotto said that some patients had a prescription for Seconal. Aunt Pearl would had to have taken doses prescribed for someone else at Glory Heights.

That left a couple of options open. In contemplating suicide, perhaps Aunt Pearl had talked someone else into saving up and handing over his or her doses. Or, maybe Aunt Pearl had found access to another patient's prescription for Seconal, and stolen it for her own use, which could have been part of a suicide plan. She might have even taken it to ease her pain over the loss of Sonny from her life.

Jordana didn't believe Aunt Pearl had tried to kill herself. She still longed to marry Sonny. She also didn't seem like the type of person who would deal with her pain by numbing it with drugs. She had too much hope for a better life, hope that someone else was attempting to squash.

An unexpected rustling coming up behind her interrupted her thoughts. She turned to find a man she had never seen before shuffling his way over to Aunt Pearl. Instinctively, Jordana folded her arms around herself. He was dressed in an unfashionable wide-striped, button-down shirt with long sleeves, and work pants. The outfit struck Jordana as odd for a hot summer morning. He was carrying a small bouquet of flowers, the kind displayed in a grocery store kiosk.

When he saw Jordana, he stopped. He looked as surprised to see her as she was to see him. At first neither of them said anything. He looked nervous. He looked at Pearl and then back to Jordana. A spark of fear shot through his eyes. She didn't know if it was for Pearl's condition, or something about Jordana that made him flinch. He put a finger to his mouth and gnawed. Looking like he should say something, but not having a clue what, he blurted out, "I came to see Pearl."

Jordana unfolded her arms and stepped forward with an outstretched hand. It had dawned on her who he was. She felt compelled to make him feel welcome. "You must be Sonny. Aunt Pearl's told me a lot about you. I'm Jordana Barlow, her niece."

Relief softened Sonny's face, and he grinned at her. Eager for her kindness, he nervously shifted the flowers from one hand to the other, as if deciding which hand he should use. Then he turned and placed the bouquet on a table, wiped his hands on his pants leg, and extending his right hand, gave Jordana's arm a good yank. "Pleased to meet you. I'm Sonny, all right. Sonny Capshaw. Pearl's my fiancée." He paused and gazed at Pearl with a look that could only be blatant love. Then he asked Jordana if Pearl was going to be okay.

"We sure hope so."

"Rebecca, Pearl's friend from Glory Heights, called me last night. Said she didn't know what was wrong with Pearl. Rebecca only knew that Nurse Charlotte had sent Pearl to Mercy Hospital by ambulance. Said Pearl hadn't come back yet. I was up all night wondering what to do. I'm not supposed to see Pearl, and I was afraid I'd get caught trying to do just that. I hadn't slept all night just worrying about her. Come this morning, I decided to call work and tell them I'd be late. I had to come see my Pearly, see what was going on with her." Abruptly, Sonny smacked his mouth closed, as if he realized his rambling.

Jordana felt sorry for him. He loved Pearl and she him, but no one had called him to let him know Pearl was in the hospital. Someone named Rebecca at that godforsaken place had taken a chance. God bless Rebecca for having the heart and mind to do the right thing.

Jordana explained what had happened to Pearl. Then, smiling amicably at Sonny, she moved closer to Pearl, inviting Sonny to do the same. Sonny followed suit and stepped closer to the bed, opposite Jordana. She watched while he hesitated, then leaned over and kissed Pearl's cheek. When he straightened, his eyes were wet with tears, for which he seemed to hold no embarrassment.

He wiped the drops on his sleeve and sniffled. "This is all my fault."

Sonny's words startled Jordana. Had he something to do with Aunt Pearl's overdose? However, as he continued, Jordana realized that he only felt responsible for asking Aunt Pearl to marry him, the event that had set off an avalanche of maladies for her.

Sonny openly sobbed. "It's not that I don't want to marry

Pearly, because of course I do. It's just that since I asked her so many things have happened to her."

Jordana thought, Sonny's right. Not that he's to blame, but since Aunt Pearl unveiled her plans to marry him, she's had one horrific misfortune after another. Was it just bad luck, or was someone doing this to her? It was not lost on Jordana that the person Pearl first revealed her intentions to was Mother. Jordana hated how her thoughts kept coming back to that. What if the things she had been thinking about Mother were unjustified? What if she was innocent of the crimes Jordana had begun to suspect her of? What kind of a daughter would do that? One that didn't believe in coincidences. One that knew Mother all too well. Yet, she had no proof. Until they could ask Pearl about the overdose, all she could do was speculate.

Sonny interrupted Jordana's reverie. "Do you think she'll hear me if I talk to her?"

Nodding, Jordana responded wholeheartedly. "She might. Maybe if she hears your voice she'll wake up. We, Nurse Charlotte, Matthew, and I, have been trying since Saturday morning without any luck. You give it a try."

If anyone could wake Pearl from the depths of unconsciousness, it would be Sonny. The one Pearl most loved. The one for whom her heart beat. Jordana was even willing to leave the room a moment to give them some privacy. If he were alone with Pearl, he would probably feel more comfortable saying what he wanted, anything he might think fitting between he and his love.

A miracle had taken place and it had manifested itself in Sonny Capshaw. Jordana had gone to the cafeteria looking for something to eat. She had just bit into a blueberry bagel slathered with cream cheese when she heard her name over the hospital's PA. "Jordana Barlow. Jordana Barlow to room 337. Jordana Barlow."

She threw the bagel in the dumpster and sped to the nearest elevator. But it was too slow, leaving too much time to speculate on why they had paged her. She could think of at least two reasons. One, the best one, was that Aunt Pearl had woken up. The second one was that Sonny Capshaw had in some way gone berserk. My God, she'd left him alone with Aunt Pearl! It was too horrible to think about. Jordana forgot the elevator and ran the stairway.

When Jordana reached the room, it was full of doctors and nurses. Sonny was there too, and Jordana was relieved to see that he wasn't in restraints. He hadn't done some unspeakable thing that she would never forgive herself for giving him the opportunity to do. Later she would laugh and roll her eyes at the absurdity of her thoughts. But now she was happy to see Sonny standing excitedly against the wall with a big smile on his face. She was even happier when he shouted for the world to hear, "Jordana, Pearly's awake! My Pearly's awake!"

Chapter Twenty-Nine

It felt like a party. All they needed were some party favors, wild music, and a few beers. Pearl lay propped up on pillows in the hospital bed reveling in this festive spirit. After all, it was for her. She knew her hair was wild and tangled in several directions, bed hair at its best, but it made no difference to anyone, least of all her. She smiled at Sonny, who stood next to her holding her hand as if he would never let it go.

Matthew stopped at Cub Foods and bought chicken salad, fresh fruit, and French bread. Doctor Sotto grabbed a banana and headed out the door, on to other patients. Charlotte bustled in with paper cups and a bottle of sparkling grape juice. She also had a change of clothes for Jordana, right down to the underwear.

Charlotte greeted Pearl with a big hug and a thank God, you're safe, before she turned to Sonny. "You must be Sonny Capshaw. I'm Charlotte, Pearl's nurse, rather, her ex-nurse. I hear you're the one responsible for waking this sleeping beauty."

Sonny smiled, but he was at a loss for words. He wasn't used to being the center of attention. He shifted uncomfortably, turned red, and then resumed his puppy-love gaze at Pearl.

Charlotte set the clothes on the bed next to Jordana. "I guessed you to be no bigger than a size eight. Am I right?"

Jordana looked surprised that Charlotte had taken the trouble to buy clothes for her. "Size eight is good. You didn't have to do that." Then she smiled. "Honestly, I'm glad you did. I'm beginning to feel like these clothes are attached to my skin."

Everyone laughed, as they did at anything remotely funny since Pearl woke. A combination of exhaustion and happiness had made them giddy. Only Charlotte, who had gotten some sleep, took a serious note. "I hate to be the one to break up any good mood. But I want to know something, and I have to be on duty at Glory Heights in an hour."

Jordana quit eating, sat up on the bed, and brushed crumbs from her lap. Matthew looked attentive from his chair on the other side of the room. Pearl and Sonny looked at Charlotte, not knowing what she was going to say next.

Charlotte looked at Pearl. "I presume Doctor Sotto told you that Seconal was in your bloodstream."

"He already asked me how I thought it got there. I told him I didn't know," Pearl hurried to say. "I sure as hell didn't put it there." They all laughed again. Not because Pearl was trying to be funny, but because she had said it with such veracity. That, and no one was used to hearing her swear. Pearl had even amused herself.

Charlotte continued. "Doctor Sotto said your phenobarbital levels were okay. Nurse Shelby allots two pills for you to take in the morning at breakfast, and then she brings your medication to your room after you're in bed at night. Right?" Charlotte spoke slowly, as if willing Pearl to add to that, or challenge it.

Pearl didn't know what Charlotte expected her to say. Pearl nodded. "Right. She brings me that with a cup of warm milk to wash it down. She really is so kind. But not as kind as you, Nurse Charlotte." Pearl added that for loyalty's sake.

Charlotte grinned. "Thanks, girlfriend."

The group went silent, as if no one knew where to take this line of questioning next. Before things got uncomfortable, Matthew spoke up. All eyes turned to him. "Pearl, has anyone else brought anything to your room, or have you taken any other pills lately? Maybe you didn't know you were taking the Seconal. Maybe you thought you were taking something else instead."

Pearl was bewildered. "I haven't taken any other pills. Not even that Tylenol you all thought I tried to kill myself with last week."

Sonny found his tongue. "What happened last week?"

Patting his hand, Pearl explained, "Don't worry, dear, there's nothing to it. When I started getting sick, I fainted and they were all speculating that I tried to commit suicide. We know now why I fainted. Seconal and phenobarbital don't go so well together."

Everyone chuckled. Pearl felt herself beaming at being able to amuse this group so. She liked the attention.

Matthew seemed amused at her recollection of events. "No, no, Pearl, we didn't think you tried to overdose with Tylenol. We were just grasping at straws, I guess. Kind of like we're doing now."

Pearl peered over at Jordana, wanting to include her in the conversation. Having Sonny in the room lit a spark in her heart. Having her niece here, too, intensified its gleam. "What do you think, Jordana?"

Jordana was standing at a small hospital table pouring grape juice for everyone. She shook her head. "It's really strange. That's what I think. For example, you fainted in Matthew's office on Wednesday."

Pearl pitched in, "Yeah, and I slept all night Wednesday. Thursday I spent the whole day in bed. Friday, I started feeling better."

"At the concert Friday night, you seemed tired, but were nowhere near collapse," said Jordana.

"And we all know what happened Saturday morning," added Charlotte.

Matthew sat forward in his chair and rested his arms on his knees. He looked as if he were concentrating hard on something. "Pearl, if you were sleeping, were you woken up to take your medication?"

Pearl touched her arm where they had given the shots. "No, they just give me shots in the arm if I'm asleep. I had one on Wednesday and Thursday night and then again Friday morning because I'd slept through breakfast."

"What about Friday night?" asked Jordana. "Did you fall asleep before they brought your medication to you?"

At the memory of spending Friday evening in Jordana's company, Pearl sat up in bed. "Oh, no, Jordana. I was far too excited to sleep. I had so much fun."

"Did Nurse Shelby bring pills for you to take then?" Jordana asked.

Pearl was nodding. "Yup. And the warm milk."

Charlotte looked like she had had enough of hearing about Shelby's milk. "What's with this warm milk Nurse Shelby brings you? I never brought you warm milk. Maybe I should have. Not that you don't deserve something extra, but if we brought warm milk to every patient to down their meds with, we'd be in the kitchen warming the stuff up half the night."

Matthew laughed, "Nurse Charlotte, you are from the South, aren't you!" But he abruptly stopped laughing when he saw the beleaguered look on Charlotte's face, and thought that somehow he'd offended her. "I'm sorry," he said. "It's just that I like your accent."

Charlotte waved him off. "Don't you worry about that, Matthew. That's not it. I'm from the South and proud of it." Her black eyes widened. "I was just thinking of something." She turned to Pearl. "Pearl, does Nurse Shelby bring you that dang-blasted warm milk every night? Does she ever miss a night?"

Pearl was baffled. She didn't know where this was leading. "Every night since they reassigned her to me. Except Wednesday and Thursday night when I'd fallen asleep before my med time."

"That's it!" shrieked Charlotte.

Everyone in the room turned to look at Charlotte and spoke in unison. "What?"

"Nurse Shelby's freakin' warm milk."

"What?" Jordana's temper flared. "I'll see that Nurse Shelby woman behind bars. How dare anyone treat my aunt that way? I'll move Aunt Pearl out of that depraved establishment myself."

Pearl listened, amazed. While sad about what they thought Nurse Shelby did, she was excited too. Perhaps Jordana was overly tired from sticking with her through the entire ordeal. It may have been exhaustion as much as the disbelief that a nurse responsible for Pearl's care would drug her. But, Jordana was really upset now.

Matthew looked sorry for the whole circumstance and tried to calm Jordana down. "Don't worry, Jordana, I'll handle this."

"If you don't, I will." Jordana shouted. Then she started to cry.

Charlotte stepped forward to pat Jordana on the back. Matthew looked like he didn't know what to do.

Pearl, trying not to smile, thought it was all quite wonderful. She secretly thought it worth the overdose to have Jordana claim her and stick up for her the way she did.

After that, the three left for Glory Heights. Every one of them ready to shoot bullets.

Chapter Thirty

Matthew and Jordana had gone into Matthew's office and collapsed side by side in the chairs in front of his desk. Neither of them spoke. Matthew stretched his long legs out in front of him. He laid his head back and closed his eyes. Rubbing his fingers over his eyelids, he relieved the tired itch plaguing them. Then he remembered his manners. He sat up, looked over at Jordana, and was about to ask her if she wanted the directions to his house. There she could stretch out on his bed and get some sleep. Although, when he turned toward her, she didn't budge.

Wearing the knit shirt and shorts from Charlotte, Jordana was half-curled into the chair. Her head tilted sideways, and her chin hung down toward her shoulder. Long strands of soft auburn hair lay across one side of her face. In the moment's silence, she had fallen asleep.

Matthew thought that only someone overly exhausted from lack of sleep and emotional stress could fall asleep in that position. Being the nurturing sort, he wondered how he could make her more comfortable without waking her. Maybe she would like a blanket—not that it was cold in the room, but the cover might be comforting.

He quietly left the office and went to the nurses' station

to ask for a pillow and blanket, ignoring the questioning looks from the loitering staff. Giving only a smile and no explanation, he made small talk until he got what he came for.

The only movement Jordana had made during his absence was to turn her folded body to the other side of the chair. He took a chance lifting her head and sticking the pillow under it, but she didn't wake up. After spreading the blanket over her, he was satisfied that she was as comfortable as he could make her. Grabbing a pen and paper off his desk, he then left the room, closing the door behind him.

Back at the nurses' station, he checked the staff schedule, running his finger down it until he found Shelby's shift. She would be coming on duty in a few hours. That gave him time to think. The first thing he thought of was that he'd stopped thinking of her as *Nurse* Shelby. If she drugged Pearl, she was no nurse.

Finding a quiet bench overlooking the river at the back of Glory Heights, he took a moment to take in the peace and the swell of the water. He admired the sun dancing on the current, and the slight breeze felt good on his face. It was a nice respite in a hectic day. Breathing deeply, he tried to calm the nervous energy he'd started to feel soon after learning about Pearl's tainted warm milk. He could barely believe Shelby would do a thing like that.

Although, when he began to write about events surrounding the overdose, circumstances easily traced back from one duplicitous person to another. The warden coming to see him, Shelby suddenly becoming Pearl's nurse—he'd heard the rumors about Shelby and the warden's affair, Pearl becoming frail and exhausted, the overdose.

The drugging began right after Nick called the warden, spilling the beans about Pearl's escape. Immediately after that, Shelby took over Pearl's care, replacing Charlotte, who would never have succumbed to the warden's pernicious demands.

Matthew hadn't thought it odd at the time. He never suspected that Shelby was doing anything other than rotating clients, a typical occurrence at Glory Heights. Had he known, had he any indication of what they were doing to Pearl, he would've done something to stop it.

He didn't believe that Shelby meant to cause an overdose. She was just following the warden's demand to sedate Pearl. However, Shelby was careless, overstepping her bounds with a dangerous drug. The warden was ruthless. No one checked what the increased level of barbiturates would do to Pearl.

The reality of it more than angered him; it made him fighting mad. Taking another deep breath, he took hold of his desire to pummel the warden and shake Shelby. Still, he vowed that they would pay for what they did to Pearl.

He knew it was unjustified, but he partly blamed himself for Pearl's sedation. Sitting at her bedside, waiting for her to regain consciousness, he'd wracked his brain over it. Yet, he thought of nothing that he might've done differently to stop the onslaught of drugging. That, however, hadn't stopped the guilt.

What Jordana thought of all this had a tremendous affect on him. She was incensed, ready to do battle, and he didn't blame her. He did worry about how she would handle it, however. They had all admitted—Charlotte, Matthew, and Jordana—that the only thing they had so far was suspicion. Suspicion that Jordana's own mother was behind all of it. Believing her mother could do something so evil had to hurt, even as she vowed to take a stand against all who had mistreated and demoralized her aunt.

After the park concert, he noticed a marked change in Jordana's view of Pearl. Jordana had grown fond of her. At the concert, her first opportunity to get to know Pearl, they chatted away, acting more like mother and daughter, sharing girl secrets. He couldn't hear what they chatted about, not that he even tried. Not wanting to intrude on their reunion, he kept his back to them for most of the concert. It seemed to have been a life-changing experience for both of them.

Matthew couldn't think about the concert without his thoughts going to the Block Party afterward. Despite everything, he smiled. Being alone with Jordana was the most incredible fun he'd had in a long while. He loved getting to know her, even learning about her work as an account executive. When she spoke of it, her voice changed. It lowered and became stronger than when she spoke about personal concerns. He suspected that she was good at her job. She seemed confident in her ability to negotiate with high-powered clients.

He realized that, between work and home, a person could be quite different. A shy, reserved person at the office could be demanding and overbearing at home. Another person who was successful and adventurous in their work might be less confident in their personal life. This one he believed to be true of Jordana.

After discovering the most likely cause of Pearl's overdose, Jordana blew up. Then, as if that had been difficult or embarrassing for her, she broke down and cried. Matthew wanted to put his arms around her and comfort her, but he didn't want to push his affection on her. Friday night, she allowed him to kiss her before leaving the Block Party in separate cars, and he was ecstatic. He was falling in love with her, but he didn't know how she felt about him. He couldn't presuppose that she required his comforting arms. He had kept his arms at his side and offered her the only thing he could: that he would take care of whoever hurt Pearl.

Matthew stretched his back and checked his watch. An hour had passed. Although he'd like to, he couldn't sit there all day thinking about Jordana, and there was nothing more to add to his analysis of events. He quickly wrote a report, and then went back to his office.

Peeking his head around the door, he saw that Jordana was still asleep. She'd moved from the fetal position. Her legs stretched out in front of her. She cradled the pillow against her bosom, her arms snugly wrapped around the downy fluff. He only wanted to check on her, to make sure she wasn't awake and waiting for him.

Satisfied, Matthew left again. He had other residents to meet with. He wanted to catch them before they traveled down to his office. What they found there would surprise them, and Matthew didn't need that.

He allowed half an hour for each meeting, after which he

went to the nurses' station. Charlotte was there, updating patient charts. "Has Shelby signed in yet?" he asked.

Charlotte nodded and then flicked her head, indicating the repository behind her. Shelby was filling a cart with medication and other supplies, getting ready to make patient rounds. Matthew walked around the counter and stood in the doorway to the supply room.

"Shelby?" Matthew spoke calmly, yet in his voice hung an eerie drape of denunciation. He had heard it himself.

Startled, she looked up, and seeing Matthew blocking the door, her face blushed crimson. "Matthew. You surprised me."

"Sorry about that, but I'd like to talk with you."

Shelby looked nervously over Matthew's shoulder to Charlotte, who was standing right behind him. "Of course. What is it?" Although Shelby spoke compliantly enough, she took a step back and away from Matthew. First she clutched the buttons on her uniform, then she grabbed at her reddening neck. It was obvious she knew what was coming. She started talking, as if to diffuse the situation she had placed herself in. "Charlotte says Pearl is fine now. She's come out of her coma. That was welcome news." Shelby tried to smile.

Matthew moved further into the small supply room. He rotated a half-turn, and with a tilt of his head, he motioned for Charlotte to follow him in. If Shelby confessed to anything, he wanted a witness. Charlotte stepped inside, never taking her dark, accusing eyes off the unstrung Shelby. Matthew shut the door behind them.

Matthew looked directly into Shelby's eyes and got right to the point. "Somebody drugged Pearl Witherby with Seconal. We think you might know something about that."

"Wha-what would I know about that? When Charlotte told me about it, I couldn't believe it myself."

Matthew and Charlotte looked at each other, then back at Shelby. Matthew tried a different tack. "I understand from Pearl that you brought her cups of warm milk at night."

Shelby assumed an unnatural look of incomprehension.

"Warm milk?"

Charlotte broke in, barely able to control her animosity. "What was in the warm milk, Shelby?"

With the next thing Shelby said—"What warm milk?"— she sought to relinquish herself from blame and cast doubt on Pearl's sanity.

It only served to strengthen Matthew's conviction that she was guilty of all he had suspected. He glared at her and said, "You won't need to finish your rounds." Then he stood back and let her slink past him and out the door. She left without saying another word to defend herself.

Shelby hadn't counted on the perceptiveness of Karoline, whom Matthew had stopped to question while he was on his rounds. Karoline had seen Shelby with the milk. Nor had Shelby counted on his unexpected position of taking the word of two Glory Heights residents over hers.

Matthew reported his confirmed suspicions about Shelby to Glory Heights' director of personnel, who immediately suspended Shelby, pending further investigation.

Proving the warden's involvement would be more difficult. Realizing the shambles her career was in, Shelby refused to admit her guilt. Having taken that position, she made no implications toward the warden. Although Matthew was sure that Shelby would inform the warden of the situation every step of the way.

When Matthew went back to his office, he found Jordana standing up with her arms reaching over her head, stretching. Her shirt separated from her shorts in the stretch, and he had to admire the soft skin of her torso. Seeing him, Jordana quickly dropped her arms and wrapped them around her middle. "Where've you been?"

Matthew gave her a slow smile. "Out playing detective."

She gave him a searching look. "Did you catch anybody?"

"They have suspended Shelby, pending an investigation." Matthew waited for Jordana to sit again, and then he sat beside her to explain what had happened. He finished with a caution that she could expect Glory Heights to be slow to investigate. No one would want any negative publicity surrounding Glory Heights, particularly the warden, whom they couldn't accuse without Shelby's assistance. As long as the warden had control of Glory Heights, no one would get very far in their investigation.

Jordana's reply to that reflected Matthew's. "That sucks," she said.

He couldn't have said it any better. "I know, but the important thing is that we've removed the person posing immediate harm to Pearl."

Apparently, that wasn't good enough for Jordana. "I now realize what's best for Aunt Pearl. I've seen it with my own eyes, and it doesn't include remaining at Glory Heights." She blazed her beautiful, wide eyes directly into Matthew's and laid the ton of bricks on him. "I'm going to help Aunt Pearl marry Sonny."

Matthew stared at her. The look on her face told him she had no doubt about her intentions. As serious as she might be, legal, medical, and personal issues would keep her from carrying out her decision. "Jordana, Pearl can't leave here."

Jordana stood up and put her hands on her hips. "Why the hell not?"

Matthew stood up to face her. "Because your mother signed Pearl in here. She's committed here." Jordana's mouth dropped open. Matthew felt sorry for her and hated to relay the rest of the bad news. Yet he thought she should hear all of it. She would at least know what she was up against. "Pearl wrote to your mother telling her of her wishes to marry Sonny and requesting her help. In essence, Pearl was asking for her permission. Susan never personally responded to Pearl, but she plainly refused, starting the perilous chain of events leading to Pearl's admittance to Mercy Hospital."

Jordana's eyes filled with angry tears, but her voice was more determined than Matthew had ever heard it. "You leave me to deal with my mother. Aunt Pearl will have her dreams come true."

Matthew continued to be the voice of reason. "But there's

Pearl's medical condition, and she's never lived on her own. I've already laid out all the obstacles to you."

"I heard what you said. Still, I don't see any obstacles that we can't get around."

"She has to better manage her medication," Matthew argued.

"You told me yourself, she's managing it. At least she would be if it wasn't for your compassionate medical staff practically murdering her with barbiturates. They can teach her to take care of her personal needs, how to shop, how to take the bus. She's no dummy." Having said her mind, Jordana stepped away from Matthew, suddenly looking uneasy against the intensity of his glare.

Matthew had had enough. He never implied that Pearl wasn't smart; in fact, he believed just the opposite. An angry silence suffocated the room, but no one was willing to say another word. Matthew sat, painfully aware of Jordana standing behind him facing the door. He hoped she wouldn't walk through it and leave on such an angry note. Although most of what she said had been unfair, some of it made sense. He had to think. Was he in some way holding Pearl back from what she deserved? He had been trying to protect her, but maybe she no longer needed it. With Jordana helping her, maybe she could gain independence. Then, as if to throw out one more argument that needed disputing, he murmured, "I don't think he's capable of taking care of her."

Jordana swung herself toward his chair, apparently unwilling to accept this argument either. She placed her hands on either side of the chair, and got in his face. "Hell, I feel a little incapable some days, don't you? Sonny lives on his own. He has a job. He adores Pearl and would do anything for her. You, Matthew Kincaid, are grasping at straws."

Matthew sat very still, staring into her blue eyes, beautifully wild with anger. Her tenacity amazed him, and he could no longer see a reason to fight her. She was winning the argument in a matter that had seemed to him against all odds. He softened his glare and broke into a smile. Taking it the wrong way, Jordana's face instantly hardened, as if certain he was mocking her. She leaned into him, looking ready to strike again, but he spoke first. "If Pearl's going to live on her own, she's going to have to learn to read bus schedules. Do you know anything about bus transfers?"

Chapter Thirty-One

By Tuesday afternoon, Pearl could sit up in a wheelchair for a few hours without getting dizzy. Doctor Sotto had stopped by earlier and said that if she continued to recover at this rate, she would be going back to Glory Heights in a few days—maybe Saturday. She supposed that was good news. At the time, she had donned an enthusiastic smile, not wanting to appear ungrateful for his exceptional care, and thanked him for all he had done.

However, the thought of returning to Glory Heights was enough to make her ill again. She was secretly enjoying her stay at Mercy Hospital. Sonny came to see her each night after work, as did Jordana. Pearl was getting more attention here than she had in years. Other than the dizzy spells she continued to experience, the lingering symptoms of oversedation, and the sting of open blisters still healing on her limbs, she was thrilled to be here, she realized. The irony of wishing to remain at Mercy rather than go back to Glory Heights, her supposed home, briefly occurred to her. The sadness of it occurred to her too.

If she left the hospital, she would lose the chance of seeing Sonny. Jordana might not be so attentive, might not come to Glory Heights to see her. Here at Mercy, Pearl had both of them attending to her. She didn't want to give up either of those goldmines. The eventuality of it was depressing her. Also, the sad facts surrounding her overdose still disturbed her. She had believed that Nurse Shelby cared about her. However, the nurse only meant to cause her harm. How was Pearl ever to know whom she could trust?

It was the shits, she thought. She giggled at the phrase. She was happy sad, or sad happy. She had good reason to feel both of those emotions simultaneously.

There was a soft rap on the door, and Pearl turned her wheelchair to see a young nurse's aide entering her room with a cart. It looked like a makeshift sink. Sonny was coming to see her again after work, and Pearl wanted to pretty herself up for him. The aide was here to help wash her hair. Pearl thought that Jordana had something to do with arranging it.

The aide smiled. "Are you ready for your beauty treatment?"

Pearl grinned back, feeling excited about it. "I sure am."

After washing her hair with some good-smelling shampoo, which Pearl loved, the aide combed it out and blow-dried it. Then, the aide rolled the wheelchair over to a mirror so Pearl could see the results. Their eyes met in the mirror, and they smiled.

With eyes glowing, Pearl said, "This is really fun. It's just like being in a beauty salon."

"You like it, then?" the aide asked.

"Love it, but I've got something to put in my hair." Then Pearl showed her the cherished barrette. She tried to get it in just the right spot, holding back a curl at the side of her head, but her hands were still shaky. The aide helped her with the clasp, and then, noticing Pearl's hands, she asked, "Would you like me to polish your fingernails?"

Pearl liked that idea. After applying a beautiful coat of red nail polish to Pearl's nails, the aide collected her things and left. Pearl watched *Wheel of Fortune* on television with her hands stretched out in front of her, waiting for the paint to dry. She was extra careful for a long while, keeping her hands still in her lap, for fear of a smudge.

Starting to feel good about herself, she applied a small amount of makeup using a hand mirror. The aide had already moved on to other patients or Pearl would have asked her for help. The small tube was difficult for Pearl to balance against her lips, making a red mess of the outline she made on her mouth. Grabbing Kleenex, she wiped off the color and started over. She reapplied the lipstick, being successful this time. Then, moving her head back and forth, she tried to catch every angle of her face in the mirror, smacking her lips together to ensure an adhesive color, touching the ends of her hair, testing for bounce. She smiled at herself. If she ignored the drab old bathrobe she was wearing, she almost felt pretty.

Thinking the time was getting on, she checked her watch. Then she maneuvered the wheelchair over to the window. Sonny's work shift was over by now. He would catch the city bus, which would soon be dropping him off in the parking lot. Fortunately, her room had a scenic view of the parking lot.

Her stomach gurgled with giddy anticipation of seeing her love. Yesterday was so much fun, too, she remembered. Sonny called in sick to work, and then he stayed with her all afternoon and into the evening. Jordana stayed for most of the day as well. They'd watched game shows and chatted away like a family. In the afternoon, Jordana went home to rest and check in at work. She was back by early evening and stayed for a couple more hours. But, saying she wanted to give Pearl and Sonny the last hour alone together, she left before visiting hours were over. Pearl smiled, thinking about it. Jordana was a considerate niece. Sonny left only after a nurse poked her head around the door telling them that visiting hours had ended. She had to do that twice before he left her side. Letting him go was hard.

The bus drove into the lot. Pearl stretched her neck out, looking for Sonny. There he was. Sonny. Dressed in a navy short-sleeve work shirt and matching pants. Pearl rolled the wheelchair to a cabinet that held her toiletries. She had already prepared herself for his arrival, but she wanted a last look. Holding the mirror, she primped. She touched the bottom of her wavy hair, testing for the spring in it.

She hurried, not wanting Sonny to catch her gawking at herself. She again focused on her lipstick, and after giving the notch above her top lip an adjustment, she was satisfied that she was ready to see Sonny—just in time, too. She barely had time to crank her wheelchair around when he came bounding into the room carrying a bouquet of fresh flowers and with a big smile on his face.

"I've been waiting all day to see you, Pearly." He hugged her and planted a loud kiss on her cheek. "I bought these flowers in the gift shop downstairs. I hope you like them."

Pearl took the flowers from him and smelled the bouquet. "Oh, Sonny, they're absolutely beautiful. You didn't need to do that. Those gift shop flowers are expensive. They're absolutely beautiful," she repeated.

Sonny's face beamed. "Beautiful, just like you. They're chrysanthemums," he added, prideful at knowing the name of the flowers.

"Yes, I know they're chrysanthemums. I like them because they last the longest."

A nurse came by and placed the flowers in a hospital vase, setting them on the window ledge alongside Monday's flowers from him. The elegant bouquets of roses with baby's breath, orchids with miniature delphiniums, and daisies with anemones she'd received from Matthew, Nurse Charlotte, and Jordana were there as well. The room smelled like a summer garden. Pearl gazed at the beautiful floral scene, the most beautiful arrangements she had ever received, and rejoiced in its pleasantness. "I'm starting to really like it here, Sonny," confided Pearl.

"Oh, but Pearly, you don't want to do that. You have to get better and get out of here."

"But then I won't be able to see you."

Sonny's face fell to a sulk. "Maybe you better stay here as long as you can, then."

Not wanting anything to sadden the occasion, Pearl offered something to give him hope. "I shouldn't have said that.

After all, Matthew has let you come here. He's not said a thing about it. Maybe he's ready to help us now."

Sonny's face brightened. "That's what I was hoping for."

"If that's the case, we've got a lot to talk about, Sonny. I've been thinking about what needs to be done."

Sonny's face went blank. "Like what?"

"Lots of things, silly. I was watching *Wheel of Fortune* earlier, and I realized that I don't know the price of anything. We'll have to budget our money so that we can live properly."

"Oh. I know what things cost. I do my own grocery shopping, you know." Sonny stretched his body out and put his hands on his waist. He was proud to know this over Pearl.

"That's right, Sonny. I'd forgotten. Well, we are just going to have to help each other out with things."

"We will, Pearly. I'll take care of you."

Over the next two hours, they talked about their future together, laughing and hugging each other. Dinner came on a tray for Pearl, and Sonny left her to eat it, going down to the cafeteria for his own meal. When he returned, they played cards and watched television until Jordana arrived.

Jordana came in carrying two beautifully gift-wrapped packages. One was quite a big box. She set the presents down on the vacant bed, and said, "Hello, you two." Jordana hugged Pearl and then smiled at Sonny.

Sonny waved at her, and smiled back.

"Hi, dear," Pearl said. Keeping her eyes on the boxes, she wondered what was in them. She thought they must be for her, and that was an exciting prospect. However, before she could ask about them, Matthew arrived, surprising her. "Matthew, I didn't know you were coming tonight too."

Matthew smiled. "I'm here for only a few minutes. I have Cory tonight. Jordana has some good news for you, and I didn't want to miss out on it." He shrugged. "I guess I have some good news too." After giving Pearl a hug, he nodded and smiled at Jordana. Sonny had retreated to the wall, but Matthew walked over and shook his hand.

"Is the good news in those boxes?" Pearl clapped her hands together like a child.

Jordana laughed. "No, that's something else. Don't worry, those packages are for you, Aunt Pearl," she teased. "I have something important to tell you first."

Pearl couldn't imagine what it could be. She grabbed Sonny's hand and pulled him away from the wall and closer to her. Both looked at Jordana.

Jordana stood next to Matthew at Pearl's bedside. "Matthew and I talked yesterday about you and Sonny. I told him I wanted to help do whatever it takes to get you on your feet, checked out of Glory Heights, and able to do as you wish. I'm going to help you two get hitched."

Sonny's reaction was the funniest. He jumped up and down. Then he skipped, wiggled, and danced around in a circle, yelling, "Hooray, hooray!"

Pearl laughed, and found the energy to stomp her feet and clap her hands in the wheelchair. Matthew and Jordana beamed at each other and at them, sharing in their excitement.

A nurse poked her head around the door to see what all the ruckus was about, to which Sonny informed her. "We're getting married. My Pearly and me are getting married. Toot, toot, toot."

Everyone laughed at his vivacity, although the nurse, who had met Sonny the day before, looked skeptical. Yet, unable to resist becoming part of the group's excitement, she stepped inside the room to congratulate Pearl. Giving Sonny a sideways glance, she added, "If that's what you want." After bidding the happy couple to keep it down, she left, firmly shutting the door on her way out.

Pearl caught the tone of the nurse's congratulations, but didn't say anything. She glanced up at Jordana, who had also noticed it, as did Matthew. They briefly looked at each other, all knowing it was an attitude that Pearl and Sonny often faced. However, it would not defeat them. They had too much love between them. Overcome with happiness, Pearl began to cry. Dabbing her eyes, she looked first to Jordana and then to Matthew. "I knew you'd help us. We can't do it by ourselves. But, I have to ask you, what made you change your minds?"

Matthew spoke first. "It's Jordana's doing. She convinced me that after all you've been though, and after seeing Sonny care for you the way he does, and you him, there was no more fighting it. There was no more fighting you. That, and no one has the right to harm you. We're going to teach them a lesson."

Matthew stopped abruptly and looked at Jordana. Pearl knew it had come out spontaneously. Too late, it seemed Matthew realized he was referring to Nurse Shelby and the warden, as well as Jordana's mother.

Jordana touched his arm. "It's okay, Matthew. I agree. It hasn't been a fair fight, and we'll put a stop to it. I'll call my mother to forewarn her that I'll be helping Aunt Pearl gain independence." Jordana lifted an arm in triumph, as if she had already accomplished the mountainous task.

Pearl's face glowed. "Are you really going to help me, Jordana?"

"Yes, I'm going to help you. You must learn to do things before you can live on your own, or with Sonny. Things like shopping, managing money and a household, and cooking." She laughed, "Heck, maybe I'll learn to cook in the process."

"We already discussed it. I know how to do those things," Sonny interjected.

"Yes, but Pearl needs to learn them too. She must learn to be as self-sufficient as possible. That doesn't exclude what she needs from you. You can help her learn what you know."

Pearl's elated face held a hint of concern. "How are we going to do that?" Then she said, "I think I remember how to cook."

Matthew opened a folder he had carried in with him. "We're going to help you, and I have the independence plan right here." He emphasized the words as if he was unveiling the road to happiness, which, in some respects, it was for Pearl. "Nurse Charlotte has also signed up to help you. She wanted to be here tonight, but she's working a double shift. She sends her regards.

Or as Nurse Charlotte said it, 'Tell that girlfriend of mine I send her my best regards.'" Matthew mimicked a Southern accent, and they all laughed while he pulled a piece of paper from the file and set it on Pearl's lap.

Pearl glanced at it. "What is this?"

Matthew explained what the independence plan was all about. "Yesterday afternoon I thought about the things you will have to do for yourself that someone has done for you since living at Glory Heights. It's a list of things for you to learn. Things that will help you live on your own.

"Your three amigos," he said, referring to Charlotte, Jordana, and himself, "have divvied up the tasks to support you along the way." Matthew pointed at the list. "Look here. You mentioned cooking. Since I'm no cook, and Jordana would rather eat out, we decided that Nurse Charlotte was the most experienced person to get you up to speed on that. Jordana's going to help you figure out the bus routes to and from work, shopping, and the pharmacy. That's after you and Sonny decide where you'll be living."

Now Pearl looked worried. She began to stutter. "Oh, dear, I knew I had things to learn. But looking at this list, there seems so much to do."

Matthew tried to alleviate her fears. "Don't worry. I know it looks overwhelming, but it's not as bad as it looks. I wrote it down so that we don't miss anything. Besides, I have faith in you."

Jordana touched Pearl's hand. "This is something you've wanted, and you're going to get it. The good news is that you won't be doing any of it alone. I'm going to be with you every step of the way."

"So am I," added Matthew. "You don't think I'm going to let go of you that easy, do you? There's something else, also."

Pearl looked at him expectantly. "You mean Nurse Charlotte?"

"Well, yes, Nurse Charlotte wants to help, but I'm talking about volunteers that will check on you every day. I'm talking with a social worker from Rum River's Social Services to have them available for you when you move into your new home."

"My new home?"

"Yeah, you and Sonny aren't going to live at Glory Heights, are you?" Everyone moaned at that thought. "Well, after we get some of this independence plan under your belt, you will want to move out on your own, and, I'm presuming, marry Sonny. That's what this is all about, isn't it?"

Matthew's reminder that it was all about getting out of Glory Heights, being with Sonny, and having a life of her own tickled Pearl to no end. "Yes, that's it. I can't thank either of you enough."

"Me either," chimed Sonny.

"When do we begin?" asked Pearl.

"As soon as you get yourself out of this hospital," piped Jordana.

Matthew held up a cautionary hand. Everyone quit talking and looked at him. "I hate to bring any of us back down to earth so soon, but we need to discuss some things. Pearl, we're going to have to be discreet about this. The warden mustn't find out what we're doing, not until I want him to know. That means not telling anyone, like Karoline or Rebecca, until the time is right." Then Matthew addressed Sonny. "Sonny, I have to tell you that it will be better if you don't come to Glory Heights." Sonny's face sunk with dejection, but Matthew waved him off. "Don't worry, I'm not going to keep your Pearly from you," he smiled. "We'll get Pearl over to see you." Sonny brightened at that news, and gave Pearl's shoulder a squeeze. Matthew continued, "Pearl has a lot of work to do, and she's going to need your support on this."

Sonny nodded his head in full agreement. "Don't worry about me, Matthew. If it means I can be with Pearly, I'll do whatever you need me to."

"Good. I wasn't worried. I knew we could count on you."

Pearl smiled at her support group. "Doctor Sotto says that I can leave here in a few days. Maybe Saturday. I'm so happy right now. I can't wait to get started." Leaving the hospital no longer seemed like such a bad idea. Pearl grinned at Sonny, then Matthew, then Jordana.

Looking into Jordana's face, Pearl suddenly remembered something that would destroy her plans. "Susan's my legal guardian since Mother and Dad died. She has to sign me out of Glory Heights. She'll never do that." Pearl's head sank to her chest. After the elation she had felt over her independence plan, her gateway to Sonny, the disappointment of remembering that Susan would still have to agree to her marrying him was too awful to bear.

Jordana put her hands on her waist. "I will talk to my mother. I know she'll be furious, but when she sees how much I want to help you, perhaps she will consent."

Matthew looked as if he thought it sounded like a pipe dream, but wasn't going to douse Jordana's newly found courage with that conviction. "If that doesn't work, we'll look at the legalities involved. Miss Pearl Witherby, you've said on several occasions that, if there is a will, there is a way. Let's hold onto that thought."

Pearl believed in Matthew's confidence more than she believed in Jordana's ability to fight Susan. She knew what Jordana was up against. However, what Matthew had said was true. Pearl did believe that if there was a will, there was a way. Nothing greater existed than Pearl Witherby's will to leave Glory Heights and marry Sonny Capshaw. Together they would find the way.

Feeling that they had discussed what they could for the time being, Pearl's gaze wandered back to the boxes on the bed. Jordana's eyes followed hers. "Okay, okay, I won't make you wait any longer," she laughed. "I bought you some things today." Matthew, being the closest to the bed, picked them up and held them out to Jordana. Taking the smaller gift first, she passed it to Pearl.

Like a child at Christmas, Pearl hastened to unwrap it. Digging through tissue paper, she found a beautiful purple print nightgown, a velvety soft bathrobe of the same deep purple, and matching slippers. "Oh, my goodness, they're beautiful. I love the color." Then she patted the sleeve of the gown she was wearing. "Now I can throw this rag away."

Jordana's eyes softened, happy that Pearl enjoyed the gifts. "I thought the color would look good with your eyes and hair. Purple has always been my favorite color."

Sonny touched the soft robe. "It really is pretty. Purple is our favorite color too."

Matthew was still holding the larger box. "Are you ready for her to have this one, Jordana?"

Taking the box from Matthew and handing it to Pearl, Jordana teased, "Oh, I suppose I can let Aunt Pearl open this one too."

Pearl again ripped into the beautiful wrapping paper, trying to get to the treasure inside. Having gotten the paper off the box and opened it up, Pearl stopped. Another box rested within. A beautiful box covered in deep purple and fuchsia flower designs with a gold rope handle on top. Pearl looked in awe at the box, wondering if what was inside would be too good for her.

She looked at Jordana, who had put her hands to her face, as if preparing for an emotional moment. Pearl whispered, "What is it?"

With tears in her eyes, Jordana nodded her head. "Go on, open it."

Pearl lifted the cover and pulled out a delicate-looking straw hat, ivory-colored, with small multicolored rosebuds surrounding its band and ribbon strings for tying at the neck. Lifting the hat from its box was more difficult than Pearl had expected. It was heavier than an ordinary hat. Gently turning the hat over she saw where the extra weight came from.

Tears slid down Pearl's face. Jordana had listened to her, and heard. She said, "It's a helmet. One no one would know about. It's disguised inside this beautiful hat."

Jordana helped Pearl place the hat on her head, moving her dark waves into place around it. Pearl had to have a look. She let Jordana finish tying the ribbons, securing the bonnet into place, and then retrieved the mirror from her bedside table. Pearl held the mirror up high in front of her and stared at herself. Her eyes roved from her hat to her face and back again, serious one moment, elated with laughter the next. Tilting the mirror from side to side, as she had done earlier, she got a better look. "It fits perfectly. Ah," she cooed over it. "It's so fashionable and the colors are perfect. It'll match anything I wear. Just look how great it looks with the bathrobe you gave me."

Pearl reached up, almost out of her chair, and hugged Jordana around the neck. "Thank you, Jordana, thank you. I love it. I love you. You are so wonderful, Jordana. Who would have thought of such a thing, a bonnet with padding? I'll wear it always. There'll be no more ugly helmet for me. I'll never hang my head in embarrassment again. I'll hold my head up high wearing this very special bonnet." The lip of the hat served to frame the shine of happiness swelling in Pearl's eyes.

Chapter Thirty-Two

Jordana was finishing up in her office Friday afternoon, procrastinating really, before placing a call to Mother in Washington. It was time to tell her mother that she planned to help Pearl. Seeing the couple's happiness had brought Jordana great joy. She knew she was doing the right thing. Pearl and Sonny needed each other. They needed to be together.

Being a part of something so good had affected Jordana. It gave her courage, and courage was exactly what she needed. Her mother was going to be livid. Jordana feared her wrath, which she'd never before aimed directly at Jordana. It would be now. Well, she thought, there's a first time for everything. She straightened a stack of client folders atop her desk for the second time.

Pearl left Mercy Hospital Saturday as the good Doctor Sotto had anticipated. Jordana had picked her up and returned her to Glory Heights, staying with her long enough to get her settled. Before leaving, Jordana assured her that they would be seeing each other very soon—this upcoming weekend, Pearl would be a guest in her home. The furlough from Glory Heights would be the kickoff to Pearl's independence plan. Pearl had cried happy tears, overwhelmed by the prospect.

Midweek, Jordana called to check on her. Jordana found

her to be quite chatty, as if relieved to hear from her. For the most part, she had resumed her life at Glory Heights and her work at Brambles. Above all, she was doing a remarkable job of keeping her temporary stay at Glory Heights a secret. Other than Nurse Charlotte, she had talked to no one about it, she reported.

Thankfully, Charlotte was again caring for her needs. The whole incident so appalled the nurse supervisor that she willingly obliged Matthew's request to reassign Charlotte to Pearl. Pearl shared with Jordana that, after what Nurse Shelby had done, she was having difficulty feeling safe. Although having Nurse Charlotte caring for her again certainly helped, she said.

As serious as the conversation was, Jordana chuckled, remembering what Pearl said just before hanging up. She'd quipped, "I'm never going to drink warm milk again. I've lost my taste for it."

Jordana found that she, too, was excited about the upcoming weekend. It would just be an overnight stay from Saturday to Sunday, since she wasn't used to caring for anyone that might at any moment have an epileptic seizure. In addition, Pearl was not used to being away from Glory Heights. No matter how much she wanted to escape the place, the sleepover would be a challenging experience for her too, but a necessary first step toward autonomy.

Jordana was excited, but nervous. She was especially worried about Pearl having a seizure. Matthew had told Jordana what to expect, and then he said not to worry about it. Uh-huh, easy for him to say, thought Jordana. He had also reminded her that she wouldn't be spending much time alone with Pearl. Jordana had invited Sonny, Charlotte, and Matthew, along with his son, Cory, to dinner Saturday night. Charlotte would come over early to help with the culinary aspect of the evening and, simultaneously, give Pearl a lesson in simple cooking. Jordana would take Pearl home Sunday morning. Matthew was right. Jordana wouldn't be alone with Pearl for long.

Still, the thought of Pearl having a seizure while in her care scared Jordana. She took a deep breath and told herself to buck up and face it. If she was going to help Pearl with the independence plan, that's exactly what she was going to have to do. She could do it, she reasoned. What seemed more difficult was the phone call she was avoiding making.

Jordana tapped her pencil on the phone, thinking it over. Should she call Mother now, or wait until after the weekend? Mother had called several times over the last couple of weeks, leaving messages on the unanswered phone. Jordana hadn't returned any of the calls. She was too fearful of Mother impinging on her thoughts while she processed all that she had learned about Pearl. Jordana was also appalled at Mother for hiding Pearl from her for so long. In the last message, Mother shrieked her dismay, demanding that she return her phone call immediately. That was before Pearl went into the coma. Jordana really owed Mother a phone call.

"Jordana," Mother cooed, "I was frantic with worry over you. It's about time you called your dear old mother. Is everything okay? Tell me everything you've been doing. Are you still dating that Ryan executive? I won't have long to talk, I have a vote in half an hour."

"He's an account executive, Mother, and we broke up. I'm fine, and this won't take long." Jordana hoped it wouldn't take long, although she wondered how Mother expected her to tell her everything she had been doing if Mother didn't have time to talk.

"You broke up? What did you do to him? He sounded exactly right for you."

"He wasn't at all right for me, Mother. Anyway, that's not what I called to talk about."

"Oh? What is it dear? You sound worried. Ryan didn't hurt you, did he?"

"No, no, it's nothing to do with Ryan. It concerns Aunt Pearl."

"What do you mean it concerns Aunt Pearl?" She'd emphasized "aunt" as if Jordana had said a dirty word. "I told you not to worry about her. You're not still thinking about that phone call she made to you, are you? She has nothing to do with—"

"Mother," Jordana interrupted, "Could I get a word in here?" Before Mother could speak again, Jordana told her everything. She started with visiting Pearl at Glory Heights, stuck in going to the concert, and finished with Pearl's stay at Mercy. Mother remained speechless throughout Jordana's monologue, but even through phone lines, it was obvious that Mother's breathing had grown heavier and faster paced with aggravation. Jordana envisioned the steam rising from Mother's ears. While relaying that a nurse at Glory Heights had sedated Pearl, causing an overdose, Jordana's voice shook. "Aunt Pearl could've died. She shouldn't be in that place."

Jordana was too afraid to say, "Did you order this done to her?" Instead, she began to cry, as she often did when confronting Mother on a battle she feared she would lose. However, this time she couldn't lose. She had made a commitment to Pearl. Pearl needed her and depended upon her. She couldn't, wouldn't, back out now. No matter what Mother said about it.

Mother remained silent while Jordana cried. Jordana felt a fool. Before she had even completed her intentions, she had broken down sobbing. She slumped in her desk chair, ashamed at her outburst of emotion, and waited for Mother to speak.

When she finally did speak, the words were slow and hostile, as if growled through gritted teeth. "I told you, she has nothing to do with us. She is exactly where she belongs. She will stay at Glory Heights, and you will stay away from her. Do you hear me, Jordana?"

The coldness emanating from Mother's voice struck Jordana, the way she called Pearl "she," as if she was someone vile and undeserving of a name. The unkindness was too much for Jordana. She loved her mother, didn't want to lose her love, but the senator's selfishness was beyond her. It was something Jordana couldn't understand and would no longer tolerate. The newfound courage that had temporarily abandoned her tweaked its mighty head. The courage, obtained from knowing she was doing the right thing in an injustice beyond redemption, would pull her through. She straightened her back to its fullest length and began to do battle with Senator Susan Seymour.

Chapter Thirty-Three

If not so many people were working in the offices outside her door, Susan would've let loose the violent scream exploding inside her pressurized head. She paled and wrenched with tormented anger like she had never before felt for her daughter. Sitting at her desk, Susan stomped her high-heeled feet into the carpet. Picking up the legal pad she had been writing notes on before Jordana called bearing the news of an enemy, she threw it across the room and hit the torchier lamp. The thrust was enough to unbalance it, but it didn't knock it over. Unsatisfied with the notepad's impact, she picked up a stapler and belted that at the wall. The stapler snapped open. Springs and staples flung through the air. She picked up a paperweight next, ready to do damage, but realized that the item was a gift from a fellow senator. He had presented it to her after winning votes on a major bill the previous year. He visited her office often to discuss issues before the senate and would notice if she broke it or if it disappeared. Reconsidering, she set the paperweight back down. However, unfinished with her tantrum, she picked up Jordana's picture and whacked it down upon her desk, shattering the glass and chipping the gilded frame.

 A knock at the door averted her attention. She stared at the door, but didn't answer. "Senator, is everything all right in there?"

It was her executive assistant, Emily. She most likely had heard the rampage and was afraid to open the door. Susan looked around at the mess, the one she had made to suppress the scream she'd had bottled up inside her. Emily had heard her furor anyway. Susan might just as well have screamed her lungs out and gotten it over with. She cleared her throat. "I'm fine, Emily. Please tell Nick I want to see him."

Emily spoke through the door. "Ah, sure, Senator, but you have a vote on increasing the allocation of emergency funds to flood victims in Iowa in five minutes. I thought I should remind you."

"I'll vote! I'll vote from here!" Susan yelled. "Just get me Nick. Now."

With shaky, abrupt movements, Susan prepared an electronic entry for the vote. She sent it, and then realized too late that she had voted "yes" when she had meant "no." Nick came through her door without knocking. Not knowing or caring how to fix the error, she turned off her computer and dramatically pointed to a chair for Nick to sit in.

Without saying hello, Susan let go of her rage. Realizing the sensitive ears of the outer offices, the details of Jordana's phone call came out in a loud, hoarse whisper. His face solemn, Nick leaned forward in his chair and listened intently.

"Jordana says she's going to help her marry that man. Can you believe it? My daughter is going to defy my wishes, and in the process, ruin all that I've worked for. If the news hounds find out what my daughter is up to, and they will, it's all over for me. We have to stop her."

Nick stared at Susan, not knowing how to respond to her tirade. He had been in his office diligently studying the latest revisions to the Water Protection Act, and he longed to go back there. The senator's personal problems no longer interested him. He had unexpectedly received an offer to work with the Environmental Protection Agency after the next month's vote on the Water Protection Bill. It was an excellent offer, and he was seriously considering it. He only had to get Susan through the vote, and then he would be free to leave. Nick expected a tight tally in the senate, making each aye important, including hers.

Nick no longer had the time or energy to save the senator from her luckless sister's attempt to spring free of Glory Heights and marry. However, the news that Pearl had suffered from an overdose disturbed him. Daris McFinley had promised that he would cause her no harm. Nick had had enough and wouldn't allow himself to be party to any further defilement against Pearl Witherby. The trick was to bow out without the senator realizing it.

"Well?" Susan was expecting some kind of answer.

"Well, what?"

"What are we going to do about this? It can't come out that I've a sister in Glory Heights whom Jordana is trying to help 'lead to independence,' as she put it. Especially with that snoop Taylor on my scent. Ever since I promised to visit an epileptic treatment center, which, by the way, you have to get me out of, she's been hanging around asking questions. We simply can't have Jordana involved with my sister. Someone has to go to Minnesota and stop her fruitless efforts. Talk some sense into her."

"Ah, shouldn't that someone be you? You're her mother."

"I know I'm her mother," snapped Susan. "You don't need to remind me of that sordid fact. Until she comes to her senses, I've disowned her. To answer your question, I simply can't go. I have far too many important issues to attend to here. Moreover, I've tried talking to Jordana, and she won't listen to me. Perhaps she'll listen to you."

"Me? Why would Jordana listen to me?" Nick was trying to think of a solution, other than him, to offer the senator, to get her off his back. "She's almost thirty years old. She can do whatever she wants to do. Nothing you or I say can stop her."

Susan stared at him, astonished by his brazen declaration. It had never occurred to her that Jordana would ever be out from under her control. The thought frightened her. "Don't say that. There must be something you can say."

"Look, even if I could say something that would make a difference, I can't leave right now. I'm working on the senate's version of the Water Protection Bill. The House is going to pass their version any minute. Things are heating up, and I have to be here."

Susan glared at Nick, probably incensed by his cheeky attitude. "Well, excuse me. I didn't know you had become the important one in my office. I thought I was the senator, not you. I'm sick and tired of hearing about the Water Protection Act. That's your baby, not mine. We have far more important bills in Congress than that one."

Nick realized his mistake. He inwardly admonished himself for allowing a hint at his derailment from her troubles and simultaneously wondered what acts of congress Susan thought important. The only opinions she had about government were those of her constituents, the poor unwitting Minnesota folks who voted for her.

He wisely kept those thoughts to himself and tried waving away Susan's anger. "No, no, that's not it. You misunderstood what I was trying to say. Of course you are the important one here, Senator." He smiled, watching her face soften. "Of course many important bills are going through Congress, of which you are involved and for which we need your powerful influence. The Water Protection Act, I admit, is important to me. But, I know you favor it too. The speech you'll deliver on the bill next week is going to knock the socks off your constituents. It's important to them too. It affects the lakes abutting their state. I'm working on your speech right now. That's why our presence, both of ours, yours specifically, here in DC is so important right now." Nick felt like he had just given a speech, one that he hoped had some effect on his lone audience. He had laid it on thick.

Susan looked appeased and appropriately sugarcoated. "That's right, I have to be here to give that speech. What do you suggest we do about Jordana?"

Nick had an idea, one Susan might buy. "Move Pearl to another home."

Susan's eyes brightened. She was listening now and said, "Somewhere Jordana wouldn't find her. Jordana would then have to give up this idiotic conduct."

Nick grinned conspiratorially with Susan. "Exactly."

"You'll take care of that for me?" A hint of uncertainty faltered her voice.

"I will," Nick stated, inspiring confidence. What Susan didn't know wouldn't hurt her.

Chapter Thirty-Four

"McFinley. Nick Ballantine here. You promised me no harm would come to Pearl Witherby. . . . Yeah, yeah, don't bother making excuses to me. . . . How'd we find out? My associate's daughter. Seems she's taken an interest in Ms. Witherby, and her dilemma. In fact, Ms. Witherby plans to spend the weekend with her at her home. . . . Didn't know that, huh? It seems to me there's a good deal you don't know, McFinley. . . . Just shut up and listen. I'm going to make this short and simple. Ms. Witherby's benefactor wants her moved. . . . That's right, to another home. The problem is, I don't have time to do that right now. So, you keep Pearl Witherby out of the hospital and the public's eye, or I'll find the time. Do you understand me? . . . I thought you would."

Chapter Thirty-Five

Pearl stood in the parking circle in front of Glory Heights holding Charlotte's hand and trying to act nonchalant. However, she reached up for the third time and touched the padded bonnet perched proudly atop her head to ensure it was there. She brushed imaginary lint off her shorts. She smoothed down the back of her hair. She rocked back and forth on the heels of her shoes. Nonchalance was difficult. She dressed comfortably in beige walking shorts, a cotton shirt, and thick-soled black shoes, which she was using to move a pebble on the sidewalk. She stopped fidgeting for a moment and looked down at the overnight bag sitting on the pavement at her feet. Tapping it with her toe, she wondered if she had remembered everything. The bag was on loan from Nurse Charlotte, who had helped her pack it. Pearl put a hand to her chin and went over the items in her mind. A simple cotton dress for the dinner party, her new nightgown, robe, and slippers, a change of clothes, and a few toiletries. That was really all she needed. She put a hand to her waist. No, she thought, she hadn't missed anything important.

The warm sun beating down on her reminded her of sunglasses. She wondered where she had put hers. She looked up at the sky; there wasn't a cloud in it. She blinked and looked away.

She thought it would surely get hot later in the day, but the morning air felt good. She was about to check her handbag for the sunglasses when she glanced sideways. Was she driving Nurse Charlotte nuts with all her wiggling around? Pearl peeked over at her. If she bothered her, the pleasant-looking Nurse Charlotte didn't show it. She loosely held Pearl's hand, occasionally giving it a pat, and surveyed the road. Pearl followed her gaze. They were waiting for Jordana to arrive.

Every time Pearl thought about it, she practically gurgled with happiness. She would be spending the weekend with Jordana, and the stay included shopping for new clothes. Knowing how badly Pearl needed new clothes, Matthew had orchestrated withdrawing some of her Brambles money, just for the occasion. She had the greenbacks tucked securely inside her purse, along with her medicine.

For the first time, she would be on her own managing her medication. Jordana was given instructions on how much medicine Pearl should take and when. However, Pearl already had that memorized. She was confident in her ability to give herself medicine, at least.

Satisfied with that thought, Pearl patted the side of her purse and realized her sunglasses were inside it. Squinting against the sun, Pearl turned toward Nurse Charlotte. She squinted back, and they exchanged goosey smiles. Pearl quickly dug out her glasses and put them on her head, still holding onto Nurse Charlotte's hand.

Even with the excitement of shopping for new clothes, Pearl was having a difficult time overcoming her apprehension. She suddenly felt silly at the mixed bag of emotions running through her. She reasoned that it was just that she hadn't been anywhere in so many years. She didn't know how to act. Or feel, apparently. Now, waiting for Jordana, knowing she would be here any minute, Pearl's unease grew. She wrung her hands around the handles of her purse, twisting the tubular straps. "I sure hope I do okay," she lightly stammered. "I don't want to be a bother to Jordana."

Charlotte automatically slung an arm around Pearl's shoulders and squeezed. "Girlfriend, you are going to do just great. Do you know why?"

Pearl looked at her. She felt a shy, childlike expectancy. "Why?"

Charlotte let go of Pearl's shoulders to clasp her hands. "Because, young lady, you really want this, and you are so capable. Remember what I told you before. It's normal to feel nervous. I'd be wondering about you if you didn't feel this way. Heck, I'm nervous, but only because it's such a new and wonderful experience for you. I want you to have a great start to your independence plan. Remember, we're having your kickoff party tonight. Everyone will be there: Sonny, Matthew, me, and Jordana. And we all love and care for you."

Pearl smiled. She got a kick out of Nurse Charlotte calling her "young lady" again. "I can't wait for that."

Charlotte grinned back, her big white teeth showing through her beautiful face. "If you get nervous while you're out shopping, just tell Jordana about it. She'll talk you through it. Your niece loves you and is as excited about this weekend as you are.

"And, this is important to remember: if you feel too apprehensive, you always have the option of coming back to Glory Heights and trying it again another time. Don't be afraid to say that's what you want to do. It doesn't mean failure. No, not at all. It just means that we take smaller steps. Not that you are going to want to do that. Just understand that the decision, the power, to change plans is yours."

Pearl thought that over, remembering that at a meeting earlier in the week Matthew had told her the same thing. She felt empowered by the fact that she had some control over her life again. It was quite a change from everyone telling her what to do and how to do it. She was beginning to relax. She swung her purse from side to side and checked the road for Jordana. No sign yet.

Charlotte moved her weight to one hip and then shifted back. She pulled the nylon fabric of her new white pants, the ones Pearl had pulled a price tag off of earlier that morning, away from her leg. "I'll be over later today to give you a cooking lesson. Girlfriend, wait until Sonny tastes the dinner we're going to make for him! We won't tell him how easy it is to do." Charlotte winked conspiratorially, making Pearl laugh.

Charlotte had successfully eased Pearl's tension. She had stopped writhing the handles of her purse and her stammer had vanished. "What are we going to make?" Pearl asked amid chuckles.

"Yankee pot roast with all the vegetables. Can you believe it, with me being from the South?" she laughed. "We'll put it all in one pan and roast it. Easy as one, two, three." Charlotte clicked her fingers three times.

"It sounds good. I like to cook. At least I used to enjoy it, from what I remember."

"You're gonna love cooking for your man!"

Pearl laughed again. She had to agree with that. She took a deep breath and let it out. "Oh, just smell that fresh air, Nurse Charlotte. That's a sweet breeze coming in, and it's not too hot yet. It's a beautiful day for shopping. Hey look, here comes Jordana."

After retrieving Pearl, Jordana drove straight to Ridgedale Mall. Pearl chatted the whole way there and her face glowed with the prospect of getting new clothes. Jordana was excited too, but didn't really know what to expect. She chose Ridgedale because it wasn't too big or crowded. Benches were scattered throughout the mall. She planned to stop and rest as often as Pearl required.

From the minute they got out of the car, Pearl surprised her. While slower moving, Pearl's step had a spring in it, and she held her own. They found several stores inside which Pearl wanted to look. Some were a quick look. In others, they lingered, finding things they couldn't live without. Jordana began to tire long before Pearl showed signs of it.

Pearl mentioned that a lot had changed since she had last been to a mall. Many shops were unique or specialized, like the ones selling coffee and tea. Toward the end of their shopping spree, they stopped at Gloria Jean's and ordered lattes. After finally parking themselves on a bench, Pearl sipped her first coffee drink and laughed. "I love it! Can I learn to make this at home?"

"Oh boy," Jordana laughed, "You're as bad as I am. I love my coffee. We're going to have to buy you a cappuccino maker if you want to do that. I have one at my house. Tell you what: we'll make lattes tonight after dinner. How does that sound?"

Pearl clapped her hands. "I can't wait! I also can't wait to try on the outfits we bought, to figure out what I should wear tonight. I'd brought a dress along, but I want to wear something new. I want to show off my new duds to Sonny." Pearl laughed.

Jordana, caught up in the excitement, laughed too. "I like the red knit tee shirt and pants. It really looks comfortable, and the red is so good with your hair coloring."

"Hey, speaking of that. Does it take long to dye your hair, I mean to put a rinse in it or something?" Pearl clasped the ends of her hair. "I'd like to get rid of the gray."

"Well, I like the gray, the salt-and-pepper look. A lot of people do."

"You mean I shouldn't change it?"

"I wouldn't, but we can if you want to."

Pearl thought a minute. "I think Sonny likes it too. Let's keep the hair." Then she looked shyly at Jordana and lowered her voice, speaking confidentially. "I have something else to ask you about."

Jordana leaned forward.

"You see this?" Pearl pointed above her upper lip to a sprinkling of dark hair.

Jordana squinted at it, nodding her head.

"How can I get rid of that? It's so embarrassing."

Jordana smiled. "I know just the thing for that. It's easy to take care of, and I have everything we need at home. We'll wax it. It'll be done before the party tonight."

Pearl looked as if she couldn't believe her good luck. "Really? It's that easy?" She beamed. "Is it something I can learn to do by myself?"

Jordana touched her hand in reassurance. "I think you'll

find it easy to do. It's something you'll have to do about every four weeks. You'll know when you see the hairs growing back that it's time to wax again. In fact, I see a Beauty Mart. Let's pick up your own jar of wax. It doesn't cost much, but it goes a long way to making us feel better about ourselves."

Pearl followed Jordana's gaze down the length of the mall and then looked questioningly back at Jordana.

"What?" Jordana asked.

Pearl blinked at her. "You mean, you have to wax too?"

Jordana smiled. "I wax my eyebrows and I have a mole on the side of my face that grows hair. I wax there too." She pointed to a mole near her ear. "Shh, don't tell anyone." They giggled at the secret.

After the Beauty Mart they stopped at a Regis hair salon for a long-overdue trim to Pearl's beautiful waves. The two women then decided to head to Jordana's house for lunch, and a well-needed rest. Later, they'd pick up groceries for dinner.

After lunch, Jordana showed Pearl to the guest room. She lay down on the double bed and looked as if she'd be fast asleep within five minutes of lying her head down on the feather pillow. Jordana thought they had made the right decision to rest before grocery shopping. Shutting the door behind her, Jordana smiled, pleased that their trip to the mall had been so successful, with no incidents or seizures to ruin their morning. She was keeping her fingers crossed for the rest of the visit.

With Pearl tucked away for a nap, Jordana felt free to relax too. She grabbed a book off her nightstand, returned to the deck, and stretched out on a lawn chair with the intent of doing just that. She let the warm sun tan her bare arms and legs and tried to concentrate on the novel, but found it to be a difficult quest. The previous day's phone conversation with her mother kept interrupting her solace. Disturbing thoughts. Perhaps she shouldn't have told Mother about her plans to help Aunt Pearl, she thought. Jordana worried about what her mother might try to do. Mother's fury had raged through the phone lines. She seemed on the brink of losing control and had never been so angry with Jordana.

Jordana couldn't make her understand the good in what she was trying to do. Why couldn't Mother see that helping Pearl was the right thing to do? It seemed that the senator thought only about her precious career, Jordana brooded. The exposure of having abandoned an invalid sister so many years ago would destroy that. Therefore, she wouldn't listen to any of it. Instead she ordered Jordana, as if she were still a child, to stay away from Pearl. The familiarity of it infuriated Jordana to no end.

Little did the senator know that she could no longer order her around. Jordana would do as she knew best. The time spent with Pearl only confirmed Jordana's belief in what she was doing. Jordana had temporarily forgotten that she still had to attain the insurmountable task of convincing Mother to sign Pearl's release from Glory Heights.

Chapter Thirty-Six

Matthew was in his office, just catching up on a few things before the dinner party, when his door came busting open. It was the warden, and he looked more pissed off than usual. Matthew grinned at him. "What's up, McFinley?"

"You know perfectly well what's up, and you better put a stop to it."

Matthew decided to play coy. "Don't know what you're talking about."

McFinley placed his hands on his hips and squinted at Matthew. "I want you to stop Pearl Witherby from seeing anyone, particularly her benefactor's daughter."

"What benefactor?"

"None of your business. I don't even know who she is. Nick is my contact, and he said he's going to move Pearl if we don't put a stop to this. If you don't put a stop to it."

"It's too late, McFinley."

"What do you mean, it's too late?" He looked worried.

"Never mind. Just tell me, what's your involvement, McFinley? They paying you?"

McFinley turned red. Shaking his finger at Matthew, he said, "You take care of this, or there's going to be trouble." Then he turned and all but ran out the door.

Chapter Thirty-Seven

Grocery shopping was a kick. Pearl said it had been twenty years since she was in a grocery store. She was amazed at the combination grocery, deli, and bakery under one roof. Jordana tried to find a store that was similar to one Pearl would frequent in Rum River and decided on Cub.

Jordana wanted to acclimate Pearl to grocery shopping. Before leaving the house, they made a list. They would get items for dinner and breakfast. Charlotte had provided the recipe for Yankee pot roast, which they used to make the list, adding ingredients for salad and dessert. They agreed to make lattes to serve with dessert, but Jordana already had the coffee beans, milk, and special flavorings to make them with.

Wearing her bonnet and walking with the same spring in her step Jordana had noticed at the mall, Pearl pushed the cart and read from the list. She easily found the canned goods and produce. She then steered the cart through the aisles, correctly picking out the remaining items, only getting stuck once on the type of roast to buy. Jordana was also stuck on that, which made them both laugh. After staring together into the packaged meats, they took a guess, and selected a large rump roast.

After that, Jordana showed Pearl how to read the signs

hanging from the ceiling indicating the contents of the rows of canned goods, condiments, and toiletries. Jordana didn't need anything from the health and beauty section, but Pearl wanted to see what they had. She ended up buying some Dove soap, a new toothbrush, and toothpaste.

She also had to look in the cards and magazine section, commenting that the magazines at Glory Heights were at least two years old. She picked out two magazines: *Better Homes and Gardens* and *Taste of Minnesota*. Both touted easy one-dish meals. By the magazines chosen, Jordana could tell that Pearl was spiritedly thinking of her upcoming life with Sonny. By the look on her face, she was delighted to have the new issues too.

After arriving home from the grocery store they waxed eyebrows and other facial hair. Pearl winced at the sting of the wax strip coming off, but after seeing the results, she smiled. "I waited a long time to get rid of that mustache. To think it took less than five minutes and, poof, it's gone. I can easily do it myself. I also love what you've done with my eyebrows. They're all shaped up, no stragglers."

Jordana smiled too. "You look great, Aunt Pearl."

Pearl preened in front of the mirror. She checked out her new bouncing haircut, her hairless lip, the smooth line of her eyebrows, and the glow in her face. Pearl finally felt good about herself. Turning to Jordana with open arms and tears in her eyes, Pearl hugged her for a long time, quietly thanking her. Smiling, Jordana hid her face in Pearl's shoulder and fought back her own tears.

Charlotte promptly arrived at 3:30 to begin preparing the meal. She wore shorts and an oversized blue tee shirt with the words "Don't give me an attitude, I have one of my own" printed on it. The bold blue in the tee sparkled against her dark skin.

Jordana graciously turned over her kitchen to the confident culinary skills of Charlotte. She was more than happy to do it and she smiled, thinking she would be paying as close attention as Pearl to Charlotte's instructions.

Charlotte went to work. She looked through all of the

groceries, commenting on everything. "That looks good, carrots, uh-huh, good, good, red potatoes just the right size." Then she shrieked, "What the hell is this? A rump roast? Girlfriends, you don't make Yankee pot roast with a rump roast!"

Stunned, Jordana and Pearl looked at each, not knowing whether to laugh or cry. Seeing the looks on their faces, Charlotte decided for them. She burst out laughing. "I see Pearl isn't the only one that needs culinary training." They all erupted into fits of giggles, causing Pearl to make a beeline for the bathroom.

The sight of Pearl clamoring to the bathroom added to the hilarity. Jordana wiped tears from her eyes. "Now what are we going to do? Can we use the rump?" The word made her double over into a belly laugh. Snorting and sputtering, she choked out, "Or are we going to have to go back to Cub?"

"No, no, we'll use the rump." They again broke into hysterics.

Pearl returned from the latrine, more composed than Jordana and Charlotte, and thought to ask, "What were we supposed to buy?"

Charlotte stopped laughing long enough to answer. "I usually use a chuck roast, but," as if afraid to say the word again, "this cut will do." Still, they laughed.

Under Charlotte's expert direction, dinner was underway. Pearl did the work, carefully following instructions and reading the recipe. Jordana's only concern came when Pearl tried to cut the vegetables for the pot roast, particularly the carrots. Her motor skills weren't what they used to be, and she struggled with the knife over the cutting board on the kitchen counter. Charlotte finally lowered the cutting board to the table, giving Pearl more leverage as she stood over it. Charlotte then showed Pearl how to cut the carrots the long way first, and then into one-inch chunks, making the vegetables easier to manage.

After Pearl prepared the vegetables, she arranged them around the pot roast and set the pan in the preheated oven to cook. Next, she rinsed and chopped the lettuce, both green leaf and romaine, for a Caesar salad, and then set the bowl in the refrigerator to chill. They had purchased croutons, shredded Parmesan cheese, and a prepared Caesar dressing to toss with the greens just before serving. Charlotte stood nearby, ready to offer directions. Jordana just tried to stay out of the way.

Pearl commented on how easy everything was to do. Cooking was something she had enjoyed doing when she was young and living at the Silver Dollar, before epilepsy struck. It seemed to have come back to her quite naturally.

Dinner preparations were as far along as they could go, so Pearl took the opportunity to change for dinner, before their guests arrived. She couldn't wait to show Sonny her new look and wear a new outfit. She wondered out loud if he would notice.

"He better notice, girlfriend!" Charlotte piped up.

"I'm sure he will," said Jordana.

Pearl shared her decision not to say anything about it, to see if Sonny noticed by himself. Jordana grinned at her aunt's sly pension for fun.

While Jordana was setting the table, Matthew arrived with Cory and Sonny in tow. More laughter and excitement permeated the air. Pearl had not seen Sonny since the last day of her hospital stay and greeted him with a big hug. Matthew made introductions to Cory, who shyly said hello and waved. Then Pearl, wanting to be the hostess, got everyone a cold drink and led the way out onto the deck.

The first thing Jordana noticed when she stepped outside was how pleasant the evening had become. The sun was still warm, but by then the maple trees shaded a good portion of the deck. Two red-crested cardinals, lovebirds themselves, perched in a tree chirping, as if they knew it was a special occasion. She couldn't help feeling a certain harmony with nature and humanity.

Everyone found a place to sit, and then Matthew led a toast to Pearl's independence. Pearl stood, positioning herself directly in Sonny's view, waiting for him to notice her. She patted her hair and fussed with the gold barrette. Striking a pose, she smoothed imaginary wrinkles from her new red shirt and matching pants. Nothing. She pranced in front of him, back and forth, but still got no reaction. Jordana was half-listening to something Matthew was telling her while keeping an eye on Pearl. Jordana started to feel sorry for her.

Finally, it appeared Pearl couldn't take it anymore. "Sonny!" she exclaimed.

Jordana smiled and winked at Charlotte. Matthew, who had just finished telling Jordana that he had something important to tell her, clammed up and glanced at Pearl. Sonny and Cory stopped talking, too, and looked at her. Sonny looked surprised to hear his name spoken so shrilly. He looked uneasily at Pearl, then back at everyone else, and then back at her again. "Ah, what, Pearly?"

Pearl placed her hands on her hips and bent down closer to him. "Don't you notice anything new about me?"

Sonny was bewildered. "Ah, like what, Pearly?" Then he said, "To me you look as beautiful as ever, Pearly." He tried a smile.

Suddenly, it was as if Pearl realized why dear Sonny had never complained about her mustache or ragged clothes. He never saw them, though they were obviously plain to see. He looked past what she believed to be inadequacy. He looked inside her. He saw into her soul. Then, if she had not confused poor Sonny enough, Pearl first burst into tears, and then started to laugh. Then she said, "Well, you sure know how to say the right thing." Jordana and Charlotte laughed with her.

Still not knowing what Pearl was getting at, but grateful that he had somehow said the right thing, Sonny laughed too. Charlotte helped Sonny out. "How do you like Pearl's new haircut and outfit, Sonny?"

Sonny finally caught on. "That's real good, Pearly, it's a real pretty outfit. Red's my favorite color."

"I thought purple was your favorite color," said Matthew. Jordana touched Matthew's arm. "Today he likes red."

Cory, at first shy around all the adults, soon became quite comfortable, not seeming to notice or care that Pearl and Sonny had disabilities. In fact, Cory had turned out to be the real gem of the evening. He regaled them all with stories about school and summer fun, proudly revealing rollerblading scars and recounting baseball triumphs. Matthew beamed with pride. Pearl and Sonny listened with interest to the boy's tales and delighted in having a young person in their midst.

Charlotte listened with a look of reminiscence. Jordana wondered what she was thinking about when she finally shared that she had a son in college. Matthew and Pearl gaped with astonishment at not having known anything about it. Matthew then prompted Charlotte to tell more about her family, which opened a floodgate of stories, entertaining everyone right up to the time when she and Pearl went inside to toss the Caesar salad and bake the garlic toast.

Matthew silently indicated that he wanted to speak with Jordana, alone. He seemed eager to get something off his chest. She couldn't imagine what. She stood up and, with a nod, suggested that he should follow her.

They walked down the steps into the yard below, leaving Cory and Sonny to entertain each other. The yard was lush green from the recent rain and stretched out amidst a row of maple trees. Matthew followed Jordana to a quiet spot beneath the trees, out of Sonny and Cory's hearing range.

Matthew arranged himself on the grass so that his shoulder touched hers. "You're not going to believe who barged into my office this morning."

Jordana looked bewildered. "Who?" Then, "You went to work this morning?"

"Yeah, just stopped in to get a few files before picking up Cory from swimming lessons."

"Who barged in?"

"The warden. For a guy who avoids Glory Heights like a vampire avoids a crucifix, he sure finds his way to my office often enough. Just lucky I guess."

Jordana gasped. "I bet I know what this is about. Friday I phoned my mother and told her my intentions to help Aunt Pearl and Sonny. Did Mother call him?"

"No, but her liaison Nick Ballantine did."

"Nick?" Jordana was baffled. "That's Mother's right-hand man in Washington."

"He's also your mother's liaison with the warden. The warden doesn't know who your mother is."

"Mother has Nick do her dirty work? Quite the coward, my mother."

Matthew wisely didn't respond to the rhetorical comment. "The warden was beyond livid," Matthew laughed.

Jordana looked surprised. "You laugh? You don't sound too worried about him finding out about our plans."

"I'm not. If push comes to shove, we'll instigate an investigation into his administrative practices." Matthew stressed the word "administrative," indicating how he felt.

"What did he say exactly?"

"He said he wanted me to stop Pearl from seeing you."

Jordana straightened up. "Uh-oh. What did you tell him?"

"I told him he was too late. You should have seen the look on his face! It was disbelief at its best." Matthew laughed again, as if delighting in the memory. "You'd already picked Pearl up for the weekend. Not that I would have stopped it from happening if you hadn't." Matthew kissed Jordana on the cheek. "Don't you worry, he won't take a chance getting his hands any dirtier than they already are. Not with the investigation into Shelby's misbehavior going on. Besides, he knows I'm on to him."

"You think so? What makes you say that?"

"I told him."

Shocked, Jordana mouthed but didn't say the word "wow."

"He's been taking bribes from your mother, via Nick. Why else would he have taken such a personal interest in Pearl? There was no other reason. I called him on it. I told him to stay out of my way or else I'd expose him for the ruthless thug he is. Boy, was he pissed! Ah, sorry, excuse my language. Anyway, he made a quick exit from my office after that. I'm sure he's up in arms about what to do next. However, that's his problem." Matthew smiled confidently and kissed Jordana again. She wished she shared his confidence.

Pearl placed garlic toast in a pan and then, from the package it came in, she read the directions for preparing it. Charlotte held her breath and watched like a mother hen while Pearl donned oven mitts and placed the garlic toast into the oven next to the roast, resisting the temptation to help.

"We had a gas stove back home," said Pearl. "This oven seems easier."

"The important thing to remember is to turn the burners and oven off when you're done cooking. I say this as a reminder, not because I think you'll forget, but because it's a fire hazard if you do." Pearl nodded, and then went about getting the lettuce, Parmesan cheese, and salad dressing from the refrigerator. She tossed the salad while the garlic toast baked.

The oven's timer buzzed—the pot roast and toast were done. Pearl again put on mitts and removed the steaming hot food from the oven. Then, without being reminded, she turned off the oven. Pearl turned to Charlotte and smiled. Charlotte expelled a contented sigh and nodded her approval. Dinner was ready.

After eating, the lattes turned out to be more trouble than they were worth. Pearl abandoned the idea after making just one, which she offered to Sonny, who turned up his nose. Instead, she made a pot of coffee, offering a cup to everyone except Cory, who had milk. She served the coffee with a luscious turtle cheesecake that she and Jordana had purchased at the store. The meal was a complete success. Charlotte beamed with pride at her student, although she had to admit that Pearl hadn't needed much guidance.

After dessert, everyone played hearts, including Cory. By this time, Pearl was patting him on the head, looking at him with affection. It made Charlotte miss her own son. After several rounds of hearts, everyone was tired and talk slowed until Matthew suggested they call it a day. Sonny offered some resistance, only because he didn't want to leave Pearl, but he finally conceded that he was exhausted. With one last toast to Pearl, Jordana declared day one of the independence plan a success.

Chapter Thirty-Eight

Jordana was in her office at Curic and McCall trying to catch up on her workload. She had really fallen behind in the last three weeks. Since Pearl's independence plan kickoff party, Jordana had been out several nights of the week and on weekends with her, ticking off the items she needed to learn to make it on her own.

From riding city buses to managing money, Pearl was getting a crash course in independence and managing quite well. She was back at Glory Heights, but knew it wouldn't be for long, and she seemed to be in good spirits when Jordana last talked with her. They still had a lot to cover on the independence plan, and while Jordana had enjoyed her time with Pearl, she was pleased when Charlotte offered to collect Pearl that afternoon for more cooking lessons at Charlotte's home. They'd also cover how to use a washer and dryer.

That's where Pearl was, which gave Jordana time to tend to her clients. Although she was so excited about the progress Pearl was making, keeping her thoughts on her work was hard. She had always felt so focused on her work, but since Pearl had come into her life, she was easily distracted. Fortunately, no one at Curic and McCall or any of her clients had yet complained about her inattentiveness. She hoped she had built up enough of a reputation that she could get by with it until Pearl met her goals.

Satisfied that that was probably a true assumption, Jordana ran down to the skyway and got a cup of coffee. Once there, she sat inside the coffeehouse and reviewed Pearl's progress—and hers, if she was honest about it. She had grown as much as Pearl had in the last few weeks, but for different reasons.

On three separate occasions, Jordana had taken the city buses with Pearl from Sonny's apartment to downtown Rum River. Jordana wanted to make the experience fun for Pearl, something she could look forward to. Each time they rode the bus, they took a transfer ticket and went as far as Bronte's Tea House before they got off to celebrate the first leg of their journey with a pot of oolong tea and buttery orange-cranberry scones.

Afterwards, they boarded another bus to Cub Foods, where the future independent Pearl would be shopping for groceries and picking up prescriptions in the in-store pharmacy. At Cub they picked up a few goodies or new magazines for Pearl to take back to Glory Heights.

One trip stuck out foremost in Jordana's mind. She blew on her hot coffee, then smiled to herself at the memory. It was at Bronte's, while sitting at a tea table, sipping a cup of hot, sweetened oolong, when Pearl had a seizure. The first one Jordana had ever witnessed. She barely knew what was happening before it was over.

In the middle of a conversation about Pearl's wedding plans, a dazed look crossed Pearl's face only seconds before a short scream passed her lips. She fell forward in her chair. By the time Jordana got out of her chair and around the table, Pearl was coming out of it. Jordana helped straighten her in the chair, when Pearl looked up and said, "Did I just have a spell?"

Jordana smiled at Pearl, feeling an odd sense of peace, a sensation typically uncalled for under the circumstances. It was just that she had personally made it through her aunt's seizure. She could have laughed at the absurdity of her response to Aunt Pearl's epileptic fit, but she didn't. After that day, she knew what it was all about.

Jordana had been afraid that something horrible was going to happen to them while they were out alone, much as Pearl feared having a seizure or getting claustrophobic in the bus. That something had just happened and she had survived! They had both survived!

Only the bewildered stares from the ladies at the table next to them stole a piece of the peculiar moment. Jordana simply looked at them and smiled that everything was okay. To Jordana's satisfaction, they smiled back, after which she cocked Pearl's bonnet back into place atop her head, sat down, and ordered another pot of tea.

During Pearl's fourth city-bus trip, Jordana drove her car behind the bus, nervously supporting Pearl's first solo venture into public transportation. At Pearl's final destination, she smiled big, searching for Jordana's face in the Cub Foods parking lot. To say that an aura of pride surrounded the aunt and niece in the following jumping-up-and-down embrace would be an understatement.

One day, they took a trip downtown and opened a checking account for Pearl at US Bank. Judging by Pearl's mystified stare into her first checkbook, money management was going to take some getting used to. "What do you do with this?" she asked Jordana.

Both of them stared at the plastic-covered checkbook from US Bank. Jordana thought a minute, figuring a way to explain the depositing, withdrawing, and, most important of all, balancing of Pearl's money from Brambles. It would be her own money to manage once she left Glory Heights.

Jordana finally responded with, "Does Sonny have a checkbook?" knowing she was deferring to an easy way out.

It didn't work. Pearl had no idea whether Sonny used a checkbook.

Jordana looked back through the windowed doors of US Bank from which they had just stepped out. Taking Pearl's hand, she led her back inside and asked for an account representative to explain the basic mechanics of banking. Pearl learned about automatic paycheck deposits, how to write out a check, and the pluses and minuses of balancing her checkbook, both figuratively and literally.

Managing spending money and creating a budget was going to be another story for another day. And another person. Jordana typically used charge cards, which she paid off at the end of each month, preferring that to carrying cash. She didn't think it a good idea to introduce Pearl to credit.

As Jordana and Matthew talked it over later, he offered to create a budget so Pearl would know how much she had to spend on rent, utilities, personal expenses, etc. Jordana and Pearl both wholeheartedly took him up on the offer.

Finishing her skyway coffee, thoughts of the budget reminded Jordana to call Matthew. She wondered how he was doing on his end of things. She promised herself she would work another few hours before calling him and headed back up to her office.

Matthew was going through files in his office. While Jordana and Charlotte prepared Pearl for life with Sonny, Matthew worked on setting up community service volunteers to fill the gaps in Pearl's independence. He also worried over how to secure Pearl's release from Glory Heights before Nick moved her to another facility. When Matthew told Jordana about the warden's visit, he had purposely left out the part about Nick's threat to transfer Pearl. Matthew hadn't wanted to worry Jordana with it. He had only later mentioned it to Charlotte, giving her a heads up, in case she observed the warden or anyone else attempting to move Pearl. In that event, Charlotte was to contact Matthew immediately. He had a lot to think about. Getting volunteers to look in on Pearl each day, and perform a myriad of other tasks, was the easy part.

Jordana hadn't mentioned the fact that Pearl couldn't leave Glory Heights without Susan's consent since the day she decided to help her aunt. Matthew didn't think for a minute that Jordana had forgotten it. Perhaps she was ignoring it, hoping it would either go away or resolve itself.

Matthew knew they would have to address the problem

soon. The women had all but picked out Pearl's wedding dress and set the wedding date. He knew that Pearl and Sonny had looked at a couple of furnished apartments. They had considered living at Sonny's current place, but ultimately opted for a fresh start in a new home.

Construction crews had built several apartment buildings in Rum River over the last few years. Finding affordable, furnished housing on the bus line, near work and shopping, was not going to be a problem.

In Matthew's mind, everything was coming together in a very big way, except the most crucial factor: they had not secured Pearl's release. They still had to climb over, knock down, drive around, bore through, or move the biggest mountain of all: Senator Susan Seymour.

Matthew had searched through old files looking for anything that might help Pearl's release. He had found nothing, and only a few files remained. He was considering calling the senator himself when all hell broke loose.

Chapter Thirty-Nine

"Senator Seymour?"

She hesitated. She didn't recognize the voice on her private line. "Yes. Who is this?"

"Anton. Anton Capiscerelli. I drive Pearl Witherby to work."

Gasp. "How did you get my number?"

"Nick Ballantine gave it to me. Said he's no longer the one to talk to."

"Talk to? About what?"

"Well, I'm just wondering if I've still got a job driving Ms. Witherby. See, she's taken to riding the van with the others."

"You mean she's still at Glory Heights?"

"Of course she's at Glory Heights. Where else would she be?"

Chapter Forty

"Senator Seymour?"

Gasp. She recognized the voice on the other end of her private line. "What do you want, Ms. Costica?"

"I understand that you backed out of your commitment to tour the epileptic treatment center in Los Angeles. Will you confirm that?"

"No, I certainly will not. I've not backed out of it. I've simply delayed the tour. I can assure you that's all it is."

"Delayed it? Until when?"

"Well of course, I don't know. Emily, my secretary, keeps my calendar. However, I can assure you the tour is still on. As I said, it's just delayed."

"Delayed? Huh."

"Do you have anything else, Ms. Costica, because I really am very busy."

"Just one more thing, Senator. I've spoken with Emily. She said there's nothing on the calendar. I've spoken with LA. They said you backed out and refused to reschedule. What *was* that speech you so eloquently delivered to the Epilepsy Foundation in New York? A dog and pony show?"

It wasn't until after Susan had recovered from the unsettling phone call that she wondered how Taylor knew her private number.

Chapter Forty-One

"I'll kill the freakin' bastard!" screamed Susan. She was alone in her office, pacing, waiting for Nick, and muttering obscenities with undeniable fury. She walked the length of the wall in front of her desk, turned and stomped back again, digging her high heels into the plush congressional carpet. "How dare he bail out on me? The jackass didn't even have the decency to forewarn me. The disloyalty of it is unforgivable. Abominable. I'm going to kill him!" she repeated.

"Who are you going to kill?" Nick had opened the door and stepped into her office without knocking or announcing himself.

The senator, pacing toward the wall, stopped mid-step and then swung around to face him, fire and battle emanating from her eyes. With an outstretched arm she pointed at him. "You. You are abominable, Nick. You've exposed me. Compromised my privacy. My position."

"What are you talking about?"

"You know perfectly well what I'm talking about." She shook a finger at him. "You gave my sister's driver, Anton Capoochi somebody, my private phone number. What in hell did you do that for? How dare you do that to me? And that's not the extent of it. What the hell is she still doing at Glory Heights? I told you to move her. That meant immediately."

"I wouldn't call Anton—and its Capiscerelli—a threat to your identity. Your sister is still at Glory Heights because I was too busy with the Water Protection Act and everything else we have going on around here to move her." Nick took a deep breath. He wanted to tell the senator that he didn't take orders from her anymore, and that Pearl Witherby was her problem to deal with. Anton had called him about Pearl's refusal to ride with him. She'd insisted on riding where she pleased, which was on the bus with her friends. He'd called amid high tension surrounding the bill. In a moment of exasperation, with no time to deal with the senator's personal problems, Nick gave Anton the senator's private number. Now Nick wished he hadn't been so hasty. The Senate vote on the Water Protection Act was two days away, after which he would be resigning his position with Susan. He still needed her. He would have to find a way to console her.

He said, "Look, I'm sorry about Anton calling you. He called when revisions to the bill were at its peak, and I thought it better to have you deal with it than to put him on hold for any length of time. Maybe I didn't make the right decision. I've been under a lot of stress lately, just as you've been." He quickly added this last part, remembering how she was the important one in the office. Nick tried to think of some way to appease her.

Susan glared at him, watching him talk his way out of it, or try to. If she knew he was leaving after the vote, she wouldn't be so haughty. However, she had no way of knowing that, and he wasn't going to tell her now. He would let her have her moment over his groveling. In the long run it meant nothing to him. Tiring of her hostile stare, he decided to make a promise he wouldn't keep. "If it will make you feel better, I'll move Pearl. There's a small home in Iowa I've heard good things about. Just give me a couple of days, until after the vote."

"Oh, you and your damn vote. I need this done now. Jordana has her out doing who knows what, probably shopping for a wedding gown by now, and I want it stopped. I can see that

I'm going to have to take care of it myself. I'm going to slide in and out of Minnesota so fast no one will know I was there."

Nick was stunned. "You can't go now. The vote . . . ." He stopped himself. He didn't need to aggravate her any further.

"I'll be back for the damn vote. Unfortunately, my career depends on that as much as yours does. My constituents expect my vote to pass the bill. I'll be here."

"But what are you going to do? What about your fear of exposure?" Nick tried, completely working his way around mentioning the Water Protection Act again.

"I have no choice but to go. The longer she's left to roam public streets, the worse things get for me. I'll be discreet. I'll talk to Jordana, convince her to leave my sister alone. My daughter must have some sense of loyalty left in her." The senator shot another powerful glare at Nick, and then she sat down at her desk, indicating she was finished with him. She hadn't needed to add the "Now get out of my office," but it seemed to restore her sense of control over the situation. Over him.

Nick had never seen her so pissed. He decided to take her up on her dismissal and get the hell out of her line of fire. He placed his hand on the door and had almost made it out when she called him back.

"By the way, Nick, how did Taylor get my private number?"

He turned slowly back to her and responded with a blank, "I have no idea" look on his face. Now that was something he wasn't going to confess before the vote. His relationship with Taylor was private.

Chapter Forty-Two

Now August, and while the summer's heat hadn't cooled by much, it was a perfect morning for the 10K Run for the Homeless. The sun was shining bright in the sky, humidity was down, and everyone was in good spirits.

Jordana and Cory had stood on the sidelines throughout the race passing water to thirsty runners. They were now waiting at the finish line as the competitors made their way to the end of the course. Watching the racers come around the last bend, Jordana realized she had been holding her breath. Until now, she hadn't known she had such a competitive spirit. Right now she was filled with it.

Matthew had held the lead for most of the race with a swift, easy pace, but was now nose to nose with another runner. Matthew's muscular arms and powerful legs pumped in unison beneath his mesh tank and running shorts, both clothes and limbs soaked with perspiration. The expression on his overheated, crimson face was one of relentless determination. Around his handsome head, dark hair swirled in sweat. His eyes darted to the finish line and then sideways to his opponent. Then, as if remembering his supporter's pledges and the warden's promise to match them with Glory Heights' funds if he won, Matthew sprung from his opponent's side. With an assertion of energy that contorted the muscles of his face and clenched the tendons in his neck, he reclaimed the lead. The contender lunged forward, attempting to gain on Matthew. However, being too tired to pump past the faster, better runner, the attempt only made him lag further behind. With fists pounding the air in victory, Matthew plunged through the finish line. Spectators noisily cheered his accomplishment. Through the clamor, Jordana and Cory's elated whoops and hollers came through the loudest.

Jordana had agreed to spend the rest of the day with Matthew and Cory. They first stopped off for a celebratory lunch at the Crab Shack. After a toast to Matthew's success, he confided to Jordana that he loved the roar of the crowd, but the sound of them cheering for him had been the sweetest to his ears. Jordana smiled at his sentiment.

Afterwards they headed over to Jordana's to get her swimsuit and rollerblades for an afternoon at Elm Creek Park. However, the stop home didn't turn out exactly as planned. In fact, the surprise waiting for them in Jordana's townhouse was unexpected, unwanted, and nerve-wracking, to say the least.

Susan arrived in Minneapolis on a midnight flight, sitting in coach and wearing a large hat and sunglasses, the typical guise of a person wanting to conceal their identity. Little did she know that following her from Washington was one person she hadn't fooled.

From the airport, Susan took a taxi to Jordana's townhouse. At the door, Susan briefly considered whether to ring the bell or to use the key that Jordana had given her. The key was a precaution, in the event that something dire happened to Jordana and Susan needed to get inside. Susan decided this was one of those times; she opened the door and let herself in.

It was 3:00 a.m. She expected to find Jordana tucked in bed sound asleep, but such was not so. To Susan's surprise, Jordana was not at home. She wondered where Jordana was at this hour. A sliver of satisfaction slid through her mind when she imagined that Jordana had gotten back with Ryan, that successful executive, and was spending the night with him. However, remembering the adamant tone in Jordana's voice when she had told Susan they were finished ended that thought.

Susan took a shower and then donned a silk gown and robe. With little else to do, she nosed around Jordana's home. She found Jordana's briefcase in the dining room and searched inside it for clues to her activities. What Susan unearthed infuriated her. Jordana appeared to be developing a list of daily tasks for Pearl. At the top of the paper was typed: "Aunt Pearl's Cheat Sheet." Jordana was deeper in cahoots with her aunt than Susan had expected. She angrily shredded the cheat sheet and tossed it in the garbage.

Next, Susan checked the refrigerator for something to eat. Finding nothing appealing, she set about waiting for Jordana to come home. To her dismay, she didn't come home all night. Slouched in the corner of the couch, Susan had tried to stay awake. However, she ended up dozing in the wee hours of the morning and falling into a deep slumber by midmorning. Much later, the sound of giggles and laughter—some of which she recognized as belonging to Jordana—approaching the front door woke her.

Jordana placed her key in the door and was disturbed to find it already unlocked. She was sure she had locked it before leaving the house the previous night when Matthew had picked her up for dinner. When the door swung open, she turned to Matthew with a shrug. "I thought I'd locked this last night."

But, Matthew was looking beyond her into the foyer. Cory had followed his gaze. The shocked look on their faces made Jordana turn back to the entryway. The grim sight of her mother in silk bedclothes, hands on hips, bleached hair wiry and tousled, glaring at her with jaws set firm sent an acidic shiver of too much morning coffee prickling through her abdomen. Jordana felt an immediate need to pee.

Matthew, who had guessed the identity of the stiff, daunting woman, felt an immediate need to use the phone.

Young, affable Cory smiled, raised his hand in a wave, and said, "Hi, who are you?"

Susan ignored the boy, turned, and walked up the steps leading to the living room. Jordana shared a discouraging look with Matthew, and then she ushered Cory inside and up the steps. Jordana didn't bother with introductions. "Mother, what are you doing here?"

Standing in the middle of the living room, Susan propped her hands back onto her hips and confronted Jordana. "Is that any way to greet your mother, Jordana? Your mother who's been waiting here for you all night? Where in heaven's name have you been all night?" Jordana involuntarily glanced at Matthew. She hoped her mother hadn't noticed the dead give away, but the look on Susan's face told her she hadn't missed a thing. Cory, who had spent the night at his mother's, looked confused by the questions. When he sought his father's face for clarification, Matthew put an arm around Cory's shoulders and gave him a reassuring look, one that said he would explain later.

Jordana, angered by her mother's attempt to again reduce her to a child, mustered up some of her newfound courage. "I am an adult, and where I've been is none of your business."

Susan waved a hand in Jordana's direction, dismissing her response. Instead, she nudged her chin at Matthew. "Who's this?"

Matthew beat Jordana to the punch, as if he couldn't wait to explain who he was. "Matthew Kincaid, senior caseworker at Glory Heights Healthcare Facility. I work with Pearl Witherby, your sister, Senator." He didn't offer his hand and he didn't introduce her to Cory.

Susan's mouth sagged with disbelief. She looked at Jordana. "What the hell? You've spent the night with a social worker from Glory Heights? You've fallen further away from the family tree than I could ever have imagined."

"Mother!" shrieked Jordana, horrified at the insult to Matthew.

Matthew laughed at the senator, showing her his contempt. Again puzzled, Cory looked from one adult to another, resting his eyes on his father. Matthew looked like he had something to say to the senator that he didn't want Cory to hear. "Cory, do me a favor and step outside. I'll be right out. We're still going to the beach." Cory, seemingly pleased at his release from the uncomfortable gathering, practically ran out the door, closing it firmly behind him.

Matthew stepped toward Susan, his masculine frame looming several inches over her, causing her to take a step back. "I don't know why you're here, lady, but if all you have to do is insult your daughter and her taste in men, then I suggest you go back to Washington on the next flight. If you've come to further disrupt Pearl Witherby's life, I still recommend that you hop the next plane out of here.

"I'm on to you, Senator. You're not as anonymous as you think. You hide behind your congressional seat, claiming to have the interests of all Americans, including the disabled, devalued, and stigmatized, at the heart of your senatorship. All the while you keep your sister Pearl under wraps in a place you think they won't discover her as related to you. You belong to the long line of idiots who think that having epilepsy in the family will somehow taint your life, ignoring what it might feel like to the person who actually suffers from the disease. A disease that, by the way, can be controlled so that most of its victims can lead fairly normal lives. Something you've done your best to deny your own sister. In your attempts to control Pearl's life, to keep Pearl down where you think she ought to stay, you've tried to take away from her what she loves best: Sonny Capshaw. In a heartless attempt to immobilize Pearl, you ordered that she be sedated."

Matthew drew up closer, within an inch of the senator's face, and jabbed an index finger under her nose. He spoke slowly, his voice low and heavy, emphasizing every word. "You almost killed Pearl."

For a silent moment, the weight of his words hung in the air. His eyes ominously penetrated the senator's stoic bearing. She visibly winced and took another step away from him. She looked at Jordana for support. There was none. Susan defiantly lifted her chin and stared back at Matthew. He wasn't finished with her. "If you have plans to do anything other than sign a release reversing Pearl's commitment at Glory Heights, I promise you, Senator, I'll make you regret it."

The senator suddenly found her voice. "What commitment papers?"

At first, he couldn't believe what he had heard. She'd said it spontaneously; there was no forethought. Finally realizing what it meant, he worked to keep from smiling, and from running out the door to recheck Pearl's files. Somebody had signed Pearl into Glory Heights. If Pearl did it herself and just didn't remember doing it, which was entirely possible considering her medication's effects on memory, they were home-free. The infamous Senator Seymour was toast.

Matthew wasn't a vindictive man, but he knew he would find great pleasure in telling the senator that she had no control whatsoever over Pearl. Sadly, for too many years, the senator had made Pearl believe otherwise. If it was true that Pearl had signed herself into Glory Heights, she could leave of her own free will. Whatever consequences the senator would face from that turn of events were her own problems to deal with.

He suddenly turned his face to Jordana and said, "I think it's time for the beach."

Matthew Kincaid's abrasive speech left Susan without a word of defense. She was stunned by this stranger's attempt to intimidate her from doing what she knew she had to do. Then, to her open-mouthed wonder, immediately following Matthew's tasteless monologue, Jordana left with him to go to the beach, of all places, leaving her alone in the townhouse.

Fuming, Susan showered and dressed, all the while talking to herself, analyzing her precarious situation. She hadn't gotten to be senator by sitting on her laurels while rugrats told her what to do. If she couldn't convince Jordana to regain her senses, she would have it out with Pearl, threaten her with displacement from Glory Heights. That was the best thing for everyone involved. Pearl had used Jordana to further her own incredulous causes. The senator would put a stop to that. By the time she was done with Pearl, she wouldn't be able to do anything but crawl in a corner of Glory Heights, or some other obscure facility for the mentally impaired, and rot.

As for Jordana, Susan wasn't finished with her either. When Susan got Jordana alone, away from that lowly caseworker, she would straighten her daughter out once and for all. Susan had hoped to have a simple discussion with Jordana over dinner and then catch the midnight flight back to DC. She could see that was most likely not going to happen. She would have to postpone her flight home another day, dangerously gambling against her required presence at the Water Protection Act vote. Which reminded her: damn Nick for not resolving this for her! Had Nick moved Pearl away from Glory Heights like she had asked him to, *when* she had asked him to, she wouldn't be stuck here in Minneapolis doing the job for him.

Susan dressed in a pale pink pantsuit and meticulously applied makeup that complemented her white-blonde hair. She tried her best to soften the anger in her face: the anger that obliterated her reasoning, causing her to forget that discretion was of the utmost importance. She was ready to take care of business. Again nosing around Jordana's home, she found a set of keys to the Mustang parked in the garage. She was going to Glory Heights.

Chapter Forty-Three

Taylor had followed Susan on her midnight flight from DC to Minneapolis with amused curiosity. It was obvious that Susan didn't want to be discovered taking the midnight flight. Using a Corolla rental car made ready and waiting for her at the airport, Taylor trailed Susan, who had hired a taxi, from the Minneapolis-St. Paul International Airport to the northwest side of the city. When the senator alit from the taxi, she went inside a townhouse. From the street, Taylor watched her enter the townhouse without knocking; she had a key. Placing a phone call to an associate in DC, Taylor easily discovered that it was the home of Jordana Barlow, Susan's daughter.

Taylor received a tip from her lover Nick Ballantine that the senator was on a mission Taylor would be very interested in, although he wouldn't reveal what it entailed. Taylor's part of the deal was that she could not break the story until after the vote on the Water Protection Act, scheduled for the following afternoon. Intrigued, she easily discovered the senator's travel arrangements, booked her own flight, and set about discovering circumstances that might be the gloom and doom of Senator Seymour.

On the flight over, Taylor had time to consider her obsession with Senator Seymour. Taylor easily came to the same conclusion that she always did when considering her. Susan was a blatant fraud, and Taylor believed the public deserved to know the truth. The senator had been fairly cunning throughout her tenure in the Senate, but Taylor knew Susan Seymour wasn't true blue. Now, if she read Nick correctly, she was going to get her chance to prove it.

Taylor had watched from the street for about an hour when someone turned the lights off inside the townhome. Feeling reasonably safe that the senator was asleep and would be for a few hours, Taylor pulled out her travel alarm and set it for 7:00 a.m. Moving to the backseat of the Corolla, she took out a small pillow and blanket she always packed for just this type of surveillance. Then she curled her compact frame quite comfortably against the seat and went to sleep.

She awoke when the alarm went off and called for a Rainbow taxi. The senator used the same service the previous evening. Wearing her own form of disguise—a New York Yankee's baseball cap pulled low to cover her fair hair, dark Rayban sunglasses, and a nylon jogging suit— she jogged a block down the street and waited for the taxi. It arrived within fifteen minutes, transporting the requested breakfast: two large Starbucks coffees, four creams, and two blueberry scones. The driver, a young ethnic man, got out of the car to hand her the breakfast. His car radio crackled in the background, transmitting all of the fares called into Rainbow's main telephone line. Drivers picked up their CBs to respond if they were in the area. It gave Taylor an idea. After taking the breakfast, she offered the driver a smile. "Is this your normal area for fares?"

"Yes. You need me, you just call up. I am here fast. Was here last night. Right over there," he said with an Eastern accent, pointing at Jordana's townhouse. He was polite and a talker. "I told the lady there too, you call me if you need me."

She paid the driver for the goodies, the fare for his trip to Starbucks, and a big tip before heading back to her car to wait for the senator to reappear. The senator hadn't called for a taxi yet this morning. Taylor stared at Ms. Barlow's closed garage door, wondering if there was a vehicle inside that would take the senator to her final destination. Taylor was eager to learn where that would be. She sipped her coffee slowly and ate one of her scones, while keeping her eyes on the door to Jordana's home.

It was early afternoon before she saw any activity at the Barlow residence. A man, a boy of about ten years, and a woman she assumed to be Jordana pulled into the drive in a beat-up Honda Accord. Taylor hadn't thought Jordana was married or that she had any children. She did think that the senator's daughter would drive a better car than that. The car most likely belonged to the handsome man accompanying her.

To Taylor's surprise, they didn't stay long at the residence. Perhaps she was mistaken. Maybe the woman wasn't Jordana. The boy came out of the house first with a bewildered look on his face. He sat on the steps and flopped his head, placing his hands on either side of his cheeks, looking as if he didn't know what to do next. Within ten minutes the man and woman came out of the house. By the way they hastily moved the boy to the car and swung its doors open, Taylor knew something had happened inside. She smiled to herself. That had to be the senator's daughter. Moreover, Jordana didn't look pleased to see her mother. Taylor rolled down the window of her car and aimed a telephoto lens at Jordana. Through the lens Taylor saw Jordana's face splotched with pink, her long auburn hair splaying wildly across her shoulders in a violent swing. Snap. Snap, snap. Taylor took Jordana's picture just before she entered the car and slammed the door, and she also took a picture of the car as they drove away.

An hour later the garage door opened and Susan appeared, rolling a red Mustang convertible with the top up out of the driveway. Now that was the type of car Taylor expected Jordana to drive. Taylor snapped a picture of the senator driving the car as she passed her on the street, and then Taylor took off after her. Her heart was pounding. She was finally going to nab the senator. At what, Taylor didn't know. However, she was sure that Nick, who would soon be leaving Susan's employ, wouldn't have given Taylor the tip if it wasn't going to be big.

Chapter Forty-Four

Matthew wasn't interested in going to the beach anymore. On the way out of Jordana's driveway, he used his mobile phone to call Charlotte. As he spoke with her, he became painfully aware of Jordana sitting in the car seat next to him. She silently listened to his account of Susan's arrival and his suspicion that she would be making an appearance at Glory Heights. Jordana's face showed signs of the upsetting quarrel with her mother. He was also aware of Cory's curious ears listening, getting the scoop on what had been happening around him for the past half an hour. Still, Matthew plunged ahead. He filled Charlotte in on what he suspected. He was saying he hadn't had a chance to finish going through all of Pearl's files when he received a small tap on his shoulder. From the backseat, Cory had something to say. "Go to work, Dad. We can go to the beach any time. Aunt Pearl needs us now."

Jordana's eyes, previously filled with frustration, now misted with tears. She turned, and leaning over the car seat, gave sweet, benevolent Cory a bear hug. Matthew gave his son a warm look in the rearview mirror. Then he told Charlotte that they were on their way. Before hanging up, knowing that time was of the essence, he added, "Get started on those files."

Upon reaching Glory Heights, Jordana and Cory went to find Pearl. Matthew went straight to his office. Charlotte was already there, sitting on her haunches, digging through files.

When Matthew entered his office, Charlotte turned to him with a jerk. "Oh, you startled me. I must be more nervous than I thought."

"No sign of the senator?"

"Not yet. I let Pearl know what was going on."

"How'd she take it?"

"You mean how did she take that her sister might drop in on her after all these years to personally harass her? I'd say she seemed amused. I thought she would be frightened. Hell, I sure am, knowing what it could mean for Pearl. But Pearl just smiled and said she looked forward to seeing her."

Matthew laughed. "She was probably talking smart. That, or she's feeling a lot more confident these days. I know she is, with all the progress she's made on her independence plan." He picked up a folder and started thumbing through it.

Charlotte stretched her back and looked up at Matthew, smiling. "I've never seen her so happy, or doing so well. We can't let anything spoil that now. We have to find her a way out of here. Pearl and Sonny found an apartment that's coming open next month. It's perfect for them."

Concerned, Matthew shook his head. "Oh brother, I knew this was coming together quickly. Too quickly for me. You women sure know how to move along a wedding. Unless we find who signed her in here, Pearl's not going anywhere."

Charlotte made her way off the floor with a folder in her hand. She laid the file open on Matthew's desk and tapped a fingernail against a document, brittle and discolored with age. The faded writing within the document was barely legible. "What's this?" she asked.

Matthew gave her a curious look. "What did you find?" He looked over the document. "My God. She signed herself in. Pearl signed herself in." Grabbing Charlotte by the shoulders, he kissed her. "You Southern women are good investigators. You found it! This is exactly what we need!" He took hold of Charlotte and spun her around in a circle dance. "I knew it. I knew it. The senator slipped up. She had never heard of a commitment document. That's when I knew."

Charlotte, caught up in the dizzy dance, grabbed the back of a chair for balance and then pulled down the edge of her skirt that had slid up her thighs during the jig. She laughed at the boyish grin on Matthew's face and the light shining through his eyes. A light that could only have come from his heart. A convergence of emotion pressed against her chest, and she recognized the elation for what their discovery meant for Pearl, but she also recognized her own redemption. She could finally forgive herself. In her mind she had failed her mother, but she had helped find victory for Pearl. "We did it! We did it! Let's go tell Pearl."

Chapter Forty-Five

Susan couldn't help but notice how the bored security officer easily allowed her inside the halls of Glory Heights. All she'd had to do was say that she was visiting a relative. The officer didn't ask her name or whom she was there to see. He just let her in. No wonder Pearl had so easily escaped, Susan thought miserably. *I'm paying someone for this?* That did it. She would move Pearl to the place in Iowa Nick had mentioned. She wasn't going to waste good money paying Daris McFinley to keep Pearl under wraps when she could see for herself how easy it was to come and go. Susan would have to get the name of the home from Nick. After that she would find a new liaison to arrange things and move Pearl. Susan no longer trusted Nick to get the job done. Without his obvious failings, she wouldn't be in this god-awful place right now putting her career at risk. But she couldn't think about that then.

She walked down a hallway toward what looked like an information desk. Her palms grew cool and sweaty. The sudden realization of where she was and whom she was going to see wasn't sitting so easily. As if to counteract her nerves, she stiffened her chin upwards and gently wiped her hands on the sleeves of her suit. The nonchalant gestures did little to erase the sudden chill running up her arms.

She stopped at the nurses' station. The nurse sitting behind the desk doing paperwork had bobbed, streaked blonde hair and was wearing a thick headband. Midwesterners, Susan thought irritably. "I'm looking for Pearl Witherby. Where may I find her?" She was abrupt, all nerves.

The nurse looked at Susan curiously, as if she somehow recognized her, but didn't know from where. "And you are?" the nurse asked.

"A friend," snapped the senator.

"I see," said the attendant, looking like she didn't have time for the rudeness and really couldn't care less who was there to see Pearl. "I believe Pearl is out in the backyard. Go through those doors down there," she said, pointing with a pen toward a door at the end of the hallway.

Susan felt the nurse's stare on her back as she walked down the hall, but arrogantly ignored it. Something she wished she could ignore but couldn't find a reasonable way to do it was the woman coming toward her dragging her left foot, also staring at her. Susan tried to pass the woman, but the woman came up in front of Susan and stuck out her hand.

"Pretty hair ya got," said the woman, reaching out to touch it.

Startled, her eyes nearly popping from her head in fright, Susan swatted at the woman's hand. "Get away from me," she hissed.

The woman backed away, holding her hand. "Sorry, didn't mean anything."

The walls seemed to be caving in on Susan. She could actually feel the perspiration in her armpits. She continued through the hallway, stepping quickly, passing patient rooms without looking. She had almost reached the door when a loud barking sound assaulted her senses. She clutched a hand to her neck and involuntarily jerked toward the sound. A man was standing at the doorway of a room in his underwear, gaping at her. He barked at her. She let out a shriek, jumped, and ran the rest of the way to the back door.

Five minutes later, Matthew and Charlotte hurried toward the nurses' station, chatting good-humoredly. They stopped at the desk to inquire about Pearl's whereabouts. The nurse sat back in her chair with her hands on her hips. "Outside. In the backyard." She shook her head, seeming bewildered at the sudden and unsurpassed onslaught of people interested in Pearl Witherby. "She's certainly popular today."

Matthew and Charlotte laughed, believing the attendant was referring to Jordana and Cory.

The attendant called after Charlotte. "Are you almost finished with your break? I could use one too."

"I'll be back in a flash, girlfriend," said Charlotte, before disappearing down the hall to the backyard.

Taylor stood in front of the building that Susan had just entered, reading aloud the sign: "Glory Heights Healthcare Facility." Baffled, she wondered what the senator was up to. Was this her idea of touring an epileptic treatment center? If that was the story, she thought, Nick could have told me as much and saved me the trip.

Taylor walked to the front steps with her hands on her hips, staring up through the double doors to Glory Heights, wondering if she should go in. She had seen the security guard through the door window when Susan had gone in. He couldn't have asked her for an ID. Within seconds of entering the building the senator had continued down a hallway. Either they knew the senator here or the security guard was a puppet. She wondered how she could find out whom the senator was here to see. No one had met her in the lobby. Maybe the person she had come to see was in one of the patient rooms.

Taylor opened the double doors. "Good afternoon. Are visiting hours still open?"

"Sure, go on in." The puppet waved her inside.

She stopped at the nurses' station. The attendant looked at her warily, then blurted out, "Don't tell me you're here to see

Pearl Witherby too."

Taylor smiled broadly. "I am. Where can I find her?"

"Is this a party or something for her? Because she's going to marry Sonny?"

Thinking fast, Taylor whispered conspiratorially, "Just a little shower." Then, realizing that she should be toting a gift for the bride, she patted her large handbag. "I'm giving money. I'm sure they'll need it."

"How nice," prickled the attendant, adjusting her headband as if an itch was going on beneath it. "They're in the backyard. Down that hallway." She pointed again with a pen to the back door. "Will there be anyone else? I'm starting to feel like I should put up a sign."

They were sitting on the bench at the edge of the river. Cory was energetically replaying his dad's race to "Aunt" Pearl. He had taken to calling her Aunt Pearl after the dinner party at Jordana's house. Jordana knew that Cory had come to work with Matthew on the weekends a few times just so he could visit with her. They were now enjoying the easy comfort of a fond, doting adult and a child loving the uncomplicated attention.

Jordana sat on the bench sideways, with a view of the building, in quiet contemplation of the earlier conversation with her mother. Therefore, Jordana saw her mother first, and froze. She worried about what the senator would do next.

Jordana's first reaction was that she had lost the battle for Pearl. That her mother had personally come to Glory Heights was fearsome. It meant her mother was taking over. She would do her best to put an end to all they'd accomplished. That Pearl had accomplished. Jordana had hoped to have found a way for Pearl to get out of Glory Heights before this.

Mother had not yet noticed them. She had bolted through the back doors like a cannonball burst from a howitzer and was trying to regain her composure. Her hair was mussed and she was reaching a hand to flatten it back into place. She touched her fingertips to her face as if to stifle the sweat that had broken there.

Jordana wanted to laugh at the scene, remembering her first impression of Glory Heights, and what it had probably just done to her mother, but concern over what her mother might try to do to Pearl stifled its humor.

She wished Matthew was with her. She didn't want to face her mother without him, although she knew she would have to sometime. Matthew was still inside looking through files. There was no way to get to him without leaving her mother alone with Pearl, something she wasn't willing to do. She needed to protect Aunt Pearl from Mother's coercing nature, she thought. It just wasn't an even match. Besides, Matthew needed to find something to help Pearl. If Matthew couldn't find a way for Pearl to leave Glory Heights, they were doomed.

When her mother stepped away from the building and began a slow look around, Jordana stood up, clearing her throat to get Pearl's attention. Cory stopped talking and followed Pearl's gaze back toward the building.

When Jordana stood, Susan noticed her immediately. Her glare then went to the boy that had been with her daughter and Matthew Kincaid earlier. But she hardly recognized the woman struggling to stand between the two. If not for the dark, wavy hair sticking out beneath a woven bonnet and a resemblance to their mother's nose, Susan might have disbelieved her eyes. Pearl somehow looked better than she expected. Younger than she expected. There were no lines on Pearl's face. Strands of gray filtered through her hair, but her tresses were as thick as Susan remembered.

There was something different in her sister's eyes. Susan had remembered the dull cast of someone beginning a life with only epileptic conditions to look forward to, but that expression was gone. In its place shone a warm light, radiating life. As Pearl pulled up from the bench and turned, a smile sat on her lips, full of confidence, satisfaction, and something else that Susan could not place.

She swallowed dryly, trying to keep the bile from coming

up in her throat, and started down the cobblestone walk toward the three people staring at her. From all the stares she had received in the last ten minutes, Susan felt something foreign to her: at Glory Heights, she was the odd person out.

Pearl watched Susan walk down the cobblestone steps toward her. She would have gone to meet her, but her legs would not allow her to move from her place near the bench. The emotions running through her went from high to low and back again, and all at once she felt fear, bitterness, forgiveness, love, regret, hatred, and kindness. Susan didn't belong here, she thought. Her discomfort showed in her every movement. Pearl felt sorry for her, although Pearl knew from what Jordana had told her that Susan was coming to cause more trouble for her. From the looks of Susan's approach, she was having some trouble of her own. Pearl didn't know what to make of it. She reached out, grabbed Jordana's hand, and pulled her closer to her side. Cory grabbed Pearl's other hand. Seeing the unmistakable unity of hands, Susan's step slowed.

Apparently wanting to ward off whatever Susan was going to attempt, Jordana spoke first. "Mother, give it up. Don't you see the harm you do? Turn around, go back to DC, and stay there." Her tone said more of what she thought than did her words.

Susan stopped a few feet away from the bench and gaped at Jordana. Pearl assumed that Jordana had never talked to Susan like that before. A struggle appeared on Susan's face, as if the need to regain control not only over herself but also over her daughter and everything around her had forced its way through. Or maybe it only claimed its rightful place in the forefront of her mind. "Listen here, I'll not have you talking to me like that, Jordana. I—"

"I believe Jordana is old enough to decide how she will talk and to whom." It was Pearl, speaking calmly.

Susan tried to speak, but the smooth and easy voice coming from Pearl, whom Susan had believed to have long lost any knack for intelligent communication, had left her senseless. Why, Pearl's eyes even twinkled.

Just then, Cory yelled out, "Yeah, leave us alone." Susan jerked her head to him and snapped her mouth shut. It looked like the rugrats were winning. She wouldn't have it. As she inwardly struggled to make her next move, Cory reached up his arm and waved wildly. "Hey, Dad, over here. We're over here. Look who's here."

Matthew hurried down the walk with Charlotte. Susan spun around to look. "You again. Leave us alone. This is family business. And take her with you," she said, pointing to Charlotte.

"Ah, so you do recognize Pearl as your family. Is that what you're saying, Senator?" cracked Matthew.

Susan stumbled over her response. "Er, I came to talk with my sister. I'll decide what is best for her. That's none of your business, or hers."

"Lady, and I use that word lightly, this lovely woman is your sister's nurse. Say hello to Nurse Charlotte. Your sister is my business and hers. Your sister, as you keep referring to her, has a name. It's Pearl Witherby. Would you like me to introduce you or have you already said hello?"

Pearl chuckled. "Actually, we hadn't said hello yet. Hi Susan. Long time no see."

Susan reluctantly nodded at Pearl, and then she glanced at Jordana. Susan thought, at least Jordana had the good grace to look worried. Her friend, Matthew, was sarcastic, Pearl was laughing, and Jordana's own mother was fuming. What next? At least that nurse had the good sense to look pleasant and keep silent. Matthew looked jubilant, as if he was enjoying himself. Jordana now looked confused and said to anyone who would listen, "Maybe we should go inside, sit down, and talk about this."

"I'm not going anywhere with that man," snapped Susan.

Matthew was quick to respond. "Have it your way, lady. I can make this short and sweet standing right here."

"What are you talking about? Get out of my way." Susan shooed her arms at Matthew and then reached out to grab Jordana's arm. "You're coming with me, Jordana. I'll take care of this my way."

Matthew cut off Susan's reach. "Not so fast, Senator. Take a look at this." He waved a paper in front of Susan's face.

Jordana, Pearl, Cory, and Susan said in unison, "What's that?"

Matthew, enjoying himself, said, "Senator Seymour, this is Pearl Witherby's ticket out of Glory Heights. Be happy for her, won't you? She's getting married. Sonny Capshaw's the lucky man. I'll give him a call. I'm sure he would love to meet you."

Click, click, click, went Taylor's camera. Scribble, scribble, scribble, went the pen in Taylor's notepad. The beep, beep, beep of the speed dial to the *Washington Post* is what got everyone's attention.

Susan took off after the reporter, shrieking obscenities. "You, you freakin' bitch. I'll have you arrested."

Cory said, "Who's that, Dad?"

Jordana studied the piece of paper that was going to save Pearl's life. Charlotte sat down on the bench with Pearl and enjoyed the show.

Chapter Forty-Six

Matthew broke up the catfight between Taylor and the senator. Taylor was taking a beating while refusing to give up her camera and notepad, and Susan was determinedly trying to pound them out of her grasp. Matthew wished he'd gotten a picture of that. However, Jordana was screaming that someone was going to get hurt. So he yanked the camera from between the two women, handed it to Taylor, and ordered them both to leave the premises.

Susan left in a hurry, making her way to a Radisson. It was the nearest hotel she could find. She intended to stay there, out of circulation, until she figured a way out of the mess she had gotten herself into. She knew that, having discovered Susan's secret, Taylor would try her best to sabotage Susan's career. Taylor would show no mercy. Angrily, Susan cursed her. She wondered how Taylor found out about her trip to Minneapolis. She couldn't suspect Nick. She needed him too much.

Taylor took her time pulling herself together after the assault, all the while smiling to herself. Matthew smiled with her. "You look pretty proud of yourself."

Taylor threw back her head, took off her baseball cap,

tossed it into the air, and laughed. "Hell yes! What a story!" She threw her fist into the air. "Yes!"

Jordana, Charlotte, and Cory quickly approached Taylor. Realizing that Jordana was the senator's daughter, Taylor reined in her enthusiasm. She looked at Jordana with a hint of concern. "Ms. Barlow, is it?"

"Yes." Jordana spoke quietly, looking uneasy at what she had just witnessed.

"I'm sorry about this, but I sense that you and your mother are on different sides of the ballgame here. I'm thinking you're winning, but I'm not sure. Tomorrow morning, the story, some story, will run in the *Washington Post*. Does anyone here want to help me make it accurate?" Taylor said the last to all clustered around her.

Walking slowly, Pearl had lagged behind the others. She reached them just in time to hear Taylor's request. Pearl moved to the front of the group. "I would like to say a few things. I'm Susan's sister, Pearl Witherby."

The next morning Taylor's story ran on the front page of the *Washington Post*. An unflattering picture of Susan running away from Taylor's camera was printed with it. It hit the AP wires and spread across the country in midday newscasts, striking particularly hard and often in Minnesota news media. The headlines alone had the potential to end Senator Seymour's career: "Senator Susan Seymour Hides Invalid Sister"; "Head Nurse Drugs Patient—Minnesota Senator Suspected Involvement"; "Chief Administrator Accepts Bribes from Senator Seymour"; and "Minnesota Senator Misses Vote on Water Protection Act."

Upon locking herself behind the hotel room door, Susan placed a call to Nick. She needed him to bail her out of this dilemma. Nick was unavailable. She stayed in her room for the rest of the afternoon pacing the floor in between unanswered calls and more messages to Nick. Later, she ordered room service and drank a bottle of wine to help her sleep. After unsuccessfully trying Nick once more at his home, she went to bed. By morning she had still not heard from him. Furious, not knowing what else to do, she called the prestigious Sterling Public Relations firm, demanding that someone meet her at her hotel room, immediately.

They were notorious as top players in the management or "handling" of scandalous press, clandestine client behaviors, and careers sinking like the Titanic. Under this umbrella of misgivings, Susan's present situation securely fit. They jumped at the chance to represent her. Silver-haired Jack Sterling met with her himself. His hair made him look older than his forty-seven years, although it added to his distinguished, polished appearance.

Worrying about her quickly declining career, Susan explained to Sterling what had happened in the most honest sentiments she had used in years. While explaining the details, she completely forgot about the Water Protection Act until minutes before vote time. Scrambling, she interrupted their meeting and tried to place another call to Nick. He was still unavailable. The minutes ticked past the final moments when votes were cast. Surely the Congress realized her absence on the Senate floor. The vote took place without her. Susan felt the demise of her career profoundly falling beneath her grasp.

News spread that Susan was not in DC to personally support and vote for the Water Protection Bill. Through an enthusiastic desk clerk, reporters discovered her whereabouts. The only good news Susan heard, as she watched media accounts of her demise on television, was that the Water Protection Bill had passed without her assistance. In a moment of self-denial, she thought she had a chance at public absolution.

Happily, she thought, now Nick will call. The vote is over. He'll have time to talk now. He'll help me. Between Sterling and Nick, there would no doubt be hope for recovering her career. Not willing to wait for Nick, she placed yet another call to her office. In livid frustration over Nick's absence, she verbally pummeled Emily into confessing that Nick was no longer working there. He'd quit.

After the Water Protection Bill had passed, he took a job with the EPA. Soon after Emily's confession, news of Nick's departure also hit the airwaves. Ironically, not used to solving a problem of this magnitude without Nick, Susan stayed inside the Radisson, refusing to come out to talk with reporters.

"There must be some way out of this," Susan begged her PR manager.

"The best thing to do now is concede your error and make amends. People understand fear, emotion. They won't understand you locked in your hotel room," said Sterling.

"What are you suggesting?" whimpered Susan.

"We'll write a speech. You'll pay for Pearl Witherby and Sonny Capshaw's wedding. You'll attend the wedding, smile, and pose for photographs. You'll donate a large financial sum to the epileptic treatment center . . . out of your own pocket."

Susan winced. "How much money are we talking about?"

"A lot," said Sterling.

"What if my sister won't let me come to her wedding?"

"Listen, you have to make amends with your sister. Why wouldn't you want to do that?"

"Make amends?" The thought had never occurred to Susan.

"Yes. If you're going to admit you were wrong, it would seem to me that you might want to seek her forgiveness."

"Forgiveness? For what?" Susan wasn't following along.

"For being wrong," said Sterling.

"What exactly have I been wrong about?" It wasn't a sinister question. Susan was trying to understand. She cocked her head and crinkled her eyes, trying to grasp what Sterling was suggesting. The concept was out of her reach.

He looked at her sharply, but sincerely. "If you want me to get you out of this, and I think I can, you're going to have to listen to some straight talk. You have to hear what you need to change to be successful. I hope you don't fire me for it, but it's the only thing left to do."

Susan stared at him, nodding her head, ready to listen. "Go ahead then."

Sterling looked her square in the eye. "The world has progressed since the 1950s. Epilepsy is a disease of the neurological system. It's not insanity. It shouldn't be a humiliation. A person shouldn't be stigmatized or devalued for having it, as reported in the *Washington Post* article."

Susan winced at his mention of the article.

Sterling continued, "If you've done all of the things you are accused of, you've treated your sister shabbily. That's just plain talk." He stopped and stayed silent, letting her react to what he had said.

Susan wondered how she could've missed it. How did the rest of the world understand but not she? Her drive to succeed had amplified an already-clouded image of Pearl. Susan had been living in the past; her view of Pearl had remained what it had been when they were teenagers. What had happened to Pearl had scared her so intensely that all she could do was run away from it.

Seeing Pearl again had left its mark on Susan's heart. She wondered if Pearl would ever forgive her. Pearl was a kinder person than she was, a better person than she could ever be. Susan suddenly burst into tears. She cried, not for her career, but for the wasted years she had caused her sister. Pearl. Pearl. Her insides screamed: Her name is Pearl! As if she could expunge her guilt through the pores of her skin.

Chapter Forty-Seven

A call came from an operator at Radisson Hotel Suites. It had to be her mother calling, using the concierge as a secretary. Jordana hesitated a second before allowing the call.

"Jordana? It's Mother." Her voice was quieter than Jordana ever remembered it being. It was an unfamiliar sound of resignation.

Jordana had been so angry with her mother over the many attempts to destroy Pearl's life. However, the newspaper accounts in the Minneapolis *Star Tribune* repeating the *Washington Post* story had stirred some misplaced pity for her. Between the article that would most likely end her mother's political career and the sadness in her voice, concern jarred Jordana's insides. She couldn't hang up on her. "Are you okay, Mother? I read the papers."

"I'm fine. I'm staying at the Radisson in Plymouth. I've still got your car."

"What are you going to do?"

"I've hired a public relations firm. They'll figure something out."

"What can I do for you?"

"I . . . I would like to speak with Pearl . . . if I may?"

Jordana was ridden with disbelief. While there was no

longer the piercing level of hostility in her mother's voice, Jordana still felt protective. She gazed over at Pearl, who had been napping on the sofa. The blaring ring of the phone in Jordana's quiet home had interrupted Pearl's slumber. Sonny had been over to see her the night before and had stayed late wrapping up their wedding plans. Earlier in the day they had signed a lease on an apartment. Brambles, after hearing of the conniving that occurred over the loss of Sonny's job, had reinstated him. Too many good things had happened to let anyone, particularly Susan, disrupt it all now. "What is it that you want to talk to Aunt Pearl about?"

Hearing her name, Pearl shifted herself off the sofa and maneuvered her way over to Jordana. "Who is it? Is it for me? Sonny?" she whispered.

Her eyes wide, indicating wonder, Jordana mouthed to Pearl: "It's my mother."

Pearl clapped her hands and laughed. As if it never occurred to her to continue being angry with Susan. "Let me have the phone."

Susan was saying, "I don't mean any more harm. I just want to make amends." The words seemed to choke off at the end, so hard were they for the senator to get out, even with the impetus of sincerity.

Jordana worried what her mother was up to and didn't want to be deceived. Once again, conflict surrounded Jordana's feelings toward her mother. Pearl was waving at her to give her the phone. Without responding to her mother, Jordana turned it over to her in a slow, wondering motion.

"Hello, Susan. Some news report, huh?"

Pearl seemed sincerely unaware of the tremendous impact the article would have on Susan's career. Susan took Pearl's naïveté with a grain of salt, a first for her. "Yes, that was some report. Look, Pearl, I just want to say I'm sorry. I didn't know what I was doing." While it was true that her self-righteous ego had blinded her from the truth, the confession didn't sound right coming from her own lips.

"You're sorry, Susan? For locking me up, you mean?" Pearl quipped.

"For . . . everything."

"That's okay, Sue. Want to come to my wedding?"

Susan's voice perked up on the line. "Why yes, Pearl, I'd love to. As a matter of fact, I don't know if you'll agree to this or not, but after all I've done, I'd like to be the one to pay for your wedding. For everything."

"That seems fitting," said Pearl.

Susan couldn't tell if she was being witty or sarcastic. She guessed it didn't really matter after all that had happened. "Are your wedding plans set, yours and Mr. Capshaw's?"

"We figured it all out last night, right down to the flowers. Maybe you should talk to Jordana about all the details. She was going to arrange everything for us, even the flowers."

Jordana, feeling her mouth agape and her eyes pools of stupefaction, listened to Pearl's end of the conversation. Jordana took back the phone and listened while her mother spoke of the financial details she would need in order to pay for the wedding. Jordana found herself promising to fax the name of the florist and discussing a myriad of other details. She then made an instantaneous decision to change the reception from a small luncheon at her home to a banquet at Sunsets, as long as her mother was going to pay for it; she even promised to send a check for Pearl's wedding dress and Sonny's tux. She ended the call with, "Whatever Pearl needs, let me know. See you at the wedding."

That night Sterling appeared on *Larry King Live.* Matthew watched it from his home in disbelief. Sterling read a prepared letter from Susan: "I have learned a lot in the last few days and now apologize for any harm that it has done to any one of my constituents, but more importantly to my sister, Pearl Witherby. I have spoken to my sister, and am making every effort to mend our relationship. She will marry Sonny Capshaw next month. This morning I offered to pay for their wedding, and Pearl accepted.

In my sister's name, I am donating $500,000 from my personal finances to epileptic treatment centers, to be disbursed at their discretion. I hope my constituents will bear with me as I learn to forgive myself for what I've done and atone for it all. I will return to Congress a better person for it."

Matthew got in his car and drove straight to Jordana's to confirm what he had heard. She had barely gotten the door open before he blurted out his confusion. "Did you see *Larry King Live*? Your mother's statement?" Jordana pulled him inside, acknowledging that she had.

It was late and Pearl had already retired for the evening. Matthew was pleased at finding some time alone with Jordana. Jordana looked happy to see him and hugged him and invited him to sit with her on the sofa. She dimmed the light and they sat together, speaking softly. Jordana snuggled into Matthew's arms; her body felt warm against his. Her face, tilted up toward him, looked tired, but more peaceful than he had ever remembered seeing it.

"It was a big day around here today, Matthew," yawned Jordana.

"I guess. What happened?"

"Mother called from the Radisson. I think she's afraid to leave her room after all the negative publicity she's had." They couldn't help chuckling together over the thought of it. Then Jordana continued, "Mother said she wanted to talk to Aunt Pearl, to make amends. She actually said Aunt Pearl's name."

"Wow. Did Pearl talk to her?"

"She did." Again Jordana laughed. "I must be tired, because the whole conversation strikes me as funny now. Aunt Pearl was almost flippant in her cheery mood. As if, now that she was going to marry Sonny, nothing else mattered. Nothing else could upset her." Jordana explained the conversation she had had with the senator. Matthew listened with an amused look on his face.

"The senator isn't really going to attend the wedding, is she?"

"It looks like she is."

Matthew was suspicious. "Are you sure you want to let her pay for it? It's not some kind of trap, is it?"

The questions irritated Jordana. "Her voice, it held a tone that my mother's never used. She sounded sincere. Like she had learned a lesson." Jordana sounded defensive. She sat up, pulling away from Matthew's side.

"I hate to say it, but people don't always change that quickly. I suppose that with the tremendous blow to your mother's career, and her ego, it could have happened." Matthew thought he had better walk the middle ground. He had come between Jordana and her mother enough in the last two days to last a very long time. "Does she know I'm going to be the best man?" He laughed, and pulled Jordana back against him.

Relenting, Jordana laughed too. "I didn't mention it, or that I'm the maid of honor."

They bantered like that for a while, still in soft tones so as not to awaken Pearl. They talked about the Larry King show. They decided to give the senator the benefit of the doubt, even if the only reason was that she was still Jordana's mother. Jordana believed that her mother wanted to make amends. Matthew couldn't help adding that even if the senator made no effort to stay in Pearl's life after the wedding, the recent publicity would keep Susan from ever hurting Pearl again. Pearl would accomplish her dream. Jordana conceded that her mother could very well revert back to the way she had always been, putting her career first. But Jordana agreed that even if her mother did go back to her old ways, it would no longer affect anyone else's life the way it had Pearl's. They felt safe in that notion.

Matthew stroked Jordana's hair, and then lifted her chin so that her eyes met his. "It's coming to an end, isn't it?"

Jordana's blue eyes grew round with confusion. "What's coming to an end? Us?"

Matthew's response was immediate and louder than he had wished. "Good God, I hope not. I meant this whole ordeal. Pearl, Sonny, your mother. I want it to come to an end with a happy conclusion for everyone. Most of all I want it to end so that we may begin."

"We've not had much time for ourselves, although I really feel like I have gotten to know you. Your soul, I mean."

"Same here. But I want time just for us, to have fun while we're learning more about each other. If that's okay with you, that is."

Jordana squeezed his hand. "It's very okay with me."

Matthew pulled her close and tipped his head to kiss her, when suddenly they weren't alone in the room.

"Matthew, when did you get here?" Pearl entered the living room wearing the purple robe Jordana had given her and a big smile. "Did you hear? Sue says she's sorry." Pearl settled in the chair next to the sofa and told Matthew of her conversation with Susan. She then relayed all the wedding plans to him.

With all his heart Matthew had wanted to be alone with Jordana, but Pearl's contagious excitement over a love she had fought so hard to have was worth the concession. He would soon have Jordana all to himself. He began to count the days.

Chapter Forty-Eight

Dressed in a black, tailed tuxedo, tears in his ever-wide, round eyes, Sonny waited at the altar. He nervously fidgeted with his tie, something he wasn't used to wearing, and watched while Matthew walked Pearly up the aisle. Sunlight filtering through the stained glassed windows illustrating the stations of the cross at Prince of Peace Catholic Church added to the feeling of reverence he felt for the occasion. Sonny started to chew on his nails, but remembered he promised Pearly he wouldn't during the ceremony and abruptly dropped his arm to his side.

Until now, he had collected no courage to look into the audience of family and friends waiting in the pews for the ceremony to begin. Feeling more confident now that all eyes were transfixed on the bride, he stole a glance up and down the aisles. People from Brambles, the ones Sonny and Pearly worked with, including Hazel Dentry, whom they'd argued over inviting with Pearly finally giving in, and Mr. and Mrs. Bramble sat on one side. Seeing the Brambles made Sonny happy. After reading the newspaper accounts of the calamities that he and Pearly suffered, they'd hired him back to his old job. They gave both Sonny and Pearly a raise and a large amount of money as a wedding gift. Sonny and Pearly just had to invite the Brambles to the wedding after that.

The crowd gathered outside in the fresh September air outnumbered those inside by tens. The uninvited guests set up in the large front lawn of the church were television crews and newspaper reporters, Minnesota media being highly represented. Close to the entrance where she had waited for hours before the morning ceremony to get the best possible angle stood Taylor and her camera crew. Pearl Witherby's wedding had become a media event.

Taylor had learned of Pearl Witherby's wedding plans from the desk clerk at the Radisson. The clerk had read a fax sent from Jordana to Senator Seymour before delivering it to the senator. He had made copies of the fax listing details of Ms. Witherby's wedding, including time, place, and cost, and given one of them to Taylor. The information was not news by itself. The item that perked Taylor's interest most was the handwritten note at the bottom of the fax that said, "See you at the wedding, Mother."

With a hopeful glimpse at fifteen minutes of fame, the clerk had kept Taylor abreast of the activity and communication to and from the senator's room. Through him, Taylor learned many things before any other reporter: the color and style of dress the senator would wear to the wedding; that Pearl Witherby had changed the wedding reception from a small gathering at Jordana's home to a private room at a supper club named Sunset's; that the banquet menu included Chicken Kiev, roasted garlic potatoes, and asparagus spears in lime sauce; that the cake would be carrot with cream cheese frosting; and that Susan was paying for it all. The clerk was unscrupulous enough to open the senator's outgoing mail. Therefore, Taylor knew of the checks sent to Ms. Witherby, the one paying for the bride's custom-tailored suit and hat and the wedding present of $5,000.

Through the clerk, Taylor became privy to many of the senator's political machinations. Before other reporters smelled the scent, Taylor knew the senator obtained a public relations manager: the very prestigious, very expensive Sterling. He was a big gun hired to handle her pitiful deluge of problems. Though the clerk tried to give her the scoop, she already knew about Nick Ballantine's flight from the senator's employ. Taylor chose to leave him out of her reports. Other reporters pounced on that aspect of the story, but after giving Taylor the tip-off to the story of the year, she respected Nick's wishes for privacy. However, Sterling was fair game. Taylor knew about the Larry King interview before it aired.

Along with a myriad of other reporters, Taylor now captured a few shots of the bride and groom as they separately entered the church. She took photos of Jordana with Matthew and Cory as they followed the bride from the limo to the inside of the chapel. She took even more of the attendees from Glory Heights Healthcare Facility lingering outside, mouths agape at the commotion, hesitating to go inside for fear they would miss something.

Taylor had sent a camera crew to the Radisson to shoot Susan's departure for the ceremony, although they'd kept their distance and used telephoto lenses. Now, by mobile phone, a car tailing the senator kept Taylor abreast of the senator's pending arrival. Taylor directed another crew to set up and aim their cameras in the direction of the limo bringing her to the church. Taylor stayed at the church entrance.

With Sterling as her escort and wearing a pale gray suit with a single strand of pearls, Susan alit from the car and smiled for the cameras. Taylor was disappointed. She had hoped the senator would be hiding her face, trying to duck the photographers.

Sterling led the way, breaking through the throng of eager journalists, holding onto Susan's elbow. "Let the senator through, please. Let Senator Seymour through."

Reporters ran toward the senator and pounded out questions, trying to get sound bites: "Senator Seymour, do you think you can salvage your career?"

"Senator Seymour, look this way, one picture please. Has Ms. Witherby really forgiven you? Do you think your constituents can forgive and forget?"

"Senator, will you run for office again?"

"Senator Seymour, the rumor is that you are resigning your Senate seat. What is your response to that?"

"When the ceremony is over, could I get you to pose for

the camera with the patients from Glory Heights? They're inside the church."

The mention of Glory Heights rankled the senator. For a second her smile wilted and her eyes drooped. Taylor's cameraman caught it on tape.

Susan hadn't asked for a list of attendees. She assumed no one would be there. It didn't occur to her that Pearl had friends. The mention of patients from Glory Heights suddenly made her ill. A tight squeeze on her elbow quickly vanquished the slightest falter in her demeanor. Alert, Sterling noticed her hesitation and quickly propelled her forward.

She was the last to arrive, but Sterling had planned it that way. They had suspected the desk clerk of searching for a piece of notoriety and had fed him information. It worked like a charm. The media was right where they wanted them to be, although they would gladly have skipped the presence of Taylor Costica.

Midway through the short walk from the limo to the wide church steps where photographers hung over steel railings waiting to get a shot at her, Susan noticed Taylor. Their eyes met, a brief contest of wills. The senator, with a smile as wide as the Pacific Ocean, and Taylor, with her unflappable calm, faced off. Neither would turn away. A photographer jumped in front of the senator and Sterling before they reached the stairway. Sterling took the opportunity to crisply whisper into Susan's ear, "Don't look at her." Then they smiled for the camera snapping an up close and personal shot, breaking the stare down.

Also as planned, Susan and Sterling, on the steps of the church, turned toward the swarm of journalists and addressed the crowd before entering the church. Susan smiled and waved. "Thank you for your great show of support," she said, as if the people in front of her were constituents and not story-hungry reporters. "I'm happier than I can tell you on this great day. My sister and I are reunited, and she's taught me a great lesson that I will use to better further the causes of my constituents." With a senatorial wave, she entered the church, and Sterling locked the door behind them.

Inside, Susan lost her smile and looked around. She was late, and Pearl was already at the altar. A short, rotund man stood next to her. That must be Sonny Capshaw, thought Susan. How odd looking. She wondered if he was all right. He kept moving a hand to his mouth as if to bite his nail, then jerked it down to his side. The caseworker and that child stood next to him. The sight of Matthew still galled the senator. Jordana, then Charlotte, stood beside Pearl. Jordana was lovely, dressed in a tea-length taffeta gown with beads framing the scooped back of the dress. The lilac color accented her auburn hair beautifully. Despite everything, Susan was proud of her daughter and wondered what kind of relationship they would have now. Jordana had changed; she wasn't yielding to Susan's demands anymore. Regrettably, Susan sensed that it would be up to her to mend their relationship too.

Susan and Sterling started down the aisle, but an usher put an arm out, stopping them. Surprised, Susan raised her eyebrows and looked at the odd thin woman taking her ushering quite seriously. "I'd like to be seated," Susan said.

To her astonishment, the woman pointed into the church and repeated her words, "I'd like to be seated, I'd like to be seated." The woman struggled to stop the flow of words.

With a malignant sigh, the senator tried to regain composure and move forward, but she hesitated. As family, she could have sat in the front pew. She had previously agreed with Sterling that she would do this. However, after one look around the church seated mostly with patients from Glory Heights, Susan couldn't do it. Jack looked at her questioningly. She gave a short shake of her head. Fortunately, there were no cameras present, save those photographing the wedding party. Susan led the way to a back pew and sat next to a distinguished-looking Asian man. She would later learn that she had sat next to Doctor Sotto, who had saved Pearl from the overdose.

Pearl wore an ivory lace suit, which, at Jordana's suggestion, was custom-made for the occasion. Susan said nothing about the change from an off-the-rack dress to the tailored outfit, and paid for it. Pearl wore nude nylons with a dainty seam up the back. Expensive shoes matched her dress. A bonnet, made especially for her wedding day, was laced with orchids and baby's breath matching a corsage at her wrist. Susan had to admit that Pearl looked lovely. Her eyes sparkled with the same look Susan had witnessed before at Glory Heights. It was an expression of achievement, happiness, and love. Susan wondered if she would visit Pearl after the media attention died down. She couldn't be sure. She got the heebie-jeebies when she looked at Pearl's intended.

When Pearl said, "I do," tears stung Susan's eyes. It wasn't as much for Pearl's happiness as for her sorrow. Sorrow that Susan had inflicted upon her for the sake of her career. The emotional moment was brief, conflicting. Susan's career was still important to her.

The ceremony was short, which pleased Susan. When the blushing, glowing bride came back up the aisle, Susan stuck out a gloved hand and waved to her. Pearl left Sonny's side for the brief moment it took to run over and hug Susan. Matthew Kincaid and Jordana, following behind Pearl and Sonny, silently nodded in Susan's direction. Susan nodded back. Charlotte and Cory fell into the reception line behind the rest of the wedding party, greeting the guests lining up to congratulate Mr. and Mrs. Capshaw. Susan held back in the pew, letting everyone go before her, again as Sterling had planned for her to do. The reporters were still lurking outside. Sterling wanted to ensure a shot of Susan smiling, offering congratulations and blessings to the newly married couple.

Pearl was a nervous bride, but not in the customary sense. She fretted that a seizure would spoil her wedding. Now, having made it to the reception line, she glowed with the knowledge that she had reached her goal. She would spend the rest of her life with Sonny who remembered her soul. That alone made her happier than she could ever have imagined. Add to that the euphoria she felt for having made it through the ceremony without an epileptic spell, and she felt truly blessed.

Pearl shook hands and accepted kisses from Rebecca,

Karoline, Kenny Holmes, Cora Wilson, who had ushered for her, and Hazel Dentry, but she had her eyes on Susan. Pearl harbored no hard feelings toward Susan, who was at the end of the reception line making her way to her. After each guest congratulated Sonny and Pearl, they went through the church doors to the sidewalk outside. Each time the doors opened, the shutter of flashbulbs and questions yelled out from reporters broke the sense of serenity inside the church.

Susan approached Sonny and Pearl with a flashy smile, causing Pearl to look around her. Hazel Dentry, designating herself as the presenter of Mr. and Mrs. Capshaw, held the doors open and waited for the bride and groom to emerge. Glory Heights patients lined the sidewalk, pushing against reporters, their hands filled with birdseed, ready to perform the customary marriage blessing.

Pearl turned back to Susan, who was standing in front of Sonny, introducing herself and shaking his hand. Susan didn't apologize for the pain she had caused him. She had never laid eyes on Sonny Capshaw before now and might not ever again. When she opened her arms to receive Pearl, Pearl first held back, but then relented and accepted the hug. Susan whispered, "Pearl, please forgive me. I truly am sorry." When Susan pulled away their eyes met, both telling a story that would set the stage for their future relationship.

Pearl saw that the apology was genuine. She also saw that Susan could not help what she had become. She was first a politician. In the long list of things important to the senator, Pearl had not been one of them.

Susan saw that Pearl was complete without her. Just as Pearl hadn't mattered to Susan for too many years, Susan no longer mattered to Pearl. She would love Susan because it was her nature to be kind and forgiving. Beyond that, what Susan needed to do with her life was not important to Pearl. Susan could no longer hurt her. Pearl had found happiness, and no one could take it away from her. She had triumphed.

She squeezed Susan's hands and gave her a last look that emanated her achievement, joy, and love. It would purchase a permanent picture in Susan's mind. It would replace the one of a slack-jowled epileptic she had embraced for so many years. When Pearl let go of Susan's hands it was with a gentle push toward the door. Toward her public.

Susan exited the church and attempted a smile for the cameras, but the expression on Pearl's glowing face remained with her seconds too long; it occurred to Susan that she shouldn't have given up on Pearl. Susan suddenly realized that she'd missed out on a relationship with a sister whose life was richer and happier than her own.